Here is what some of the girls who ... 's brilliant 'Girls Like You' books have said:

Some of ... I first read *Maddy* and I got ... ' books].
Jasmin (

[*Hannah*] ... reflected teenage life.
Hannah (13)

I read [*Hannah*] in less than 24 hours! I loved the book.
Chiara

I thought they were great! I've even got my mates on to them now!
Hannah

I've never read anything so good.
Jenna (12)

I couldn't put [*Hannah*] down.
Chloe

. . . every chance we get we are reading one of [the 'Girls Like You'] books (I'm starting to think our form teacher is getting seriously sick of us reading all the time!).
Emma

When I was reading them, I felt like I was there, watching everything happen. [The 'Girls Like You'] books are soooo cool!
Kate

I've read [*Maddy*] three times so far!
Amy (12)

I love them so much I can never put them down.
Sophie

Also by Kate Petty

Makeover

For younger readers

The Nightspinners

KATE PETTY

Summer Heat

Dolphin Paperbacks

These books are for Rachel, who approved

First published in Great Britain in 2004
by Dolphin paperbacks
an imprint of Orion Children's Books
a division of the Orion Publishing Group Ltd
Orion House
5 Upper St Martin's Lane
London WC2H 9EA

Reprinted 2004

A catalogue record for this book is available from the British Library

Typeset at The Spartan Press Ltd,
Lymington, Hants

Printed and bound in Great Britain by
Clays Ltd, St Ives plc

ISBN 1 84255 162 0

Summer Heat

Hannah

ONE

When Sophie rang and asked if I'd like to come to a sleep-over on their last night of term, I was really pleased. Sophie, Charlotte and Maddy are still my best friends even though I go to a different school from them now. My terms are shorter, so I'd already been vegging out for a few days. I wouldn't say I was bored exactly, just in need of a better class of company than my nerdy older brother Jeremy can provide.

My parents are awesomely high-powered. Dad is a barrister and Mum is a financial consultant. You'd think they'd enjoy a bit of high-powered leisure as well, but they both seem to find their work endlessly fascinating. Holiday is a word that barely features in their joint vocabulary. Actually they don't have a joint vocabulary. They don't really choose to spend a lot of time together, which might explain why jolly family outings don't appeal. As far as they're concerned, holidays are time out from school when J and I are expected to brush up on subjects extra-curricular. So it's music courses for me – I play the flute – and genius stuff like astrophysics for J. He's heading for Oxford and I'm expected to excel in one way or another. All very stressful.

So. I made the most of my extra week's holiday (before the parents complain that I don't get up until lunchtime), and I felt nicely de-stressed, but the other three were still high as kites from their last day of term.

Maddy and Charlotte were already there when I arrived. Maddy's a laugh. She'll be on the telly one day, that girl. She's absolutely stunningly beautiful, everything I'm not, with a lovely figure, a terrific tan, honey-gold hair and black eyelashes. Makes you sick really. She wears expensive scent and she's very touchy-feely. Loads of kisses all round. She speaks in italics – 'Hi, *Hannah*. How are *you*? You look amazing. You *do*. *Really*.' You know the sort of thing. Not an enormous brain, but you can't help liking her.

Now Charlotte I'm very fond of. She's your original sweet girl. Smallish, mousey hair, big blue eyes, very shy and self-conscious, but really nice. Her self-esteem is zilch, which I blame on her brassy older sister myself. Perhaps she'll come into her own when her sister leaves home. She blushes a lot, which she hates because it makes it so easy for people to tease her.

We were all in Sophie's loft. It's typical of Sophie that she even has a loft. She's tall and cool and things seem to work for her. Her older brother Danny is very straight, but not half such a geek as J, and her parents always seem pleasantly chaotic and easygoing. Unlike mine. It would be easy to be jealous of Sophie, and sometimes I am. It's not as if she has more material things than I do, just an enviable home life. But she's a good friend and always has been.

Sophie's mum lays on great food, and they had set out mattresses round the TV so we could all watch a DVD later. Charlotte was feeding her face. Maddy was regaling Sophie with tales of their maths teacher. Maddy reckons he's got a crush on her – he probably has. I went and sat with Charlotte and the dips. 'Hi, Hannah. Save me from eating all this stuff. I'm fat enough as it is!' (See what I mean?) I laid into the doritos and guacamole.

'Now you lot have finished term I feel the holidays have really begun,' I told her. 'It's not the same when everyone else is still at school. You're not going to the Lake District straight away, are you?'

'I've got a few days to get ready, thank God.'

'Me too.' I was going to savour these next few days.

Maddy was turning through the DVDs. 'Shall I set the DVD going now? Are we all here, Soph?' she asked. Typical Mads. Can't she count to four?

'No, let's wait for my brother to go out first,' said Sophie. So we were treated to a Maddy and Sophie dance special instead. I still can't figure out how they know what to do – just watch endless MTV, I suppose. I'm a radio person myself. I'm more interested in what's new than what's popular.

Dan went out with a slam of the front door and we had the house to ourselves soon after that. So then the fun and games could begin. We let the DVD roll while some of us concentrated on eating and others on drinking. My posh schoolfriends (i.e. not Sophie, Maddy and Charlotte) are all spoilt brats, and drinking's a big thing with them – those that haven't expanded their minds still further with other stuff. I suppose you could say that I'm finding out about alcohol, but not in a big way, honest. I've decided that I like red wine better than white wine because the parents always offer me wine with dinner (when they're there), very French, don't you know. Gin's nice with lots of tonic, but it makes you drunk; vodka doesn't taste of anything – so I don't see the point – but it doesn't give you a headache; and whisky's plain horrible. My schoolfriends like Bailey's and other sticky drinks, but I think they're a waste of money. So sophisticated, aren't I? Anyway, I'd nabbed a bottle of Dad's Law Society wine – he buys it by the case – and we shared it out. There was some cider too, but I do know not to mix my drinks.

I don't remember much about the food – or the DVD, because it was some horror thing I'd already seen a million times. Good special effects, though. I'd love to watch them making some of these things. But as far as I'm concerned, the best bit of a sleepover comes next, once we're all in our nightclothes. Maddy wears tons of make-up, not that she needs to, and spends hours with cleansers and toners and face packs and stuff getting it off, so we usually muck about with it too. Mum wears minimal make-up (and of course she's far to busy to chat with her only daughter about such things) and we practically get expelled if we wear it for school, so I'm not much good with it. Also I'm dark, so my eyebrows and eyelashes are dark already – not that you can see much behind my specs. But Maddy decided to give me a makeover once I'd taken my glasses off for the night. Eyeshadow, eyeliner, mascara and blushers and lipstick. I looked quite good actually. Perhaps there's hope for me yet! I kept it on because the others wanted to turn the lights out and talk about guess what.

All-girls school plus a brother who doesn't seem to understand the essential difference between boys and girls means that my hands-on (so to speak) experience of the opposite sex is pretty flimsy. So I just keep quiet when they're talking about the boys in their year. Maddy's been out with loads of boys. Sophie and Charlotte go to the same parties as she does, so I'd guess that a certain amount of hands-on experience is exactly what they have had. The name Ben Southwell cropped up rather frequently with the fascinating fact that 'he kisses like a fish'. Obviously I wasn't missing much! But then they got on to Orlando Bloom and Brad Pitt. Well, they're OK, but sadly for me all my favourite men are dead. I mean, how can you improve on Louis Armstrong – or John Lennon or even Kurt Cobain? Perhaps it's time I got a little more realistic. I'm sure I could find someone who *looked* like John Lennon.

The others had gone back to Ben Southwell, but before I switched off again they were quizzing Charlotte about her sister. Between you and me, Michelle's a bit of a tart – all blonde from a bottle and pierced navel, but she's the only older sister we've got between us, and we're kind of fascinated to have some of her experiences second-hand. Michelle gets away with murder as far as I can see, running Charlotte's parents ragged with her parties and clubbing. Michelle goes out at night when Charlotte comes in. All of which means that their parents are tougher on Charlotte because they can't stand the strain a second time around.

Luckily Charlotte's a very different kettle of fish – clubbing's not her scene anyway. Right now Michelle's in Corfu with her friends after their exams, so I hope she doesn't blow that one for Charl as well.

And so the subject turned back to boys – on holiday this time. Charlotte gets to be with the love of her life each year in the Lake District – not that she stands much of a chance, because he's eighteen. Maddy's a complete romantic – she's determined to meet a 'real lovey-dovey Mr Darcy' of her own. Sounds like the older man to me. She'll probably get one on a trip to Barbados with her dad.

It was Maddy's idea that we should all have holiday romances. Fine for her – perhaps not so easy for the rest of us. 'Let's all agree to have holiday romances, and we'll have another sleepover on the last weekend of the holidays and report back.' She was warming to her subject. 'We'll go round and say where we're going. Age order. I'm nearly fifteen – God, would you believe it – so I go first. OK. I'm going to Barbados with my dad. Two weeks. What about you, Duck?'

Duck is me. I'd better explain. As if being called Hannah Gross wasn't bad enough, I answer to the ghastly nickname of 'Duck'. Most people just think it's a term of endearment, but in my case it's because I waddle – or used to, when I was still wearing over-large lace-ups (of course my mum had to buy expensive sensible shoes big enough for me to grow into, never the trendy ones I really wanted) in the juniors. And the nickname's stuck, even at my secondary school. It could be worse, I suppose, but sometimes I almost forget I've got a nice ordinary name like Hannah.

I thought about the romance potential of the music course. It's a residential for the good musicians in our area, so it's subsidised, which means that rather than the usual wet boarding-school kids whose parents don't know what to do with them in the holidays, some of the guys are quite normal people. I've played in concerts with quite a few of them and – well, yes, there are one or two I could fancy. In fact, there's even one who looks like John Lennon . . . Still, I don't expect anyone to notice a four-eyed waddler like me. And even if they did, I can't see myself having the confidence to work it into a snogging situation, let alone anything more. Then again, it's high time I did a little experimenting in that direction . . . Not so fast, Hannah old girl, I told myself. Anyway, I might not want to when the time came. No – I wasn't promising anything. The others were looking at me. Oh yes, they wanted to know what I was doing on holiday.

'Me? Oh the usual boring old music course. Ten whole days with a load of musos in sandals,' – which was actually the most likely scenario.

Charlotte went all wide-eyed. 'But I thought you really liked doing your music. And mightn't you meet a wonderful double-bass player or a sexy saxophonist or someone?'

Well, she had a point – the John Lennon one plays the saxophone as well as the flute – but I wasn't going to get my hopes up. 'I might,' I said cautiously, 'but I don't promise to talk about it afterwards.'

'Spoilsport!' said Sophie – but I wasn't going to say anything I might regret, so I kept my mouth shut. Sophie carried on, 'I'm going to yet another campsite in France. With one boring older brother. Mum and Dad read and drink and go to museums and markets. I'm left with dear Danny to mingle with all those other campers. I suppose I might just find myself a Campsite courier on a bicycle . . . You're so lucky, Mads. Barbados, huh? You'll have to have a wonderful exotic time for all of us.'

Some time later, when Charlotte and Maddy were asleep, Sophie and I carried on in whispers. 'I think you're a fraud,' said Sophie. 'You're just as keen as the rest of us. And just as likely to pull. You've got a heaving bosom there, Duck. Don't think we haven't noticed. As for the smouldering eyes behind the librarian specs – ' here she put on an American-movie accent and a deep voice – 'My, but you're beautiful, Miss Goldbaum . . . ' Sophie doesn't miss much. And heaving bosom sounds more promising than top-heavy. Obviously it's all a matter of attitude. Where would I be without my mates? It's amazing how a couple of well-chosen phrases can make you feel good about yourself. I snuggled into my sleeping-bag and dreamed of a passionate encounter with John Lennon. In his younger days of course, when he was alive.

Two

Sophie lives round the corner from me. I've known her even longer than the others – since we were toddlers. We pop in and out of each other's houses all the time during the holidays – I like the sense of a caring family and the comfortable muddle in hers and she likes the lack of it in ours. She called round at lunch time. J was out, so I was on my own. Sophie followed me through the hall to our newly done-up kitchen. 'Wow, Hannah. This must have happened since last time I came over. It looks like something out of a magazine.'

'That's because it is. Mum said, "That's a nice kitchen, I'll have that." So, three weeks and ten workmen later, hey presto!' I took her on a tour. 'Walk-in fridge, industrial stainless steel hob, double oven, microwave, breakfast bar, dishwasher . . . ' Everything's disguised behind identical doors, so you need the running commentary.

'Cool,' said Sophie. 'OK, where's the deep-freeze with the pizza? I'm starving.'

'How about on the end of the phone?'

'But I haven't brought any money for food—'

'No worries. Guilty parents pay all.'

'I'm not complaining,' said Sophie. 'Quattro formaggi, please.'

I ordered pizzas with extra garlic bread. 'What shall we do this afternoon?'

'We're going shopping,' said Sophie. 'I want a bikini for France and I said we might meet up with Charl at the shops. Why don't we try some on?'

'I'm not sure they make them in 36D. Anyway, my black regulation swimsuit is probably about right for the nasty pool at the school where the course is being held.'

'Oh, go on. You'd look great. Knock 'em dead.'

'Thanks, Sophie.'

'No – I mean you'll look stunning—'

'It's OK,' I laughed. 'I know what you mean. All right. I'll try. So long as they have cubicles in the fitting room and you promise not to laugh!' I looked at my watch. 'Pizzas'll be here in about twenty minutes. I'll go and shave my legs.'

'Wait for me,' said Sophie.

We got on the bus to the shopping centre feeling fat from the pizzas but with wonderfully smooth legs. Sometimes I wonder how I look next to Sophie. Just all wrong compared with her all right, I expect. All tense and anxious compared with her laid-back and hip. Oh well. 'Where are we going to look, Soph?' Sophie knows about clothes and the right places to shop for them. If my wretched mother had her way, I'd be buying everything from John Lewis or Marks and Sparks with a quick turn round Next for something 'up to the minute': Sophie wouldn't be seen dead in Next (really, she just won't even go in) and Marks is strictly for underwear. She'd really like to buy stuff from Diesel and Miss Sixty but Top Shop and Hennes will do. As far as I can tell, it's more important where you *don't* go . . . but I'm perfectly happy to leave that to Sophie and her highly tuned cool-detectors.

'Top Shop.' Sophie was leading the way. 'First stop.'

Top Shop it was. And there was Charlotte over by the bikinis. Sophie grabbed a handful of hangers. She seemed confident that she'd look fine in almost anything – which is probably true. Charlotte was wavering. I spotted her discarding the horizontal stripes – she's as self-conscious about her bottom half as I am about my top half. As for me, I just wanted something underwired. And I actually found it, in a tasteful greeny colour. I hovered over the black – I always do – but Sophie noticed and reprimanded me, 'Hannah! No!' So I moved towards the more interesting colours.

Not long after, we all emerged from our cubicles. I had to peer at myself because I'd taken my glasses off, but I actually didn't look so bad, especially if I stood up straight. Sophie of course looked gorgeous. But so did Charlotte. Quite a surprise! 'Buy it!' I told her. 'You can seduce Josh in it!'

'And you buy that one, Hannah,' said Sophie to me. 'You look fantastic! As I said earlier, knock 'em dead!' I pretended I hadn't heard precisely what she'd said, and bought it anyway.

Charlotte had to go and finish her packing so she came as far as Boots with us and then left. Sophie wanted nail varnish and I, worse luck, needed to stock up on the really exciting things in life, like sanitary protection. I bought several varieties to be prepared for all eventualities. Sophie looked pityingly at my basket. 'Looks like you're all set for a marvellous holiday, Han, hon,' she said. 'Come on, let's go and buy you some gorgeous make-up like Maddy used on you the other night. Just so you can *look* as if you're enjoying yourself even while you're doubled up with period pains.'

'Like, paint a false smile on my face?'

'Something like that.'

Between us we sorted out eyeliner and the brownish eyeshadow. Finding the right lipstick was harder because you can only try it out on your hand. Sophie picked one that I reckoned was darker and vampier than Maddy's, but by then I wanted to pay for my embarrassing basketload and get it all hidden away in a nice carrier bag, so I tossed it in anyway. The queue was full of people buying stuff for going away. I put my basket down and Sophie and I got intrigued by all the different sun preparations the couple in front of us were buying, not to mention the colourful selection of condoms. Terrible how nosy you get in the chemists. At last my things were going through, but by then I was distracted all over again by a loud Scottish voice coming from the large Scottish woman in the queue behind us. She was with a teenage boy who looked totally excruciated and as if he'd rather be anywhere else than in Boots with his mother. 'Donald,' she boomed, 'do you really shave often enough to need your own shaving cream to take away with you? Couldn't you manage without for a week? I'm sure very few of the other lads your age will be shaving. And do you really need this expensive anti-dandruff shampoo? And Donald, the OXY TEN is a very costly (she pronounced it 'corstly') brand of spot cream.' She picked up the offending article and scrutinised it. Then she tutted, 'You don't have to believe all this advertising nonsense, you know. Now TCP always worked for me . . . '

Sophie was heaving in silent agony next to me. I was sobered by the thought that the boy would no doubt have seen all my ghastly purchases. I glanced back at him after I'd paid. My God! He was tall with longish hair and round glasses and looked remarkably like John L—

'Outta here! Now!' said Sophie and dragged me outside to a bench where we both collapsed. 'Dornald!' she said in her best Scottish accent. 'Dornald, you are a pubescent git with bumfluff, dandruff and zits, and as you're my son I think you should be ashamed of yourself . . . Sad bloke, eh, Hannah?'

I hesitated, thinking of the poor guy's embarrassment, not to mention the way he looked, but then I joined in with her helpless giggles. 'Yeah. Unbelievable.'

Sophie was still gasping on the bus and barely over it when we got off and bumped, literally, into yet another embarrassed teenager, the famous Ben Southwell. 'Hi, Sophie!' His voice was rather gruff (no bumfluff, zits or dandruff though).

'Oh, hi, Ben,' said Sophie languidly and started to walk away.

I wasn't having this. 'Aren't you going to introduce me?' I asked.

'Ben, meet Hannah,' said Sophie. There was a silence. 'Hannah, meet Ben,' she added.

I was aware of Ben groping for something to say. 'Maddy gone off somewhere exotic then?' was what he came up with.

'Oh yes,' I said quickly, terrified that Sophie was going to remain silent. 'Hasn't she, Sophie? She's gone to the West Indies with her dad, lucky thing. And Sophie's going to France—'

'You never told me that,' cut in Ben to Sophie. 'I'm going to France too. Isn't that a coincidence?'

'It's a big place, France,' said Sophie. 'Sorry, Ben. Hannah and I are in a bit of a hurry . . . '

'Are we?' I started to ask, but she just linked her arm grimly in mine and walked me away.

'See ya,' said Ben, forlornly I thought, to our departing backs.

All Sophie's mirth had evaporated. 'Why did you have to tell him I was going to France?' she wailed.

'I'm sorry. I didn't know it was classified information. Anyway, it's a big place, France.' Sophie managed a partial return to normality.

'No. I'm sorry. Sense of humour failure on my part. I'll tell you about Ben Southwell some time . . . '

'I know about Ben Southwell. He kisses like a fish . . . '

'There's more.'

'Well I can tell you one thing. He fancies you like mad.

And he's fit. And I'm jealous. And I'll tell you another thing. Donald is coming on my music course. I recognised him, though he was about a foot shorter last year.'

'Hanny, sweetheart . . . ' My mother was using a tone of voice that meant bad news. I'd just packed my bag, folded my music stand and checked that I had a selection of pencils with rubbers on the end – standard music course requirement. Conductors love humiliating kids who don't have their pencils with them. 'Hannah?' Mum's voice came wheedling up the stairs again. 'We need to sort something out, darling. Could you come down?'

I went down slowly, sliding against the banister. 'What?'

'Don't say "what", Hanny.'

'What do we need to sort out?'

'Your lift to the course tomorrow morning.'

'What is there to sort? You're taking me, aren't you?'

'Well. You see, I hadn't realised you started on a Thursday and unfortunately I now have a meeting . . . '

'But, Mum! You promised. Cancel the meeting. Say you've got a prior engagement. You *have* got a prior engagement.'

'I'm afraid it's rather an important meeting.'

'It's important that you take me, Mum! I've got loads to carry. How am I supposed to get there?'

'I was thinking perhaps you could ring one of your friends on the course and ask for a lift?'

'Mum! I don't have any *friends* on a music course. At least, there's no one I know well enough to cadge a lift from!' I was feeling ridiculously upset.

'There is a train, too. You could get a cab from the station. I don't mind giving you the money!'

'I bet you don't!' I snarled. 'You never mind giving me money! It's just a tiny bit of your precious time that you can't give me! You've known about this for ages. Why should your bloomin' meeting be more important than your bloomin' daughter? Why can't your bloomin' daughter come first for a change?'

My dad came home at this point. He always looks dreadful when he comes in from work. 'Now, now, what's all this?' he asked in diplomatic tones as he poured himself a drink. 'No need to fight, surely? Not just before you go away, darling.'

'Mum won't give me a lift tomorrow. She wants me to go on a train. It'll mean leaving at some unearthly hour—'

'You've stayed in bed till lunchtime every day of the holidays so far,' said Mum unnecessarily. 'It won't hurt you to get up—'

'That's not the point!' I shouted. 'You said you'd take me. I want you to take me. All the others arrive with their doting parents. Why can't I?'

'Maybe I can take you,' said Dad. 'I've got a late start tomorrow.'

'That's because you're taking J, Dad, in the opposite direction.'

'You can't let J down,' said Mum. I couldn't believe this.

'But you can let *me* down? Typical!' I stormed out of the room. God, I hate that woman sometimes. She upsets me so much. I stomped upstairs and slammed my door. Why can't I have nice parents, like other people? Dad's not so bad, I suppose. Just feeble. I can't imagine him at work, I really can't.

A while later, J knocked on my door. Ever the peacemaker, J. 'Hannah, why don't you let Dad take you and I'll go on a train. I don't mind. It's about time I got around on my own a bit.' Dad was hovering outside. He followed J in and sat on my bed.

'What time do you start, Hannah?'

'We have to be there by half-past ten.'

'And you, J?'

'Half-eleven.'

'OK. I'll take you first, Hannah. You'll be there a bit early, I'm afraid. And then I'll dash back and take J.'

Not-so-feeble Dad. 'Thanks, Dad. I'd rather be early than have to find my own way there. I just wish Mum would put me before her work sometimes. And before J, sometimes. It's so unfair.'

Dad didn't say anything. There wasn't anything he could say. Then he gave us what was supposed to be a jolly paternal smile. 'Pizzas all round then, for a treat? I think your mother's too tired to cook tonight.' I kicked J to make sure he didn't tell Dad that we'd ordered pizzas for practically every meal so far this holidays. It would be bewildering enough for Dad when he rang them up and found they already knew his address.

Sophie rang quite late. 'Have a cool time, Hannah. Don't do anything I wouldn't do!'

'That gives me a lot of scope then!'

'By the way. Ben Southwell. It's a bit difficult. He cornered me last week and came out with all this stuff about being in love with me and wanting me to go out with him. And I blew it somewhat. Because I do like him but I just don't fancy him – and told him so. And, Hannah, it was awful, because he nearly cried. I didn't know what to do. So then I tried to give him a hug and he shook me off. He said, "Don't do that! I know you don't mean it!" So I said something about not liking to see a friend sad, especially if it was my fault. Anyway, he went quiet for a bit and then just said – "We are friends, aren't we?" So I said, " 'Course, " and he went away. And today was the first time I'd seen him since. Difficult one, huh?'

'Poor guy,' I said. 'And poor you, too.'

'I'll say. Anyway, have a fabbo time. Think of me in sunny France. And I'll think of you' – and here the Scottish accent came on again – 'and Dornald!'

'Thanks a bunch!' I said into her barrage of giggles.

THREE

They always smell, don't they, schools? This was a boarding school where they'd spent the last few days cleaning up after the term, so actually it smelt chiefly of polish. Writers try to identify the components of school smells, like chalk and disinfectant and socks, but it can't be done. I'll leave it to you to imagine the smell of the school I found myself in, a long way this side of lunch, on a boiling hot Thursday that was about to turn gorgeous. Sophie would never allow herself to be in this situation. Nor would Maddy. And there was I, sitting on a bed in a spotless dormitory for four, swinging my legs like a five-year-old and unable to make up my mind what to do next.

Dad had delivered me and driven off. As the first arrival I was met in the foyer by all three women staff, smiling far too brightly for the early hour, and one goat-bearded man (even I knew him as the Goat, though his real name was Mr Galt), who was always in charge of getting everyone to the right place at the right time. I was duly welcomed and sent to consult the notices on the boards: endless lists that told us which orchestra we were in, what pieces we were playing, where we were sleeping, what we would be doing the rest of the time – meals, organised games, outings – aargh! What was I doing here on a lovely hot day in July? What had happened to my freedom?

The notice boards told me that I was in 'Daffodil' (ouch!) dormitory on the first floor, sharing with two sixteen-year-olds I knew slightly, Jessa and Gemma (Jessa was first flute), and another girl my own age. Her name was Adela. Alarm bells rang when I read her name but I wasn't sure why. The notice boards also told me that I was in the first orchestra playing second flute and piccolo. I am good, though I say it myself, so I wasn't surprised. Fourth flute was one Donald Ogilvie. Thank God we were to be separated by the third flute, another Hannah. (There are a lot of us Hannahs.) I scanned the lists for other names I recognised. There were a couple of horn players I was looking forward to seeing again (from afar) and a drummer who everyone fancies. He would liven things up a bit. There were several other girls I get on with, so perhaps I wasn't in for such a terrible ten days after all.

I'd hauled my stuff upstairs. Still no sign of anyone else arriving. The bright chatter of the three women floated up the stairs after me, punctuated from time to time by the gruff voice and the dry laugh of the goaty man. Each bed had a chest of drawers next to it and there were 'dress cupboards' in a small room down the corridor.

I put my clothes away. I put my toothbrush in the toothmug on the chest of drawers. I went and looked out of the window. The grounds of this school were rather beautiful. There was a covered walkway with roses and honeysuckle growing up it, and a huge ancient chestnut tree with a circular bench around the trunk. Beyond the dried-out playing-fields in the distance I could see the swimming-pool, with its Portakabin changing rooms. School buildings and staff houses merged into the trees and hedgerows of the surrounding countryside. Everything shimmered in the heat. Then I heard a couple of cars draw up on the gravel at the front of the school, but that was round the corner where I couldn't see. All of a sudden my solitude seemed precious. I went back to my bed and curled up with a book, so that if anyone came in I could look busy.

Someone swung into the room and hurled a backpack on to the bed next to mine. 'Wattadump!' was what she said. 'You Hannah?'

'Yup.'

'Gemma and Jessa are older, aren't they?' she said. I

realised that this bright-eyed girl with wiry black curls, shredded jeans and a tight T-shirt that said *I Like the Pope, the Pope Smokes Dope* on it, was Adela Borelli. Half-Italian, brilliant violinist and total wildchild. 'I'm just nipping outside for a cig,' she informed me. 'Don't go away. I'm relying on you to show me the business. Never done a residential before.'

'Just don't get caught smoking,' I said, rather primly.

'Huh! They won't get me!' laughed Adela. 'Considering they *begged* me to come and lead the orchestra, they're hardly likely to kick me out for something as boring as smoking *cigarettes*, are they?' She stuffed her packet of 20 into her jeans' pocket and disappeared.

Jessa and Gemma arrived together. Jessa is an English rose; Gemma more of a British bulldog, but they're both nice, dead sensible types, with steady boyfriends.

'Hi, Hannah,' said Jessa, recognising me. 'I see we've been promoted to First and Second. They should have made you First, really, but then I don't do the piccolo.' Our instruments were all we had in common at this stage.

'Hi,' said Gemma. 'You realise we've got Adela to contend with!'

'She's OK,' said Jessa, testing the springs on her bed.

'You wait until she gets up to her tricks—'

'And what tricks might they be?' Adela came into the room, reeking of cigarette smoke. 'Come on, Hannah,' she said, as if we were already best mates, 'everyone's going in for this meeting and I want to check out Kevin Hazell, you know, the drummer. I want to see how anyone called Kevin can be as sexy as he's supposed to be. Perhaps it's just because he's got his own car.'

A faraway look came into Jessa's eyes. '*He*'s here, is he? Kevin! Let me tell you that Kevin Hazell is – a god. He is tall, he is dark, he has these melting brown eyes that just turn you into a little puddle, he—'

Gemma was looking at her strangely, but Adela was tugging at my shirt. 'Come *on*, Hannah,' she said. 'No time to waste.'

The introductory meeting was held in the old school hall. It was one of the original school buildings, more like a church, with pews. I slid in after Gemma and Jessa, and Adela squeezed in next to me. It looked like I was stuck with her. I felt the temperature rise all down the row as the famous Kevin Hazell sat down next to Adela, followed by a number of the older boys, including, to my horror, Donald. (I couldn't even think of his name without hearing it spoken by the Scottish mother from hell.) Adela managed to elbow Kevin in the ribs and get his attention while we were waiting. Jessa was practically fainting with envy, but Adela simply said – 'So you're Mr Skins, are you? I'm Adela, your leader.'

'It's like policemen!' said Kevin, smiling confidentially at the rest of us, 'Leaders get younger every year.'

'Infant prodigy, me,' said Adela, without a hint of embarrassment.

'Ssshhh!' said Gemma. Our introductory meeting was about to begin.

As the Goat told us all about being punctual for rehearsals and quiet after 11pm I glanced around the hall. There were about seventy of us. Half were exceedingly small. They were the junior orchestra, annoying little brats to a kid. The other half were the senior orchestra – us. Most of us were fourteen or over, with a good proportion of sixth-formers. If my row was anything to go by, there were some OK people here. By the time one of the smiley women was talking about what was on offer apart from music I was beginning to think it might even be quite fun – if only to watch Jessa and Adela doing battle over Kevin. He was nice though. When he'd smiled at us I could almost believe he was smiling just at me . . .

Our days were to go something like this: sectionals in the

morning and whole orchestra sessions in the afternoon. The afternoon sessions didn't start until about three, so there was a big break in the middle of the day to rest or swim, play tennis, go to the town or whatever. The rehearsals went on until half-five, when everyone rushed to the TV room before supper at half-past six. And then the long summer evenings were our own. Friday nights were disco nights – sarky shrieks and whistles in response to this. It didn't match up to the clubbing habits of the more sophisticated ones.

The juniors trooped out to the other school hall to be briefed about the music they were going to be playing while we stayed behind to hear about ours. This was to be quite a big, showy concert with a Beethoven symphony, Rimsky-Korsakov's *Capriccio Espagnol* – which has loads of solos for all the different instruments, and the Mendelssohn violin concerto, starring guess who? Adela rolled her eyes at me and wriggled like a little kid. We were also going to put on a chamber concert. We'd form our own groups and choose our own music, including jazz and rock as well as old stuff. Only the really dedicated parents make it to the chamber concert on the last afternoon. Mine never do. They just about manage to arrive in time for the evening concert before whisking me home.

The meeting finally came to an end with, 'You'll be working hard, but we'll try to make this an enjoyable ten days for you. You're all excellent musicians or you wouldn't be here. You all have plenty in common. Get to know each other. (Cheers and jeers.) Have fun. But first have some lunch. The canteen is along the covered way and round the corner. Your afternoon rehearsals are in the gym at three. Sectionals in the music block in the morning.'

We filed out in our rows to the canteen. I was keen to avoid Donald. I'm not sure why. I associated him with feeling horribly embarrassed. From where I sat in the canteen I had a good view of the boys' table. Adela and Jessa were gazing at it – and Kevin – unashamedly, but I just sneaked little looks every now and then. Kevin was unbelievably attractive. Kind of dark and hunky with eyes like deep pools. I couldn't help noticing that Donald's longish, light-brown hair was clean and silky (and dandruff-free!) today. His pointy nose and glinting granny glasses still made him look like John Lennon, but the part of his face that intrigued me most was his mouth and the way the corners went up when he smiled – and that was *just* like John Lennon . . .

'Cool guy, Kevin,' said Adela. 'Jessa was right about his eyes. When he fixes you with his gaze you kind of – wibble.'

'I'm surprised anything makes *you* "wibble", Adela,' said Gemma sharply.

Adela scraped her chair noisily and stood up. 'Anyone else coming for a smoke?' she asked loudly. There was no response so she swaggered off on her own.

'Nice butt,' came a comment from the next table, but it wasn't from Kevin, or from Donald.

'Nice but what?' someone else asked.

'Naughty,' I said, and left the canteen, thinking I might join Adela, at least for a wander round the grounds, if not for a smoke. There was always a chance that some of the attention showered on her by the boys might rub off on me.

The afternoon rehearsal was going fine until I felt a familiar griping sensation in my stomach and realised I was going to have to get to the loo fast. My period had chosen this precise moment to begin. I lasted out to the end of the section and then made a dash for it. Of course I sent my music stand flying, but I couldn't hang around to pick it up. When I came back the entire orchestra was waiting for me. Why is a girl's life so ghastly? I picked my way over to my desk. Someone had righted my music stand. Jessa and the other Hannah were poised ready to play. It was Donald who leant across and pointed out which bar we were starting on. I sensed his sympathy but I couldn't bear to look him in the eye. Of course, he would *know* why I'd had to go out. Ooooh. Horrible! I cringed and tried to concentrate on the music in front of me.

FOUR

At quarter to eight on Friday morning we were all woken by a nasty buzzing sound. As I surfaced I realised that this was the 'rising bell'. 'Wozatt?!' Adela shouted in alarm. Jessa looked distinctly bleary, but Gemma sat up and looked at her watch.

'Time to get up,' she said, and swung her legs out of bed.

'When'ssectionalsh?' asked Adela.

'Ten o'clock,' I told her.

'Wake me at ten to,' she said, and burrowed back under her pillows.

I had a vague memory of Adela going out in the night. Perhaps that was why she was tired. I decided not to mention it. Jessa wasn't thinking about Adela. She was hugging her knees and looking dreamy. 'When I'm with Kevin I wonder if I should stay with my boyfriend,' she was saying. 'Is it fair, d'you think, to stay with one boy when really you fancy someone else?'

'Doesn't everyone fancy Kevin, though?' I asked hesitantly. *I* fancied him. He even made Adela feel wibbly.

'Well, yes,' said Jessa. 'But he is very nice to me. He just makes me feel . . . so . . . special when he talks to me.' So the confidential smile hadn't been for my benefit after all.

'Ah well,' she sighed. 'Perhaps I'll get a smoochy dance out of him at the disco tonight . . . '

'Dream on,' said Gemma, returning to the dormitory. 'You're awful, Jessa. You've got a perfectly nice boyfriend of your own. Maybe I should tell him you're more interested in someone called *Kevin.*'

'Oh don't be so boring, Gemma,' said Jessa mildly, and drifted off to have a shower.

'Sectionals' are when each section of the orchestra – strings, brass, woodwind and so on – practise separately. So my section, the woodwind section, consisted of four flute players, three oboists and one cor anglais player, three clarinettists and two bassoonists. Two of the clarinettists, Josie and Helen, were girls I knew slightly from another class at my school. The third, Max, was a boy a bit younger than me who I've played alongside for years. No one had arrived to take the sectional when I got there. Jessa, Hannah and Donald were all in their seats. I had to squeeze past Donald to get to my stand but I was spared looking at him because Josie and Helen were tugging at me.

'Duck! Duck!'

Donald ducked, but I chose not to notice. He wasn't to know it was my nickname. Yet. 'Duck,' said Josie, 'give us the goss on Adela. She's in your room, isn't she? Did you know that she went up to the boys' rooms last night? Apparently she just walked into the room Kevin was in and asked if any of them wanted to come out and wander around with her. They were out for hours. Max says they went for a swim.'

'What did I say?' asked Max, sitting down and adjusting his stand.

'About Adela and the boys last night. Didn't they go for a midnight swim or something?'

'I didn't hear about a swim. I just heard about a hip flask . . . '

'I heard that she was snogging Ke—' Helen was interrupted by the piercing voice of Miss Claggan, the woodwind tutor.

'Quiet, everyone please. We're going to work on the

Beethoven this morning, but we're starting with the slow movement – that's page six in your music. Now hands up if you *haven't* brought a pencil with you . . .'

'Here we go,' muttered Jessa.

We had a coffee break at 11.30, and then carried on relentlessly. The worst bit in sectionals is when you have to deal with a particularly tricky bit and everyone has to play those few bars on their own. That way the tutor can find out precisely who is playing the bum notes. The flutes had a difficult ten-bar section. Jessa played it. Most of it was OK. I played it. I fluffed the first few notes and then it went fine. The other Hannah made a complete mess of it. 'Again,' said Miss Claggan. Hannah managed a bit better. 'Once more,' said Miss Claggan. Hannah scraped through. Then it was Donald's turn. I hadn't really heard him play solo. He played it with a very breathy jazzy tone, but it was all in tune and on time. Miss Claggan didn't say anything. Donald started to go red. Then – 'We have a problem here,' said Miss Claggan. Donald looked around desperately.

'Sounded fine to me,' I said to Jessa, as Donald wiped his sweating palms on his jeans.

'Not your playing,' said Miss Claggan, preoccupied. 'No, it's your names, flutes.' Donald looked relieved but we were all puzzled. 'Two Hannahs,' she said. 'What shall I call you, Hannah One and Hannah Two? Hannah with the specs and Hannah without?' Great, I thought, but worse was to come. 'Or your surnames?' (Yeah, call me Gross, why don't you?) 'Does either of you have a nickname I can use, perhaps?'

Oh God. 'Hannah Gross is always called Duck!' squeaked Josie.

'Duck?' said Miss Claggan.

'I'd rather not,' I said, but I said it too quietly.

'OK, Duck it is!' said Miss Claggan cheerfully.

And then someone said what was bound to be said sooner

or later – 'At least she's not sitting next to Donald!' Total collapse of woodwind section. Donald Duck! Ha ha! At my expense. And Donald's, I suppose. He looked over at me but I looked away. It was all too painful. Fancy being 'Duck' here. From now on our names would be horribly, inextricably linked.

In fact the sectional was fine after that. In a funny sort of way the business over the names had broken the ice and made us a group. The only person really suffering was the other Hannah because she was terrible at sightreading and minded about being shown up. But she was a great one for locking herself into a practice room for hours, so she'd sort herself out over the next few days. The piece was even beginning to take shape by the end of the morning. This is when I realise how much I enjoy playing in a orchestra. It's the team thing. You all work away at your little bit and then suddenly you put it all together and it sounds terrific. That part never fails to give me a buzz.

But I wanted more than ever to avoid close encounters with Donald. I stuck with Helen and Josie for lunch, rather than sitting with my room-mates, who were sharing a table with the boys. I caught sight of Adela squashed in between Kevin and Donald, flirting outrageously with both of them. Jessa was looking grumpy and Gemma was being aloof.

'Thanks a bunch for telling the world my nickname,' I said to Josie, as we finished eating.

'Sorry. It just seemed the obvious solution. All your friends call you Duck, don't they?'

'My *friends*, yes. But not the whole world.'

'I really am sorry.' Josie was genuinely apologetic.

'Just don't do it again!' I said, and we all laughed.

Adela scampered over to our table. 'Coming for a walk, Ducks?'

'Not you as well! Anyway, it's Duck, not Ducks. OK, Adela. I've had enough of this lunch. See you later, you two.'

The bright sun blinded us after the dark of the dining room. High noon in high summer. Mad dogs and Englishmen. The short grass was dry and prickly. The path was a glare of white concrete. Adela was making for an avenue of lime trees which ran along one side of the games pitches. There was a dip between the two rows of tall trunks, so you could sit in the shade with your back against a trunk, well hidden from the passing world. Obviously the perfect place to smoke. Adela lit up. 'Sure you don't want one?'

'No thanks.' But I let out a tremendous exhalation when she did. 'Phew. It's good to be away from everyone.'

'You bet. Everyone's been on at me about last night as if I'd done something really out of order. Such a bunch of goody-goodies. The rumours are cool, actually. Much better than what really happened.'

'Well, what did happen? I vaguely remember hearing you go out in the night.'

'What have you heard?'

'Oh, most things. Drink. Sex. Nudity.'

'I told you the rumours were cool! I went over to the boys' block – just for a laugh. Most of them were tucked up in their little beds. Some of them were watching a TV. The younger ones were having a pillow fight, for God's sake! They barely noticed me, but then Kevin came along in these really vile pyjamas to stop them. *He* certainly noticed me! So I said, "You're not really going to bed before eleven o'clock on a hot summer night, are you? Why don't you come outside with me for a bit? We could go skinny dipping." I only said it to freak him out. Anyway, he told the kids to go to bed and then said that he couldn't *possibly* set a bad example by coming with me, but behind their backs he made swimming motions and held up ten fingers. Then he said, all prefect-like, "You'd better get out of here before someone catches you, Adela." I told him that no one had even noticed me so far. It's because I look like a boy, Hannah. Short hair and no bum. Do you know, I walked down the stairs and out of the front door and still no one saw me?'

And that's what she wants, I thought. Attention. All the time. People to notice her. Look at me! Adela is quite unlike anyone I've ever met in my life before. Not a kid, but certainly not grown-up either. I'm not sure I like her but I can't help feeling envious of her confidence.

'Anyway, I had a swim and then Kevin turned up. He had his jeans on but I could see his pyjama trousers sticking out underneath. And a T-shirt. Gorgeous and hunky he may be, but secretly I think he's a bit of a mummy's boy. He sat on the edge with his feet in the water and said he didn't want a swim. So I pushed him in! He was furious at first – all his clothes wet – but then he just started mucking about, like me. It was cool. Then we came over here and had a bit of a chat while I had a cig. He's OK. Bit of a wuss, but OK . . . '

'OK?' I said. 'OK? He's so fit, Adela. I can't believe you're being so casual. I mean, he followed you out to the pool – just you and just him. I suppose he must fancy you . . . '

'Probably,' said Adela. 'But I suppose I really wanted all of them to come out. It's daft, everyone being in their rooms. It wouldn't happen in Italy. We're all out in the summer evenings, kids, everyone. I thought Donald and the Horns might come out too.'

She looked at me in that direct way of hers. 'What do you think of Donald? Don't you think he looks like John Lennon?'

I was thrown, so I played for time. 'Yes. He does look like John Lennon. I don't know what I think of him.' I thought of Sophie and me in Boots and my dash to the loo and the Donald Duck jokes and the memory of each occasion made me cringe all over again.

'I think he's sexy.'

'Sexy? Donald?' (I thought of the dandruff shampoo and the spot cream.) 'I don't. No. I don't think Donald's sexy—'

Adela's butterfly mind was darting all over the place. 'You ever been to Italy?'

'We stayed in a hotel once, but I don't remember much about it.'

'I go there every summer. It's where I'm going after this is all over. I stay with my nonna – my Dad's mum. And she lives in this brilliant place with all my dad's other relations. I've got five uncles and loads of cousins. Dad's a bit of a dead loss. He has what we call a drink problem, does my darling papa. Wonderful singer but can't stay upright. That's why Mum has to work so hard. Concerts every night.'

'What does she play?' I didn't want to halt Adela's flow. All this was fascinating.

'Cello. Surely you've heard of her? Celia Barnes? That's her maiden name. Anyway, holidays are a bit of a bummer, or they would be if I couldn't go to Italy.'

'So do you speak Italian with your grandmother?'

'Of course!'

'And do you take your violin?'

'Of course!' she said again, and laughed. 'OK, so they forced me to practise when I was little. No way out when both your parents are musicians. But yes, I still do loads of practice out there because someone always rolls up to listen. And you know me, I love an audience.'

Adela's mind darted back. 'I refuse to be treated like a six-year-old. No one's making me stay in bed if I don't want to be there . . . ' And off again. 'I think Donald's sexy. I think you're lucky sitting almost next to him. He's very tall, isn't he? I like tall blokes. I think he fancies me. I think Kevin does too. And I think I'll probably go for Kevin. Just to annoy Jessa!' Adela leapt to her feet. 'Come on, let's go and see what everyone's doing. There's still an hour before you have to listen to me in whole orchestra rehearsal.'

We spent most of that hour touring the various places

people had scattered to. Jessa, Gemma & Co. were sunbathing by the pool. Kevin, Donald et al. were getting sunstroke on the tennis courts. Josie and Helen, Max and some of the younger boys were on the bench under the chestnut tree. Most people were drifting back to the dormitory blocks to get ready for the afternoon rehearsal. Adela abandoned me and went to practise. We were doing the Mendelssohn – her big moment, or rather, moments. It is a difficult and showy solo part, though I don't think anyone doubted that she would manage it.

An hour later, 'manage' wasn't the word I'd have used to describe Adela's performance. Wretched girl had us spellbound. I had that silly lump in the throat and lurking tears you get when something is just completely brilliant. There was little Adela, looking like a sprite or an elf with her short hair, short shorts and a green top, completely into it, ducking and swaying as she played, in a world of her own. We all burst into spontaneous applause when we got to the end. Kevin gave her a drum roll. Jessa leant over to me and said 'Wow. Why do the rest of us bother?'

Adela came and took up her place at first desk again and we carried on the rehearsal. There was plenty of work if we were going to do Adela justice. And even when the rehearsal was over and we were having our dose of pre-supper TV, people were still talking about her. I began to feel I was sharing a room with royalty. The coming evening's entertainment – the disco – hardly got a mention. The boys were all over her at supper, I know, because Adela forced me to sit at their table. Jessa tried to distract them by talking about the disco. 'You are coming, aren't you? You won't all just go to the pub?'

'Now there's a good idea,' said Kevin.

'I don't fancy our chances,' said Donald, who I know is at least two years under drinking age (not that I'd dream of saying anything). 'Staff are all on their guard. I expect *they'll* all come to the disco, Jessa.' And he grinned at her. And it was at that precise moment that something happened to me. That grin. A shake of his hair, his fine silky hair. His eyes dancing behind the glasses. His lanky body leaning towards her. A stab of pure jealousy shot through me. I felt jealous of Jessa because Donald was smiling at her.

Get a grip, Han, old girl, I thought. I remembered with renewed pangs all the times he'd tried to be nice to me. How unpleasant he must have found me. Always looking the other way. Always blanking him.

Adela was talking to me. 'You OK over there? You won't catch me going to a totally narcotic-free rave-up, but you'll go, won't you, Hannah?'

Oh yes. Dreary innocent little me. Disco queen. Sure. 'I might.'

'Well *we're* going,' said Gemma, linking arms with Jessa and heading for the door, 'and we expect to see you all there.'

'What an incentive,' said Kevin. But I couldn't tell whether or not he was being ironic. My brain was shot to pieces.

FIVE

I hate discos.

Adela was nowhere to be seen, but Gemma, Jessa and I spent the next hour getting ready. I had clammy hands (why was I nervous?) and couldn't decide what to wear. I tried on a dress of Jessa's. It looked OK, but then I thought jeans would be better, so I tried on a variety of everybody's tops until I came up with one of Gemma's that suited me. Jessa made me up, so I decided to brave it without my glasses. In the end we tottered over to the new hall, Jessa looking like a tart and me almost completely blind.

The hall was bleak. There were a few older kids, including

Max, but mainly there were about fifty brats skidding around to some girl band in the half-darkness. No sign of any of 'our' boys. Jessa (bless 'er) hauled some bloke on to the floor and called to us to join them. Well, we tried dancing, but it was hopeless. I couldn't see much anyway – though I knew it was Max I was dancing with at that point. Later, when he was over at the hi-fi checking for any half-decent CDs, Adela burst in. 'Come on, you guys. We're all going to the pool. This is for the kids. Blimey, Jessa,' she added as Kevin and the other boys drew up at the rear, 'you going somewhere special?' I couldn't see Jessa blushing but I felt it. And Adela's next little gem was for me. 'Don't suppose you'll want to swim in your condition, will you, Hannah? You could always come and watch.' I couldn't think of anything to say to that, so I just stood by helplessly as the evening crumbled before my (misty) eyes and everyone over the age of twelve left the disco and followed Adela to the pool. Along with Kevin, Donald, the Horns, Max and anyone the tiniest bit worth spending time with. Except Jessa.

Jessa grabbed my arm and hissed, 'Bitch! . . . I hate her!' as she wheeled me away from the hall in the opposite direction. In fact, on that occasion I think Adela was just opening her mouth without thinking first. But poor Jessa. We found ourselves drifting around the gardens. A warm breeze blew through the evening and it would have been quite romantic in different circumstances. We sat down on the grass. 'How dare she show me up in front of Kevin, like that. And you for that matter.'

'I don't really mind what Kevin thinks of me,' I said, realising with a pang that I *did* care what Donald thought.

'Well I mind a lot. And she knows it. Little madam. She thinks that just because she's a genius on the violin she can get away with anything. She flaunts herself in front of the boys all the time. Why doesn't she just wear a sign saying "I am available. Queue here"?'

'I don't reckon she *thinks*,' I said, ' – she just acts on impulse.'

But Jessa wasn't having any of it. 'Don't you believe it. She's a scheming little bitch. She knows I fancy the pants off Kevin and so she's determined to get off with him herself. All right, I know I've got a boyfriend and all that, but that's my problem, not hers. I mean, I don't think she even appreciates just how gorgeous he is, that he's nice as well as good-looking. It's all just a game to her.'

Jessa had a point. It wasn't even animal attraction that drew Adela to Kevin (which it certainly was with the rest of us). It was simply that he was the coolest guy around so she was out to prove herself and annoy Jessa by getting him. Rather a waste somehow.

'We have to make sure that the next disco isn't as rubbish as that one,' I said.

'Perhaps we should get them to have it by the pool and cut out the competition,' said Jessa. 'Actually, that's not such a bad idea. There's a big area between the two changing rooms, where we were sunbathing. We could do a barbecue as well. Perhaps it should just be for the older ones – it'll be our last night.' She was really getting her teeth into this idea. I could see her setting up the big romantic scene with Kevin. 'We could get some fairy lights from somewhere . . . ' At least it had taken her mind off Adela for the time being.

The grass was beginning to feel damp so we got up and walked around. We could hear the thud of the music from the disco and the squeals that drifted over from the direction of the swimming pool. Jessa was talking about Kevin but I found that my mind was filling up with images of Donald – or Donnie, as the boys called him. 'Donnie lad' in Kevin's tones sounded a lot better than 'Dornald' as shrilled by his mother. To think that Sophie and I had found him sad! He was so cute. And that smile. If only he'd direct it at me again. I'd like to have him look down at me from that height with a smile specially for me. Really for me, not just for anyone, like Kevin. How was I going to sit so near him all the time with my newly found awareness? It would be torture. Or would it be bliss? And what if he did bother to look at me? Would it be written all over my face? And then I remembered Adela saying that she thought he was sexy. And me saying I didn't think he was sexy. Oh, what if she told him! Donnie, Donnie, I *do* think you're sexy now . . .

'What did you say?' I must have been gnashing my teeth audibly. And I'd no idea what Jessa had been talking about. It suddenly felt quite late. As if to rub it in, a bell rang from the belltower – time for the younger ones to go to bed.

'What shall we do?' asked Jessa. 'I don't really want to go over to the swimming pool now. I don't know what I want to do, apart from finding Kevin on his own. Come on, Hannah, think of something. We can't possibly just go to *bed*! Not on a beautiful romantic evening like this!'

I thought about it. 'Let's go over to the pool then. There are over thirty senior orchestra kids around the place. I'm not going to let stupid remarks from Adela stop us from doing what we want to do – which for you is being with Kevin and for me is just being with a bunch of us and not being left out.' (I didn't say what I really wanted to do. Actually, I wasn't sure what I'd do right then if I was on my own with Donald.) So we ambled over towards the pool. We could hear people splashing about and shouting, but when we opened the high wooden gate we didn't know who we would find there. Faces just look like blobs to me when I haven't got my glasses on, especially in fading light, so I wasn't bothered, but I could sense the tension in Jessa as we went in.

'Adela's not here—' she hissed.

'Probably in the boys' changing rooms then,' I said tactlessly.

'Hi, you two!'

'Who was that?' I asked.

'Max and the two Horns,' said Jessa, still distracted. 'I can't see Kevin either. Or Gemma. Or Donald.'

'I expect Adela's dragged them off for a smoke or something,' I said, not liking to think about it.

'Guess what!' said Max, near us now. 'Big scandal! Adela was swimming topless when the Goat came along. Not that *we* minded, of course. She said she was only doing what they do on every beach on the Continent, but he wasn't having any of it. He told Gemma to get her a towel and ordered Adela to get out straight away and get dressed and go over to the office. She's in for a rocket.'

'So where are the others?' Jessa asked.

'Well. Gemma went with Adela to the office. A bunch of blokes went off somewhere else. My guess is that they went somewhere in Kevin's car.'

'Right gang of delinquents we are!' I was a bit shocked by Adela's exhibitionism, though not surprised. She was perfectly right about Mediterranean beaches. I mean, my *mother* goes topless there, though I wish she wouldn't.

'No,' said Jessa through gritted teeth. 'Just normal teenagers. Who happen to play musical instruments. The only thing that's abnormal is that we have parents who think it's OK to send us to prison camp in our school holidays.'

'It's not that bad!' said Max. 'We were having a brilliant time until the Goat came along.'

'Max,' said Jessa grandly. 'You are fourteen. I am nearly seventeen. I'm old enough to have left home and I don't like people who aren't even my parents telling me what to do.' This amused me because Jessa is hardly a rebel, but I knew she was sore at that moment. Her darling Kevin with a topless Adela. Hang on! My darling Donald with a topless Adela too, and all the other darlings. Actually, I could only think of it as funny. If Adela wanted to take her clothes off it was up to her. I can't say I felt threatened. And it had obviously made Max's day.

*

'Lemmego!' Gemma was struggling to get something from Adela's hands as we walked back in.

Definitely a situation that needed defusing. 'Hi, Adela! You've made a lot of guys very happy tonight!'

Adela finally shook herself free. 'I can't see what the fuss is all about. Fascists. They make me furious!' She glared at Gemma. 'And you, you're as bad as the rest of them! So I want to have a fag. I'm upset. OK? And you get it into your head that I'm going to set fire to things.' She flicked her lighter on under Gemma's nose. 'Angry, yes. Stupid, no. Not like everyone else around here.' She went to the door.

Jessa stepped forward. 'Adela – don't you think – if everyone's cross already—'

'Oh give me a break!' screamed Adela and pushed past her on her way out.

'Thank God you're back,' said Gemma. 'She's completely out of control. Honestly, when the three teachers told her off she went berserk. Two of them frogmarched her back here. They said her behaviour was disgusting and immoral and that they would tell her parents. So she just shouted, "Fine! Do that. My dad's an alcoholic. My mum's a professional workaholic. Oh yes, they'll be so upset to discover that their daughter removed her bikini top won't they – like they *really* give a cuss. Well, believe me, they don't!" '

'Adela's just on a different planet from the rest of us,' I said.

'No she isn't,' Jessa said. 'She's a spoilt little brat and a complete exhibitionist. I don't think we should start feeling sorry for her.'

'I don't understand her at all,' said Gemma.

It occurred to me that maybe I was the only one who had any time for Adela. 'I think I'd better go and get her. I know where she goes.'

'She can stay out all night for all I care,' said Gemma.

'As long as she doesn't decide to include Kevin in her plans,' said Jessa, suddenly alarmed.

I managed to slip outside again. I don't know quite how Adela does it so easily – I had to play hide-and-seek with the teachers and the Goat quite a bit before I crept out of one of the back doors. I wasn't sure how we were going to get in again. I found Adela in the lime avenue as I knew I would. She was alone. 'I came out to keep you company,' I said and sat next to her.

She didn't say anything. She finished her cigarette and stood up. 'We'll go back past the music block,' she said. 'The jasmine smells fantastic at night.' Like a lamb she came back with me, sliding in the back door, past the voices coming from the staff sitting room and up the stairs in the subdued light to our room.

She stripped off, got into bed and whispered, 'G'night.' So ended the most important day of my life to date, the day I fell in love with Donnie.

SIX

The first Saturday on a ten-day course is just like a weekday. (The following Wednesday is an outing and then the second Saturday is the concert before we all go home.) But I woke up feeling completely hyper – like I do on a weekend in school-time – and wondered why for a while before I remembered. Donnie. Don. Donald. 'Dornald' even. Oh God! I didn't know if I wanted to see him or not. I couldn't decide what to wear. I wished I didn't have to wear my glasses. I wanted it to be a hot day so we could sit outside but then I thought I'd prefer a wet day so we'd be confined indoors. Maybe I'd just stay in bed and daydream for a bit. Adela was dead to the world, but Gemma, in her usual efficient way, was ready for breakfast, and so was Jessa. They looked over to where I was sitting in my nightie with three tops laid out on the bed. 'The black one,' said Jessa. 'Come on, I'm starving.'

'She means that she wants to get over to the dining room to see Kevin,' said Gemma, 'and check that he hasn't been corrupted. But we'll wait for you if you hurry up.' Did I want to have a shower and wash my hair or did I want to see Donald?

'You go. I'll skip breakfast. I want to wash my hair. Bring me back an apple or something.' So I had a shower and washed my hair. I blow-dried it so it hung straight and shiny. Black top. Jeans. Trainers. Glasses. Damn. I wished I didn't have to wear them. If Mum wanted to buy me off this holiday she could get me some contact lenses . . . Squirt of body spray.

'Oi! Hannah! You smell!' Adela was waking up. 'It smells OK actually. Can I borrow some?'

'I suppose so. Hadn't you better get up, Adela?'

'I'll get up when I want to, thank you very much. I'm not letting those cows get to me, you know.'

'Well, sectionals start in half an hour. See you at lunch time?' I could hear Gemma and Jessa coming back from breakfast and I really didn't want to be there when they saw how late Adela was. It was a gorgeous day outside. I gathered up my flute and went out to intercept them. 'Did you bring me back some food?'

'Oh sorry,' said Jessa. 'We forgot. If you run you might still get some. They were only just starting to clear away when we left.' Again I dithered. Did I want food, or did I want to get to the sectional long before Donald so that I didn't have to squeeze past him? I set off towards the dining room, saw the boys leaving it and changed my mind. I headed towards the music block. I was hungry. Well, sort of hungry. I had butterflies in my stomach and my hands were clammy again. I wished I wasn't on my own. I felt self-conscious. What if I bumped into the boys? I thought of Sophie. She wouldn't be fazed like this. She thought Donald was a pubescent git. I looked around guiltily as if someone could read my thoughts. I don't think you're a pubescent git, Donnie. *I* think you're cute.

Needless to say I arrived ten whole minutes earlier than anyone else for the sectional. Max was the next to turn up – with Donald. 'Bit early for sex aren't you, Hannah?' said Max, and grinned over at Donald before they both cracked up. Helen and Josie came along next. There was definitely an air of hysteria.

'Toothsome twosome,' remarked Max, and they cracked up again.

'OK, OK, what's the joke?' said Jessa from the door. 'Are you talking about Adela? Everyone else is.'

Max strutted around pretending to be Adela unclasping her bikini top and tossing it to the crowd. He mimicked: 'Don't gawp, Max. Never seen a girl naked before? I just prefer an all-over tan. You'll get used to it.'

Helen took over. She minced around with one hand on her hip. 'Anyone would think I was doing something *wild*. Where have you been all your sad little lives?'

Then Donald became the Goat arriving on the scene. He stepped back and put his hand over his eyes. 'Good gracious, girl! COVER YOURSELF UP!' And the entire section who had now gathered fell about laughing. Jessa caught my eye and silently commiserated. At least I wasn't the only one who'd missed the drama. I couldn't help feeling a bit sorry for Adela being the butt of everyone's jokes, but Miss Claggan was there and organising us before sympathy got the better of me.

People became businesslike as they sorted out their stands and their music. I dared myself to glance sideways at Donald once or twice when I knew he was turning pages or looking at Miss Claggan. The day was becoming hot and airless. I felt aware of my whole body: the way I was sitting, my feet, my hands, my glasses. I realised I was sensing Donald rather than seeing him – his concentration, his nervous smile when he played a wrong note, his outstretched legs when he wasn't playing and the way he tucked one foot under his chair when it was his turn.

What with one thing and another, I was pretty tense. And then – my guts started to speak. During the twenty bars' rest my empty tummy started to protest loudly – and musically. Jessa and the other Hannah were the first to titter, and then, as the rumbles became more pronounced, everyone else in the section. Donald and Miss Claggan were the last to surrender to helpless giggles. 'Now, really!' scolded Miss Claggan.

'Those were the most musical notes I've heard all morning!' said Max.

'Donald Duck lives!' said Helen.

'Lunchtime, I think,' said Miss Claggan firmly. 'And Duck – eat breakfast in future!'

Why is my life one big embarrassment? Now everyone was talking to me in Donald Duck voices. Everyone, that is, except Donald. He'd disappeared. He didn't turn up for lunch either. 'Where's Donald, Duck?' Why was everyone asking *me*?

'How should I know?' I said to Gemma.

'Well, you sit with him don't you?'

'And it's funnier to ask you,' said one of the Horns.

'I know where he is.' It was Adela speaking. (How did *she* know?) 'I saw him being kidnapped by the Loch Ness monster – a monstrous Scottish female – straight after your sectional.'

'That's his mother,' I said.

'Oooh, so you *are* very familiar with the life of Donald, Duck!' said Jessa.

'Well – I—'

'Don't protest too much . . . ' said the other Horn.

Adela was impatient to finish her bulletin. 'When I asked him where he was going he said it was his grandparents' golden wedding party and his mother wouldn't let him miss it. He's coming back tonight though. So cheer up, Hannah.'

'What? Me?' What was Adela up to now?

'Yeah. You should have seen your face just then.'

'Oh shut up, Adela,' said Jessa protectively. 'Come on, Hannah. Let's go and sunbathe before the weather breaks.'

'I thought I heard thunder during the sectional,' said Max with a wicked grin.

Did I dare to ask Jessa what was going on? 'Jessa, why do I get the feeling everyone's always taking the mickey out of me?'

'They don't.'

'Well, it feels like it. All this – ' I hesitated, not wanting to give anything away – 'Donald Duck business. And what was Adela on about?'

'Oh, ignore her. She just wants to make people think that she knows more than they do. And . . . well . . . I suppose it's because you do look rather anxious all the time. But it's a cute sort of anxious. And the boys probably fancy you and try to cover it up with teasing.'

'ME!' I couldn't have been more surprised. Maddy, Sophie, yes. Charlotte, maybe. But *me*? There must definitely be signals out there that I was not reading.

'Yes. Why not?'

'Glasses? Bad hair? Top heavy—'

'Exactly. Where've you been, Hannah? You know what blokes go for!'

'Yes. Leggy blondes. Without glasses.'

'Nobody minds glasses these days. It's like train tracks. You won't have them forever. And you're cool. You know about things and you don't blather like most girls.'

I was struck dumb with amazement. With my old friends I was just the Duck. And with the girls at school I was just one of the swotty ones. I wasn't sure I could cope with being noticed.

'So what was that about Donald?'

'Adela thinks he fancies you. Didn't she say? And she

can't stand the fact that someone might fancy anyone other than her, so she's going to make it difficult for you.'

'Oh, Adela's not that spiteful, you know.'

'She is, Hannah. Watch it.'

It was pain and pleasure together to have Donald absent. I didn't have to worry about shooting off to the loo, my glasses steaming up, bumping into him, or anything like that. On the other hand, I missed him. I would glance over to his desk and feel disappointment at his empty chair. Life was dull without the possibility of one of his smiles in my direction. And now Jessa had planted the idea in my brain that *he* fancied *me* . . . Oh well. I was so flustered that I would have blown it anyway.

The thunder came towards the end of the afternoon rehearsal. It was loud and close and made people scream, but it was also a huge relief as giant raindrops hit the windows of the hall. There was to be an early evening concert for the public given by the tutors on the course, followed by a barbecue and silly outdoor games for us. The rain would put paid to our games, though I don't think many of the older ones minded. Saturday night telly was OK entertainment for most of us.

We had to sort out the old hall for the concert. I don't mind humping chairs around and I felt relaxed for almost the first time. No Donald to worry about. The fact that people quite liked me. Having a laugh with Max and Jessa and Gemma and the Horns. No silly games, just a few hours in a darkened common room watching *Blind Date* and other undemanding programmes. So I didn't blush or flinch when Kevin came over to where Jessa and I were setting up music stands (though Jessa did). 'You're sorted for chamber music, aren't you, Jess?'

'Yes,' said Jessa comfortably. 'I'm in the wind quintet,' she added, not without pride. The wind quintet was a prestigious group consisting of first flute, first oboe, first clarinet, first horn and bassoon.

'What about you?' Kevin turned his melting gaze on me. I melted. It was a Pavlovian response.

'Me? Oh, I expect I'll just wind up with one bunch of dregs or another. It's all us non-principals, I expect. Piccolo, triangle and double bass trio or something.'

Kevin smiled. I wibbled. Another reflex action. And the smile was just for me – sorry, Jessa. 'You wouldn't like to join our jazz group, would you?'

I saw Jessa's jaw become completely unhinged. So did mine. 'But what would I play?'

'Well, we really need a saxophonist, but a flute will do. Donald has to be on keyboard, I'm on drums and Sam's on double bass. I do some of the vocals too. You know, the dark brown voice.'

To match his eyes, I thought, not that I was really capable of rational thought at that moment. Or rational speech. This was just so cool. My favourite music, with, it has to be said, my favourite guys. And they actually *wanted* little me! My glasses were steaming up. I could see Jessa trying desperately to think of a way of weasling out of her wind quintet and offering herself, but she didn't really like jazz, or any sort of busking.

Sound came out of my lips. 'Fine,' I said, sounding a thousand per cent cooler than I felt.

'Excellent!' said Kevin and drifted off, leaving me and Jessa completely poleaxed.

'I won't pretend I'm not jealous,' said Jessa when he was out of earshot and we'd sat down on a couple of stacks of chairs. 'Fancy all that close contact with Kevin. *And* you're one of the younger ones. There, what did I tell you? I said they all fancied you.'

'Jessa! There is no way that Kevin fancies me. If he's any sense, he fancies you. So rest assured on that score. You two are out of my league.' I was about to say that, anyway, I wasn't interested in Kevin, I was interested in Donald. But good sense prevailed.

'Adela's nose will be seriously out of joint, too. Still, there isn't really any call for a violin in a jazz band, is there?'

'She's in the string quartet. I know, because she mentioned it yesterday. I'm so chuffed, Jessa! Things are looking up at last!' And they were. I hadn't thought about Donald for a whole minute.

The 'barbecue' had to be sausages and baked beans in the common room. It suited me. It felt very cosy with everyone huddled round the TV and the rain pouring down outside. Admit it, Hannah! I was enjoying myself. A lot. Embarrassment and curse notwithstanding. Two hours of telly was enough for some people and there was a move afoot to have a table tennis tournament. Some people obviously still wanted their silly games. Kevin was one of them. In fact, Kevin turned out to be an organiser, and before we knew it we were all involved in round-the-table tennis – even flat-footed me. And we'd been tearing round the table for a while before I noticed that Donald was playing too.

'Hi, Hannah. Has Kevin asked you yet?'

Don't faint, Hannah. And don't presume. 'About what?' I asked coolly.

'Will you be in our band?' Great. I'd wanted to hear it from him too. 'I can't play flute or sax because I do the keyboard. Have you ever played sax? I could teach you if you wanted. It's the same fingering as the flute.' He looked closely at my mouth. 'And you've got the right sort of mouth.' Who was babbling now?

'I told Kevin I'd do it.' How did I manage to sound so calm?

'Oh, great. That's brilliant.'

'HANNAH!' shouted Max. 'It's your turn. Stop gassing!'

'Sorry!' I said, and smiled at Donnie. He smiled back and the ball shot past my left shoulder.

*

As it was Saturday the staff didn't shove us off to bed until well after eleven. Too early for Adela, but I was knackered. The boys were in a huddle as we went off. It didn't occur to me to be suspicious, though I should have been – there was a lot of sniggering going on.

Adela caught up with me. 'I didn't see you this evening,' I said to her, already slightly nervous about her reaction to me being in the jazz band.

'I went to the concert,' she said. 'And then I practised. I think playing table tennis is a bit juvenile.'

'Kevin doesn't.' I was still smarting from her comments at lunch time.

'That's only because I wasn't around,' she said smugly.

I started to say that it was nothing of the sort and then held back. I wasn't interested in Kevin anyway, and it seemed that she didn't know about the band. I had the feeling that Adela was like an unreliable kitten. Stroke her in the wrong place and she'd scratch.

I fell into a deep and happy sleep which turned into an amazingly vivid dream about Donald telling me I had the right sort of mouth and kissing me. I could feel his hair. I could hear his laugh. Wait a minute. I *could* hear him laughing! And Max, and two other boys. I opened my eyes in the half dark as I heard drawers being opened and shut and the sound of things being shoved into a plastic sack.

'What the hell's going on?' Gemma was sitting up, but the culprits had legged it.

'Oi!' Adela was half out of bed.

'I don't believe it!' said Jessa, outraged. 'We're the victims of a knicker raid!'

'Ha!' Adela loved it. 'Brilliant! At last! A bit of life round here! Who was it? Where have they gone? What did they take?' And she rummaged, thrilled to bits, through her drawers.

'They've taken all my underwear,' said Jessa, not knowing whether to laugh or be cross.

'Mine too,' I said. I'd been through my drawers, but so had the villains. They'd taken everything except the sanitary towels.

Total joy in the evening gave way to total mortification.

I curled up, miserable. Would the embarrassment never end? 'Night, all,' I said, wondering how on earth I was going to face anyone in the morning.

SEVEN

'It wasn't me who told, honest.' I was angry with them, but I don't grass. Kevin, Don and Sam looked at me, unsure. Predictably it had been Gemma who'd reported the crime in the morning, but it hadn't brought the underwear back. Between them the boys had managed to empty the top drawers of every single one of the senior girls before disappearing into the night. Fortunately we all had our swimming gear to wear instead, but there'd been an uproar. I had a sneaky admiration for the feat they'd pulled off, but I needed a change of knickers. And I didn't like the fact that they'd gone into places that were essentially female and private. Perhaps I wouldn't have been so cross if I hadn't had the curse. But that was part of the point. Girls need their privacy and boys should respect that.

All the boys had been called into the hall for a talking to – nobody knew precisely who was responsible – and warned that when the culprits were discovered their parents would be told. The usual threat.

'Nothing to do with us,' said Kevin, Sam and Donald, all innocence.

I looked at Donald. 'Oh yes it was,' I said. 'I *heard* you laughing.'

'Such naughty boys,' said Kevin, smirking.

'You'd better tell us where they are – the knickers,' I said. I wasn't feeling shy right then, and I sensed that they were abashed, slightly.

'Ooh,' said Donald. 'It was *knickers* they took, was it now?' Underneath the bravado he was smiling up at me anxiously from behind his glasses.

'I *heard*,' said Sam, 'that they'd stashed them in the freezer.'

'Yes, that's what I *heard*, too,' said Donald.

'Never mind the knickers,' said Kevin. 'Let's get started.'

'I mind the knickers!' I said. 'Just because you smelly lot wear one pair all week doesn't mean to say that we do.'

'Well—' Kevin was quite embarrassed.

'They'd better come back very soon, or the girls are all going on strike.' I'd just made this up. 'And this quartet, for one, will be a trio.'

'OK, OK,' said Kevin. 'We wouldn't want that, lads, would we? See to it that the knickers are returned forthwith!'

'Aye aye, Cap'n,' said Don and Sam together, still leering, mind you.

Donald was actually the natural leader of this group. Even Kevin accepted that when Don sat down at the keyboard he was king. I hadn't known he played anything other than a breathy flute and the saxophone. He noodled around for a while and then said, 'Why don't we just start in with something we all know. You all right about jamming, Hannah?'

I nodded. I was.

'What shall we do then?'

Sam started plunking on his bass. '*Yesterday*,' he said. Everyone knows that.

Phew.

So Donald started us off. I just let myself go and tootled in whenever I felt it was right.

The song drew to a close. 'Wow!' said Kevin. 'Hannah, what a star! You're a natural! Did you know that?'

'I like playing without music,' I said. 'I love jazz.'

'You can tell,' said Donald. And he looked triumphantly over at Kevin. 'See? Told you she was the one to ask!'

'After Jessa,' I added.

Kevin coughed. 'Well, I knew Jessa was fixed up really,' he said.

'I didn't want Jessa!' Donald said. 'Thank God she was fixed up! I said to ask Duck. You're impossible, Kevin!'

I smiled to myself. Jessa would be over the moon to know that Kevin had invited her against his instructions. It was a wet Sunday afternoon. We'd been allowed a lie-in in the morning – it was that or church. Adela, rather surprisingly, had been to Mass, which meant she wasn't back in time for lunch. I realised how much more peaceful life was without her. Now we were working on our chamber group stuff, and here I was in a large practice room with three guys, and I was getting to know them fast. My righteous anger over the knicker raid gave me an advantage because it meant they were just the tiniest bit deferential. It also overrode my shyness. But more important than anything, they rated me as a jazz player! For the past few days I'd simply admired Kevin from afar. Now I could tell that, as Jessa kept saying, he was a really nice bloke – and an excellent drummer. I liked the way he played, totally relaxed and cool, lots of sexy shoulder movement. When we were playing without music I had every reason to watch him, to try and anticipate what he was going to do with the beat. I enjoyed watching the muscles in his back, and the suntanned gap between his T-shirt and his jeans.

Of course I had even more reason to watch Donald closely, since he led us from the keyboard most of the time. Now here was a difference too. As a fluteplayer he was slightly stiff-fingered and uncomfortable looking, especially jammed up with the rest of us in the woodwind section. But on keyboards he was all over the place, head down, hair shaking; or head tilted back, beatific smile on his face; or standing as he played and making eye contact with the rest of us. Wow! Respect! Not only was I in love with the guy but I thought he was brilliant. I felt humbled, so grateful that he'd chosen me. How could I ever have thought he was laughable?

Sam was the quiet one. He just grooved away on his double bass. Like me he took his cues from Don and Kevin. He's tall with heavy dark eyebrows and a serious face which breaks out into a rare cheeky smile.

I found out a lot about myself in that session too. Ever since I was a little kid I could copy tunes I heard and get them right. I thought everyone could, but I still have memories of people exclaiming when I sang some song note for note. I've never had any trouble reading music, but I've always been happiest busking, just like when I was little and playing the notes in my head. So here I was doing this for real. And still impressing people. But these people were not my parents' friends. I wasn't compelled to be an extension of my mother's ego. I was with cool guys. Was I happy? Was I ever! I didn't want the session to end.

At teatime we gave Sam our orders for drinks and chocolate and he went off to fetch them while the three of us sat around watching the rain. Kevin went off to the loo and I was left with Don. I suspect he felt as shy as I did. He stood up and stretched. 'Phew, it's a bit rank in here. Do you think we can open the French windows?' He loped over and managed to wrench them open. A rush of sweet-smelling air came into the room.

The temptation was too great. I stepped outside and stood in the teeming rain for a few seconds. Bliss! When I came back in my hair was wet and my glasses were streaming. I took them off and flicked my hair out of my face, scattering raindrops on to Don. I looked up at him. 'Sorry about that! It's beautiful out there. You've never smelt anything so gorgeous!' And I was rewarded by the briefest of smiles – yes, down at me and me alone – before Kevin returned, closely followed by Sam and the drinks.

I felt more at ease with the others there. We sat on the floor and shared out the picnic. 'OK, guys. So where is the underwear?' I asked.

'You could try looking in the place I *heard* they'd been stashed,' said Sam.

'I could,' I said. 'But I'm in the middle of a chamber group rehearsal, aren't I?'

'They'll be returned,' said Kevin, as if he knew.

'They will indeed,' said Don solemnly. And then they all laughed at their own private joke.

Boys! I don't know.

We stood up and brushed the crumbs off ourselves. 'We can do another hour or so if we're up to it,' said Kevin. 'Perhaps the rain will have stopped by this evening and we can have a swim.'

By the end of the wet afternoon we had worked out four things to play: *Yesterday, The Entertainer* (possibly), *In the Mood* and *Take Five*. All tired old favourites, I know, but not when *we* played them! Under Don's direction we worked really well. The only problem was with *Take Five*. 'It's no good,' said Don. 'The flute's all wrong in this.'

I gulped before he added – 'Not your playing – that's brilliant, especially the improvising. It's just that the sound's wrong. It really needs a sax. Can you play the piano, Hannah?'

'Not well enough for this,' I said.

Don thought for a bit and then said, 'How about I teach you the sax then, like I said before? It wouldn't be difficult for someone like you.'

I tried to hide my excitement at the thought of being taught the sax by Don. 'OK. I like trying new things.'

Kevin interrupted. 'Look, I've got to go. I promised Adela I'd listen in on her masterclass.'

I felt buoyed up and brave enough to say, 'Ooh, Adela's masterclass, eh?' in a suggestive way, but I soon shut up when Donald also said that he'd promised to go.

'Oh no you don't, Donnie lad,' said Kevin. Could it be that he wanted to keep Adela for himself? 'You have knickers to rescue. Don't pretend it wasn't you. We all know it was, amongst others. And I know a certain young lady who won't be happy until her knickers are restored, and we wouldn't want that.'

Donald flashed a glance at me. I looked down demurely, fighting a jubilant heart.

'OK, Duck. Can't have our star player unhappy, can we?'

The cold store was behind the kitchens at the back of the main building. No one was about in the pouring rain. The kitchen staff were still at home recovering from Sunday lunch. Donald and I had to run from tree to tree to get there without being soaked. We moved more furtively as we got closer, and finally made a dash for the cold store door. The padlock hinge was open. I lifted it and pulled open the door. The chill struck us at once and brought goose bumps to our wet skin.

'All right,' I said, surveying the range of chest freezers I could make out in the crack of light from the door. 'Which one?'

'Well,' said Don, 'it wasn't actually me who hid them, you understand.'

'Why in a freezer, for God's sake?'

'Why not?' Donald was peering into a freezer full of frozen chips. His face was eerily lit up by the blue light inside. 'He said he put them in an empty one. Nothing unhygienic, naturally.'

'Naturally.' I lifted the lid on a freezer full of chicken and fish. 'They're bound to be in the last one we open, aren't they?'

'Got them!' yelled Don triumphantly, and held up a frozen bin liner, presumably full of frozen underwear. But then he suddenly ducked behind the freezer and frantically motioned to me to do the same. Someone was approaching. Two people were coming in.

It was two of the kitchen staff with a metal barrow. They switched on the light, a single bulb. 'We'll need three tubs of frozen minestrone from the third freezer on the right,' one of them said. 'Then come and help me load up with baking potatoes from this bunker.' The bunker was by the door. Donald and I held our breath.

They seemed to take forever. We heard all seventy potatoes bonging into the barrow. Donald was clutching the bin liner to him, trying not to let it rustle, though I could see that its icy coldness was just about killing him, until a large wet patch started to develop on his T-shirt as the contents began thawing. At last the cooks had everything they wanted. But then disaster struck.

'Turn out the light, can you? I'm going to lock up for the night.'

Aaagh! Did I really want to be locked in a dark cold store for the night – even with Donald?

We heard the padlock snapping shut and their footsteps getting softer as they went into the kitchen. 'Oh dear,' came Donald's voice through the darkness. 'What now?'

EIGHT

At first we just giggled. The whole situation was so ridiculous.

'It could be a long wait,' said Don gravely.

'I know.' I echoed his tone. But that just made us both laugh again. 'I haven't even got my mobile.'

'Me neither.' Don kept on his serious voice. 'They're not

going to like it!' he said. 'Not one little bit . . . Oh well!' He put the bag of knickers down. 'I'm rather cold and wet. But I expect I'll warm up. How about you?' Cue, I thought, for something huggy. But no. Anyway, I'd have been too embarrassed just then. 'We could do some jumping-around type exercises,' he suggested.

'No thanks,' I said. It wasn't what I had in mind. 'You can. It'll pass the time.'

He stood up. 'Do you mind if I take off my wet things?'

'I—'

'My T-shirt,' he added, and pulled it off.

My eyes were only just accustomed to the tiny amount of light that came under the door. I didn't want to look. But then he started flinging his arms around, doing what I considered to be bust-improvement exercises.

'Canadian army stuff,' he panted. 'They make us do it at school.' And he did some knee bends. I was mesmerised. I've never been that close to a bloke being so physical. His torso gleamed in the faint light. It was a nice, well-built torso. At last he came to rest. 'Phew! Sorry about that. I was getting really chilled. And I lose my inhibitions in the dark!'

Promising, I thought. What next? He pulled his damp T-shirt on again and paced about the cold store. 'I wonder if there's anywhere warm in here?'

'We probably ought to be by the door,' I said. 'Then we can shout if we hear anyone outside. And it might be a bit warmer too, if the sun comes out. If!'

'Fat chance,' said Don. 'You're right though, let's set up camp here,' and he sat down against the wall by the door. He patted the ground beside him and I sat down obediently. There was just enough room for the two of us between the potato bunker and the door but very little to spare. I managed to keep an inch between us, on tenterhooks in case we should accidentally make contact. I wanted to squash up against him, really I did, but then the shy part of me took over and held me rigidly at a distance. God, I hoped someone would let us out soon. The fact that this was a situation made in heaven didn't help. I couldn't cope.

'Sorry – what?' I'd been so wrapped up in my own paranoia that I hadn't heard what Don was saying.

'Oh, nothing really. I was just making conversation.' (Oh dear, was it that difficult?) 'I just asked if you had any brothers or sisters. Not important.'

'I've got one older brother,' I said, 'called Jeremy. Unfortunately.'

'What, that you've got him or that he's called Jeremy?'

'Oh he's not bad, as nerds go. No, I meant that he's called Jeremy. I call him J, which sounds better somehow.'

'Huh.' There was a short silence. 'I'm not in a position to laugh at other people's names. I mean – Donald! It's not so bad if it's said in a Scottish accent, but I'm used to people falling about when I tell them. Funny, isn't it? John's OK, Dan's OK, but Don just isn't quite. It sounds like a sixties pop star.'

I really didn't want to talk about names. Or how ours were linked. 'What about you? Your family, I mean?' I couldn't imagine there being any more where he came from. Especially after seeing his scary mother. But I was wrong.

'I've got two older sisters. Quite a bit older. I was what you might call an afterthought. Or a mistake, more like. When I was little, my friends thought Ma was my grandmother and that Dad was my grandfather.'

'My parents are normal-parent age,' I said. 'But I don't see much of them. I don't think they could be any more useless than they are.'

'Ooh, *bitter*!' said Donald. 'Mine are OK. Mum's bark is worse than her bite. And Dad can be quite a cool dude when she lets him. Really into jazz, you see. But can't play a note – and can't get over the fact that I can! So he's always been a bit indulgent towards his Donnie-lad. Apparently he was resigned to never having a son to wear a kilt with him and then I came along . . . '

'You don't really wear a kilt, do you?'

'If you were christened Donald Angus Bruce Ogilvie you'd get to wear a kilt, too! I wore one yesterday, if you must know.'

'You must show me some time . . . What about your sisters then? How old are they?'

'Ancient. Twenty-three and twenty-five. I'm a bit like an only child really. It's quite good having big sisters, though, because they make a fuss of their baby brother. I really missed them when they left home and I only had Ma and Dad for company. That's when boarding school was a good thing. Not any more, though. I'm going to sixth-form college next term.'

'I don't think I could ever call my parents "company". They're desperate for us to achieve great things, but all without their help. Sometimes I just feel mine would prefer a photo of me and a sheet of brilliant exam results. They're not interested in the flesh and blood, and certainly not the heart and soul.'

'Bet that's not true,' said Donald, shifting round slightly so that he was facing me.

I was taken aback. My grotty parents are a fact of life. Who was this boy to say that things should be otherwise? 'So I'm a liar?'

'Not at all. But you know, at school, at night, we quite often talk about our families. Especially with the younger ones, when they're homesick. And so many kids think their parents don't like them. And then they turn up on parents' day and you can see that they're like all the other parents – thrilled to see their little darlings. I just think some adults aren't very good with children. They love them, and everything, but they just don't know how to behave. No one's ever taught them and it doesn't come naturally.'

I thought for a bit. 'Well, my dad tries. He's a feeb, but he tries. It's Mum who really gets me. She never puts me first. Work yes, J yes, but never me.' I was getting quite worked up.

'What was her family like?'

'Her mum died when she was about twelve and—'

'Ah! Don't you think that's your answer . . . ?'

'Donald, that's too pat! And anyway, what's with all this psychology stuff? Why can't I just hate my mother like any normal teenage girl . . . '

'Because it's not in character. You're far too sw—'

But he didn't finish his sentence. He stood up, out of range, and skipped about a bit. 'Leg's gone to sleep,' he told me, by way of explanation. So much for hugs. I felt confused. Donald had touched a nerve, a real point of dissatisfaction in my life. I felt exposed. I couldn't think of anything to say. I wanted to tell him I really liked him, that I thought he was fantastic. I wanted to talk about life, the world, the future, our future, but we'd talked about my mother and I felt cheated. Bloody mother. Always spoiling things.

'Hannah?' He sat down on the edge of the bunker. His feet were swinging somewhere round by my nose.

'Yes?' I shifted so that I could look up at him.

'Do you ever write any music?'

'Only what I've done at school. I prefer making it up as I go along. Why?'

'I've got an idea for a song. Well, I'm not much good on the words but I think the tune might be OK. Can I play it to you some time?'

'Of course. If we ever get out of here!'

He peered at his watch. 'It must be getting on for six. I could do with something to eat. I need a pee too.'

'Thank you for sharing that with me.' I needed a loo, too, but I wasn't about to say so. 'There's plenty of food around!'

'And not a bite to eat. Actually, I bet there's some ice-cream!' He jumped down from the bunker and started to lift the lids on the freezers. 'Over here! Wow! They've got Magnums and Feasts and things. Want one?'

I stood up on my cramped legs and went over to have a look. The light inside the freezer lit up his intent face. He looked all excited, like a little boy. 'Here, bet you'd like a white Magnum,' he said, handing me one.

'Yes. How did you know?'

'I got you sussed, kid!' he said, closing the lid and tearing the wrapper off his lolly with a flourish. 'Ah. What do we do with the evidence?' He crumpled it up. 'Pockets, I suppose. You just seem like . . . My sister Fiona likes them, that's why.'

We stood leaning against the freezer with our lollies for a bit. It was good having something to do. I was catching plenty of the amazing smiles (well, gleaming teeth in the darkness) and loads of chat, but nothing more. *Hannah!* I gave myself a mental slap on the wrist. I was in love with Donald. But I had spent the first few days either avoiding him or giving him a hard time. He had no reason to like me. No other boy had ever fancied me as far as I knew. He was probably really hacked off. Fancy being stuck in a cold store with Duck! I could imagine him telling the others after. How much more fun to be stuck in a cold store with Adela, say . . .

I jumped when he said, 'I suppose Adela's masterclass is over by now.'

'I'm sorry,' I said. 'Kevin made you miss it because of me.'

'Kevin didn't want me there. Nothing to do with you.'

'I thought Kevin liked Jessa,' I said, and wished I hadn't.

'He does,' said Donald bluntly. 'But he's fascinated by Adela.'

'Him and all the others,' I said, and he didn't bother to contradict me.

He carried on as if I'd never interrupted. 'If the masterclass is over they might start to miss us soon. Kevin had this idea we might go for a swim if the weather cleared up. You ought to come, you know.'

'Some time,' I said vaguely. Funny, I'd been so positive Don knew all about *why* I hadn't been swimming. It occurred to me for the first time that he hadn't a clue, that he didn't even know who I was in Boots, let alone what I had in my basket. Why should he have cared anyway? Maybe I should review events in a different light . . .

'I think we should go and sit by the door again,' said Don. 'Look, Hannah, I'm really sorry about all this. It's my fault we're locked in here.'

I wanted to say that I didn't mind at all. That having him to myself was everything I could have wished for. But all I could manage was a wry-sounding, 'I suppose it isn't exactly *my* fault . . . ' There was no answer to that, so we squatted down by the door again in silence. Neither of us said a word for several minutes. My mind was ablaze with 'what is he thinking?' thoughts, and I was taut as a wire with trying not to brush against him.

I could sense his agitation. He stood up suddenly and knocked me off balance as I sat back on my heels. He put out a hand to steady me, a firm, gentle hand on my arm. I thought for an agonising moment that perhaps he was going to hold me, but then I realised he was just being his caring self. Aagh.

'Sorry,' he said. 'Didn't mean to send you flying – Hey! Listen . . . ' We could hear definite sounds of people approaching, scrunchy gravel sorts of noises, chatter and laughter.

'That laugh sounds like Gemma—' I suddenly thought about how it would be when someone discovered us. What would they think? Kevin or Sam would know the situation, but what about Adela, or even Jessa, or one of the girls? What would rumour-monger Max make of it? What conclusions would people draw when they knew we'd spent over an hour alone together, or worse still, what if it was one of the staff and we were caught, knicker haul and all?

'How can we get their attention?' He seemed to lose his nerve. 'D'you think we should shout?'

'We could bang on the door,' I said. We both banged, furiously. But to no avail. They were obviously going in to supper, but no one heard us.

Despondent, we crouched down by the door again. As if to raise our spirits, a ray of sunlight crept under the door. Donald looked at his watch again. 'It's quarter to seven. We've been here nearly two hours . . . My, how time flies when you're enjoying yourself.'

But he didn't say it as if he meant it, and my heart was plummeting at the thought of how I had wasted the opportunities of two whole hours. All I wanted to do was to find out if he liked me, and I hadn't a clue how to go about it.

'They'll be coming back again in a while. They must have missed us at supper. Kev will expect me to go swimming with him. I'm starving—' He paused to draw breath and laughed at himself. 'Sorry—'

'Stop apologising! Neither of us can help it about being locked in. Actually, this reminds me of when I'd been naughty when I was little, and my parents used to shut me in my bedroom and say I couldn't go down and eat with them until I'd apologised. It's that same mixture of guilt and rebelliousness and – hunger.'

'We mustn't talk about being hungry. It just makes you hungrier. God! No one ever shut me in anywhere when I was a kid. They were all far too indulgent.'

'Lucky you.'

'I dunno. It made boarding school all the more of a shock. Kids don't forgive you for anything. And you can't go rushing to Mummy. The trouble with boarding school is that you just have to get on with people. I've thought about this a lot. Day kids can go home, sound off and be thoroughly nasty if need be and, generally, their parents know they're just letting off steam. But if you're a boarder it's all too easy to be really evil just once and you've got a reputation to live down ever after. I think I cottoned on to that very quickly. Survival. So as a result it takes people a long time to find out what I'm really thinking. It's something that gets in the way of being spontaneous.'

Was he trying to tell me something? 'Just think how much you'll enjoy being 'orrible from now on. No more being sent to Coventry in the "dorm" . . . You can take out the frustrations of the day on your parents or the cat, and everyone'll go on loving you just the same.' Scary Mum and me both.

'Yeah, s'pose so.' He was distracted again. 'You know that song I was talking about?'

'The one you've written? What's the accompaniment?'

'Oh, it's still in my head at the moment. I suppose I could play it on the sax until I work the words out. But – when could you listen to it?'

'Don! We're stuck in here! You can hum it to me if you want!'

'Now? Oh God, no. No way! I need a keyboard for security. I really only sing in the shower. Kevin's our singing boy—'

'OK, OK!' I had heard him singing harmonies and at least he could sing in tune, but he clearly didn't want to now. 'Whenever. I mean, once we're out of here. Whenever.' I was repeating myself. I couldn't work out what sort of answer he wanted.

'Tomorrow evening?'

'As I said, whenever.'

'I don't know if it's any good, you see.'

'Don, whenever you want to play it I'm happy to listen. OK?'

'Thanks.'

So what was all that about?

'I can hear them again!' We both leant with our ears to the door. 'Let's shout this time, and bang,' I said. There went the voices and the laughter. It was so tantalising. We could even hear Kevin saying, 'Who's coming for a swim then?' and a general smattering of replies.

'KEVIN!' we both yelled. 'WE'RE LOCKED IN HERE!' and we banged vigorously on the door. But they went past.

'I really don't believe this,' said Don. 'It calls for another ice-cream I think. Want one?'

'No thanks.' I was desperate to get out, to get to a loo, to get out of my uncomfortable swimsuit that I'd been wearing all day. 'Hang on! I think they might be coming back!' I could hear laughter outside.

It was Kevin! 'Oi! Donnie lad. What you up to in there?'

And Jessa. 'Duck! Are you in there?'

And Max. 'Donald! Duck! Donald! Duck!' followed by lots of silly Donald Duck quacking noises.

'We're locked in!' we both shouted.

'You'll need a key!'

'Don't panic!' came Kevin's voice. More laughter. 'We could break this padlock. Tell you what would be better . . . Jessa, do you reckon you could charm someone into giving us the key? Try the caretaker's house by the old building.'

'OK, Kevin.'

I smiled to myself. That's my Jessa. Anything to please Kevin. Kevin and Max came back to the door. It didn't sound as if anyone else was out there. 'You two OK?'

'Hungry!' said Don.

'Anything to be alone with a woman!' Max bellowed.

'Shut it, Max. We don't want everyone to hear us,' said Kevin.

Yeah, shut it Max, I thought.

'Jessa's been really quick,' Kevin reported. 'She's running back already, and it looks as though she's holding a bunch of keys.'

'I wonder what she told him?' I asked Donald.

'Do we care?'

I cared a lot about what people said when we got out. Clearly Don didn't.

We heard a lot more sniggering and the sound of someone sorting keys. Then one was fitted in the padlock. I could have cried when I heard it snap apart. The doors were wrenched open from outside and sunlight flooded into the cold store that had been our prison. Jessa linked her arm in mine. She was full of her good deed. 'The caretaker was a real sweetie. Said he wouldn't ask any questions, but to get the key back straightaway. And why not have an ice-cream each while we were about it. I couldn't believe it . . . '

Meanwhile I was aware of Max running rings round all of us, saying, 'Nearly two hours in the storeroom! I don't know, Don. You're a quiet one!'

And then I caught sight of Kevin raising his eyebrows at Don and Don clutching the black plastic sack and mouthing – 'I wish!'

'Go on,' Jessa was saying, walking me away from the boys. 'You jammy woman. Tell me what happened! I want to know all the details.'

'Oh, nothing,' I said, 'Nothing at all!'

'I don't believe you,' said Jessa.

'Well, you'd better, because it's the truth,' I said. But to myself I thought *I wish*.

NINE

Gemma got up first as usual on Monday. Adela was spark out and Jessa and I were still lying in bed talking about yesterday's events. Our first problem the night before had been over the redistribution of the knickers. Then Jessa had had the brilliant idea of putting them all in a laundry basket and leaving it somewhere conspicuous. She managed to do this completely openly without anyone seeing her. Somehow no one expected Jessa to be up to anything. It worked a treat. Word got around and everyone went and sorted out their own knickers.

Jessa had definitely rescued me in my hour of need but she hadn't let up about Donald and me being locked up together and whether or not we fancied one another. I found I was protesting and then wondering whether I was protesting too much. She made me very flustered. I kept thinking how differently Sophie would have handled this situation. Every now and then Jessa gave me a break and waxed lyrical about the possibility of being locked in with Kevin. Once when she'd fixed me with a piercing gaze and said, 'Now, look me in the eye and deny that you fancy Donald,' I'd nearly caved in. In some ways it would have been lovely to share my secret with someone, but I was terrified of making a fool of myself. I couldn't risk it.

She was at it again this morning. 'Just imagine if you *had* fancied Donald. Nearly two hours alone with him. Or if he'd fancied you. I suppose,' she added, somewhat thoughtlessly, 'he can't have fancied you or he would have tried it on. He had plenty of opportunity.' I'd considered this possibility. But I'd also thought about the various conversations we'd had and about what he might have been trying to say rather than what he actually had said. On the whole I felt hopeful, so it wasn't great to hear Jessa's views on the matter.

It was even less great to hear Adela mumbling thickly, 'Butt out, Jessa. Hannah doesn't rate Donald's sex appeal. She told me that ages ago, didn't you, Duck?'

I didn't know how to reply. So I just pretended I hadn't heard and went off for a shower.

If I'd thought Jessa was bad, I'd reckoned without Max. He was already having a go at Donald when we turned up for sectionals. 'Weyhey, Donald! Here comes your ice maiden. Two hours! Kuh! Two hours and he says nothing happened—'

'Shut up, Max,' said Donald, apparently unperturbed. 'Hi, Duck! Sax lesson after lunch then?' But underneath the bravado he was giving me the worried glance that I was coming to recognise.

'Yeah, great,' I said, ignoring Jessa's pointed looks and Max's muttered 'sax after sex' comments. I tried to focus on the sectional.

We all ended up at the same lunch table, so of course my forthcoming saxophone lesson was up for general review. In some ways the openness of it all made it easier to handle. I found I could even pretend that music *was* all it was about. That's the way Donald was playing it, because that's the way it was for him. He didn't have to pretend, I realised sadly. 'OK,' he said, when lunch was over. 'Sax masterclass time, Duck.'

'Now this I must see,' said Kevin, attaching himself to us.

'And me!' said Jessa and Adela together.

'Oh no,' said Don. 'This is one small practice room. Three will be a crowd, five would be an orgy . . .'

I was quite glad to have Kevin as a chaperone. Maybe Don was too. He detached the head from his saxophone and showed me how to blow on it. He made the right embouchure with his mouth and made me copy it, so we spent a lot of time mouthing at each other. Kevin found this all very amusing and kept saying that he felt like a gooseberry. But he didn't go away. Once I could make a decent sound, Don assembled the sax again. He was about to put it to his lips when I realised that the mouthpiece must be covered in my spit. 'Er – do you want me to wipe it?' I asked, embarrassed as usual.

'Nah,' said Don. 'I'm sure it'll taste lovely,' and proceeded to show me how to finger the notes. 'There. You try. It's just the same as the flute. I don't think you'll have a problem.'

He handed me the sax again. I felt self-conscious as I put it back to my lips. It seemed a terribly intimate thing to do, but I had no choice and Don was concentrating on teaching me to play *Take Five*. I thought I did quite well for a first-timer, and so did he.

'What d'you think, Kev?' he asked.

Kevin was less than enthusiastic. 'We-ell . . . '

'Kevin!' Donald wasn't having it. 'This lady has never picked up a sax before. If she can do that now, by Saturday we'll have a pro on our hands!'

'OK, OK!' Kevin laughed. 'If you say so! Come on both of you. Time for the afternoon session.'

'I'll see you there. Thanks for the lesson,' I said, and made a dash for it. I needed some fresh air, and the chance to savour the taste of Don's lips. Wow.

I met up with Jessa coming down from the girls' block. 'Well?' she asked. 'How was it?'

'Cool,' I said, giving nothing away.

'Can I come and listen this evening? We're not having a quintet rehearsal today. I'd like to be near Kevin with*out* Adela for once. That girl is driving me nuts!'

'Yes, sure,' I said. 'So long as you realise I'm only a beginner and don't go all critical like Kevin did.'

'Oh, I'm *sure* he didn't mean it!' Jessa leapt to his defence. 'Kevin would never be unkind. I mean, you should hear how sweet he is to Adela, even when she's being irritating as hell. Everyone else is wincing, but he's still nice as pie.'

'I wouldn't call that *kind*, exactly—' I started, but Jessa came down on me like a ton of bricks.

'Well, it couldn't possibly be for any other reason. Everyone knows she's just a little slapper who happens to be very good at the violin.'

I kept quiet, but I wasn't so sure that that was how guys saw Adela or, if they did, that they minded in the least.

*

After supper I set off for the music block with Donald. I was beginning to relax with him. It wasn't difficult when he was being all enthusiastic. If I suppressed my romantic notions and assumed that he had none of his own, it was perfectly possible to be good mates – because he was so, well, nice! Jessa and Kevin and Sam followed behind.

'I meant to try out my song on you after lunch,' said Donald. 'But I didn't really want to with Kevin around. Perhaps we'll get a chance later on. Would you mind?'

Before I had a chance to answer, Adela came rushing over to join us. 'Can I come, too?' she asked. 'Quartet's cancelled. I'm longing to hear you and Kevin doing jazz, Donnie. Are you sure you don't need a violinist? Or female vocals?' She caught hold of Don's arm and skipped alongside him, ignoring me completely. Perhaps it was time I stopped defending that girl. I fell back to be with Jessa, just as Kevin strode forward to be with Donnie and Adela. Jessa and I exchanged snarls. For once I could understand just how she was feeling.

I wasn't sure how I felt about playing in front of an audience. The first three pieces were OK. Adela mercifully kept her mouth shut, though Jessa was clapping away after each one. The lads were being complimentary, so I suppose Adela couldn't be too critical. Then it was time for my saxophone debut.

'We'll take it really slow, OK?' said Don. 'In fact, you go at a pace you can handle, Duck, and we'll follow.'

Adela started muttering, 'Good job we don't all need that sort of treatment,' but she was drowned out as we got going. I managed to get through it, but I made an awful lot of squeaks and odd noises along the way. Kevin shot me some amused looks, and so did Jessa, but Adela just creased up with giggles. It was really offputting. I wanted Kevin to shut her up, but in fact it was Don who had a go at her.

'This is only the second time Duck has played a saxophone, Adela. And she's doing bloody well. If you can't be sympathetic, bog off. We need to rehearse.'

'I'll say,' said Adela, stung. I could see that for once she felt awkward. She didn't like being dismissed. So she went on the charm offensive. 'Sorry. Honestly I am. I didn't mean to laugh. You're all sounding great. Really,' and she pulled the sleeves of her jumper down over her hands and wrapped her arms around her legs, settling in. Hatred was oozing out of Jessa. She was ominously silent during this exchange.

We played *Take Five* a couple more times. I felt a little more confident, but not a whole lot. Kevin and Sam packed their gear away. As Sam left, Don caught my eye. 'Hang about,' he said. 'Don't forget my song.' I wasn't sure how this was going to work. But I'd forgotten the Kevin magnetism. When he moved towards the door Adela and Jessa followed him as one.

Don laughed. 'What's his secret? Sure you don't mind listening to this, Duck? I wouldn't ask, but . . . ' He trailed off.

'Get on with it! Are you going to sing?'

'No. I know what the song's about, but I haven't sorted the words yet.' He looked away.

'Go on!' I sat on the floor by the keyboard.

He smoothed out a sheet of manuscript paper and started to play. I could feel him looking down at me, but I didn't dare to look up. It was a sweet, romantic tune. It made me think of rain and flowers. It was beautiful. I felt that Don was trying to tell me something with it that he couldn't say in words. The song drew to a close. I sat with my forehead on my knees, overwhelmed, just longing for him to come over and put his arms round me—

The door crashed open and Adela and Jessa stormed in, screaming at each other. I stood up, shocked. They were heading for me. 'Girls! Girls!' said Donald nervously.

'Tell her, Hannah!' Jessa was shouting. 'Tell her to leave Kevin alone. He doesn't like her following him around—'

'Tell *her,*' shrieked Adela, 'that Kevin is a lot more interested in someone like me than a sad nun like her!'

'I don't believe this,' I said. '*I* don't know what Kevin wants, but this is ridiculous! Calm down!'

'I'll be off then,' said Don, with an apologetic smile at me.

'I'll come with you,' said Adela, attaching herself to him like a limpet. Alarm bells should have rung again at that point, but Jessa was claiming all my attention.

They left. 'Do you *know* what she did?' Jessa was still blazing.

'Tell me. I don't think anything Adela did would surprise me any more.'

'Well. The three of us, Kevin, me and Adela, all came down from the music block together after we'd left you. Kevin was talking to me and Adela didn't like that at all. And she was so – so blatant. Do you know, Duck, she just came up and grabbed his arm and said, "Kevin, come with me, there's something I want to show you," or something corny like that. Can you believe it? More to the point, he *went*! Like a little dog. She said "Bye, Jessa, Kevin's coming with me now, aren't you, Kev?" There didn't seem to be much I could do so I just went back towards the dormitory. But I decided to follow them and there was Adela trying to snog him! I could see he wasn't really happy about it – he kept pulling away, and saying things like "Hang on, Adela! I think there's been a misunderstanding" and stuff. So, I'm ashamed to say, I hung around to listen. And Adela went on and on, pressing herself up against him, stroking his hair, putting her hands in his back pockets – you know the sort of thing. She was really trying to seduce him. And she kept saying, "Oh come on, Kevin. You know you fancy me!" The way she was going on I'm surprised he resisted, but he did. He suddenly pushed her away quite roughly and shouted, "Look, Adela! Stop it! You're making a fool of yourself. I don't fancy you. And—" Then they walked on, back in this direction again. It was so frustrating! I was dying to hear what he was going to say next! Anyway, I decided to go round and intercept them. And that's when I heard Adela still saying, "Oh come *on*, Kev!" . . . And I just flipped. I walked up to them and told her to leave him alone! Kevin looked really shocked and started to back away, and that's when I dragged Adela over to you. I don't know what got into me. Sheer jealousy, I think!'

All the fight had gone out of Jessa. 'Sorry, Duck,' she said weakly. 'I really don't know what came over me. Arguing with that *child*, it's pointless.' She looked slyly at me. 'And what did we barge in on, eh? You and Donald alone again?'

I told her the truth. 'He wanted me to listen to a song he's writing. He's shy about it.'

'Wish Kevin wanted me to listen to his songs. I love him so much, Duck. You can't imagine how it feels.'

I thought I could.

TEN

We didn't bother to wake Adela in the morning. Jessa had calmed down. It was a gorgeous day with blue holiday skies and we wanted to get out there. I felt blissfully confident about Donald and, what's more, I was looking forward to going in the pool at last. Things were definitely looking up. There might even be a romance in the offing to surprise the others with when I got home.

Everyone was affected by the good weather. We threw the doors open for the sectionals and caught snatches of the other groups rehearsing. It sounded like a mad party.

Donald was giving me a quick sax lesson after lunch and then Kevin was organising everyone for a swim. Whole orchestra rehearsal was starting half an hour later than usual, so we'd be able to make the most of the afternoon sun. My lesson was fun. After yesterday's raw beginnings I was getting the hang of it. Donald was very professional this time and just gave me hints rather than demonstrations. Then he sat down at the keyboard and we vamped through *Take Five* together. I even did some pretty cool improvising. He grinned at me and said we made beautiful music together, though he didn't look me in the eye as he said it.

On the way out he asked me if Adela was OK. 'Yes,' I said. 'Why shouldn't she be?'

He hesitated. 'Well, she seemed to be in quite a state yesterday evening. We – she seemed very upset about Kevin.'

'She was fine when I last saw her,' I said, and thought no more of the conversation.

Jessa and Gemma were gathering up their swimming things from our room. 'Kevin's been organising again,' said Jessa excitedly. 'Apparently he's found all these inflatables – turtles and sharks and lilos.' I had my new bikini on. 'Wow, Duck, you're really brown. When did you get your tan?'

'Still left over from the south of France last summer.' I looked down at myself. I wasn't really brown but at least I wasn't completely white. I can't swim in my glasses so I decided to leave them behind. 'Are we off then?'

The pool was heaving. I slipped in for a couple of lengths. It was blissfully cool but a bit of an obstacle course. I kept bumping into squealing kids on giant spotty things. Jessa called out to me. 'I've bagged a couple of lilos, Duck. Come out and sunbathe with me. I want to borrow your suntan lotion.' I hauled myself out and blindly located Jessa and two red lilos. 'Over here,' she called, seeing me peering at people.

We settled ourselves in for the afternoon. We had suntan lotion, books, bottles of water, even some crisps. For the first time it really felt as if we were on holiday.

Our lilos became a sort of base camp. Gemma, Max, Helen, Josie and the Horns pitched up alongside us. Kevin, Don and Adela had some elaborate waterfight going on. I was far too lazy to want to join in. Then Max and the Horns went to join in the battle and Adela came and sat nearby. It was obvious she thought that we were where the action was, but she didn't want to sit too close to Jessa. I was peering closely at my book and just then I really didn't care.

I could hear Kevin chatting to Jessa. They were sitting together on her lilo. I shaded my eyes and turned to speak to them. 'Hi! How's the battle going?'

'Hannah!' said Kevin, surprised. 'I didn't recognise you—'

'—without your clothes on!' Jessa finished for him.

'Nice – erm – bikini,' he finished lamely.

'It's like Brighton beach here,' said Jessa. 'And, oh God, Adela is going for the all-over tan again!'

'Now?' I turned over to look in Adela's direction. It wasn't quite as bad as Jessa made out. She was lying on her front, reading. One of the boys was pouring suntan lotion into his hand, about to anoint her. I couldn't really see who.

'Good old Donald!' I heard Kevin say. I peered short-sightedly in Adela's direction again. The man with the oil was indeed Donald. But Kevin was talking to me again. 'You look great, Hannah,' he said appreciatively, and smiled at me with those melting eyes. I suffered a major wibble. 'Come for a swim, cool off a bit,' and he reached out a hand to pull me to my feet. He didn't let go either but carried on pulling me to the water's edge.

'Remember I'm blind without my glasses!' I yelled.

'Don't worry! I'm looking where I'm going! Jump now!' And we both landed up in the pool.

We splashed around for a bit but the pool was still crowded. Once I'd cooled off I decided I'd rather be sunbathing. 'I'm getting out again,' I told him. 'Time for a bit of heavy-duty basting and roasting I think.'

'Good idea,' said Kevin. 'I'll lead you back again,' and he grabbed my hand.

'Over here!' Jessa waved and we picked our way towards the lilos.

Jessa sat up and moved over to accommodate Kevin again. I flopped down on my front. 'Someone do my back?' I asked and held out the lotion. I had meant Jessa, so I was slightly surprised when Kevin took it and said, 'Yes, I will.'

I could hear the bewilderment in Jessa's voice as she said, 'Will you do me too?'

'Oh. Yes. All right then. I'll do you both.'

Kevin and the suntan lotion was an experience not to be forgotten. I'll freely admit it's the closest *I've* ever been to having sex. God. When I'd had oil firmly massaged into every centimetre of skin on my back (and thank God I didn't have spots there) I turned my head to see how Jessa was enjoying her turn. As I thought, she was in heaven. Then I turned to look the other way. Donald appeared to be asleep but Adela, I could tell even from this distance, held us in a steely gaze. Kevin lay on the other side of Jessa. They were chatting in a desultory sort of way. I couldn't hear what they were saying, and anyway my addled brain was drifting idly between Don's song and Kevin's massage and Don's smile and the taste of Don's lips . . . Jessa was too hot and got up to cool off in the water. Kevin slid on to her lilo.

'How're you doing, Hannah?'

'Fine.'

'That's good.'

The time for the afternoon rehearsal drew closer. No one seemed to want to move – we were like beached seals. Jessa stood up – she did look lovely in her lilac bikini, all slender with soft curves – 'Come on, Duck. I want a shower before the rehearsal.' I certainly didn't want to walk out of there alone. So we picked our way through the bodies again, reaching Adela just as she was fumbling with the clasp of her bikini behind her back, and Don just as he was offering to do it for her.

'Tart!' said Jessa as she dragged me away. 'Still, thank God she's turned her attentions to Don. Good job you don't fancy him, isn't it!'

I didn't like it one bit. Donnie was mine. I excused him on all fronts, of course. He was just being nice to Adela. He felt sorry for her. I hadn't been there. I'd been with Kevin.

Oooh. There must be an explanation.

I went into the rehearsal. Don leant over. 'OK for jazz practice after supper, Duck?' He'd washed his hair. I could smell its clean scent.

'Sure,' I said. Please God let everything be all right. There didn't seem to be any major change in Don's behaviour. But then I had no proof that he felt anything special for me anyway. All I had were my feelings for him – that I'd kept to myself.

Adela's concerto took up the second half of the rehearsal. It was coming on really well. At those moments, when the notes soared above us or dipped below or sang out alone, she was ours and I could forgive her anything.

Kevin was paying me a lot of attention. This was a totally new experience for me and I didn't know how to handle it. When he came up to Jessa and me after the rehearsal I assumed it was to talk to Jessa, but it soon became apparent that it was me he was focusing on. It was the 'Hi, Hannah – oh, and hi, Jessa,' sort of thing. And, 'Do you two do *every*thing together?' After supper, when it was time for our jazz practice, he practically dragged me away from Jessa, saying, 'Have a good toot, Jessa. Come on, Hannah, Donnie tells me you're getting brilliant. Can't wait to hear you.' Jessa cast me a reproachful look, but there wasn't a lot I could do.

Our practice was really great. My sax playing had come on in leaps and bounds in only two days. I felt mighty proud of myself, but the best part was that the guys seemed proud of me too. I began to feel like one of the lads. Not that Kevin was going to let me. He commented on the clothes I was wearing, talked at length about how good I'd looked without my glasses, told the others to see how cool I looked when I played sax. I really couldn't believe it.

We emerged from the practice room into a beautiful romantic summer evening, the sort I seemed to have spent with either Jessa or Adela so far. The sky still glowed pink and the scented jasmine flowers shone out like stars. I waited a little, letting Kevin and Sam go ahead so that I could walk with Don. Tomorrow was the day of our outing to Cambridge and the instrument workshops. I knew he'd been there before and I wanted to ask him about it. He came out humming. 'Don?' I longed to put my hand in his and wander off into the sunset with him. He looked down at me and my stomach lurched.

But I never got any further. Kevin had come back to us at the same time as Jessa and the others in her quintet spilled out of their practice room. And that was unfortunate because Jessa arrived on the scene at the same time as Kevin was saying, 'You are coming on the outing tomorrow, aren't you, Hannah? It will be so cool to get away from this place for the day.'

'Yes, we're coming,' said Jessa, linking her arm in mine and giving me a funny look. 'See you on the coach, guys,' she said as she steered me away from them. So here I was about to spend the evening with Jessa again.

But Jessa had fire in her eyes. She walked me firmly to the bench under the chestnut tree and sat me down. She checked that no one else was around. In fact most of them had gone up to the dormitories. 'OK, Ms Duck,' she said a tad fiercely. 'Tell me. What precisely is going on between you and Kevin? It hasn't escaped my notice that he has been buttering you up nonstop since the moment he saw you in a bikini. So what's it all about?'

'Honest, Jess, I don't know myself. I promise I haven't done a thing to encourage him! I agree with you that he's totally gorgeous, but he's not really my type. Anyway it's—' I stopped myself. I had come so close to telling Jessa about Don so many times I almost forgot that she didn't know. Perhaps now was the time to tell her. But she wasn't really listening.

'I don't understand it. I could have killed Adela last night for muscling in, and I ought to want to kill you, but it's just so weird. I mean, you have to admit, he seems to chat you up in front of me, almost on purpose. But why? Why now? I really thought he liked me, Duck. I really thought I was beginning to get somewhere. And with Adela, well, I can dismiss her because I don't think much of her, but you! That's different!'

I decided the time had come to lay my cards on the table. 'Jessa. Listen to me. For what it's worth, I'm not the slightest bit interested in Kevin. I – the only person I'm interested in is Don.'

Jessa was gawping at me. 'So I was right all along. I *knew* you and Donald had something going, you sneaky thing. I could tell he fancied you rotten. *And* you lied about the cold store episode. Duck! You are a dark horse!'

'No, Jessa. No. We haven't got anything going at all. That's the problem. I'm crazy about him but I don't think he's the slightest bit interested in me, not like that, anyway. In fact he seems a bit keen on Adela now.'

'Cow,' hissed Jessa, not for the first time.

'So. I haven't got a clue what Kevin's up to. I thought you two were getting on really well too. I think it's wait-and-see time, Jessie-baby. All will be revealed . . . '

'Yes. Perhaps by the time we get back tomorrow we'll understand a bit more.' She gave me a hug. 'Oooh, Duck! I'd so love you and Donald to get together. You're perfect for one another. Teehee! Donald Duck!' And she ran off to the dormitory block with me in hot pursuit.

ELEVEN

Another gorgeous day. Our room was a whirl of strappy dresses and short tops, shorts, short skirts and sandals. Even Jessa and Adela weren't glaring at one another as we discussed what to wear on a hot day out. We picked up our packed lunches after breakfast and bundled on to the coach.

The plan was this: coach to the workshops of the Instrument-makers' Guild just outside Cambridge, where we would see the whole range of musical instruments being made and repaired by hand. It sounded boring, but Don had been before and said it was worth it, if only to meet the flute-maker, George Hooper, a real craftsman of the old school, who made some of the most expensive flutes in the world. Then picnic by the Cam. Then the choice of an afternoon on the river or looking round colleges, with a bit of time for shopping afterwards. Supper was being laid on in one of the college canteens and then there was a short concert in King's College Chapel before the coach took us back again. They'd been to Brighton one year, Oxford another. Parents obviously approved of University towns for days out. Personally I'd have preferred Chessington with the juniors, but with weather like this, the river trip sounded good. As Kevin had said, it would be great to get away from the course for a day.

Jessa was keeping very close to Kevin as we boarded the coach. And Kevin was keeping quite close to me, while I was looking out for Donnie – though I couldn't see him. Kevin sat by a window and Jessa dived in beside him. I sat across the aisle from her, but then Adela told me to shove up to the window and I ended up there instead. At least if Adela was sitting next to me she wasn't sitting next to Don. I saw him at last, definitely one of the stragglers, along with Sam. They were deep in conversation and sat down together, still talking, near the front, along with Max and the Horns, Josie and Helen. Gemma was also at the front, sitting with Miss Claggan, but that was Gemma for you.

Adela grinned slyly over at me and cast a glance towards Kevin. 'I'd say you're in, there, Ducks. Poor old Jessa.'

'What makes you think I want to be?' I really didn't want to spend the coach journey being goaded by Adela, but I couldn't let her get away with it.

'Weyhey! I saw him applying the suntan lotion by the pool yesterday, Duck! And I have to say, I was almost too embarrassed to watch!'

'Oh come off it. He put some on Jessa as well!' I was going to add something about Donald doing the same for her, but I was scared of giving myself away. Fortunately for me, the coach lurched into action at that moment. 'We're off! Great! Today should be cool.'

'Bit educational, if you ask me,' said Adela. 'Wish we could have gone to Chessington with the little ones. Still, going in a punt could be good. I've always fancied that. Bit like a gondola in Venice. Not that I've ever done that. Too touristy.'

'Isn't punting on the Cam touristy?'

'Well, I'll be a tourist there, won't I?' Adela leant across Jessa to Kevin. 'You'll come in a punt with us, won't you, Kevin?'

Jessa looked up crossly, but Kevin smiled and said, 'Possibly, Adela, very possibly.'

I looked out of the window at the unfolding countryside. It was already hot. The cornfields were bleached pale gold and ready for harvest. The trees looked dark by contrast and cast dark shadows. There was a heat haze already. Constable harvest weather. Picnic weather! I wanted to share it all with Don. Damn it, why wasn't he with us? As if she'd overheard my thoughts, Adela suddenly said, 'Poor old Don. I tried to cheer him up yesterday, but I think I'm going to have to look after him today as well.'

'You what?' I couldn't believe what I was hearing. But I checked myself. I wanted to hear what Adela was going to say next without giving my feelings away. 'Sorry, Adela, I hadn't noticed Donald was upset about anything.'

'Well, you wouldn't have done, would you? Not with the gorgeous Kevin all over you. I mean who would notice droopy Donald with cute Kevin around?'

'What are you saying, Adela? I told you – ' I lowered my voice so Kevin couldn't hear – 'I didn't necessarily want . . . '

' 'Course you do! And that's what I said to Donald when I told him not to make a fool of himself over you. I said you'd told me you really didn't fancy him. He looked so upset that I thought it would soften the blow a bit if I told him it was because there was someone else –' she nodded in Kevin's direction, '– you know.'

My jaw must have dropped as I looked at her in sheer horror. 'Adela,' I said, 'did you do this just to spite Jessa?'

She looked at me coolly. Her eyes looked slightly out of focus. 'No, no,' she said vaguely. 'I admit I was upset about Kevin leading me on and then letting me down, but then of course I realised *he* must like someone else. He couldn't have had any other reason for not wanting *me*, could he? But I was pretty unhappy that night after Jessa had shrieked at me, and Donald was so sweet and kind when we came away from the music block. And he did look a bit as if he was mooning over you when we burst in on you. And I *know* you don't think he's sexy, Hannah, you must remember telling me so yourself.'

I must have been glaring at her. She said, 'I was doing you a *favour* for God's sake. Jessa can look after herself, but I was trying to help you.'

I opened my mouth to speak, but no sound came out. Poor Donald. Poor me. So many things explained. But what was Adela playing at with Donald?

'Don't worry, I'll look after poor Donald this afternoon,' she said. And she gave me her impish look. 'I've *always* thought he was fit . . . '

I turned to look out of the coach window and took some deep breaths. This was like a bad dream. Donald thought I didn't fancy him. He thought I preferred Kevin. He must have told Kevin. He must have decided to show me that he didn't care. I glanced over at Jessa and Kevin. They were getting on fine. Kevin must have realised that I wasn't very rewarding . . . God what a mess. I felt completely helpless. Thanks, Adela. Thanks a lot.

We arrived at the workshops. They were housed in a group of beautiful converted barns attached to a seventeenth-century farmhouse that was now the showroom. A river ran beneath a row of willows behind them. The barns were clustered round what was once the farmyard, now a tasteful carpark. More than thirty of us piled out of the coach. I looked for Donald, but he was definitely keeping his distance. Sam, who I knew was interested in making instruments and genuinely enthusiastic about the visit, was talking with him. Jessa hustled Kevin as far from Adela as she could, so there I was again, with my old friend Adela. I had a sudden sharp sense of the day going horribly wrong.

We were organised into six groups to go round the six workshops. Needless to say, Adela and I weren't with either Jessa and Kevin or Donald and Sam. But we were with Helen and Josie and the Horns, which suited me fine. In our first workshop they were making harpsichords and clavichords. Sunlight slanted in on to the fragrant piles of woodshavings that surrounded the two craftsmen. The scene reminded me of a painting I'd seen once. Already the day seemed to be passing in a series of picture frames. I loved the little clavichord, with its black keys where the white keys on a piano are and pale wooden keys for the 'black' notes. When I touched the keys a soft silvery sound came out. Why can't my parents spend their money on something like this rather than the latest BMW? I carried on playing quietly as Adela chatted up one of the makers. I remembered some of the chords of Donald's flowers and rain song . . . the clavichord was such a private and personal instrument . . . I imagined him sitting down at the same gentle keyboard. It would suit him. Perhaps he'd know that his music had been played on it . . . Oh Donnie! What was I going to do?

It was time to move on. We went through guitars, woodwind instruments and brass before we arrived at the violin maker, Wolf Prosser. He worked alone on his violins. Prosser was a feisty old gentleman, who obviously did not appreciate gangs of schoolchildren interrupting him, and we were the fifth group that morning. We hung back slightly, scared to touch anything. But then Adela, impulsive as always, saw a finished violin lying in its plush case and picked it out. She tuned it. We looked on nervously, but the violin maker seemed not to notice and carried on working. Suddenly Adela broke into her Mendelssohn. Dwarfed by the ancient rafters of the sunny barn she played like an angel. The Horns and Josie and Helen – who of course had refrained from showing anything other than polite interest when they saw their own instruments being made – raised their eyebrows at one another, but I could feel the tears pricking as they always did when Adela worked her magic. And I thought of Donald, and I thought of the beautiful day, and the fiasco it was becoming, and the tears welled up, clouding my glasses. I wasn't the only one affected. Adela finished playing and laid the violin back in its case. The violin maker stood up and went over to her, his eyes glistening. He put a gnarled hand on her arm. 'My dear,' he said simply, 'thank you. For this I make violins.' And he went back to his bench.

Humbled, we crept on to the final workshop, where

George Hooper made the famous Hooper flutes. He was a craftsman metalworker, wearing an apron and with his sleeves rolled up. 'Have a good look round,' he said. 'Ask me anything. And I've got some heads over there if you want a blow. Any of you flute-players?'

'She is.' They all pointed at me.

'You seem a nice careful girl. Here. This is a gold head. See what you make of it.'

I'd heard about gold flutes, but I'd never tried one. 'Give it a wipe. Lad from the last group blew a lot of germs into it. I wouldn't want you to catch anything!' He gave a raucous chuckle. I made an elaborate play of wiping the lip plate and blew. Wow. A gorgeous golden sound. 'See? It makes you all sound like Jimmy Galway!'

We thanked him and went out into the bright sunlight, the last group out. 'A quick look round the showroom, everyone,' Miss Claggan was saying. She looked at her watch, 'And then back on the coach. It's midday already – I expect you're all gasping for something to drink.'

Jessa came and found me. 'Did you try the gold flute head?' she asked. 'I did, and so did Donald. Amazing, wasn't it? Donald told Mr Hooper to make sure you tried it. Oh, and I sorted Kevin out . . . Tell you more later,' she said as Kevin came towards us.

So Donald was definitely avoiding me. I wasn't imagining it. Jessa, Kevin and I found a tree to sit under for our picnic. But as soon as we were off the coach Adela ran up to Donald and Sam, linked an arm through each of theirs and steered them as far away from us as possible. I could hear her starting to tell them about trying out the Prosser violin. To her credit she only told them about how wonderful it was, not how her playing moved the maker himself to tears, but then I never heard the end of the story because they were so far away. Jessa and Kevin were getting along really well. I found myself feeling distinctly left out. It wasn't that they weren't nice to me, just that it was definitely 'them' and me. And there in the distance was Adela being all animated and cute – pass the sick bag – with Donald and Sam, I could tell. I gave up. I took my glasses off, and lay back in the sun.

'You coming punting, Donnie lad?'

'Come on, Donald,' Jessa was saying. 'Come with us on the river.'

I heard Adela. 'Nah. River's for tourists, isn't it, Don?' But I didn't hear his reply. It wasn't what Adela had said before. I sat up and rubbed my eyes. Glasses back on. Ah, hello world.

'You'll come on a boat with us, won't you, Duck?' Jessa asked me. But I was getting mixed messages here. Jessa's voice wasn't as imploring as her words. And her expression seemed to be saying 'Please let me have Kevin to myself . . .'

I looked at her hard and said hesitantly – 'I thought I might have a wander round the colleges.' I'd read her expression right. She didn't ask again.

So, colleges it was. I attached myself to the colleges party while the boating lot went off to the boatyard to hire boats. I looked around our group. It did not contain Don and Adela.

Swine.

King's College Cambridge is a beautiful place. So is Queen's College and so are Trinity College, St John's, Peterhouse, Pembroke, Clare – and any others you'd care to mention. They soon merged into one. The heat was merciless. My newish sandals started to give me blisters. My friends were all out on the cool river. Donald was with Adela and they had skived off somewhere, together. I didn't have anything else to do until six o'clock, unless I felt like shopping – which I didn't – and I didn't have anyone to do it with anyway. We were all meeting up at the Clare canteen at half-past five. Tea was being laid on there before evensong next door in King's College chapel at six-fifteen. I told the others I'd see them at Clare for tea. I bought a bottle of Evian and went back through King's to the river. I lay in the shade with my chin on my hands and feasted my eyes on the green water, and thought of the pre-Raphaelite painting of drowned Ophelia, and envied her.

At five-thirty I got up to go. The thought of food and the concert cheered me a little, but just then a rowing boat slid into view. The oars were shipped. Two people were in it. The rower had taken his shirt off. His passenger lay back against him, a bottle of wine to her lips, giggling. He bent his silky head to her dark curly one and said something that brought peals of laughter from her. I drew back into the shadow of the tree. I'd just seen Donald and Adela.

I don't remember much about what happened after that. Somehow I got through tea and the concert without crying too much or too obviously. Somehow I managed the journey home in the front of the coach without looking back. Somehow I got into bed without telling Jessa to stop going on about Kevin. Somehow I fell asleep. I didn't hear when Adela came in.

TWELVE

I was crying in my dream. My mum was shouting at me and someone was looking on, Sophie maybe. I was saying please stop, I really hadn't meant to be naughty . . . I woke up, great sobs rasping from my chest. Thank God it was only a dream. But I was unhappy, still. Then I remembered. Donald and Adela. I sat up in a sweat. Adela! Where was she? She was there, asleep, her back towards me. And there were Gemma and Jessa. Everything was normal. Except that it wasn't. I had lost Donald. I'd never even had him, of course, but now I'd lost him. To Adela. I looked at her sleeping form, and slid back down under my covers, overwhelmed with misery. I found myself snivelling, tears and snot combining somewhere around my chin.

The most difficult thing to come to terms with was that I hadn't seen what was going on. Everything had been fine, brilliant, until Monday night, when Adela and Jessa had had their row over Kevin. And then Adela had left the music block with Donald and I hadn't even realised.

It didn't matter when it had begun. It had happened, and now Donald obviously despised me and had got it together with Adela in a big way – I winced at the memory of them in the boat together. And Kevin was definitely interested in Jessa. Perhaps I was too young for all this. Perhaps older people had a code that I didn't understand. Or it wasn't so much older people as just less innocent people who had a code. Perhaps that included Sophie and the others. Perhaps they all just saw me as sad and hopelessly immature.

The self-pity was really building now. I pulled the bedclothes up over my head and tried to cry quietly. I cried myself back to sleep.

The morning bell cut through another miserable dream. In this dream I was drowning. I fought my way out from under the duvet and looked around. Adela was sleeping through the bell as usual. Jessa and Gemma were going off to the shower together. Jessa was definitely looking bright-eyed and bushy-tailed this morning. I thought about the day ahead and tried to decide on a course of action. If I stayed in bed I'd have to face Adela. If I got up while Jessa and Gemma were in the shower and made a run for it I wouldn't have to face any of them. But where would I run to? I was bound to bump into someone. Of course, Jessa was the only one who knew what I felt about Donald. But I couldn't face seeing Donald, and certainly not if he was all over Adela. If I carried on as normal I would have to go through a sectional with Donald and Jessa and possibly a sax lesson with

Donald. It looked like the sort of day when everyone would head for the swimming pool and that certainly didn't appeal to me. And then whole group rehearsal and probably a jazz practice. Hmmm. I felt ghastly.

That was it. I felt really ill. I would send my apologies and stay in bed for the morning. I could probably cope with whole orchestra and even the jazz practice. After all, I was going to have to face Donald some time and it would be easier to act normal with lots of other people around. It wasn't as if *he* knew my feelings had changed from 'not fancying him'. He certainly wasn't to know I'd fallen in love with him. Only Jessa knew that.

And how had *Adela*, who didn't really care, managed to get off with him, when I hadn't?

Gemma came back into the dormitory. She saw me still in bed and came over. 'You all right, Hannah?'

I sounded suitably groggy. 'Not really,' I croaked. 'I think I'll stay in bed this morning. Could you ask Jessa to tell people? Thanks.' I snuggled down again. I heard Gemma whispering to Jessa not to wake me up again, I wasn't well, and Jessa murmuring 'Poor thing'. I heard Gemma go over and talk to Adela and tell her to let me sleep and Adela grunting something in response. This was a good way out. Exhausted, I went back to dreaming.

'Hi, Hannah. Are you OK?' Donald touched my arm as I pushed past him to my seat. Emotion had drained me and I still felt a bit wobbly. He was looking concerned. Huh.

'I'll live,' I said.

He leant across the other Hannah as I sat down. He was still looking concerned. Then I realised why. 'D'you think you'll be able to manage a jazz practice this evening? We need to spend as much time as we can rehearsing.'

Of course. Don't want to spoil the music. Don't want the precious jazz group to appear unrehearsed. I looked away. 'I'll be fine,' I said, concentrating on setting up my music on the stand. We were doing the Rimsky-Korsakov *Variations* and I had to concentrate on my piccolo solo. Thank God we were giving the Mendelssohn a rest. I don't think I could have borne Adela strutting her stuff just then. Jessa caught my eye. She gave me a 'that's ma girl!' smile as the conductor raised his baton, and I felt strengthened.

I needed all the strength I could get. In the break Adela bustled over to the flute section. 'Hi, Duck. I thought you were ill! Don, darlin', come with me for a quick one. Smoke,' she added, as if she was shocking us all. She pulled him out of his seat and dragged him out, leaving a trail of rocking music stands in her wake.

Jessa took my arm. 'Let's go and grab a drink, Han. I've got things to tell you.'

The break was only twenty minutes. 'Forget the drink, let's just go for a walk.' It seemed strangely bright outside to my red puffy eyes. 'God, Hannah, you look awful.'

We found a tree to sit under. I looked at Jessa expectantly. 'I'm happy for you, Jessa. Don't worry about me. I think I'm probably over Donald already. He and Adela deserve each other.'

'Like hell!' said Jessa. 'I always knew the cow was complicated, but I never quite knew how complicated. I'm only just beginning to understand. Now. I'll try and be quick. OK. So this is what Kevin has told me. Adela goes off with Donald after I'd screamed at her. Adela is feeling all rejected, so she lays this self-pity number on Don – everybody hates me, it's because I'm so brilliant, nobody treats me normally, they're scared of my sexuality (I know – as if!). Isn't it awful fancying someone when they don't fancy you etc., etc. And THEN she says – "I know you know how it feels, Don, with Duck not fancying you but liking KEVIN instead . . ."'

'I know all this,' I said. 'Adela told me herself. But none of it alters the fact that Don and Adela are now an item. So are you and Kevin.'

'That's only because I put him straight yesterday. I said Adela was just up to her tricks. *You* like Donald. It was *me* –' here she had the grace to blush – 'who liked him.'

'So what's new? Has Kevin said anything to Donald about me?'

'Well, no, not now he's going out with Adela, but he did tell me that Don *was* mad about you.'

'We have to go back in, don't we?'

'Let's skive off supper. I'll tell Kevin that's what we're doing.'

I still couldn't look at Donald when I went back to my seat. But I had a little spark of hope. It went out, frequently, because then I thought of him and Adela and how it was too late to change anything, but I still felt a bit better. Everyone went to the common room after the rehearsal, but I went back to the dormitories. I didn't want to have to watch Don and Adela, especially now. Jessa came and fetched me. 'I don't want to stay here,' I said. Adela might come in.

'Let's go to the gardens by the music block, then you won't worry about your jazz practice.'

'I'm tempted to miss that.'

'Don't you dare let Kevin down!'

'OK, OK!'

'Right, now, where were we?'

'Kevin knows *you* like him, not me. He also knows that Donald likes me – sorry, liked. But Donald doesn't know I like him. In fact, quite the opposite, because Adela had told our Donnie what I told her on Day One – namely, that I don't find him attractive . . .'

'Do you mean – you really said that?'

'On Day One – well, our first whole day – yes.'

'So when did you change your mind?'

'On Day Two!'

'The bit I don't understand is what made Donald get off

with Adela. Witchcraft is the only thing I can think of. Something pretty bloody powerful – after all, we know it's you he has the hots for.'

'*Had*. Had the hots for.'

'No. Something happened. Someone did or said something that set it all in motion.'

'Adela didn't like Kevin making up to me, that's for sure.'

'Neither did I!'

'But you're not the vindictive sort, not to me, anyway.'

'And Adela most definitely is. And it's not as if Kevin was faking his interest, unfortunately! I think we're getting somewhere, Han.' We heard voices and sounds of furniture being moved in the music room. 'They're setting up. I'll just say hello to my gorgeous Kevin, and then leave you to it.'

Jessa made an entrance. I hung back. The boys were all in there. So was Adela. She was sitting on Don's lap, all over him. Dead sexy. I couldn't look. Jessa was brilliant. 'Come on, Adela,' she said. 'These guys have work to do.'

Adela slid reluctantly off Don's lap. 'OK.' She smiled radiantly at Donald. 'Just imagine you're playing to me.' She blew him a kiss and scampered after Jessa, sweet as pie, now they were no longer rivals.

I decided that the best way to handle things was to excuse myself by saying I still felt a bit rough. It wasn't a lie. Rarely in my life have I felt in so much pain. Don was a bit subdued. Worn out, I should imagine. So we had a very workmanlike practice. Technically it was coming on really well.

But then Sam, who doesn't usually say much, spoke up. 'What's happened to you guys? Where's the soul? This is jazz you know. You have to put your heart into it. Tuesday night it was brilliant – loads of heart and soul. Tonight it was crap. What's changed?'

'Did my best,' muttered Kevin.

'Sorry,' Don and I said in unison. I wanted to look at him

and get one of those smiles, but I didn't dare. I knew what had changed, even if I didn't understand the whole story.

In the end it was Adela herself who filled me in. Jessa had come in blissfully happy. Kevin was a dream. Kevin was just so sexy. Kevin couldn't believe why he hadn't got together with her earlier. Her other boyfriend was history. Kevin, Kevin, Kevin. She fell asleep with a sigh. Needless to say, Adela hadn't put in an appearance so far. She turned up half an hour later. I was still tossing and turning, half waiting, I realised, for her to come in from being with Don.

She seemed to know that I was still awake as soon as she saw me. 'Duck!' she hissed. 'It's too early for bed. Come out with me.'

I can't think why I agreed to, but I did. I set off for the lime grove and she danced along beside me in the summer night. 'I wanted Don to stay out all night with me,' she said (Adela didn't know the meaning of the word tact), 'but the old goodie-goodie wanted to go to bed. He's had a hangover all day, as you probably gathered.' (I hadn't.) 'He doesn't seem to be interested in everything that's on offer, if you know what I mean.'

'Perhaps you're rushing him,' I said dully.

'Maybe,' she said. 'But he was happy enough yesterday, *once* I got a bit of alcohol down him. Well, quite a lot of alcohol. I was trying to cheer him up. Bit of a lightweight though. He was nearly puking up all the way home!'

'Probably not used to it.'

'Still, he's cute. I quite like having him around. Especially if Kevin is so determined to be with Jessa. It passes the time, doesn't it?' She tossed her curls and lit a cigarette. 'Thank God this is nearly over. Two more days of prison and then – Italy! Sea, sun and you know what. I can't wait.'

I was gobsmacked. She talked about Don, *my* Don, as a plaything. And a temporary one at that. Did he know?

'I'm going back now,' I said. 'Better if we don't sneak in

together. You finish your cigarette.' I didn't trust myself to speak and my brain was reeling.

THIRTEEN

I couldn't get to sleep. I heard Adela come in, though she slipped into bed like a shadow. All my thoughts were just 'If only . . . ' I went over and over the events of the last few days – after all, I had had *a* relationship with Don, even if it hadn't come to anything. We'd been friends. He'd taught me the saxophone. We'd been stuck in a dark room together for several hours – well, two. We'd played in a jazz group. I'd listened to his song. In fact, the more I considered it, the more I realised that maybe it *had* been leading somewhere. Or it had been until Adela got in on the act.

To be fair, Adela had always liked Donald. And I had told her categorically that *I* didn't fancy him. But then . . . she didn't need Donald. She could have had anyone. Except for Kevin, of course. Jessa and I had been right. If she couldn't toy with Kevin then she was going to toy with Donald instead.

I tossed and turned until my sheet was twisted up like a rope and my duvet had all gathered in one corner. I wanted to be asleep – tomorrow was the last whole day and I had to do something about Donald. There was a complete run-through in the afternoon as well as the usual rehearsals and practices, not to mention the last-night barbecue by the swimming pool . . . But then Donald was going out with Adela. They were a couple. He was probably hopelessly in love with her by now. No wonder. She encouraged him. She made him feel good about himself. She wasn't inhibited. And he'd probably never *really* fancied me. How could you fancy someone called Duck?

I must have fallen asleep eventually, though I know it

wasn't until after the dawn chorus. I woke up at the rising buzzer, feeling wide awake in a lightheaded kind of way. Jessa and Gemma were stirring. Adela was comatose. I decided to get up quickly, to be ahead of the game.

It was another gorgeous morning. I had a shower and washed my hair and shaved my legs. I was going to be irresistible today. I dried my hair with the hair-drier and dressed in my skinniest top and nicest jeans.

I went over to breakfast with Jessa, secure in the knowledge that Adela wouldn't make it, and headed for the boys' table. 'Hi, Kevin! Hi, Donald!' Donald gave me one of those anxious grins. I battled on. 'We've got a lot of rehearsing to get in today, guys. How do you propose to squeeze it all in?'

'One after lunch and a quickie before the disco is what I thought,' said Kevin.

Max was smutty as usual. 'And that's just with Jessa.'

Jessa went pink and giggled. 'Oh shut up, Max.'

I had to say something quickly before Max could make any jokes about Donald and Adela. 'OK, I'll be there,' I said, wishing I could think of something amusing to add. But I couldn't. It was hard enough just swallowing my cornflakes.

Jessa rescued me. 'There's quite a bit to do for the disco – apart from praying for the weather to stay nice. The kitchens are providing the food and the Horns are sorting out the sound system but we need to decorate the place a bit. I wanted candles everywhere, but we're not allowed. I think I'm going to have to buy fairy lights from a garden centre somewhere. You'll drive me, won't you, Kevin?'

'Are we going to sneak in any booze?' said Max. 'Last night, and all that. There's not a lot they can do to punish us.'

'I don't really think we want hangovers on the concert day, do we?' said Jessa. 'Anyway, Max. You shouldn't be thinking about booze.'

'Ah, but I do, Jessa,' said Max. 'And all sorts of other things. All the time. You can't imagine the things I think about.'

'I don't think I want to,' said Jessa.

'We know what you think about, Max,' said Kevin. 'Because you talk in your sleep.'

'That's only because *I* don't get the chance to see it in the flesh—' I was beginning to wish I hadn't joined this lot for breakfast. Kevin and Jessa were smiling indulgently at one another and the talk was getting dangerous again. Donald was looking everywhere but at me. It was time to go, but I was proud of myself. I wasn't going to go out of the course with a whimper, oh no.

I stood up. 'See y'all. Jazz practice straight after lunch then. See you two in sectionals. I'm off to practise my piccolo part. Don't want to muck it up.' And I walked out trying not to look self-conscious and willing Donald to be watching me wistfully and hoping I wouldn't hear gales of laughter just as I got out of the door.

I was serious about practising the piccolo. This was for the Rimsky-Korsakov. I'd only realised yesterday just how exposed it was. I couldn't bear the thought of Mum criticising my performance. Actually I couldn't bear the thought of Mum – or even home – at all at that particular point. Despite everything, I didn't want the course to finish. Or at least, not until I'd resolved things with Donald. I tramped up to the music school, my mind whirring as if I'd been wound up. That was it; even if Donald didn't want to hear, I knew I needed to tell him that I had liked him all along and that I did fancy him. If he wanted to be with Adela, well, that was fine (well, not really, but that's what I'd say, anyway). I'd just been too shy to let him know how I felt. I suspected that that had been his problem, too, but I don't suppose it was for me to tell him.

I worked hard at the piccolo. It's not really an early-morning instrument, especially if you haven't slept much.

But I had such a feeling of time running out that I was prepared to work hard at everything today. I wanted to be perfect in every department. So that if things went wrong they couldn't be blamed on me. I would have liked to have had a bit of a go on the sax. I could have gone and borrowed it, I knew where Don kept it, but I didn't want to delve amongst his things. I was too frightened of what I might find. I decided to ask him for it at the sectional – at least Adela wouldn't be there. And I needed to take full advantage of those times from now on.

We had a five-minute break. Hannah – other Hannah – had nipped out for a drink. Jessa was going over her part with Miss Claggan. There was no one between Donald and me. As if in a farce, we both started speaking at once. 'Hannah—' 'Don—' I pushed on. 'I need a bit more time on the sax – any chance I could borrow it for twenty minutes before the practice?'

'Yes, sure. I'll come up with you after the sectional. Check the reed and stuff.' He looked at me as if he was about to say something else, but I cut in. Hannah was making her way back.

'Thanks.' The sectional was starting again.

Donald waited for me by the door as we came out. Maybe Kevin had said something to him. Jessa gave me a meaningful 'go-for-it' glance as she passed us. Don was looking particularly fit today – good jeans and a top that matched his eyes. We set off up the stairs to the instrument store. Somehow it felt like old times. He found the sax. 'Which practice room are you in?'

'I'll go in the one we use for jazz. I'm skipping lunch.'

'Do you want me to bring you something? You know what happens—' and he gave me one of his dazzling grins – nothing anxious about it. A bubble of relief welled up in me – brought tears to my eyes. I took off my glasses and flicked my hair back. 'Hey, Hannah – are you all right?'

'Yeah, yeah,' I laughed, and saw the look of relief on his face.

'I hoped you weren't—'

'No, I was just remembering the embarrassment. I'm fine. Really. Not hungry.'

He turned at the door. 'Hannah – I—' He was at it again.

'Donnie! There you are! Coaching the Duck again, are we?' Thanks, Adela. She tucked herself under his arm. I wanted to shut my eyes. 'Lunchtime, Donnie lad. I thought I'd come and fetch you.' And she dragged him off. But not before he'd thrown an indecipherable glance in my direction. I gritted my teeth. The day was far from over. I *would* sort it out. I *would*.

Adela came with Donald to the jazz practice. When they arrived her arm was hooked firmly in his. I chose to think that he didn't look very comfortable, but that was probably just because I felt so annoyed. I put the anger into the music and of course it sounded great. We stayed with *Take Five* and *Yesterday*, saving the other two for the evening practice. I caught Donald's eye as he sang the harmonies during *Yesterday* – and he looked away quickly, but I saw a tell-tale flush on his neck that gave me an odd satisfaction. Adela sat swinging her legs throughout and for the first time ever she was full of praise at the end. 'That was amazing,' she said. 'Even you, Duck.'

Don leapt to my defence. 'What do you mean, even Duck? Duck has more soul than the rest of us put together!'

Then Jessa appeared. It was still only two-fifteen. 'Come on, Kevin, we've got to pick up those fairy lights.'

'Oh, OK. Sorry everybody, I forgot. I promised Jessa.'

'What's all this about?' Adela didn't like not knowing what was going on.

'It's for the barbecue disco thing,' said Jessa. 'We want to make the pool look really romantic, so we're hiring fairy lights. It's all sorted, but we've got to pick them up. Kevin's driving me.'

'So you're stopping?' Adela hopped down from her seat. 'Great. Come on, Don, come with me for a fag,' and she tugged at his shirt.

'Hang on a minute.' Don shook her off. 'Not now, Adela. We have to clear up. You go, Kevin.'

'I don't want to clear up. Can't I come with you two, then?' Adela asked Kevin and Jessa.

But Jessa wasn't having any of it. 'We can manage on our own, thanks,' she said. 'We need to hurry, Kev.' They left.

Adela hung around. We were busy tidying up but she didn't offer to help. Then Sam said, 'I need someone to take my double bass down for the run-through while I put the big amplifier away. Can you give me a hand?' He looked round at Adela, who was sitting idly. 'Adela?'

'Oh OK,' she said. 'Meet me in five minutes then, Don.'

Don and I were left alone. I packed up the wind instruments while he sorted out the keyboard and stacked the chairs. He looked at his watch. 'Damn,' he said. 'She'll just have to wait. I said I'd take some chairs down for the run-through.'

I looked at him helplessly. He swept all the music into a pile and stuffed it into the Gap carrier bag he used. He picked up the saxophone case, swung the bag of music over his shoulder and grabbed a stack of three chairs by the backs as he made for the door. 'Sorry about the rush,' he said. 'I thought we'd all have loads of time. Dunno why I agreed to cart chairs around – or go with Adela. Sorry,' he said again.

'It's OK,' I said as, laden, he crashed through the door. I wanted to offer to take the chairs for him, but the words wouldn't come and he seemed intent on punishing himself in this way. Then the Gap bag chose that moment to split open, scattering a snowstorm of sheets of music everywhere. The French windows were open and a wicked summer breeze picked them up and tossed them around.

'Damn,' said Donald again, and worse. I started to chase

down the sheets and gather them up as he put down the chairs and the sax to join in. It took us nearly five minutes before we each had a neat sheaf of music. I handed mine to Don and saw a last sheet dancing through the French windows. 'I'll get it,' I said and ran after it, finally stamping it into submission in the courtyard. I bent down to pick it up. It was a piece of handwritten music. I recognised it as one of Don's songs. At the top were three titles, all crossed out. Intrigued, I tried to make them out under the scribble. The first was 'Raindrops On Her Skin'. The second was 'Girl, I Love You' and the third was simply 'Hannah in the Rain'.

I stood, dumbstruck, staring at the sheet of paper in my hand.

I stood there for so long that Don came out to find me. 'Hannah?' he called. 'Where've you got to? Are you OK?' Then he saw me. 'Oh, thanks. It would be such a pain to lose the music at this stage. What was it I was going to have to improvise then?' He held out his hand for the music. I gave it to him. He looked at it, and then at me.

'Oh,' he said.

I didn't move.

'Oh Hannah, I'm so sorry – so sorry – to have embarrassed you. Hannah – are you cross?'

I still couldn't move. He came closer. His face was bright red – I'd only ever seen it like that a couple of times before.

'*Cross?*' was all I could say.

He held the music close to his chest, as if he couldn't bear it to be seen again. I looked down, shaking my head in disbelief. I wanted to cry. I took my glasses off and rubbed my eyes, but they started to fill with tears.

'Hannah, I'm so sorry,' he said it again. He looked as if he was about to cry too.

'I – I – I wish I'd known then,' I said, looking up at him.

'Nothing's changed, you know,' he said softly, and moved closer to me, towering over me.

I was about to say, 'Yes, it has,' but then Adela appeared in person, and made the words unnecessary.

If Adela had seen us moving guiltily apart she didn't comment. '*There* you are, lover!' she shrieked. 'What kept you? I had to have my cigarette all on my own. We'll be late for the run-through!'

For some reason I was less tongue-tied than Donald (nothing to be guilty about, I suppose). 'Don's music bag exploded by the French windows,' I told her. 'Music everywhere. It took us ages to pick it all up. And we've got to take some chairs down. Grab one, can you?'

So we all set off down to the run-through. And I felt immensely gratified that Adela had her hands full and couldn't paw Donald.

FOURTEEN

'You're going to have to let Hannah off this jazz practice,' Jessa said to Kevin. She had a firm grip on my wrist. 'She can't possibly play any more or her mouth will drop off. You know she's brilliant. And anyway, I need her for fairy-light duty.'

'What do you think, Don?' Kevin needed back-up.

'Fine,' Don mumbled.

'Great,' said Adela, never far away. 'I'll come up and be your artistic adviser.'

'Whatever,' said Don, not looking in our direction.

Kevin gave Jessa a hug. They were getting *very* married. 'OK, Jess. We'll let her off this time. Just this once, mind . . . Make it look stunning. See you there later.'

I'd been dying to talk to Jessa all through the run-through, but with Don right there, it just hadn't been possible. And it wasn't as if we didn't have plenty to concentrate on. Adela's concerto had been the worst time. She played brilliantly as usual, but Donald hadn't known where to look. Well, down, in fact, but the flush on his neck was a dead give-away.

And Jessa knew none of this. She was prattling on about vegetarian and non-vegetarian barbecues, music for the disco, fairy lights and changing rooms without pausing for breath.

'Jess – hang on,' I said.

'Uh-oh. What's up? You're not going flabby on me, are you?'

'No, Jess. Listen. I've got loads to tell you.'

'Tell me while we do stuff,' said Jessa. I obviously looked worried. 'OK. Tell me while we sit down and unravel these lights then.' She put them down on a bench by the pool. 'Fire away.'

So I told her about Don and the song. And how he'd come so close to saying things and doing things, but how Adela seemed to have a sixth sense that brought her on the scene right on cue, every time.

'Blimey, Duck,' said Jessa. 'But what's going to happen? Adela won't let him go, you know. Not without a major struggle.'

I told her what Adela had said the night before. 'It's not as if she really rates him. She was so dismissive, Jessa, so patronising.'

'That's not the point where Adela's concerned. Looks like you'll just have to wait until after the course.'

'*What?* But he really likes me, Jess,' (it felt so wonderful saying that). 'He said that nothing had changed. And we've got this whole romantic evening ahead of us.'

'You'll have to fight Adela for him.'

'You didn't have to fight her for Kevin.'

'I almost did. Anyway. Then she had Don.'

'Exactly. What about me in all this? Don't you think I've missed out somewhere?'

'Well, yes. But that doesn't alter the fact that Adela won't just say – Here, take him with my blessing. She's not like that.'

We carried on in silence for a few minutes. 'Maybe you're right,' I said in a small voice. 'Maybe I should wait until she's gone to Italy. It's only the day after tomorrow.' Jessa looked at me sympathetically. 'But it doesn't seem fair. And, Jess, I have to have some time with him tonight. We haven't *done* anything yet to – like – ac*know*ledge that we – *lurve* each other.'

'There's always the disco. Tell you what – I'll get Kevin to organise some of the dancing. You know, like a caller. Dance with the girl on your right, or the man opposite you, or whatever. I'm sure Kevin will be only too pleased to oblige. You know how bossy he is!'

'I'm not sure that Adela would go for all that stuff. Don would though.'

Jess climbed a ladder to hook up the lights around the 'dance area' (the patch of grass where we'd been sunbathing). 'Then we'll just get Kevin to be with Adela somehow, even though it will break my heart. The things I do for a friend . . . '

'Thanks, Jess,' I said meekly.

'There. How does it look?' She came down the ladder to admire the thread of lights.

'Not a lot, until we switch them on!'

Jessa bustled over to the power points where the Horns were sorting out the disco. 'Wait for it . . . Ta-da!'

'Wow!' The shadows were long and the August day was already fading. The coloured lights were like fireflies flitting amongst the leaves or little falling stars.

'Testing . . . 1-2-1-2' Breathy voices imploded over the sound system. The charcoal on the barbecues was glowing and smoke wafted across the pool. Jessa hugged me.

'A Midsummer Night's Dream or what? Bring on Donald! You must be desperate for him. Bring on Kevin, too. I'm certainly desperate for *him*.'

'Let's go and get changed,' I said. But all I was thinking was, what on earth would Adela *do*, if she knew I was planning on nicking her boyfriend?

Jessa and I were in the pool when the rest of the jazz band turned up. Adela wasn't with them. I had this on hearsay from Jessa – without my glasses I couldn't see a thing. 'Maybe this is your lucky day after all, Duck,' she said, and hauled herself dripping from the water to throw herself at Kevin. 'Get your kit off, fellas. The water's gorgeous.'

'Mm. *You're* gorgeous,' said Kevin, catching hold of her hand, 'and – aagh – you're all wet!'

'Of course I am! Cheer up, Donald – where's Adela?'

'Oh, cooking up something with Max, I think.' Donald was mumbling again. I couldn't really hear him from where I was in the water, and Kevin and Jessa were squealing.

'What sort of something?' Sam asked.

'Don't ask,' said Donald. 'Hi, Duck!' he called in my direction. 'Don't go away, we're coming in.'

Gulp. I nearly drowned at that point. But of course, it was safe for him to be all jolly with me.

Jessa swam up beside me. 'Hey, Duck. They'll be over here soon. Stay cool.'

'I don't feel cool. Anyway, Adela will be here any minute. Probably topless!' I wasn't far wrong. At that moment there was a commotion at the side of the pool. Max was shouting. He sounded hugely over-excited.

'Oi, Don! Don! Don't be a spoilsport! We want Adela to give us an action replay, but she says you wouldn't like it!'

Adela's voice. She sounded hyper, too. 'What do you think, Don?'

Don and Kevin were swimming towards us. I didn't dare to look. I felt we were all too naked and vulnerable. Don was saying, 'Help me get out of this one, Kev.'

Then Kevin called, 'Forget it, Adela! Look behind you!'

'Who's there?' I asked Jessa.

Jessa laughed. 'Only the entire staff – in their swimming gear!'

'Woo-oo!' Kevin grabbed me and pulled me under. Don did the same to Jessa. That was all right, somehow. But then Adela was jumping in near us, and I realised that we were all a bit wary of her. 'Hang on in there, Duck,' said Kevin in my ear as Adela popped up beside Don. 'We'll sort you young lovers somehow.'

I stared at him. 'Jess told me,' he said, and dived down to pull her feet from under her. By now the pool was so crowded it didn't matter if you were on your own or not. Adela was pulling Don towards the side. She wasn't being very nice to him – I could hear words like, 'Don't be so *boring*,' and 'It's only a bit of fun'. They climbed out of the pool.

Max was laughing inordinately. He kept shouting, 'I've got a sausage for you, Adela!' and cracking up. I couldn't bear to watch and I couldn't see anyhow, so I stuck with Jessa and Kevin, wishing Don was with me, glad that Adela seemed to be making it easier for him to be with me and faint at the prospect of him really being with me. I wanted him to strike out towards me now and sweep me up in his arms, all dripping water and muscles and cold, firm flesh and warm lips . . .

'Coming in, Duck?' My reverie had stopped me noticing that everyone else was getting out of the pool and heading for the changing rooms.

It wasn't quite warm enough to wander around in a wet bikini, but most of us had sarongs and tops of one sort and another. It felt a bit odd – but different, anyway, and at least it was warm around the barbecues and the DJ played some boppy numbers to get people going.

'What d'you think?' Jessa was justifiably smug about her efforts.

'Brilliant,' said Kevin, leaning forward as he bit into a

burger so it didn't drip down the T-shirt he'd pulled on over his swimming shorts.

Adela and Don were there. 'It's great,' said Adela. 'Especially this fizz!' and she held up her plastic cup in Max's direction. Max responded by raising his cup and hiccupping as he poured in some more Coke from a large plastic bottle.

'Good bottle, this,' he said, unsubtly. 'Duck? Don? Kevin? Jessa? Want some extra-special Coke?'

'Oh, don't bother giving Don any,' said Adela. 'He doesn't approve. I don't expect any of them do. I'll have some more though.'

'You're just mad to be so obvious! All the staff are here, for God's sake!' said Jessa.

'Oh, that's the problem, is it?' said Adela. 'Come on, Max, let's go somewhere less obvious then, where all the staff aren't. See you in a bit, guys.' And she ran off after Max, leaving the four of us standing.

'You dancin'?' Kevin asked Jessa.

'You askin'?' laughed Jessa, and they spun off into the dance area.

Don looked nervously in the direction Adela and Max had disappeared in. Then he looked sideways at me.

I looked at my feet.

'Tricky, huh?' he said, to my feet, trying to get me to look up at him.

I did, and wished I hadn't. I wanted him so badly. Still, there was no law against looking at each other. We stood there, gazing into each other's eyes.

He looked down this time. 'I'm scared,' he said. 'I'm scared of Adela, Hannah. I don't know what to do.' He spoke very quietly. 'I'm scared that if we dance together she'll find us. I'm scared that if we disappear off, she'll notice, and find us.'

'Perhaps it should be enough that we know we want to,' I said. 'She's flying off to Italy after the concert tomorrow evening.'

'I can't wait that long,' said Don.

'I'm not sure that I can, either,' I replied.

'Where did she and Max go with their booze, anyway? Good job I'm not the jealous type! Do you think it might be grounds for divorce?'

I couldn't laugh. I was so desperate to be with Don, but he was right – Adela would *know* somehow. And she *was* scary. How would she react? It didn't bear thinking about.

'Let's go and line up for a sausage and stand close to each other . . . ' Don was still capable of making a joke of it. He lowered his voice to a whisper. 'Cheer up, Han. We'll laugh about this one day – won't we?'

'OK,' I said. We got on the end of the queue. Kevin and Jessa jigged along after us and Kevin pushed Don into me with plenty of uproarious laughter.

'Anyone seen Adela?' asked Don innocently as he leant against me.

'I'm here!' God! Adela had materialised from nowhere. 'Babe!' she said, and squeezed up against Don.

'Sausage time!' said Max. 'We require sausages, don't we, 'Dela?' Max was talking very loudly.

So was Adela. And her words were slightly slurred. 'No,' she said, pouting. 'Not sausages. Smooching. Come on Donnie babe. Come and dance with me. I missed you.' And she dragged him off.

'Lucky sod,' said Max, still loudly.

'Your time will come, Max,' said Kevin.

'Thought it had,' said Max sulkily. 'I mean, look at her.'

We looked. Adela was draped all over Don as they danced a slow one. I could tell that Don was trying to be as detached as possible. But he wasn't finding it easy.

Max set off towards them. He patted a hip flask under his shirt. 'I'll lure her away,' he said.

Kevin looked at me. 'I don't advise it, mate,' he said. 'But I can't stop you,' he added as Max lurched off.

Jessa looked worried. 'We *ought* to stop him, Kev. Adela's got major stuff to do tomorrow.'

'I can't believe Max has enough there to affect Adela that much,' said Kevin.

'I shouldn't be too sure,' said Jessa. 'I know we've got to get Duck up there with Don, but I don't think this is the way to do it.'

I felt helpless. I started to shiver.

'Think of something, Kev. I'm going to force some hot food into my little friend here. Come on, Duck, we're nearly there. It's nice and warm by the barbecue.'

I suddenly felt sick and miserable. 'It's no good Jessa. Thanks for trying and everything, but I just can't bear to be anywhere near Adela and Don together. Not now. I'm going off for a bit.'

'But, Duck – after all our hard work! You can't walk out now, just when the evening's going so well.'

'It's brilliant, Jessa, really it is. But I can't honestly say it's going well for me right now. You must see.'

'Yeah. I do. Poor old thing. It must be ghastly. I wish Don could just tell her it's over. But I don't like to think about what she'd do if he did.'

'My point precisely. We're all scared of her. It's ridiculous, but we are. Especially Don.'

'Must make him feel powerful. Fancy knowing that the whole success of tomorrow's concert is in your hands.'

'What do you mean?'

'Well, if he dumps her tonight she'll probably do something really stupid, like running away. And then she won't be able to lead the orchestra tomorrow, or play her concerto.'

'Thanks for that, Jess. You've just made me realise that it's even more of a nightmare than I thought. I think I'll run away instead. See ya!'

FIFTEEN

I had to get away before I started crying. I felt so sorry for myself that I knew tears weren't far away. I thought I might just go back to the dormitory, but a part of me thought it would be more romantic to weep somewhere near a bank of scented flowers. After all, Don might just come looking for me . . .

Jasmine grew up the wall of the music block and there was a bench in the corner there. In the dusk the flowers seemed to pulsate with scent and light. I sat on the bench and hugged my knees. It was very peaceful. I could hear the music drifting over from the swimming pool, but it wasn't intrusive. The events of the evening went round and round in my head. Don. Me. Don. Adela. I just had to make it through tomorrow and then I could have Don to myself. Maybe it wouldn't be that hard. I had so much to look forward to.

I calmed down as I sat there, breathing the heady night air. Today was nearly over. I just had to make it through tomorrow . . . make it through tomorrow . . . make it through tomorrow . . .

It was dark in a late-summer, velvety way. I felt light and detached, invisible. Without my glasses I could hear and smell and sense far more than I could see. The music from the disco had slowed down and I could hear people dispersing. Some were in couples – there was laughter and furtive giggles. Two people ran past me, quite close, panting and laughing rather than speaking, the boy chasing the girl – I could hear him shaking a bottle of something ready to squirt at her. They rustled off into the distance and then the water obviously hit her. The squeals of laughter made it clear that it was Adela who had been soaked, and Max who had done the soaking. I pricked up my ears. 'Gotcha!'

'Don't!' shrieked Adela, but she was laughing.

'Now you've got to do it!'

'I don't have to!'

'Yes you do! It was your part of the bargain!'

'Oh no I don't!'

'Give me some of your drink then!'

'OK! OK! Calm down. Follow me. I've got a stash of it. Hang on . . . ' I heard the click and hiss of a cigarette lighter.

'Give me one of those, too.'

'All right, all right.' The lighter flicked on again.

I vaguely made out two little red lights moving away. What I failed to do just then was make the connection – if Adela was with Max then she wasn't with Don. I just felt glad that they weren't intruding on my privacy any longer. I hugged my knees again and allowed the scent of jasmine to beguile my senses.

Down below at the disco another slow number was starting up. The evening was definitely drawing to a close. Suddenly my skin prickled. Someone was walking towards me over the grass. She – or he – must have seen me. Damn.

'Hannah?'

I didn't answer – I didn't want to see anyone.

'Hannah, is that you?' It was Don. He was coming closer. He came over and pulled me to my feet. 'Please?'

We stood close. I put my arms around his neck. He held me round my waist and we swayed to the strains of the music that drifted up from below. He bent his head down, pushed my shirt from my shoulders and kissed my neck, gentle kisses. I breathed in the chlorine smell of his hair. He was kissing my throat and my chin and then, at last, our lips met. At some point he drew breath, only to say, 'Hannah,' and stroke my hair from my face before kissing me again.

I started to say, 'What about Adela?' but he put his finger over my lips.

'Shh.'

It's the only time I've ever wanted a disco to go on for ever, but the music came to an end and we couldn't ignore the general hubbub of people leaving and packing up. 'One more,' said Don, 'and then I'd better go down and help Kevin and Jessa.' And before I could add anything, 'Don't ask, OK?' Then he caught me up again and I wasn't able to speak for a good five minutes. I wouldn't have noticed if the whole world had come to watch us.

Don let go of me suddenly. 'Uh-oh,' he said, and then, 'I really hope she didn't see us. I'll run down the long way round. You come down in a bit!' And he was gone, leaving me to peer after a familiar sprite clutching a bottle and staggering back the way she had come.

Adela still hadn't come in by one o'clock. Gemma was asleep, but Jessa and I sat on my bed, wondering what on earth to do. I kept saying, 'Oh God, it's all my fault! If only we'd waited . . . '

'Damn her!' said Jessa uncharacteristically. 'It's her own silly fault. She should never have seduced Don in the first place. She's just *so* desperate for love and attention. Bloody artistic temperament.'

'But what can we do?' I wailed. 'I bet she's done something stupid, and then she won't be able to play tomorrow and the course will have been ruined.'

'No doubt she *has* done something stupid and we'd better find her. But she's tough. We'll make her play tomorrow. I'm sick of her calling the tune. We're all stuck here. We're an orchestra – a team, she can't let us down just because of this.'

Jessa was right, of course. She always was.

'We're going to find her, all of us, and confront her. Me and Kevin, you and Don, and Max.'

'Max?'

'Yeah. She's messed him about too, you know. Well, she's sunk to his juvenile level basically. But he's a nice guy. He likes Adela. She led him on something rotten tonight.'

I couldn't deny that. Max, Kevin and Don. All nice guys. Why wasn't Adela able just to be friends with them? Why did she always want them to fancy her, get off with her? 'OK, Jess. We'd better go and throw stones at their windows or something.'

Jess and I were adept at slipping out unseen these days, but we didn't need to throw stones at windows. As we approached the boys' block we heard the dreadful sound of someone retching. It was Max. Kevin and Don were with him. They weren't being very sympathetic.

'Get on with it, Max,' said Kevin.

'Stick your fingers down your throat!' advised Don.

Max groaned.

'Turn away, Max! We have female visitors,' said Kevin. 'Hi, Jessa! What are you two doing here?'

Don put his arm around me.

'Oi!' said Kevin. 'Enough of that. That's what got us into this mess in the first place.'

'Not true,' said Jessa. 'Leave them alone. Adela is to blame for *all* this mess. Not any of us.'

'Do you know where she is, Max?'

Max groaned. 'Snuggled up with a large bottle of vodka somewhere. Cow.'

'You didn't have to drink it, Max,' said Jessa severely.

'I didn't,' said Max. 'I drank the cider. And, er, some of the Hooch. OOOO-er – '

'Face the other way when you vomit, please,' Don reprimanded him. 'The ladies don't want to see your supper.'

'Sausages, I seem to remember,' I said.

'Thank you, Hannah,' said Jessa. Max was throwing up again. 'Oh yuk. I can't stay here.'

'I'll stay with him,' said Kevin.

'We'll wait just round the corner . . . ' Don spun me round.

'Oh God, does that mean I have to be with you two lovebirds?'

'Hark at who's talking!' I said.

''Fraid so,' said Don.'

Max was in full flow – so to speak – now.

'Hurry up and get it over with, Max,' we heard Kevin saying.

Max groaned some more. 'Leave me alone.'

'Nope,' said Kevin. 'We need you. Adela has gone missing and we've got to find her and make sure she plays OK tomorrow. It's already quarter to two in the morning. The chamber concert starts in just over twelve hours.'

'She's just drinking somewhere,' said Max. 'She saw Don and Duck snogging and she's upset . . . Ooooooh-er . . . here we go again.'

'I'm not sure I can stand any more of this,' said Jessa. 'Leave him, Kev.'

'No,' said Kev. 'We all need to go together. Come on, Max. Mind over matter. Lead us to where Adela is.'

They came round the corner to us. 'Oh no!' said Jess. 'He's got puke all down his T-shirt.'

'Take it off, Max,' said Kevin. 'Can't have you offending my girlfriend.'

'Wear my sweatshirt,' I offered. 'It's not as cold as I thought.' And I had Don to keep me warm.

'Wow!' said Max, as he put it on.

'There, you see? He's cheering up already,' said Don. 'And so he should. Come on.'

'I don't know where she is,' said Max.

'I bet I do.' I felt pretty sure she'd be in the lime grove. Perhaps, like me earlier, she half wanted to be found.

We found her curled up. The bottle was on its side and

almost empty. It was hard to tell whether she had passed out or fallen asleep.

'Adela? Wake up!' I rubbed her back tentatively. There was no response.

'Let me try,' said Kevin. He shook her quite roughly by the shoulders. 'Adela! Don't be silly! Wake up and talk to us.'

She emitted a grunt that sounded mostly like 'Go away.'

'We're not going anywhere,' said Kevin. 'Not without you, anyway.'

Another groan. 'I wish I was dead.'

'That's crazy,' said Kevin. 'We'd be bloody cross with you if you were.'

Jessa was whispering. 'She's drunk one hell of a lot. She must be pretty ill. How can we make her be sick?'

Max groaned.

'Just make her smell Max,' said Don. 'He still stinks. He makes me want to throw up.'

'I've got a bottle of mineral water,' said Kevin to Adela. 'Now I want you to sit up and glug some down. Come on, sit up.'

'I want to die,' said Adela. 'Nobody loves me! Don doesn't love me!'

'Cut the drama, Adela,' said Jessa brusquely. 'You don't love Don. Or Kevin or Max. But luckily for you we all like you. Can't think why, but we do. And we want you to feel better.' Adela was slumped against the tree now.

'Oh, the world's going round and round.'

'That's because you're drunk,' said Max. 'You'll feel better when you've been sick.'

'I'm no lightweight!' said Adela furiously, but then she started to retch, too.

'This has been the most disgusting night of my life,' said Jessa. 'You'll have to be sick on your own, Adela. I just wanted to talk to you, not go through all this.'

'Go away then,' said Adela rudely. And then her head fell on her chest again.

'Sit her up again, Kev,' said Jessa, sounding anxious. 'She mustn't be allowed to fall asleep if she's going to be sick. People die that way.'

'Jimi Hendrix,' said Max usefully. 'Funnily enough I feel a lot better now. Better out than in, eh? Come on, Adela, we're all going to prop you up, and you're going to drink water and vomit for us like a good girl.'

Adela was unwilling. Her head lolled alarmingly. 'This is not good,' said Jessa. 'Maybe it's more than we can cope with. What if she needs a stomach pump?'

'Give it five minutes,' said Don. 'After all, it's only luck – for her – that we even found her. Come on, Adela, you're going to lean against me and drink the water Kevin's giving you.'

'And then you can throw up on me,' said Max. 'See? All your favourite men looking after you!'

I was slightly shocked by his frivolity in such a serious situation, but his words had obviously struck a chord.

'Yeah,' said Adela, slurrily. 'That's right. All my favourite fellas. I love you all . . . ' She paused. 'But you don't love me . . . ' and proceeded to throw up all over Max – and *my* sweatshirt.

'Well done,' said Max, unperturbed. 'Actually, I *am* pretty crazy about you, Adela, but now isn't really the time to tell you. The important thing is that we are all fond of you and we don't want you to be dead. You muck us about something rotten – ' he paused to think – 'but then you seem to play by different rules from the rest of us.' He took off the offending sweatshirt and elbowed Don out of the way so that Adela could lean on him. 'But you really shouldn't play games with your friends, Adela. Love and war, and all that, but not with your friends.'

This was turning into quite a speech. Kevin and Jessa were looking on, amazed. I realised that Max was definitely saving the day by keeping up the chat, but I found it hard to concentrate because Don was now stroking my ear and cheek with his thumb in a way that no one could see but that I could feel intensely.

'The thing is,' Max continued, 'you might think that we all have ordinary families and boring lives, and you might even envy that, but you've got something that none of us really has – and that is, totally effing superb talent.'

I think we all wanted to say 'Speak for yourself' at that point, but we knew he was right, and anyway, Adela chose that moment to puke again. Max patiently wiped her up with the clean side of my sweatshirt, and carried on as if nothing had happened. 'You see, most people will never treat you as quite normal because you're abnormally brilliant, but it's up to you to choose whether you want that or not. We'll treat you as normal, because we're your regular friends – well, I might not, but this lot will . . . ' He put his arm around her so that her head lolled onto his chest. 'Do you think we can let her go to sleep now?' he asked us.

'Not here,' said Kevin. 'Even if that's what you want, Max! Come on, you two had better get her into bed.'

'But she's revolting,' said Jessa.

'Better than dead,' said Don.

'Marginally,' retorted Jessa. 'Oh all right then. Clean her up as much as you can, Max.'

'And then leave that sweatshirt here,' I said. 'I never want to see it again.'

We pulled Adela, grumbling, to her feet. It was a long journey back to the dormitories, but it was so late by then that we weren't too worried about making a noise. We stripped her naked and put her to bed with a large bowl and a mug of water beside her.

'Sleep tight, Adela,' said Jessa. 'We'll make sure no one wakes you until lunch time, and then you'd bloomin' well better play your heart out.' But Adela was fast asleep, and soon we were too.

SIXTEEN

We missed breakfast. Jessa and I managed to roll out of bed for a briefing at half-past ten. Don was looking out for me. I still couldn't believe that we had gone public. He hugged me tight and surreptitiously kissed my hair. Kevin and Jessa smiled on us indulgently. Max looked wan. We told the Goat that Adela had been ill last night, probably something she ate, but that we were confident she'd recover in time for the concerts. The briefing was followed by an hour of last-minute sectionals and then it was really all over bar the concerts. Parents were beginning to draw up in Jeeps and Volvos. Those who had come a long way were scattered across the lawns with picnics. Some were taking younger brothers and sisters for a swim.

Don and I sat together on the bench under the chestnut tree. I couldn't bear the thought of being apart from him for more than a moment. There were five minutes before lunch. It was hard to find time to talk between the kissing, but I managed to ask Don if his parents were coming for the concert. 'Of course,' he said. 'My old man said this morning that he wouldn't miss a jazz concert for anything.'

'Mine will only make it for the evening do,' I told him. 'They force themselves to come and support me. Makes it easier to send me off on another one.'

Don smiled down at me. I suddenly remembered what he felt about parents, but he didn't preach this time. 'Cynic,' he said. 'They must know they've got one hell of a daughter. Or do they need me to tell them?'

'Don't you dare—' I started to say.

'Oh, aren't you going to introduce me? Ashamed of me already?'

'Don, you know it's not like that! I just couldn't bear it.

My mum would be all curious and girlish. And Dad would be embarrassed.'

'Only joking. Anyway, Hannah – or should I say Duck?'

'Don't remind me! Though I suppose I don't mind being Donald's Duck . . . '

'I was going to say – this isn't – you know, *it*, is it?'

'What do you mean?'

'We can see each other once we get home?'

I couldn't imagine *not* seeing him. 'Of *course*!' I said. 'We've got the whole holidays ahead, haven't we?'

'Not quite,' he said. 'I'm going up to Scotland for three weeks now, but there'll still be some time before term starts.'

'And *after* term starts, I sincerely hope,' I said, 'Or are you planning on cutting a swathe through the sixth form crumpet at Greenwood as soon as you arrive?'

'No,' he said solemnly, 'I'm thinking of starting quite slowly with my year first . . . ' This called for some serious slapping followed by some even more serious snogging.

'Oi, you two, cut that out! You might make me vomit again and it's lunchtime!' My God, it was Adela, and she was laughing.

'Good kisser, isn't he?' she said, and darted off with a Puckish grin. That girl was so unpredictable. One minute trying to drink herself into oblivion and the next minute skipping about like a child. That was probably why she frightened us all so much. But I could have hugged her for taking the awkwardness out of the situation so quickly. We followed her. Don was still a bit embarrassed and fell in with Kev, but I wanted to see how Adela was.

'Adela! Wait! How are you feeling?'

'There's this amazing drug called Alka-Seltzer, Hannah. You take it when you've got a hangover . . . '

'Are you patronising me . . . ?'

She looked at me without laughing for a moment. 'We're all right, aren't we, Hannah? You and me?' She was almost pleading. No apologies or excuses required.

'Sure,' I said. 'We're friends.'

She changed the subject. 'When are your parents coming?'

'After tea,' I said. 'Just for the evening concert.'

'Oh, that's a pity,' she said. 'My mum just rang to say she's coming in time for the chamber concert. And I told her to listen out for the jazz group – since three of my best friends were in it.' Her eyes sparkled, and she added, 'She's been on tour for the last six weeks. I'm really looking forward to seeing her.'

The chamber concert began at four. It was informal and the doors were open on to the gardens. People could come and go between items while the stage was being rearranged. Jessa's wind quintet kicked the thing off in style and Adela's string quartet was programmed to finish it with a flourish. We were second to last – a long time to wait and get nervous. We went off to warm up fifteen minutes early and came on stage to shouts and cheers. My apprehension vanished, leaving a simple adrenalin rush. The first two pieces were on the flute – no problem. Then I picked up the sax for *Take Five*. Don smiled at me encouragingly and we took it away. Wow! Did we ever take it away! I don't think I've ever played anything so well in my whole life. It just worked. And when it finished, the audience were on their feet. Kevin had to drown them out on the drums, and then, when they were quiet, we slipped into *Yesterday*. You could have heard a pin drop. And then the audience went wild! The lads hauled me out in front and Kevin again had to shush everyone while he told them that I had only picked up a sax a few days ago, and added, 'but she had a terrific tutor . . . ' to more catcalls and whistles. I was blushing ferociously, but I have to say it felt good. We filed off and into our seats, reserved at the side, and prepared ourselves for a classy last act.

Adela led her quartet on to the stage. She looked tiny but

completely professional and in control. The wreck of the previous night didn't exist. I heard some loud clapping from behind and caught sight of an elegant blonde woman who looked familiar – of course! – Adela's mother, Celia Barnes. Like Adela she was petite, particularly next to the enormous woman beside her. I'd seen her before, too: Donald's mother in a flowery dress. And then, as I turned back to look at the stage, I caught a glimpse of a third woman, face aglow. It was Mum, sitting next to Celia!

The quartet had started. I sat back and watched them play, my hand in Donald's, trying not to be distracted as he stroked patterns on my palm with his fingers.

'Tumultuous' was the only way you could describe the applause at the end, 'ecstatic' by the time they had played an encore. The Goat came on stage and thanked us all, saying what a treat the chamber concert was for the staff, particularly as it was all our own work. Then he said that tea was served on the lawn, and that the unfortunate parents who had missed the chamber concert would soon be here for the evening concert, which started at seven.

We made our way towards the white-draped tables under the trees. I looked out for Mum, still not quite believing that she was actually there, not sure if I wanted her to see me with Donald.

But she was waiting for me. And something had changed, she looked different. 'Hannah! I wouldn't have missed that for the world!' And she turned to Don as if I had a boy on the end of my arm every day of the week – 'Well done, it was terrific. I just felt so proud of Hannah – and you all . . . '

'Thanks,' said Donald warmly. 'See you later, Han. I'm off to find my folks. Bye, Hannah's mum.' And he gave me one of his grins, which *almost* said I told you so. I waited for a comment from Mum, but it never came. She just gave me a hug. I couldn't think why I felt so choked.

'Dad will get here in time for the concert,' she said. 'He'll be really sorry he missed your jazz though, especially when

I tell him what a star you were. You know, Hannah, you just looked so at ease and cool up there. I felt quite jealous!' Still nothing about Donald. 'But I had an inkling it was going to be special when Celia Barnes said that Adela's best friends were in the jazz band. And then that lovely motherly Scottish woman told me that the young saxophonist was the one to look out for, and proudly added that she knew because it was *her* son's girlfriend . . . ' Mum smiled at me. 'Don't worry, I kept quiet. I didn't want to embarrass you.'

Well! That was what was different about Mum. She seemed – understanding. We headed for the food and I was spared any introductions by Dad arriving. J was with him and, funnily enough . . . he looked different too. Maybe he'd had an eventful week as well. 'It's all we heard as we came over here,' said J. ' "Wasn't Hannah brilliant . . . Duck was amazing . . . " So what have we missed? Another piccolo solo?'

'You've still got that to come,' I said.

'You missed an extremely groovy young saxophonist,' said Mum, 'who has only been playing for a few days but who knocked 'em dead.'

My brother looked at me with a certain amount of respect. 'You?'

'So it would seem,' I said smugly.

'Well, I'm sorry I didn't cut work like your mother. I thought your conference went on all afternoon, dear,' said Dad.

I looked at Mum questioningly. 'I don't expect they missed me. I just thought, to hell with it – I want to go and hear Hannah.'

'Mother!'

'I didn't know I was in for quite such a treat, though. Shows the best decisions are always rewarded, huh?'

The concert was, needless to say, a triumph, and Adela's performance was simply breathtaking. I felt euphoric at the way things had turned out, and I think lots of us felt that way. So when the Goat finally bade us farewell at the end of the concert and said he felt it had been a highly successful ten days and that – despite a certain amount of high spirits – the 'children' had all learned about themselves and each other as well as about music, I thought about Adela and about blokes and about love and about unhappiness and about friendship – and felt inclined to agree with him as I joined in the cheering and foot-stamping. Two people were called to the front of the stage for special mention and bouquets: Jessa for organising the last-night disco and Adela for her performance. As they stood there clutching their flowers a strange noise started up in the orchestra. It dawned on me with horrifying certainty that it was a Donald Duck noise. The Goat cleared his throat. 'And each year we also like to pick out a star from the chamber concert. There was no doubt amongst the staff that that honour belongs to Hannah Gross on the saxophone.' Aagh. I squeezed past the other Hannah and Donald for the last time and staggered to the front. 'Well done – Duck,' said the Goat, and handed me my bouquet.

Donald and I kept our parents waiting for a further ten minutes while we revisited an unlocked practice room for old time's sake. 'I know this is only goodbye for now,' said Don, 'but, Han – it's been great, this last bit, hasn't it? This will have to keep us going for the next three weeks.' He pulled me in and leant against the door so no one could disturb us. He was getting a bit carried away when there was a loud knock on the door.

Don looked out sheepishly. It was Kevin and Jessa, also looking somewhat tousled. 'Come on, kids,' said Kevin. 'I've been told to round everyone up. You're not the only ones locked in practice rooms, you know. Let's see who's in here . . . '

He knocked smartly on the next door along. 'Bogoff!'

came a familiar voice. Then Adela came out. She wiped her mouth, smiling, but her grin wasn't half as wide as Max's, who stood in the doorway, all signs of wanness long gone, and punched the air.

EPILOGUE

Don is the best thing that has happened to me in my life and I don't want our relationship ever to end. We wrote to each other all the time he was in Scotland and since he's got back it's just got better and better. We like doing the same things. We've been to hear bands and gone swimming at the lido, even wandered around the shopping mall – but mostly we've just flopped about at each other's houses. I've now heard the full version of the song – with the sweetest, most blushmaking words you can imagine. It's called *Rain on her Face* and it's all about the time in the music school during our first jazz practice when I came in from the rain and flicked water all over him! He said that's when it happened for him . . . Romantic old thing.

I've seen the others a bit, but it's Sophie I'm longing to tell. She's not coming back until the last minute, so we're having the sleepover at my house. Mum is cool about that. She's been amazingly cool about everything. She did say she was a bit anxious about me being only fourteen and Don being sixteen, but in fact I'll be fifteen before Christmas, and Don is one of the youngest in his year. She also reckons that our generation is about a year ahead of hers, so she isn't that worried. She let on that she had a serious relationship that started when she was fifteen and lasted until she went to university. 'What happened then?' I asked her.

She looked all girlish, remembering. 'He went to university in the States. We were devastated at first, but then we both made new friends, grew apart – and of course we couldn't see each other. He writes to me sometimes, though, even now . . . '

'Mum! I do believe you still have a thing about him! It's OK. I won't tell Dad.'

She laughed, wryly. 'No, it's not like that. Well, not really. But that first great romance is one you never forget. So make the most of it!'

'You bet!'

I had lots of phone conversations with Jessa before she went on holiday with her family, but somehow our age difference seems to matter more away from the course. She also lives too far away for us to meet up without quite a bit of planning. I'll look forward to seeing her next time we play together though.

I've had a couple of postcards from Adela in Italy, mostly listing her latest conquests. I think about her a lot. I've never met anyone as volatile as her before. I looked that word up in the dictionary and it really describes her perfectly: 'capable of readily changing from a solid or liquid form to a vapour . . . liable to sudden, unpredictable or explosive changes . . . ' I don't think I could ever trust her, but I am fond of her. And my lasting impression of her is as a fey, impish creature, not quite human, and of how, like Puck in *A Midsummer Night's Dream*, she ultimately brought all the lovers together.

Charlotte turned up first to the sleepover. She looked a bit how I felt – kind of self-satisfied. So I was looking forward to her story.

Mads and Soph arrived together. Soph had literally just got off the boat. She hugged me. 'Like the contact lenses, Duck! You look great! I gather there's a lucky guy out there somewhere. Mads told me as we were coming over. She said he was called John – Jonny – or something?'

'Hi, Hannah my darling!' Mads wafted in more scented

than ever, deeply tanned and immaculately made up. She didn't seem bothered about going in age order this time. In fact I sensed that she was holding back. 'Tell us all about Jonny, Duck,' she said.

'Not Jonny,' I said, and looked at Sophie. 'Donnie. D*onald . . .* '

'HANNAH!' Sophie squealed. 'Not DORNALD!'

'The very same,' I said. 'But we got him all wrong, Sophie. About as wrong as we could have done.' And I proceeded to tell them about the great guy who was my boyfriend.

Charlotte

ONE

On the last day of the summer term we had a sleepover at Sophie's. Mum would've let me have it at our house if I'd wanted, and there's plenty of space at Hannah's, but we usually end up at Sophie's. Anyway, Sophie has the whole loft to herself with her own bathroom and TV, so it's no problem for her to have three extra. In fact, Sophie's pretty cool altogether – nothing seems to be much of a problem for her, as far as I can see.

Which is not true in my case! I'm Charlotte. I've got boring light brown hair and I'm a bit fat with a big bum. 'Baby-faced' is how my sister describes me, and that's being kind. I think she was quite tubby too when she was my age, but now she just constitutes yet another of my problems. Michelle is sixteen and stunning. When the phone rings it's always for her. Michelle finished her exams weeks ago and now she's in Corfu with her friends – 'recovering'. Oh yeah. I end up doing all the chores, being on the receiving end of all Dad's sarky comments about teenage girls (laziness thereof), even though I'm doing the work of both of us and feeding her hamster and her cat as well as my own. If I'm telling you about myself, which I seem to be at the moment, I should add at this point that I'm soft about animals. I certainly won't eat them – much to Mum's annoyance – or use anything that's been tested on them. And animals like me. They don't care how fat or thin you are. If only it was the same with boys.

Back to the sleepover. There are four of us who have been friends since primary school. Hannah's gone to an all-girls' school but she lives nearby and still spends her free time with us. Hannah and I are both quite shy so we get on well, but she's known Sophie even longer because they live close to each other. And then there's Maddy. Maddy is in a totally different league from me, as you'll see. In fact I do sometimes wonder why they include me – I'd die rather than be a hanger-on. I expect it's because I make them all look gorgeous and slim by comparison!

I was the first to arrive at Sophie's. Sophie's older brother Danny opened the door. He usually says hello, but today he just bellowed up the stairs, 'Soph!' and disappeared back where he'd come from, leaving me standing in the hall, blushing furiously. To be fair, he'd just had a terrible haircut – perhaps he was making himself scarce. Sophie appeared at the top of the stairs. She'd changed since school into tiny shorts and a skinny top which had the usual effect of making me feel enormous in my baggy T-shirt and jeans. Instant inferiority complex kicked in . . .

We went to sort out the food. Whereas my mum is big on home cooking, Sophie's is happy to buy all the stuff we actually like. Pizzas, loads of crisps and dips, salad that probably wouldn't get eaten, bottles of juice and Coke were laid out on the big table in the kitchen. Sophie slapped my hand as I scooped up some cream-cheese-and-chive dip with a dorito. 'Oy! Don't be piggy! We're taking this lot upstairs. Carry some bottles!' At that point, the doorbell rang.

Sophie opened the door and Maddy made an entrance. 'Hi, guys!' Maddy addressed the world at large and kissed us both, enveloping us in a wave of her latest scent – which actually I can't stand – but you can't help liking Maddy. She spotted Danny behind the door (where had he come from?), ruffled his hair and said, 'Like your hair, Dan,' before he had time to run and hide again. Mum and Michelle describe Maddy as a 'luvvie', and I'm sure she will end up on the stage one day. She's shorter than Sophie, but taller than me, with browny-gold hair, a terrific tan, good cheekbones and browny-gold eyes with long, curling eyelashes. Sophie is cool, but Maddy, as everyone knows, has something else. Sex appeal, I suppose.

Hannah arrived last. She is a very different kettle of fish from the other two. We definitely all like her, but it's hard not to feel a bit sorry for her. She's dark and intense. She used to have a funny way of walking (I don't notice it any more), which is why she's known as 'Duck'. Her parents both work and expect her to do really well at school but they don't seem to care much about her otherwise. Hannah peers through her glasses and always seems anxious about something. Actually she can also be very funny in a quiet, dry way, but in our group you have to listen hard to hear her.

Sophie's loft is brilliant. It feels cut off from the rest of the house. She'd laid out mattresses for us round the edges with the TV and video at one end. We put the food and drink in the space in the middle and made ourselves comfortable for watching the video – a faithful old horror movie that we could all scream along to. 'Shall I set the vid going, Soph?' asked Maddy, who was closest.

'No, let's wait for my brother to go out first,' said Sophie. 'I'll put some music on.' Sophie prides herself on having the latest CD, and usually the T-shirt to go with it. Maddy tends to follow her lead, and so do I. But Hannah, who's really brilliant at classical stuff – she plays the flute and the piano – is often the first to hear a band and tell us about it. Somehow, because Hannah's not a cool person like Sophie and Maddy, we forget that she's got great taste.

Sophie and Maddy went into their usual dance routines. Sophie's not such a show-off as Maddy, and you won't catch me dancing in public, but it was fun to watch them anyway, while getting stuck into the serious business of the sleepover – eating. Then Dan went out and we spent the next couple of hours watching Freddie do his stuff. My parents still think I'm too young and impressionable to watch horror movies – little do they know . . . Personally

I'm more interested in the food than the blood and gore, and if I'm honest, I do have to look away from time to time. Hannah never seems scared and nothing is too gross or too sophisticated for Maddy and Sophie. I ate a lot of pizza and a very large amount of chocolate fudge brownie, with squirty cream. Well, I know I shouldn't be so piggy, but what's the point, when the only boy I've ever been interested in will never fancy me anyway? All that lot was washed down with 7-Up, Coke, and a sip of the red wine that Hannah said her dad wouldn't miss. Funny how often I fail to catch the end of the video at a sleepover.

Sophie's parents came home and called upstairs at some point to ask if we 'were ready for bed'. I dived into my sleeping-bag to change into my night things – I wouldn't like to offend the others with my bulging flesh (in all the wrong places), but Maddy is more than happy to flaunt herself. Hannah is a sleeping-bag changer too. Sophie does her cool-Sophie thing and gets round the problem by sleeping in the T-shirt and knickers she's wearing. We sat round with cotton-wool balls and cleansers and face packs with the usual late-night TV antics going on in the background. It was great. Sleepovers are great. It's just so brilliant being up late with your friends. The next bit's even greater. We all snuggled down in our sleeping-bags.

'Wish Ben Southwell was here . . .' began Maddy.

'That little jerk?' said Sophie, a tad viciously. 'I'd rather have Orlando Bloom.'

'Louis Armstrong! John Lennon!' squeaked Hannah.

'They're dead,' shouted Sophie, drowning out my 'Josh Rowlinson, please, God.'

'Oh, well,' said Maddy, 'if we're talking real men here, give me . . . give me JASON TIMBERLAKE! I was just talking – attainable. Anyway, Ben's cute!'

'Too young!' said Sophie. 'All the boys in our year are too young. They're titchy.'

'Ben isn't,' I said. I thought he was pretty cute myself.

And most people aren't that titchy compared with a short-arse like me.

'Well, he's not too short for you, Charlotte,' said Sophie, 'but you've got to admit he's too immature for us. And anyway, he kisses like a fish.' Before we could all ask her what she meant by that, she asked me, 'What about your loverboy in Cumbria – Josh thingy?'

I sighed. Josh is so out of the question I don't have any secrets about him. 'He's eighteen, for God's sake.'

'Sounds all right to me,' said Maddy.

'Not when you've got a skinny sister like Michelle it isn't.' The others had to agree with me. Grim as it is having a sister like Michelle, she does sometimes up my street cred with the group – to my advantage. Suddenly they were all interested in what Michelle was doing, who she was going out with, how she had her hair. I was telling them when Maddy interrupted with her old theme.

'A real man. That's what I want. A real lovey-dovey Mr Darcy of my own. Perhaps I'll meet him on holiday.'

'Well, I'll get to see Josh on holiday—' I said.

Maddy turned her full golden gaze on me. 'Oh really, Charlotte? Oh you're so lucky. Is Michelle going?' she asked crushingly.

'No, just me—'

Now Sophie joined in. 'Well then, Charl – it's your big chance.'

'Fat chance,' I said, 'with the emphasis on fat,' but the others weren't going to be put off. I let them argue it out among themselves. On the whole, Maddy thought I was in with a chance. Sophie and Hannah (who know me and my holiday circumstances a bit better) thought that maybe I wasn't.

'Tell us again, Charlotte,' said Maddy beseechingly. 'I want to imagine it all.' So, pleased to be the centre of attention for a change, I did.

Every summer Michelle and I spend a couple of weeks in

the Lake District with my aunt. This very sensibly means that Mum can get on with some work without feeling guilty in the summer holidays and that my aunt, who is a widow with three boys to look after, gets some female company and support. This isn't as ghastly as it sounds because my Aunt Viv is great, the sort of wacky, arty primary school teacher that everybody adores. And it's not like the boys are the seven dwarfs, who need a female about the place to wipe their noses – we just give a hand with the little ones in exchange for a holiday in the Lakes. Their house is in a beautiful place and all the picnics and swimming they do are cool. The boys are Ollie, Tom and Ned, in that order. Ollie's thirteen. Tom's nine. Ned's six. So who's Josh Rowlinson, you ask? Well, my aunt's house is actually half of a big old mill house. The Rowlinsons live in the other half. Little Kate Rowlinson is Ned's best mate, and Joe Rowlinson is Ollie's. And Josh Rowlinson is their eighteen-year-old half-brother who also spends the summer there. I've been madly in love with Josh Rowlinson as long as I can remember. He looks like a young version of Daniel Day-Lewis, kind of saturnine, and doesn't deserve my devotion one little bit. He's never taken any notice of me whatsoever, apart from teasing me once or twice for blushing. Sadly, he started taking notice of Michelle last year.

'But this year, Charlotte,' said Hannah romantically, 'with no Michelle, he's bound to realise what a fantastic person you are, and how kind . . .' She tailed off lamely.

Maddy was off again. 'We'll all have holiday romances! Let's all agree to have holiday romances! And we'll have another sleepover on the last weekend of the holidays and report back. Let's go round and everybody say where they're going. Age order. I'm nearly fifteen – God, would you believe it – so I go first. OK, I'm going to Barbados with my dad. Two weeks. What about you, Duck?'

'Me?' said Hannah. 'Oh, the usual boring old music course with a load of musos in sandals.'

I was shocked. 'But I thought you really liked doing your music. And mightn't you meet a wonderful double-bass player or a sexy saxophonist or someone?' I've always been jealous of Hannah's talent – felt it swept her up into a glamorous world of musicians and artists.

'I might,' said Hannah. 'But I don't promise to talk about it afterwards.'

'Spoilsport!' said Sophie, and we all joined in the jeering. Hannah kept her mouth shut, so Sophie said, 'I'm going to yet another French campsite. With one nerdy older brother. Mum and Dad read and drink and go to museums and markets. I'm left with dear Danny to mingle with all those other campers. I suppose I might just find myself a campsite courier on a bicycle . . . You're so lucky, Mads – Barbados! You'll have to have a wonderfully exotic time for all of us.'

'Well, I'm the youngest,' I said. 'But you all know about me.' I fell asleep soon after that and dreamt of Josh.

Two

Four days later I met up with Hannah and Sophie at the shopping centre. 'You all ready to go then, Charlotte? Got your bikini packed?' asked Sophie. 'Hannah and I are going to try some on now.'

'It's not a bikini sort of holiday,' I told her.

'Oh, go on!' said Hannah. 'If I can make a prat of myself, I don't see why you shouldn't.'

'Hannah! Me? In a bikini? You *are* joking?'

'Not really. You're not half as fat as you think you are. I don't think you've noticed that it's dropping off you, have you? Considering how much you eat?'

I was about to thump her, but she said, 'I dare you to try one on!'

'Oh, OK, but only if they have fitting rooms with cubicles . . .'

Three heads popped round the curtains of three different cubicles. We all stepped out like synchronised swimmers. 'Ta-da!' Sophie looked great. So did Hannah without her glasses.

'Charlotte, you look OK, really,' said Sophie.

And, though I say it myself, I did look OK. 'It seems to hide a multitude of sins.'

'Buy it!' said Hannah. 'You can seduce Josh in it!'

I conveniently forgot how useless this garment would be for swimming in the icy mountain tarns, and went ahead and bought it. Now I was ready for my holiday.

The train journey to Oxenholme from Euston took three hours and twenty minutes and it poured with rain nearly all the way. My wellies were well to the fore in my luggage. My new bikini was tucked away in a pocket. I had two magazines, a book of horror stories, a Diskman and some sandwiches to while away the time. There wasn't much to see beyond the raindrops on the window and some wet fields. I put on my headphones and let Bob Marley soothe me into a holiday mood . . .

I stepped down from the train in the hazy golden light of evening. The train pulled away and left me standing on my own on an empty platform. I made my way over the bridge and looked around the car park for Aunt Viv's battered Volvo. The cars were all empty. I was just wondering what to do when a crazy orange Beetle skidded into view. The door slammed and a tall, dark-haired guy stood up and seemed to be looking for someone. He kept looking at me and then looking beyond me to the platform. Eventually he came up to me and asked, 'Excuse me, do you happen to know if the London train has arrived yet? I'm meeting a girl—' He stared at me. 'My God, it's you, Charlotte! I didn't recognise you . . . You've changed . . . you look so much older . . .' Josh stuttered to a halt and gazed down at me with his clear green eyes. After a few moments he remembered his manners. 'Here, let me take your bag and you can get in.' I sat in the passenger seat of Josh's amazing car. 'I offered to come and meet you,' he said, starting the engine. 'Viv was really busy getting ready for you and she was still waiting for Ollie and Joe to get back from playing football. I wanted to see you again. I've always wanted to tell you how much more beautiful you are than your sister and when I heard she wasn't coming, I thought this might be my chance. I think it's going to be a wonderful summer . . .'

Hang *on*! Wake up, Charlotte! This is *Josh* I'm dreaming about? Supercilious, silent Josh? Josh who only recently woke up to the charms of Michelle? Josh who only speaks to me to tease me and laugh at me blushing? Yup. Oh well. Dream on. The last hour of the journey is always the best. The scenery got more scenic and the weather began to clear. It was still wet everywhere, but at least it was all *green* and wet. I started to feel excited, that great end-of-journey feeling when you can't wait to get there but at the same time you want the journey to go on for ever. Finally we pulled into Oxenholme. I lugged my bags out on to the platform and, almost before I'd set them down, there was Aunt Viv throwing her arms round me, Ned (my littlest cousin) grabbing my hand, Tom gallantly offering to carry my bags and Kate (Josh's baby sister) hauling on the lead of an overexcited dog. Quite a welcome.

'Charlotte, sweetheart, it's lovely to see you!' said Aunt Viv. 'Ned and Kate have been on at me all day – "'When's she coming? How long till she gets here?'" Tom's changed his meeting-Charlotte clothes about six times, haven't you, Tom?' Poor Tom blushed furiously. Just like me. He's always been my favourite.

Viv shepherded us into the car. Scrappy hopped into the

back. I'd say hello to her later. Tom was quickly absorbed in his Gameboy but Ned and Kate started telling me about all the expeditions they'd saved for my visit.

'And it's going to be Joe's birthday next week and we're all going to the boathouse to have a party for him. Him and Ollie have been planning it,' said Kate. She looked at me from under her dark fringe with incredibly clear green eyes. (Oh, Josh.) 'Even Josh says he'll come to Joe's birthday,' she added, as though a little kid could read my mind, but then she sent my hopes plummeting with 'though he's not so interested now he knows Michelle isn't coming.' And she and Ned curled up with laughter.

'Josh fancies Michelle!' chortled Ned. 'He'd really like to . . .' but his rude six-year-old sentence was too much for him and he spluttered.

I looked straight ahead and pretended to be above such smutty talk, though from the corner of my eye I could see that Tom had looked up from his Gameboy and was watching me. Even when he was tiny Tom had seemed to understand my feelings about things. He rounded on the little ones and said, 'Don't be stupid. You're just making that up. Of course Josh is coming to Joe's birthday.' He leant forward to me, 'We're going to play Water Warriors. Will you double with me?'

I laughed. Water Warriors is a game to make you forget any airs and graces. We play it nearly every year at the boathouse. It's basically a fight on boats and rubber dinghies and lilos where everyone tries to get everyone else into the water. There are all sorts of complicated rules that keep on changing every year. The only rule that doesn't change is that *everyone* has to play, grown-ups and tinies included. That's why you have to fight in pairs – one strong and one weak or two middlings. I reckoned Tom and I were a good pair of middlings. 'Josh is going to double with me!' said Kate. She's very proud of her big brother. 'Joe and Ollie have been training. They think they can go as middlings, but I think we should split them up. Joe's getting really big.'

'So why weren't Ollie and Joe here to meet me?' I asked Aunt Viv.

'They're a waste of space, socially, this summer,' she said. 'It's all sport, mostly football, for them. You think we'd get a break in the summer, wouldn't you?'

'So what's new?' Ollie and Joe have been hitting a ball around as long as I can remember.

'It's just a shame, since they're closest to you in age.'

'Don't worry about them, Aunt Viv! You're my friend among all these boys. We girls need to stick together!'

'And me,' said Kate from the back. 'I'm a girl too!'

We bumped up the driveway and pulled into the yard of the L-shaped house. I suddenly felt nervous. What if Josh was there? I composed myself to look thin and sophisticated as I climbed out of the car, but then Scrappy jumped up to greet me. 'Hello, soppy dog . . .'

'Hello, soppy cousin!' There was Ollie in the yard, much taller than last year. 'Come round later, Joe,' he called after another lanky lad – Joe! – disappearing next door. Joe nodded at me briefly before going in – to where Josh was, no doubt. I began to recall just why Aunt Viv was so glad of female company.

'Now you've seen everyone except Josh,' said Kate. 'And my mum and dad, but they don't count. Can I help you unpack?'

THREE

We have a first-night ritual of going down to the weir to watch the salmon leap. The mill house isn't far from the water-mill, which of course is on the river. The river has to be tightly controlled near the mill to make sure there's always enough water to turn the wheel, so there's a whole system of pools and weirs. Every summer the salmon make a fantastic journey to their spawning grounds up the river, swimming against the stream all the time. If they come to an obstacle like a weir they just have to gather all their strength and jump up it. They hurl themselves up the fall of water again and again until they make it. And then you imagine them going on and on, getting more and more exhausted but still driven to get upstream and reproduce. Crazy, really.

Aunt Viv stayed behind to cook supper but everyone else came down to the weir – my three cousins, Joe and Kate Rowlinson, and the dog. Kate and Ned swung from each of my hands. Ollie and Joe went on ahead and Tom and Scrappy ran between us. The rain had given way to a beautiful fresh evening with sopping wet grass underfoot and birds wheeling and calling high overhead. If only Josh had come too, it would have been perfect. But then again, I was more relaxed without him around.

We walked past the mill and over the stile into the field that runs beside the river. Each year it's the same – I'm knocked out by the sheer pounding force of the river, and the smell of it. Tom was caught between wanting to push on with the bigger boys and being with me. He took it upon himself to report back to us what Ollie and Joe were up to. 'They've gone down the bank . . . ' Off he went again. 'They're tightrope walking across the weir . . .' Away again. 'Joe's found a salmon caught in some weeds.' Next bulletin: 'Joe's rescued the salmon! He threw it up to the top and it swam away. Come on, you're missing everything.'

I suddenly realised that Scrappy wasn't with us. 'Tom, where's Scrappy?'

'Oh, nosing down a burrow somewhere. She's all right. There aren't any sheep in this field.' Scrappy is a mongrel with a lot of sheepdog in her. She can't help rounding animals up, whether they're sheep or ducks. It would be hilarious at home but in this part of the world it's deadly serious. She could get shot on sight for worrying sheep. We climbed over the final gate to the weir. Ollie and Tom stood watching. I'd hardly ever seen them so still!

'Charlotte, Joe's a hero,' said Ollie. 'He rescued this fish! It was gasping away and he managed to pull all the weeds free and then he just picked it up ever so gently and popped it up to the top of the weir. Another life saved. Lives, probably – think of all those baby salmon.'

The hero was leaning on the fence watching the silver salmon leaping through the tumbling water. 'I'd be too squeamish to hold a fish,' I said to him. 'I'm impressed.'

Joe looked at me intently and I realised for the first time that he had grown way taller than me. He's always been quiet and serious with warm brown eyes and a skin that's quick to flush. It was flushed now. You have to be careful not to tease Joe. 'I'm always impressed by people who are good with animals,' I felt I had to explain. That seemed to satisfy him and he turned back to watching the fish.

'Eleven!' shouted Ned above the noise of the water. 'I've counted eleven fish jumping!'

'I've counted twelve,' said Kate, not to be outdone.

'Well, I've only seen six make it so far,' said Tom, wanting to show that he knew what he was talking about.

'Yeah, it's six,' said Joe, and Tom looked pleased because Joe certainly knew what he was talking about.

'Where's Scrappy?' asked Ollie after a while.

'Looking for rabbits,' said Tom.

'That dog'll get herself shot if you're not careful,' said Joe. 'We'd better find her.'

Ollie looked at Joe, surprised. 'What, now?'

'Yes. You lot just can't seem to get it into your heads that sheep-worrying is a big deal round here. It's farmland, not a park. Let's find her. Dad said the other day that old Blaythwaite on Upper Farm was complaining about dogs worrying the sheep. He wouldn't know that Scrappy was just trying to round them up.'

We set off for home, calling Scrappy as we went. Sure enough, she was bounding through the brambles that edged the first field, pretending to chase rabbits.

'We needn't have worried, Joe,' I said as Ollie called Scrappy to heel.

'It's better that we did,' said Joe, and turned that intense brown gaze on me again.

After supper I bathed Ned and read him a bedtime story. Tom, who'd given up his bedroom for me, snuggled up to listen too. 'I'm glad you're here,' he said. 'Ned and Kate are too little for me and Ollie and Joe are too big. You won't stop doing things with me when Josh comes along, will you?'

'Why ever should I do that, Tom?' I asked innocently. Why indeed, when every minute since I'd arrived I expected Josh to materialise. I couldn't get him out of my mind, especially when it was quite possible that he *might* walk in at any time. Even here, in Tom's bedroom, I didn't feel safe.

'I just thought you might, that's all.'

'Don't worry, Tom. You know we're cool.' I wasn't sure I could reassure him any more than that.

When I got downstairs the TV was on and three large male figures were crouched over it. That meant Ollie and Joe – and Josh. See what I mean? None of them looked up when I went in. My heart started to thump because of Josh being there but I went into the kitchen to seek refuge with Viv.

'Take this tray of coffees into the boys, would you, love? There's one for you there and I'll come and join you in a minute.' I wasn't to be spared after all. My hands were trembling so much that the mugs shook and coffee spilled all over the tray.

'Ah, great,' said Ollie and reached out for his drink. Josh followed suit without even looking up.

'Thanks, Charlotte,' said Joe.

I took my coffee and perched on the only available seat, on the sofa between Ollie and Josh. 'Eugh! No sugar!' said Ollie and stood up suddenly. I was catapulted backwards, shooting my coffee into Josh's lap. I've never seen anyone move so fast! Josh certainly noticed me then.

'Stupid cow!' he yelled.

'I'm sorry,' I said.

'So you should be,' growled Josh, dabbing at himself with tissues.

I noticed Joe grinning nervously up at me. Ollie, whose fault it was really, finally came to my defence. 'That's no way to speak to my cousin, Josh.' But it was too late. Josh's trousers were soaked and he was going home. It was quite obvious that in his eyes I was nothing more than a stupid girl, no – worse, a stupid cow. Probably a fat cow, too.

So that, as far as my holiday romance was concerned, was clearly that.

FOUR

When I woke up next morning it took me a while to get my bearings. Ah yes! Lake District. With Josh, the love of my life, only a stone's throw away. And no Michelle. I hoped everyone wasn't too disappointed that it was only me this time. There was a gentle tap on the door and Tom came in with a cup of tea for me. Though most of it was in the saucer he was very pleased with himself for bringing it and plonked comfortably on the bed to tell me about the day ahead.

'Ned chose today. We're taking a picnic up to Black Gill. It's his favourite place.'

Black Gill was one of my favourite places too. It's high up in the fells with a pool deep enough to swim in and nothing and no one but sheep for company.

'It's just us. The Rowlinsons are going into town with their mum.'

I wasn't sure whether to feel sorry or glad about this news. On the whole I think I was glad.

Ollie washed up after breakfast while Viv and I put a picnic together. 'I hope you don't feel too grand for picnics and swimming, Charlotte,' said Viv, filling a Thermos.

'Of course not! To be honest, it's quite a relief to be able to do all these things without worrying what my friends would think. They can't quite get to grips with the concept of a holiday without a suntan! Bit like Michelle these days. Though she's still keen to come up after Corfu, even if it is only for the last weekend.'

'That's OK then. So you're not missing her?'

'Not a bit. Michelle's quite bossy – you might have noticed!'

Viv laughed. 'You forget. I've got a big sister too – your mum. You and I have quite a lot in common!'

It was a nice way of looking at things. Especially as I always think of Viv as the tough one. That could be because Mum's always had Dad to share the load, whereas Viv has coped on her own since the boys' dad was knocked off his bike and killed. Ned was still a baby. Viv's not a bit sentimental. I forget she's a widow because she never refers to it. And the boys never seem to feel sorry for themselves either. I really can't imagine being that strong myself.

Aren't other people's families complicated? And that was just my relations! Later that day I was to learn more about the Rowlinsons – and they made Viv's lot seem very straightforward.

The sun was out and great cloud shadows billowed across

the fells. I could sense Viv enjoying herself as much as we were. We drove round the curve of a hill and then along a bumpy track that stopped at the gate of a field with a spectacular view across the valley.

'Get that dog on her lead, Ollie,' said Viv. 'There are a lot of sheep about.'

'Poor old Scrappy,' said Ollie as he grabbed her collar. 'Here, girl. Sometimes the sheep are on the other side and she can just run around – but not today.'

We climbed over the gate and carried the picnic stuff and our swimming gear to the stream, scrambling down over the rocks to a sheltered stony beach right by the waterfall. We tied Scrappy's long lead to a tree. 'Swim before food,' said Viv. I wasn't that tempted. 'You can swim again later,' she added, but the boys had already stripped off and were testing the water.

Our little pool was fed by a waterfall. It was about a metre deep – just right for Ned – and roughly four metres in diameter. Ollie went in gingerly but Tom jumped in from a rock and emerged to announce that it was fine, not cold at all, even though Ned, sitting on the next rock and dipping his feet in, was already shivering visibly. Not to be outdone, Ollie dunked himself and pulled Ned in and they all splashed around saying how it was quite warm really.

'Men!' said Viv, smiling fondly at her brood. 'Put them in a group and they're all the same, whatever their age. So competitive! Just won't be beaten.'

'Look at me! Look at me!' shouted Ned. 'I'm swimming!'

'So what—' Tom began saying, but Ollie leapt on him and shoved him under. And so it went on. I liked watching them. They're quite alike, each one a younger version of the next. Tom is probably the one most like me physically, fairer and a bit more fleshy than the other two. They're very at home in the water, completely unselfconscious, which was why I felt so comfortable with them. I realised how different it was going to be when the Rowlinsons were with us. I couldn't even *imagine* baring my flesh in their presence, not that it ever seemed to bother Michelle. I seem to remember her prancing round Josh in a bikini at every possible opportunity last year.

When Ned was completely blue and even Ollie was shivering, Viv called them in. She threw a towel for me to wrap round Ned and rubbed a squirming Tom down herself. Poor little bundle. 'Come on, Ned,' I said. 'Soon have you dry, and then you can have some soup.' We peeled off his swimming trunks and pulled his clothes on over his damp, goosepimply body. I suddenly had a vision of my friend Maddy in Barbados and smiled to myself. Not glamorous, I thought, but fun all the same. Ned poked his tousled head through the neck of his sweater, normal colour restored to his cheeks. Tom was hopping about trying to put on his underpants without exposing himself. Ollie was expert at doing this under a towel. I averted my gaze and started unpacking the picnic.

'Be good if Joe was here,' said Ollie. 'We could follow the stream up the hill and build a dam.'

'You could do that with me,' said Tom, slighted.

''Spose so,' said Ollie. 'But Joe's older.'

'Well, I'll be ten soon.'

'Big deal,' said Ollie. 'Joe will be fourteen next week.'

'Fourteen?' I asked, surprised. I always thought he and Ollie were the same age.

'Yeah. I'm just thirteen but he's nearly fourteen. The Water Warriors party. Remember?'

So Joe was only a couple of months younger than me then. And I'd never realised. Though I could tell you to the day how much older than me Josh was.

'Let me follow the stream up the hill with you after lunch, Ollie. Please,' pleaded Tom. 'Can we, Mum? We could take Scrappy.'

'I don't see why not,' said Viv. 'You could let her off the

leash when the stream goes through the field beyond the wall. I don't think there are any sheep up there.'

So after we'd eaten, the two older boys and Scrappy set off. Ned wanted another swim, and as the day was warming up I thought I'd be brave and go in with him once the food had gone down. Feeling distinctly underdressed, even in my regulation black swimsuit, I remembered how cold the mountain water was. Was I crazy? No. This was what Lake District holidays were about, and I'd better toughen up fast.

My swim lasted for all of four minutes. Ned's didn't last much longer. I rather wished I could ask Aunty Viv to wrap me up in a big towel and dry me, too, but I'm a big girl now . . . I retreated behind Ollie's bush to try to replace my wet swimsuit with dry underwear under cover of a large T-shirt. Afterwards I stretched out on a sun-warmed rock with a mug of tea from the Thermos. It was heaven. Ned went down to throw stones in the water, leaving me and Viv to chat lazily in the sun.

'I gather Josh wasn't too polite last night,' she said.

'I can't really remember,' I lied. 'I suppose he was a bit brusque.'

'There's no excuse for loutish behaviour, but I do feel sorry for him at the moment.'

'Oh?'

'I can't remember how much you've picked up about the Rowlinsons over the years – but here's the story. John and his first wife split up very acrimoniously. John had been having an affair with his secretary (that's Louise, Kate's mother) for some time before the first marriage ended and it actually sent his wife a bit screwy. She's incredibly neurotic anyhow. She was passionate about Josh but never so warm towards Joe, who was quite a difficult toddler – no doubt he was picking up on all the bad feeling—'

'I always thought Louise was Joe's mother?'

'No. You see John and his wife finally agreed to take one son each. Louise was all ready to move in and more than happy to humour John by looking after his little boy. She was desperate to have children of her own but it was several years before Kate turned up. Louise is a good mother to Joe, but it's always been a complicated set-up. Josh was quite smothered by his mum most of the time but she'd sometimes just want to get rid of him so that she could have a life of her own. And that's when he started coming back here for his holidays. In fact he doesn't get on that well with John, who's quite tough with him, and he's a bit jealous of Joe – Joe's life seems pretty normal compared with Josh's. And of course, poor old Josh got shoved off to boarding school – which he hated at first – and so on and so on. One thing you can be sure of is that he absolutely adores Kate. When you see him with her, you begin to think that maybe there's a human being in there somewhere, poor boy. Right now he's panicking about his A-level results. His mum rang him last night to say how worried she is. She's not prepared to have him at home if he doesn't get into college. He was telling us a bit about it while you were reading to the little ones.'

'So does my popular psychology tell me that his mum was the stupid cow, and not me?'

'That would seem to be the size of it.'

Just then Tom came running down the hill. 'Mum! We need you. Scrappy's got in with some sheep!'

Viv leapt up. 'Stay with Ned, would you? That dog!' She ran off after Tom.

'Joe says Scrappy will get shot one day,' said Ned, on the verge of tears.

'No one would shoot Scrappy,' I consoled him. 'She's far too sweet and silly.'

Ned pulled away from me. I was clearly a hopeless townie when it came to dogs and sheep. 'No. Joe's right. He loves Scrappy but he knows that she mustn't be so stupid with sheep. They won't shoot her, will they?'

I realised that I just didn't know. So I was hugely relieved to see Tom racing towards us, shouting, 'It's OK! We've caught her!' Ollie and a very grim-looking Viv followed. Viv was gripping Scrappy fiercely by the collar. Scrappy didn't like it but knew better than to fuss because it was clear she was in big trouble.

'BAD dog,' said Viv, hauling Scrappy to the car. We saw her slapping her on the behind and slamming the boot. She came back to us. 'Come on, pack up the stuff. Let's get the wretched dog home.' She caught our disapproving glances. 'She IS bad. Stupid, stupid dog. What are we going to do with her?'

'She was fine until we were coming back,' said Ollie. 'Then we just couldn't catch her. She was off after the sheep in the near field. I was terrified the farmer would come along.'

'Well, he did come,' said Viv. 'I'd just caught Scrappy and it was obvious she wasn't on a lead. She looked guilty as hell and the sheep were all huddled in a corner bleating their silly heads off. The farmer said, "I hope for your sakes that that dog hasn't been worrying my sheep. Because if she has, and I catch her, you know what will happen, don't you?"'

'And we all just smiled weakly at him,' said Ollie. 'It was awful.'

'Yes, but nothing actually happened, did it?' said Tom (bless him). 'I suppose it was time to go home anyway.'

Scrappy whimpered all the way back, and when we went in the house she ran and cowered in her corner. It was quite pathetic. But I could see that Viv was really shaken by the whole episode. 'From now on,' she said, 'that dog goes on a lead. Always.'

Ollie and I cooked pasta for supper while Viv sat in front of the TV with a stiff drink. She'd cheered up by the time we'd eaten, though, and I even saw her giving 'that dog' a hug before she went to bed.

FIVE

Only in the Lake District can it rain as it did the following morning. The world outside the windows was a green and grey blur. I came down late for breakfast – Viv had cleared the table and it seemed that the day was well under way. 'No rush. The others are all next door playing on the computer,' she said to me. 'I'm going to the supermarket with Tom and dropping Ollie and Joe at the sports centre. Josh is looking after the little ones.' Even the sound of Josh's name made me feel slightly dizzy. 'Come shopping if you want, but if I were you I'd make the most of the peace and have a lazy breakfast followed by a long bath. There's plenty of hot water. Just make yourself at home.'

I had to admit that it sounded irresistible. 'I'm persuaded,' I said, and Viv went out into the rain.

While the bath was running I dug out my make-up bag from the bottom of my suitcase where it would probably have languished all holiday. Viv had some gorgeous designer shampoo and conditioner and Mum had treated me to a Bodyshop basket of bath oils, so I spent a blissful half-hour in their great deep bath tub. The bubbles conveniently hid my wobbly bits from view – I could even pretend I was lean and fit. I lay there soaking and fantasising about Josh. I wondered when I'd next see him. Would he be nicer this time? Or would he look at me as if I'd just crawled from under a stone? We'd got off to such a bad start.

I only got out when my fingers started to wrinkle. There were warm towels in the big airing cupboard. I wrapped one round me and another round my hair like a turban and padded to the bedroom where I put the radio on full volume. Now all I needed was a hairdryer and I was pretty sure Viv kept one in the drawer in the kitchen. I was just fossicking around down there when the back door flew open with a crash. Ned and Kate rushed in from the wet yard, closely followed by – Josh!

Well, I blushed. Under Josh's sardonic gaze I blushed from head to bare shoulders to bare legs to bare toes. I blushed all over, rooted to the spot before I finally turned tail and shot up the stairs into the bedroom and shut the door, blocking out Ned's cries of 'Charlotte! We've come to play Pictionary. Will you play with us?'

I stayed in the bedroom for what seemed like forever. I brushed through my tangled wet hair and dressed. I mucked about with make-up. Finally I turned the radio off and listened. It sounded quiet downstairs. They'd probably gone back next door. I crept down to the kitchen to look for the hairdryer again and reached for the kettle to make myself a cup of coffee.

'The kettle's on already,' said a voice from the depths of the armchair. 'They won't play Pictionary until you join us so I've stuck them in front of the TV.' Oh God. Josh is one of those awful silent people who can be there without you knowing. My heart was knocking and I couldn't think of a thing to say. I could feel a major blush creeping up my neck to my face. Then he said, 'And Ollie says I owe you an apology for last night, so . . . sorry if I was rude but if a guy's already in a foul mood and someone pours scalding water on his genitals you can't be too surprised if he's not particularly pleased to see you.' I was completely beetroot by now and utterly beyond speech. I looked at the floor. After a while I glanced up at Josh to see that he was grinning. 'You shouldn't have bothered with the blusher,' he said. 'Here's some coffee, kiddo. Come and play Pictionary.'

How do you *deal* with someone like that?

'I want to play with Charlotte!' said Ned.

'Well, I want to play with my favourite little sister,' said

Josh, picking Kate up and swinging her on to his lap. 'Can you play Pictionary with only two people on each side?'

'Easy,' said Ned. 'I draw and Charlotte guesses and you draw and Kate guesses and then we swap.'

'OK . . .' said Josh. 'Let's go.' He threw the dice and moved his counter on to D for difficult. I picked a card from the box and gave it to him. It said 'boiling water.' Very apt after our recent conversation. I hoped Josh wouldn't mention it. He drew a kettle, made lots of steam come out of it, then drew another picture of the kettle pouring into a mug. All very innocent.

'Boiling water!' shrieked Kate. She was an old hand at this. 'My go! My go!' She landed on A for action. 'I don't understand what it says. What does this word mean, Charlotte?' It said 'clone', for heaven's sake.

'I think we'd better find you another one,' I said.

'That's not fair,' said Ned, on his mettle.

'It's all right, Ned, I'll do the same for you,' said Josh. Ned was mollified. I couldn't cope with this gentle side of Josh.

It was short-lived. So what did I get to draw? 'Behind'. Josh smirked as he handed me the card. 'I can't draw this!' I was blushing all over again.

'Course you can. Ned sure as hell knows what it is.' I tentatively drew a circle with a line through it. 'Come on, Ned, Charlotte's got a big one!'

'BUM!' squealed Ned.

I think the tears came to my eyes at that point. 'Josh! You've made Charlotte cry,' said Kate, all feminine outrage.

'Ah diddums,' said Josh, and put his arms round me, though I was stiff with embarrassment. 'Can't you take a joke then?'

That's when the others came home. 'Why are you hugging Charlotte, Josh?' asked Tom. Viv gave me a funny look. So did Ollie and Joe.

'I expect he's apologising to her,' said Ollie to Joe. But Joe had gone.

'I'm not sure that game was going anywhere,' Josh told Viv without looking at me. 'I'd better give my lot lunch. See you all later.' And he steered Kate out of the back door.

We all helped unpack the shopping. 'So what's on the agenda for later?' I asked, fearing the worst. If the love of my life was to be included I could count on feeling confused and uncomfortable.

'Ollie and Joe want to watch the athletics on TV,' said Viv, 'so I thought we'd take the little ones – and Tom – ' she added, 'to the cinema. They've got the new Disney on. It's really too wet to try and do anything else today.'

It was after the film that I finally got my longed-for ride in Josh's Volkswagen. Not that I really wanted it. Well, of course I did, but I knew I couldn't handle it. I'd sat as far away from him as possible in the cinema, but now Kate and Ned wanted to go with Tom in Viv's car and Josh had the effrontery to ask if I would keep him company in his. I was still furious with him. My relationship with him this year was turning out differently all right. A voice in my head was screaming *Stop playing with me*, but I was incapable of saying it out loud, so I sat silently as he drove us home. We pulled up in the yard. He turned to me in the semi-darkness of the wet late afternoon. 'Don't mind me, little girl.' He rolled his eyes and pulled a terrible face. 'I'm just a crazy guy,' he said in a Hannibal Lecter voice. 'And when's your delicious big sister coming to join us?'

'For the last weekend,' I said flatly. When I got out of the car I had the distinct feeling that someone had been watching us.

SIX

'My expedition today,' said Ollie. 'The forecast says it's going to get warm. It'll need to be where we're swimming.'

'Oh no,' I said. 'Not the bottomless tarn with the killer pike?'

'That's the one.'

'So who's coming this time?'

'No Josh, so we've only got the one car.' (Phew. Relief overcame disappointment.) 'We can all fit in if we leave Scrappy behind.'

'Picnic?'

'Me and Tom are doing it with Mum.'

'Swimming things?'

''Course. They're all dry.'

'Anything for me to do?'

'Nope.'

I made myself a cup of coffee, found a magazine and a hairbrush and curled up in the window seat. My hair is long and thick. When it's clean and I've got it brushed out for a party or something it's possibly my best feature, even though it's a boring colour. Usually, and especially on this sort of holiday, I have it pulled back into a ponytail. Yesterday's rain had made it very scraggy, so I needed to get the tangles out. It could be a long job.

The weather was cheering up. The sun broke through the clouds and streamed through the window, catching the steam of my coffee. I could feel its warmth on my hair. The back door opened and in came Ned and Kate, followed by Joe.

Kate ran over to me. 'Oh Charlotte, can I brush your hair?'

'My cousin looks like a princess, doesn't she,' said Ned

fondly, 'with her hair all loose?' and the two of them scrambled up beside me. I grimaced at Joe as one of them tugged at a knot. He said 'Hi!' gruffly, and sat down with his hands in his pockets. He couldn't sit still. Scrappy came in and flopped down on his feet with a sigh. Then she looked up at him soulfully.

'You know she's not coming today,' I said.

'That's because she's naughty,' said Ned.

Joe consoled her. 'Aah. Poor old girl. Who's a lovely girl then?' Scrappy rolled on to her back. 'Who's a terrible old flirt then?' said Joe, tickling her tummy. Scrappy whimpered with pleasure.

'She never does that for me,' said Ned, climbing down from the window-seat.

'That's because you're not good with animals like my brother,' said Kate, still combing my hair.

'No, Kate,' said Joe. 'It's just that Scrappy thinks I'm sexier than Ned, don't you, Scrappy?'

Ned giggled and rolled on the floor by Scrappy. 'Do you think I'm sexy, do you think I'm sexy . . .'

Kate pulled my hair back and piled it on top of my head for effect. She regarded me seriously and then spoke over her shoulder to the boys. 'We think you're both disgusting, don't we, Charlotte? Look, you two, haven't I made her beautiful?'

'Oh yes,' said Joe and headed for the kitchen, Scrappy and Ned in hot pursuit.

The long, blue-black tarn lay before us. It can't really be bottomless, but it's very still and mysterious and there are certainly pike in it because John Rowlinson has caught them there. 'Come on, Charl, Joe,' said Ollie. 'Real swimming for mature people takes place over here.' He and Joe led the way to some rocks further down.

The boys stripped off to their shorts. Ollie waded in and started swimming very quickly, yelping a bit with the cold.

Joe went in more slowly, his arms crossed across his chest, gasping as the icy water worked its way up his legs. I undressed down to my swimsuit and followed.

I felt the sun on my shoulders and back. I hitched my hair into a topknot as Joe looked back at me and called encouragingly, 'It's not so bad once you're in!' He struck off in an erratic crawl to catch up with Ollie. I waded on determinedly until the bottom fell away under my feet and I was forced to get my shoulders under and swim. The water was achingly cold but silky. If I kept thrashing about it became quite bearable and then suddenly it felt fine, amazing in fact. The boys were swimming towards me, Ollie looking tousled and faintly ridiculous, Joe sleek as a seal. I rolled on to my back; it was blissful with the warm sun on my face and the cool water all around.

The boys were swimming towards me but they disappeared suddenly. I felt little nipping sensations on my legs – 'Hey!' Ollie emerged at my shoulder, water streaming from his grinning face. 'Watch out for pike!' he said and Joe also burst up through the surface, his expression all innocence.

'Pigs!' I yelled, but they had gone again. Ollie popped up a few yards in front of me. Where was Joe? I felt vulnerable. More nips, on my feet this time. 'Joe?' Suddenly there he was, right next to me, hair plastered to his head. He shook it out of his eyes and looked at me, water clinging to his eyelashes. 'I'll protect you, Charlotte. You just tell me if those nasty pike are nipping you.' And he was gone again, with scarcely a ripple.

'Joe!' I yelled.

'You called?'

'Joe . . . I—' I tried to turn in the water, but something was tugging at my feet, my feet which were miles from the bottom. I felt genuinely frightened, out in the middle of the lake. Ollie was a dot in the distance, and Joe was nowhere to be seen. 'Joe,' I called. 'Help!'

Joe was there, in front of me this time. 'Ha! It was you,

wasn't it? Grabbing my feet! You toad!' I tried to splash him, but the water was too deep for me to get any purchase. 'Can we go in now? You've had your little joke. I'm cold. I've had enough.'

Joe was grinning broadly as he ducked and spluttered. 'I thought you'd never ask. Can I practise my life-saving skills on you? Lie you on your back? Tow you home?' He swam behind me, ready to save my life.

'Oh, go on then.' I was feeling rather weak. I turned on to my back. Deftly, Joe gripped my head in his hands and pulled it against his chest, kicking out strongly as we set off for the edge. I let myself be pulled along, gazing up at the banks of white clouds and discovering how it felt to be rescued by a knight in shining armour . . . fab.

'Consider yourself rescued,' said Joe when his feet could touch the bottom. I stood in the water and regarded my knight. It was only Joe, Ollie's little friend, except that he wasn't little – he was really quite tall, and dark, with a muscular torso, and . . . perhaps some mouth-to-mouth resuscitation wouldn't have gone amiss either, but Joe had reverted to shy mode and was jogging towards Ollie and the picnic. I felt as if I had somehow missed the moment. Then I felt stupid. What was all this about? Josh was the one I cared about – not his kid brother.

It was quite hot. We ate our picnic still in our towels. Afterwards I felt sleepy and spread my towel on a rock to sunbathe. I shut my eyes and drifted, the shouts and chatter of the others fading into background noise. I could hear the older boys bantering, Viv laughing, the high voices of the little ones, splashing sounds, waves . . . I imagined myself thin as Michelle in my new bikini and Josh lying next to me, the unattainable Josh of my dreams.

'Do you mind if I sunbathe next to you?' Joe's voice was clear. I opened my eyes. I must have dozed right off, the others were all back in the water. I shut my eyes again. Joe settled himself on a nearby rock.

'Good not having to worry about Scrappy, isn't it?'

I hadn't given Scrappy a moment's thought until then. An image of her crestfallen expression as we left floated into my mind. 'Poor old thing. She's just a bit daft. She'd never hurt a flea.'

'Get herself into trouble one day, that dog,' said Joe. 'And that will be sad. We're good mates, me and Scrappy. I could have trained her properly, but your aunt spoilt her rotten. You have to be consistent with animals, you see. They need to know what's what. It's no wonder dogs find humans confusing.' He laughed. 'So do I! Give me animals any day. They don't let you down.'

We didn't say anything for a bit. Then Joe added, as if there hadn't been a silence, 'Of course, the people in my family are *very* confusing. Louise isn't my real mother, did you know that?'

I said nothing and he carried on. 'But she wanted me, for Dad mostly. I think she wanted me more than he did. My real mum can't really have wanted me that much herself, can she? Dotes on Josh, mind. Drives him mad. But she didn't want me. I hardly ever see her, you know. Weird, isn't it?'

He sat up. 'Josh is an OK guy, you mustn't mind him. No fun for him having just Mum and boarding school. I think he even misses me sometimes. And he certainly misses Kate. Josh adores Kate. I expect you've noticed! Everyone adores Kate. She's the one that makes us a family somehow. I sometimes wonder what we'd do if anything happened to Kate.'

'Kate's a cool kid,' I said. And then neither of us spoke for a while. It had been quite a long speech for Joe. I felt flattered that he had chosen to tell me about his complicated family. If only Josh were half so confiding.

A chilly little breeze whipped up the goosepimples on my arms and legs at the same time as I heard the others approaching. I pulled on my jersey and jeans, appalled that

Joe had been exposed to so much cellulite, and busied myself with the picnic basket. The little ones were going to need food and hot drinks, fast. Joe went to meet up with Ollie and I didn't speak to him again that day.

SEVEN

The next day started badly and ended worse than any day I've ever known.

Viv overslept and forgot that Ollie and Tom were doing the football course. They were dozy and she nagged at them in a very un-Vivlike manner to get washed, have breakfast, find their things. Ned got in the way and irritated Tom by playing on his Gameboy without permission. Scrappy kept tripping everyone up. Even I felt like a spare part and tried to keep a low profile. They finally got through the door and Ned and I managed to eat a civilised breakfast, but we were edgy and the day seemed doomed from the start. Not without cause, as it turned out.

Viv returned, sorry about being so crotchety but worried about the car, which had been playing up all the way home and had barely made it up the hill. She had to spend the next hour on the telephone ringing round repair services all without much joy, until she finaly persuaded someone to come out. We sat down for sandwiches and soup at lunch time and the phone went again. Ned, trying to be helpful, answered it, but didn't make matters any better by saying, 'Mum! Here! Quick! Ollie's had an accident!'

Ned and I hung on every word of Viv's half of the ensuing conversation. 'What's happened? Is Ollie all right? . . . Broken? . . . You're not sure? . . . What should I do? I don't know. Which is the nearest Casualty? . . . Oh hell – oh no – I can't come. My car's packed up. I'll have to ask a neighbour . . . I'll be there somehow. Tell Ollie I'm on my way.

We'll be there as quickly as we can. Yes, OK. Goodbye.' Then she sat down and put her head in her hands.

'I'll make a cup of tea,' I said, as the only thing I could think of in a crisis. 'Ned, go next door and get Josh. Tell him to come over here – we need him.' Ned was off like a shot.

'What's happened to Ollie, exactly?' I asked Viv.

'It's his ankle. He fell over and landed badly. They think he might have broken it.'

'He might just have a bad sprain. Michelle did that playing hockey. They X-rayed her and everything, but in the end she just had a bandage and crutches.'

'Well, fingers crossed. Poor Ollie. They said he's being brave, but I'm sure it's very painful. Oh goodness, I do hope Josh can get us there. I'm afraid you'll have to wait in for the garage men, and look after Ned and Kate, I suppose. I'm so sorry, Charl. This isn't any fun for you.'

'Less fun for Ollie,' I said. And secretly I don't mind a bit of a crisis, I think it brings out the best in me. At least, that's what I was thinking *then*.

Josh appeared, looking red-eyed and unshaven in a scruffy T-shirt – as if he'd only just got up. I even registered that he didn't look very appealing today. Kate trailed behind him, also looking less than her usual bright-eyed self. 'I've waited all morning for Josh to get up and do something with me,' she said, 'and now he's got to go out and leave me. And Mum said we weren't to bother you lot today. She said we spend too much time here and she can't return the favour.'

'Nonsense,' said Viv tartly. 'Anyway, Josh is just about to do me a *big* favour, Kate, and you'll be doing Ned another favour by keeping him company this afternoon.' She turned to Josh. 'Thanks, Josh, I'm really grateful. Let's go then.'

'Be good,' Josh warned Kate. He turned to me. 'She's been a right little madam today – don't take any nonsense from her, Charlotte.'

Scrappy saw them leaving and, ever hopeful, bounced after them, nearly tripping them up again. 'No, Scrappy,' said Viv, and 'darned dog – always in the way.' And they were gone.

'Poor Scrappy,' said Kate.

'Well, she does get in the way,' said Ned, unsure whether to protect his mum or his dog and plumping for his mum.

'Shut up, Ned,' said Kate, throwing her arms round Scrappy's neck. 'It's not my darling Scrappy's fault. She can't help it. Anyway, dogs are much nicer than humans. Aren't they, Scraps?' (Now where had I heard that before?)

'If you're going to be mean, I'm going to watch telly,' said Ned, and flounced off.

'Kate,' I said, perhaps more sharply than I'd intended, 'come on. It's Ollie we've got to worry about, and Viv's broken-down car. I don't want you two squabbling.'

'I'm not squabbling,' said Kate. 'It's been a horrible day. First Mum saying I wasn't to spend so much time with all of you – just because I wanted *her* to stay at home for once. And then Joe going off to have fun and Josh being all grumpy because he didn't want to get up. Josh isn't usually nasty to me, but he was today. And then I am allowed to come here and Ned starts being all unkind too . . .' She put her head against Scrappy's flank, and stuck her thumb in her mouth. I could see that the tears weren't far away.

'Cheer up, Kate. Perhaps we'll all take Scrappy for a walk down by the weir later. Why don't we all—' I was interrupted by a knock at the kitchen door. Scrappy leapt up, barking, and ran towards it. It was the garage men. 'Down, Scrappy!' I shouted, but Scrappy was intent on protecting us from intruders and villains. I opened the door and she rushed out, nearly knocking them over.

'Keep that dog under control, can't you?' said one of the men.

'I'm really sorry,' I said to him. 'Scrappy, get back in!' I grabbed her roughly by the scruff of her neck and shoved her back into the kitchen, shutting the door on her, ignoring the high-pitched barks that came from the other side.

'Where's this car, then? I assume you're not the owner. Got the keys?'

The keys. Viv had them hanging in the kitchen. I'd have to go back in there. I pushed open the door and immediately trod on Scrappy, who had positioned herself behind it. She yelped. 'Wretched dog!' I snarled, echoing Viv. I grabbed the keys and tried not to notice Kate's accusing little face as she wrapped herself round Scrappy. 'Won't be long, Kate,' I called over my shoulder, though I don't think she was listening. 'I'm just going to show the men where the car is.'

It was actually a relief to be out of the house, even though it was an untrustworthy sort of day – bright and windy. The two garage men followed me to where Viv had left the car. 'This it?' one asked.

The other guffawed rather rudely. 'More surprising if it *did* go!' he said, kicking the wheel.

I was about to protest, but then the first one pulled himself together and said, 'Don't worry, pet. Could be nowt more'n a dirty plug. At worst it'll need a new fuel pump, and that won't break the bank. Leave it with us. I'll come up to the house when we've sorted it out. Your mum coming back soon?'

'My aunt,' I corrected him. 'I hope so. She's gone to fetch my cousin who's had an accident. They might have to go to Casualty.'

'Fine. Right, let's get a look under this bonnet.' They turned their backs on me and I left them to it.

We always use the back door at Viv's, but the car was nearer the front, so I climbed up the steep, overgrown front path that leads up from the road below. I took my time, savouring the peace. I rang the bell by the front door and waited for Ned or Kate to let me in.

No reply. I peered in at the window of the front room

where Ned had been watching television. He wasn't there. I could see the door was open, and I tried to peer down the passage to the kitchen, but it was tantalisingly dark. 'Ned! Kate!' I called. No one came. They don't expect visitors to arrive at the front door. So I set off round to the back again. I passed the garage men bent over the engine, and walked on up to the yard. I was nearly there when I heard Josh's car toiling up the hill behind me. Tom and Joe were with him but no Ollie or Viv. Josh tooted and I waved. My heart started to thump to order. 'That was speedy,' I said.

Josh wound down his window as they drew alongside. He was fully restored to gorgeousness. 'We took them straight to Casualty. Ollie's having an X-ray just in case the ankle's broken. They're in for a long wait though. He's not exactly an emergency. I'll go back and fetch them in a bit.'

They got out of the car and Tom followed Joe into the Rowlinsons' house. Josh came with me into ours. I tried to breathe normally. 'Is Kate all right?' he asked. 'She was furious with me earlier on. It probably did her good to be somewhere else for a bit.' I didn't let on that I was worrying about Kate as we pushed open the back door. I'd barely been gone ten minutes. Perhaps she had curled up and fallen asleep with Scrappy in the kitchen where I left her. But Scrappy wasn't there. Nor was Kate. They'd probably gone to watch TV with Ned – except that there hadn't been anyone there either. I went out into the passage. 'Ned? Kate?' The house was silent.

I went back to the kitchen where Josh was filling the kettle, as usual. 'Where are the kids?' he asked.

'Josh, I don't know.' I tried to suppress rising panic. 'When I went out to the car Kate was in here with the dog and Ned was watching telly. Now I don't know where any of them are.'

Josh seemed pretty relaxed. 'Probably hiding somewhere. Let's make them sweat while we have some coffee. I haven't had any breakfast today, let alone lunch.' He passed me a mug of coffee. I took it and sat down in the armchair but quickly stood up because I'd sat on something uncomfortable. It was Scrappy's lead.

'That's OK then,' I said, relieved. Josh was probably right. 'Scrappy's lead is here so Scrappy and the kids can't be far away.' We sat back with our coffee. And then we both sat up again and said simultaneously—

'—Or Scrappy's out without her lead . . .'

'Oh my God!' I pocketed the lead and ran to the back door. 'You look for the kids. I have to find the dog.' I started yelling, 'Scrappy! Scrappy! Here girl!'

Josh raced upstairs and then ran over to their house. After a few minutes he stormed out to me, as I stood calling. He was white as a sheet. 'I thought you were meant to be looking after them. Why did you let Kate out of your sight? If she's gone after that crazy dog . . .' The force of his anger made me reel.

This wasn't the time to argue, or to try and make Josh stop thinking badly of me. I took a deep breath and tried to think calmly. What had been going on when the garage men arrived? Ned had been watching TV in the front room. Kate was with me in the kitchen. Then the memory of Kate's distressed face combined with Scrappy's yelps when I'd stepped on her came back to me: Kate, feeling that everyone was against her, and poor old Scrappy, who'd been left behind the day before and shouted at and trodden on today. I could just imagine Kate saying, 'Come on Scrappy. *I'll* take you out for a walk.' But why no lead? Even Kate understood about the need to have Scrappy on a lead. And why would Ned go too? Perhaps Ned hadn't gone too. Perhaps he'd gone *after* her. And all in such a short space of time.

I ran up the bank behind the house and called again. 'Ned! Ned! Come and help me! I need you!' Then I saw a small dishevelled figure hurtling down from the top of the field in our direction. 'Ned! What's going on? Where's Kate? Has she got Scrappy?'

Ned, out of breath, flung his arms around my knees. 'Charlotte! Where have you been? Kate wasn't in the kitchen when I went in to make friends again. And Scrappy wasn't there either. I called you and you weren't there. I thought Kate had run away so I went up the hill to look out for her. But I couldn't see her . . .'

'Calm down, Ned. I wasn't gone long. I was only out by the car – I wasn't far away. And I'm sure Kate's not far away either.'

'I hope Scrappy's with her. Perhaps she just took Scrappy for a walk. Perhaps they just went for a walk by the weir. I hope Scrappy doesn't pull too hard on her lead – sometimes even Tom can't stop her pulling . . .'

I tried not to think about the fact that Scrappy wasn't on a lead.

Josh was still at the kitchen door. He seemed rooted to the spot. I had to be the sensible one. This might be serious. Ned ran in to Joe and Tom, but they were unmoved by his panic and ambled out to join us. Josh just stared at them, paralysed. 'We've lost Kate and Scrappy,' I explained, 'and I think that Scrappy might not be on her lead.' Joe's eyes widened and I could see him visibly snapping into action. He drew himself up.

'Tom,' he said, 'take Charlotte and Ned over to the weir to look for Kate. She can't have gone far, but the dog could be anywhere. Josh, if you drive back to the hospital now, I'll come as far as Upper Farm with you and then work my way back to join the others. You know what I'm thinking: that daft mutt's a disaster waiting to happen. Send Tom back in a couple of hours to report to Viv. It's still only three-thirty – no need to phone Dad and Louise yet, but we might have to later. Ned, you stay right by Charlotte. And Ned, *think*. Kate's your mate. You know the sort of places she goes. Help Charlotte and Tom, OK? Josh? *Josh?* Come on, get moving!'

But Josh wasn't moving. He looked as if he was about to cry. 'Find her,' he said through gritted teeth. 'Find my little sister. Don't let anything have happened to her. Please God. Just find her and bring her back, and I'll never shout at her again.' He let Joe push him towards his car and they got in.

Tom and Ned turned to me. 'Let's go,' I said. The boys each took one of my hands and we set off for the weir.

The wind was really beginning to get up. The trees shook and rustled and it felt as if rain wasn't far away. Tom was worried and pulled me forward, but Ned, strangely enough, let go of my hand and danced along behind, talking to himself. Tom said, 'We must find Kate before it gets dark. Just imagine how everyone will be if we come back without her. I'm really worried, Charl.'

'It's ages until then,' I said. 'We'll find her.' We were walking past the water-mill. 'She knows not to go in there, surely?' I asked Ned.

'Kate's not stupid,' said Ned indignantly. 'It's scary in there. She wouldn't go anywhere scary.'

'What if she was looking for Scrappy?'

'Scrappy wouldn't go in there either. Anyway, Scrappy always goes in the brambles here. She's not interested in the mill – no rabbits.'

We walked on, calling Kate and Scrappy all the time. It was getting windier and the sky was darkening, building up to a summer storm. I couldn't bear to think of Kate out here on her own. We went over the stile and into the field by the river. Absolutely everything suddenly seemed hazardous to a little girl and an uncontrollable dog. Could I bear to look in the river? What if she'd fallen in? Tom read my thoughts. 'I'll walk along by the edge of the river. It's not very deep here, but we all know it's fast. We've been brought up by this river. Kate would have been careful.'

''Course she'd have been careful,' said Ned. 'Like I said,

she's not stupid.' Ned seemed remarkably calm about his friend at this particular moment. Tom went right down by the river below the weir. I could see him squatting down on the bank, pulling back branches and peering into the gloom. Ned held my hand as we watched him.

'What are you thinking, Ned?' I asked him. 'Have you had any more ideas about where Kate is?'

'I'm thinking, Charlotte,' he said. 'I'm thinking, but I'm not scared any more. After all, Kate's older than me, and I wouldn't go in the mill or fall in the river, or any of those things. So I'm still thinking about it.'

I found a big stick for slashing at brambles and long grass. We zig-zagged across the fields. I really didn't know what we were looking for. Perhaps I hoped we'd find a clue, something of Kate's that would tell us where she was. The twenty-minute walk to the weir took over an hour. I hardly wanted to look in the big pools there or under the waterfalls. I was scared of what I might find. But Tom was dogged in his search. He crossed right along the top of the weir ('Kate knows we're not allowed to do that,' said Ned) and looked among the trees on the other bank, but there was nothing to be found. We walked on past the weir towards the land belonging to Upper Farm where Joe was. I didn't really know my way round here, and it became increasingly hard to search. As we climbed through Blaythwaite's fields the wind blew cold on us, cutting right through my thin shirt. I tried to concentrate on the job in hand, poking around in hedges, calling, always calling.

There was no sign of Joe. We were all flagging. 'I'd better go back and report, I suppose,' said Tom. 'We've been two hours. Don't worry, I know the way. I'll nip across those fields there. You go back the way we came. Please have Kate with you. I can't bear to think how everyone will be if she's really lost. I can't bear to think how *Kate* will be if she's really lost . . .' He set off at a jog. (And I couldn't bear to think how Josh would be if anything happened to his sister.)

'Can we stop for a bit soon?' asked Ned. 'I've got tired legs and I want to sit down. Can we go and sit on the big boulder by the weir? I don't mind carrying on that far if it's all downhill.' Poor old Ned. I forget sometimes that he's only six. He'd done jolly well.

'Of course. We'll sit down on the boulder and have another good think.'

Tom returned to absolute pandemonium. (He told me all this later.) Josh had brought Viv and Ollie home. Ollie was on crutches, slightly miffed that he was no longer the centre of attention. Viv and Josh were reacting equally badly. Viv, tough Viv, was wailing about her car, her son and her (suddenly) beloved dog. Josh was not helping by saying that it was only a stupid dog that she'd lost. He obviously blamed himself for Kate running off, but he was taking his anger out on everyone else. Tom's arrival without Kate just made everything worse, and they all realised that the Rowlinson parents were going to have to be told. In the end, Ollie said that he would ring them at work, since both Viv and Josh seemed incapable, but in fact there was no need, because John Rowlinson's car could be heard coming up the hill at that very moment. They all stood silently and listened while John went into the Rowlinsons' empty house and then made his way next door to them.

'There you are, Josh! Where are the children? I thought you were taking care of everything today?' Of course it was the worst thing he could have said. Josh was rendered speechless, so finally it was Ollie after all who told John about Kate's disappearance. John said angrily that he'd phone the police straight away. He couldn't imagine why no one had done it earlier.

Meanwhile, Ned and I were having our little sit-down. 'Charlotte, Joe said I had to think, didn't he?'

'Have you thought some more, then, Ned?'

'Yes. I'm sure Kate's not lost. And I don't think she's hurt herself either. I think she's hiding.'

'Hiding?'

'Yes. Kate hides if she thinks people are cross with her. I was cross with her and she probably thought you were cross with her too, as well as Josh.'

Oh God. So it was my fault. 'I wasn't really cross with her, Ned. I just didn't want you two squabbling. I suppose she might be hiding. Where does she like to hide?'

'That's the thing. I don't know. You see, Kate's so good at hiding. She always finds somewhere new.'

We got up and started walking again. We still called for Kate, but I was beginning to feel that Ned might have a point. I hoped he had a point. I much preferred to think of Kate hiding. In fact, that was what Josh had suggested originally. And we hadn't even searched our two houses properly. How crazy! 'Ned, come on, let's get back and make everyone search the house. Josh only had a quick look around, so if she's ... *hiding* ...'

As soon as we rushed into the kitchen I felt really stupid. Viv was there. Both the Rowlinson parents were there. The police were there. Everyone was grey-faced. Viv and Josh had obviously both been in tears. I hung Scrappy's lead on the hook on the door where it lived. All eyes were on me. 'We came back,' I said, unnecessarily. 'We thought she might just be hiding.'

Silence.

'Excuse me,' I said, and headed for the privacy of the loo. It was while I was there that I had a sudden thought. Kate liked to trail around after me. Sometimes she followed me to the loo and hung around outside the door, dodging behind a corner as I came out. She was a very sociable little girl. She often kept a conversation or a train of thought going for ages, picking up the threads of what we'd been saying sometimes hours later. I thought about Kate trailing me. What if she'd followed me out to the car? What if Scrappy had followed her?

I whizzed up to my room for a sweatshirt and then slipped out of the front door into the windy evening. Viv's car didn't live in a garage, exactly. She kept it in what was probably once a stable or a pigsty, now almost totally in ruins and hidden by trees. The roof was a sheet of corrugated plastic weighted down with stones. There really wasn't any space around the car in which to hide. The wind rattled the roof and whistled round the old building. A few raindrops bounced overhead.

Suddenly I glimpsed a movement in the car. On the floor behind the driver's seat. Something curled up was curling itself up tighter because I was there. I tried to open the doors. The locks were down. I knocked on the windows. It was too dark in there to see properly. I prayed it was Kate, but I couldn't be sure. I called, 'Kate, it's me, Charlotte! Open the door!' Kate, if it was Kate, didn't move. I realised I'd have to get back into the house, get the keys and get out again, all without raising anybody's hopes. I needed an ally. Who should it be?

Everyone looked up at me expectantly as I went in at the kitchen door again, but luckily the police had just finished making notes and were on their way out. That was taking up the attention of all the adults. I went over to Tom. 'Tom,' I said quietly, 'go and find your mum's car keys and give them to me. I'll be by the front door.'

Tom was amazing. It's quite possible he got the keys from Viv's pocket without her noticing. 'Here. Why do you want them?'

'Because I just *might* have found Kate. I'll slip out the front again. Change the subject if anyone starts asking where I am.'

I went back to the car and opened the door. It was completely dark in there now. 'Kate?' I called. 'Kate? Answer me.' I reached nervously into the corner where I'd seen something and touched a warm body. 'Kate?'

In a tiny voice Kate said, 'Are they all cross with me about Scrappy?'

'Nobody's cross with you, Kate. They're just terribly worried that you've gone missing. Come on, come with me. They've called the police, Kate.'

'Oh no,' she whimpered. 'That's because they're cross with me, isn't it?'

'No, Kate. No one's cross. Just as worried as they could be.' I sat in the front seat. 'Come on. Climb over and have a cuddle.'

She squeezed between the seats and on to my lap. 'You were all cross with me. But I wanted to be with you and I wanted us to take Scrappy for a walk because she was unhappy, so I followed you. I left the door open by mistake and Scrappy came after me.' Kate was tearful. She went on with her story between sobs. 'I tried to get her back in but I couldn't and then I tried to find her lead but I couldn't and then I thought you wouldn't mind her not being on her lead in the garden so I came anyway, but then Scrappy went running off and she wouldn't come when I called her and then I was so frightened that Mr Blaythwaite would shoot her and I knew everyone would be angry with me so I just hid by the wall and then when the garage men left I got in the car. I pressed the button that locks all the doors and I think I must have fallen asleep . . .'

I gave her a hug. 'Let's go back to the house. They'll all be so pleased to see you, Kate.'

EIGHT

I'll admit that I carried Kate in through the back door partly for effect. I knew how relieved Josh would be to see her. Kate had her arms firmly round my neck and her face was buried in my shoulder. She peeped out at the assembled gathering as they all cried out 'Kate!' and 'Darling!' and 'Sweetheart!' I explained a bit about where I'd found her, but her immediate family were too happy to care about the details. True to form, Kate struggled down and ran over to Josh.

'Don't be cross with me, Josh,' she said. 'Will you read me a story? I want to go to bed now.'

Josh hoisted Kate up into his arms and hugged her very tightly. 'Come on, little sis. What shall it be?' It wasn't until they were all in the dark courtyard and Kate was waving goodnight to us over Josh's shoulder that she asked, almost as an afterthought, 'Where's Joe?'

'Joe'll be fine,' said Josh soothingly. 'Come on, Kate, let's get you into bed.' And that was the last we saw of the Rowlinsons for a while.

The rest of us reacted quite differently to Joe's absence. 'I don't believe it!' said Viv. 'How could we all have forgotten Joe, even in the heat of the moment?'

'And Scrappy,' said Ollie, gloomily. 'Do you think I ought to go and look for them?' he asked, obviously hoping that no one would say yes.

'Don't be ridiculous!' snapped Viv. 'You can't possibly go anywhere with that ankle.' She looked over at the two younger boys. 'And don't you two think you're going on some wild-goose chase in the dark. It's way past your bedtime! Up you go, all of you. Go on, help Ollie up the stairs!' Slightly shocked by their mother's uncharacteristic outburst, and exhausted anyway, the three boys slunk out of the kitchen door. No sooner had they gone than Viv sat down and started crying uncontrollably.

'Pour me a drink would you?' she asked. 'There's some whisky on the shelf by the DVDs.' I waited for Viv to talk while I gathered my own thoughts about what to do next.

'Hell! Hell! Hell!' were Viv's first comments on the situation. 'I can't – I just can't hack it.' She heaved some more great sighs, and sniffed. It was very alarming, my aunt behaving like this. 'I think I'm coping, and then I just can't any more! How did this happen? What can the Rowlinsons think of me – two children lost because of one wretched dog?'

'One child found,' I said, 'and the other capable of looking after himself. Don't blame yourself, Viv. None of this is your fault exactly.'

'It is,' she retorted. 'If I'd trained that blasted dog properly none of this would have happened.'

'Look,' I said, nervous that I might end up agreeing with her, 'you've had Scrappy all this time and nothing like this has happened before. You can't help the way the Rowlinsons operate. It's not your fault that Josh and Kate got in a snit with each other, or that Joe takes animals so seriously.'

'Joe!' she said, and started to sniff again. 'That poor child, out God knows where in the dark looking for *our* dog. And you saw how they practically all forgot about him. I just hope that nothing happens to him . . . If only he had a mobile.'

'Viv, Viv,' I tried to comfort her, but I didn't really know what to say.

'I'd like another whisky,' she said, 'but perhaps I'd better just sleep – unless they need me.'

'Go to bed,' I said, though there was no way *I* could have slept after everything that had happened. 'I'll wait up for Joe. Josh is right, Joe is pretty self-sufficient. I don't think he'll actually be in any danger. But you know what he's like. Once he's started something, he won't stop until it's finished. Go on, go to bed. I'll come and wake you if I need to.'

'Bless you, Charlotte. I'm just about ready to collapse. John will be out searching, that's for sure, so let's hope Joe and Scrappy come back safe and sound. We'll think positive – since there's nothing else we can do. Perhaps they're on their way up the path now.' She went upstairs.

Before long the house was silent. I wondered whether Josh was still awake next door. If only I dared go round there, we could wait together. Huh! I started to make some coffee for something to do. A cup of coffee is the answer to most things in Viv's house. Just then there was a noise outside in the yard. I ran out into the dark – 'Joe?' But it wasn't Joe, it was Josh. Here we go – my heart started pounding away. I was scared of Josh as well as being in love with him. 'Josh? What's going on?'

'I saw your kitchen light on. I hoped you'd be up – I wanted to talk to you.' I couldn't believe my ears. 'Look, sorry I was so unpleasant earlier. Seems like I'm making a habit of it. I was out of my mind with worry. Kind of felt it was my fault. And I took it out on you. When in fact you were the one staying calm.' He stepped over towards me. 'You were brilliant, Charlotte,' he said, and put his arms round me. (Wow.)

'I really didn't—'

'Yes, you did—' he said, and started to *kiss* me, right there in the yard.

'Josh—' I tried to speak, but he wouldn't let me. He was taking this seriously. He gripped my head tightly and his unshaven chin practically grazed my face. I could have started to take it extremely seriously too, if we hadn't been in such a public place. I kept expecting Viv or one of the boys to stick their heads out of the window.

Josh held me close, squeezing my arms to prevent me from resisting his incredible charms. 'Mmmmm . . . I'd never have thought it,' he said dreamily, 'but yes, you're brilliant.'

Brilliant? Me? What at?

'You found Kate. You sorted everyone out.'

Ah. So that's what he was getting at. I pulled away and smoothed myself down, too confused to speak. I'd just been *kissed* by Josh. He turned to go back into his door. 'Better get back – I'm manning the phones. I can't imagine what my little brother's got up to this time.' He punched me lightly on the shoulder. 'We'll carry on where we left off tomorrow,' he said enigmatically. 'Ta-ra,' and he disappeared.

I went indoors and sat down heavily. What's Josh playing at? He sweeps me up in a passionate embrace, leaves me a quivering wreck and then, cool as a cucumber, off he goes. What did he mean, 'We'll carry on where we left off tomorrow'? Heaven only knows. I didn't. And what was all that about? Was that his way of *thanking* me? You're a weird guy, Josh Rowlinson, I thought, but I think I love you. No change there.

I put the kettle on again, still shaking my head in disbelief. I made a mug of coffee and drank it. I switched on the radio. It was after midnight. I dozed off. It was two-thirty a.m. John put his head round the door to say that no accidents had been reported and the police were on Joe's case now, so he was going to try and get some sleep. I passed this information on to Viv, though she barely woke up, but I couldn't go to bed myself. At four a.m. the birds started to sing. I didn't know whether I was coming or going. I kept remembering Josh. I replayed that kiss – rewind, action replay, again, slow motion, fast forward, rewind – until it seemed more like a video than the real thing. Had it really happened? Had Josh really kissed me after all these years of longing? Then I went over the rest of the awful day. I wondered where Joe was.

At four-thirty the sun came up. At five-fifteen I heard the scrunch of stones underfoot. The door was pushed open. I stood up. There was Joe, and in his arms he was carrying a bloody mess that bore a very slight resemblance to Scrappy.

Joe was almost beyond words. 'Towel. On table,' was what he said. I grabbed a clean towel from a laundry basket. Gently he laid Scrappy down. She whimpered.

'Oh, Joe—' I started.

But he cut in— 'Boil a kettle and get loads of cotton-wool and some tweezers. And more towels. Quick!'

I switched the kettle on and ran to get my make-up bag. I found tweezers and loads of cotton-wool balls. I brought some extra towels and bandages from the airing cupboard too. Joe spoke softly to Scrappy and stroked her head, almost hypnotising her. 'Hold her while I wash my hands, Charl.' I carried on stroking Scrappy's head. She didn't need holding. She wasn't going anywhere. I hardly liked to look, but I could see that there were two places where the blood was coming from. Why did he want tweezers? Joe put the tweezers in a jug and poured boiling water on them. I realised he wanted to sterilise them.

'No, Joe. Let me boil them in the water in a saucepan – it won't take much longer. You can't take any risks. I've brought some bandages.' I poured some of the water into a bowl and he started to dip the cotton wool balls into it and clean around the wounds. Poor Scrappy looked so weak, almost as if she'd given up. Joe was terribly gentle and kept up a monologue – 'It's OK, girl. We'll make you better. Don't worry. We'll clean you up. I'll get them out.'

Ah, the tweezers. Joe was concentrating so hard he obviously didn't care too much about burning himself as he fished the tweezers out of the water. And I started to realise just what he was trying to do.

'Hold her down, Charlotte. Talk to her. She won't like this but I'll do it quickly. I can see the pellets. And . . .'

I held poor Scrappy down and felt her jerk as Joe inserted the tweezers deftly into the wound and pulled out a pellet. He almost grinned as he got it out. 'There! Just like in the movies!' Needless to say, I was impressed. 'Only seven or eight more to go,' he said grimly.

'What about the other wound?' I asked as he tweaked out the next pellet.

'That's just a nasty cut. It needs cleaning and she'll need antibiotics. It's more important to get rid of this shot right now. She's ever so weak, though. I don't know if she'll make it.'

We carried on the grisly operation until Joe was satisfied that all the shot was out. I counted ten pellets in all. Scrappy seemed more dead than alive. 'Joe, it's after six a.m. Couldn't I call a vet now?'

'How do you propose we get this creature to a vet? They don't do home visits for sheep-worrying dogs, you know. Not round here. Not at this time in the morning.'

'Joe, we must tell your family you're safe, anyway. Your dad would drive us. Or Josh.'

'You must be joking!'

'Viv's car's been fixed! Viv will drive us! It's her dog. Please, let me ring.'

I could see that Joe was torn between wanting to save Scrappy all on his own and knowing that she really needed a vet. 'You've done the really important thing,' I told him. 'You got the pellets out. That needed to be done straight away.' I looked at Scrappy. While I'd been trying to persuade him, Joe had cleaned her up some more. He bandaged her leg and lightly covered the shot wound with a swab of cotton wool. Scrappy seemed to be asleep.

'The bleeding's stopped. OK, ring the vet, but I don't hold out much hope. My folks might as well sleep on for the moment.'

I pulled the sofa over and he slumped into it, one hand still resting on Scrappy's flank. I looked at him. He was totally exhausted. His face was grimy and his clothes were muddy and snagged with brambles and burrs. I turned through the Yellow Pages.

'Here's one in the village. Sheila Watson.'

'That's not who they usually go to.'

I had a feeling that a female might be more sympathetic. I dialled the number and waited for the inevitable answer machine. But then a pleasant sounding woman answered. I apologised for ringing so early in the morning and told her what had happened. She listened, interested, and then – I couldn't believe my luck. I gave Joe a thumbs-up sign. 'She's coming!' I said. 'She'll be here in about ten minutes!'

I plonked myself down next to Joe, the sleepless night almost forgotten in my excitement. I looked at his face. Tears were making tracks in the grime. Josh or no Josh, I couldn't help it. I put my arm around him and he leant his head on my chest while I stroked his hair and he stroked Scrappy. Neither of us spoke. We just sat like that until Sheila Watson arrived.

She knocked briefly on the back door and came in with her bag. 'Oh my goodness!' she said as soon as she saw Scrappy. 'I wonder who took a shot at her like that!'

'Joe got all the pellets out though,' I told her as she proceeded to examine Scrappy.

'You did well,' she said. 'Luckily the cartridge only grazed her or she'd have been full of shot and never have survived. Mind you, she'd probably be dead anyway if you hadn't removed the pellets. Your first aid was excellent. We don't want any infection to spread so I'll give her a shot of antibiotics here. She might not last out to the surgery.'

Just then Viv put her head round the door. Viv! I'd quite forgotten to tell her what was going on. And Joe's dad still didn't know he was back. Well, there just hadn't been time. Sleep had revived Viv. 'Joe!' she said, hugging him. 'Thank goodness you're home. Do your family know you're OK?'

'We've been too busy sorting Scrappy out,' Joe said, embarrassed by the hug. 'But I suppose now the vet's here . . .'

'You go home, love,' said Viv. 'You've done more than enough. It's my turn now. You'd better get some sleep, too, Charl. You've been brave and wonderful, bless you both. I'll put a notice on the kitchen door so the boys don't barge in.'

Great, Viv was in charge again.

NINE

It took me a while to get to sleep. It was bright sunlight outside and I could hear the boys getting up and then shushing each other. I could hear their questions – 'Where's Joe? Is Scrappy all right? Why can't we see Charlotte?' I had so many questions of my own. I didn't know where or how Joe had finally found Scrappy or even exactly what had happened to her. We'd been too busy with the 'operation' for questions. I knew that Josh thought I was a heroine but I also knew with far greater certainty that Joe was a hero. I finally dropped off.

It must have been about lunch time when I surfaced. My first impulse was to throw off the bedclothes, leap out of bed and rush downstairs to find out all the news. Then I started remembering the various events of the night. My second, far stronger, impulse was to pull the duvet over my head and stay buried under it for as long as possible.

I thought about Josh. Josh had held me. Josh had kissed me. Josh had been strong and firm and, oh dear, incredibly sexy. Little details replayed themselves – the way he'd wound my hair round his hands to grip my head, the way his teeth had knocked mine, the taste of his mouth . . . Aaaagh! Bury face in pillow time. The way he'd held me so tightly, pinned my arms so I couldn't struggle. What was a girl to do?

And then – Joe. Joe, who once he'd started on something couldn't let it go. Serious Joe who actually *did* things, took action. He must have searched and searched for Scrappy. How far had he trudged for all those hours without ever giving up? How had he felt when he found her? How far had he carried her? And how had he summoned the energy to clean her up and take all those pellets out? No wonder the tears had spilled when it was all over. Then I thought about comforting him, too, and how natural it had seemed. His soft, tawny hair and the tears clinging to his lashes. How he smelt of wet dog (not very pleasant) mixed with the Cumbrian night (gorgeous) . . . Total mindblow, bite the pillow time.

How could I ever emerge from this room? How could I ever look either of those brothers in the eye again?

There was a discreet tap on my door. It was Tom. 'Charlotte? Are you awake? Mum told me to bring you a cup of tea at two o'clock. Can I come in?' He looked at me expectantly. 'Well? It's all ever so exciting, isn't it? Losing Kate and Scrappy and then you finding Kate and Joe being out all night looking for Scrappy and Scrappy nearly dying. I missed out on all the drama. Joe's been over and told us all about it.'

'You'd better tell me then, Tom, because Joe and I were so busy with Scrappy that I never heard the whole story.'

'Well—' Tom settled himself on the bed and told me what he'd learned about the previous night. Joe's first worry was that Scrappy had wandered over to Upper Farm, Blaythwaite's place. So he started over there, whistling and calling for her and looking in as many fields as he could. But no luck. By eleven o'clock he was starving hungry, so he called into the Ollertons' pub (Pete Ollerton's in his class at school), thinking that he'd buy a sandwich before working his way home. He specifically decided not to phone from the pub because someone else was using it and he knew he'd be home soon. (The grown-ups have all told him off for that!) But while he was eating Joe overheard a conversation that made his blood run cold. A group of farmers were having a heated discussion about summer visitors and dogs. One of them was the farmer from Black Gill. Joe heard him mouthing off about finding some picnickers near his sheep with a dog off the lead. 'Saw a dog up there again this afternoon. Could've been the same one. Completely on her own. No owner in sight. Took a pot shot at her, I did, too. Just to frighten her. Don't think I hit her, but I don't expect to see that one around again . . .' Joe knew all about our little episode with Scrappy up at Black Gill that day. And he knew that George Botham was in fact one of the best shots around.

I interrupted Tom. 'But Black Gill's miles away – it took us ages to drive there when we went.'

'It's not far cross country,' Tom said, 'especially if you wade through the river once or twice. The Rowlinsons took me and Ollie fishing there and we walked all the way.'

'Anyway, go on. So Joe thought they were talking about Scrappy, did he?'

Joe knew right off that Botham was talking about Scrappy. He also felt sure he'd hit her, otherwise she'd have come home. What really worried him was the fact that Botham didn't shoot to kill. It would have been simpler if he had. So Joe hiked over there and just walked his way round all the fields with sheep in. He followed the stream down to our swimming place, in case Scrappy was looking for us somehow. And that's where he found her, on our little beach. She was a complete mess. Botham's 'pot shot' had caught her shoulder and then she'd cut her leg running away. Joe picked her up and carried her. That's what took him so long. He kept thinking she was going to die before he got her home. He could see the wound, though, so he could tell that the shot hadn't penetrated beyond the bone – which was lucky really.

We were both silent for a bit, just imagining it all. And imagining life without a daffy dog around.

'How's Scrappy now?' I asked.

'Mum said the vet sedated her, so she just looks asleep. The vet's coming again this evening. We're taking it in turns to Scrappy-sit. Ollie doesn't mind. Says he feels they have something in common.'

'Of course! Poor Ollie! How's his ankle? There were so

many dramas yesterday I'd completely forgotten about him.'

'Ollie's just fed up. He's OK but he'll be on crutches for a while, so no sport.'

'Not even swimming?' I realised the Water Warriors fixture might be in jeopardy.

'Dunno,' said Tom, bored with the subject of Ollie. 'Are you getting up, or not?'

As nonchalantly as I could, I asked, 'So what are the Rowlinsons up to today? What day is it, anyway?'

'Saturday. They sent Joe to bed at lunchtime. He's been checking on his patient all morning, "past sleeping," he said. Then he conked out over his soup. Kate's downstairs with Ned. And Josh has gone fishing with his dad. Look, are you getting up?'

The coast was clear. 'Yeah, sure,' I said. 'Bog off, then! Can't a girl get some privacy round here?' And Tom dodged his way, laughing, out of the door.

I had a shower and dressed and went downstairs feeling almost human. There was a big notice on the kitchen door saying 'KNOCK FIRST, THEN WAIT' so I did. I heard someone creaking towards the door and realised it was Ollie on his crutches. 'Come in,' he whispered as he opened the door. 'We're trying to keep Scrappy in hospital conditions.' Scrappy had a bed of towels in the corner and she was fenced round with fire guards and airing racks. 'No little ones allowed. You are though.' He creaked back to the kitchen table, which I saw had been well scrubbed since the morning, and looked back at me. 'Very popular you are round here. Can't move for people singing your praises. Charlotte, you're blushing!'

'You know me, Ollie. I blush at anything.'

'First it was Mum – "Charlotte was *so* supportive last night," and then it was Kate – "Charlotte was *really* nice to me last night," and then it was Josh' – here he did another blush-check – '"Wasn't Charlotte *brilliant* with Kate?"' I really was blushing now, because I knew he hadn't finished. 'But your greatest admirer, Charlotte, is my hard mate Joe. He kept on about how *excellent* you were with Scrappy and how you *anticipated* his every move. I had to say "Hang on, mate. Don't get ideas above your station. It's your big brother that Cousin Charlotte is gagging for—"'

'Ollie!'

Ollie grinned. 'Sorry, Charl. I just can't see the attraction myself. Josh is such a surly so-and-so.'

'*Ollie!*' I shrieked, and lunged at him. He fended me off with one of his crutches. Scrappy whimpered.

'Now look what you've done!' he laughed as quietly as he could. 'And, Charlotte – you've gone very red!' Little did he know why.

I made myself a sandwich and left Ollie, still smirking, to his dog-sitting. I went out into the garden to be with Viv. She was hanging out the washed towels. Ned and Kate were deeply involved in some elaborate game. 'Hi, Charlotte. Come and talk to me.' Viv sat down on the grass and gestured for me to join her. 'Tell me everything.'

It was great to go over it all now everyone was safe. Viv was very complimentary about my role in the proceedings. I let her approval wash over me like the sun.

'I do apologise for coming so unhinged last night, Charl. I can cope with most things. I do cope with most things. But that dog – somehow she brings out emotions that I've kept under wraps since Jim's accident – at least, that's the only way I can explain it. I still don't know what I'm going to do about her.'

'Is it too late to get Joe to train her? I know he wants to.'

'Maybe. Perhaps her convalescence will be like a second childhood and she'll be trainable. But I don't know. You know what they say about old dogs and new tricks! Though I'm beginning to think that if anyone could train her, it's

Joe. He's got a remarkable way with animals. The vet said that Scrappy should never have survived being carried all that way, let alone kitchen-table surgery. But somehow Joe did exactly the right things. She was very impressed.'

I didn't want to get any deeper into a conversation about Joe at that moment, so I just leant back against the wall and turned my face into the sun.

'We can take it easy this afternoon. There's nothing to do but keep an eye on Scrappy, and that's something Ollie can do. Yesterday was quite enough excitement for an entire summer. We need time to get over it before Joe's birthday bonanza on Wednesday. Maybe Ollie will have recovered enough to swim by then. And maybe Scrappy will be well enough to leave behind!'

Water Warriors was a nice general topic of conversation. I could handle this. 'Who's organising it? We've never actually done Water Warriors on Joe's birthday before, have we? Are we going to have tea and cake and stuff? Will Louise even take time off work?'

'Who knows? I'm happy to organise a birthday picnic. I'm fond of Joe, he's a nice lad. And I owe him one. You'll help, won't you? We could make a cake, buy some crisps. Take ice-cream in the cool bag . . . In fact—' she jumped to her feet, 'why don't we go over to the boathouse now and case the joint? I feel like getting out, trying out the car. Joe's going fishing when he wakes up, so he'll be nicely out of the way. Ollie can stay with the dog, Tom and the little kids can come with us, and we'll be back in a couple of hours. OK?'

'Sounds OK to me.'

The little kids were easily persuaded. The boathouse is on a small private lake. Viv has known the owners for years. No one else uses it, so it's ramshackle and scruffy in the nicest sort of way.

We parked by the roadside and went in through a gate.

It's only a short walk through some woods to the lake. The boathouse is about the size of a garage, and stone built. There's a picnic bench in it and, surprisingly, a fireplace. We checked out the wooden dinghy and a fibreglass one, both very basic but still seaworthy. I came across the remains of a raft the boys had tried to construct from logs last year. With a bit of work it might be pressed into service again.

'Let's reckon on good weather, shall we,' said Viv, 'and bring the bench outside. Then the boathouse can be the changing room. We can light the fire – there's luxury!'

'How many will we be?'

'Let's see – you, me and my three, that's five – five Rowlinsons, that's ten . . . That's plenty, actually. Even eight would seem like a party if John and Louise decide not to come. Shame Michelle won't be here. Never mind. She'll be here soon enough.'

'Let's gather some wood now. The kids would be good at that.'

While we were picking up sticks Tom, Ned and Kate discussed the various boats we had at our disposal. Kate said, 'There are two dinghies, but only two paddles, so that has to be one paddle for each dingy. We've got a lilo—'

'And we've got an inflatable dinghy,' said Ned.

'What about the raft?' I asked them. 'I don't remember it being here last year.'

'Joe and Ollie started it last summer,' said Tom, 'but they never managed to finish it somehow. It's cool though. It didn't sink. Perhaps they can use it this year. Now Ollie's such a cripple I reckon we can let them be a pair. You'll still be a middling with me, won't you Charlotte?'

'I'm going with Josh,' said Kate.

'And I'm going with Mum,' said Ned.

'So that leaves my mum and dad to go together,' said Kate. 'And they're both really hopeless!'

Tom and I decided to bag the inflatable dinghy. It didn't

have paddles, but it was hard to overturn. Roll on Wednesday!

We had gathered plenty of sticks to pile up by the fireplace. A woodstore lent a homely air to the boathouse. 'It might be fun to brew up if we get a good fire going,' said Viv. 'And if we bring blankets for cold swimmers – no one will ever want to leave!'

On the journey back my stomach lurched at the thought of having to see either Josh or Joe. I tried to marshall my thoughts. Nothing had happened with Joe, after all – nothing as far as he was concerned, anyway. I'd just given a tired boy a hug. That was all. Anyone would have. His mother would have. He was only young. He wouldn't have made anything of it. As for Josh – well, you never could tell with Josh. Anything for attention, anything for effect. But he had kissed me. Properly. It hadn't just been a peck on the cheek. Or even a peck on the lips, for that matter. It had been the real thing, real tonsil hockey. Aagh. My legs turned to jelly, even there in the car. I mean, could it be that I was his girlfriend now – carrying on where we left off? (Don't be ridiculous, Charlotte.) What was I going to say? Should I go up to him and slip a proprietorial arm around his waist? I *don't* think so. No, the more I considered it, the more I thought I should just behave as normal, as if nothing out of the ordinary had happened. After all, Josh played games. Joe didn't. But Josh did.

The kids were making up silly rhymes. 'Ned the bed!' they shrieked. 'Kate the bate!' 'Tom the – Tom the bomb!' 'Mum the bum!' Ned was beside himself with laughter. 'Charlotte the harlot!' That was all I needed. Never mind the fact that Ned didn't have a clue what a harlot was.

We got home just before the vet drove up. Ollie was tired and his leg was hurting. Scrappy looked dreadful. I felt rather depressed. Anti-climax, I suppose. I had supper with the others and told Viv I was going up for an early night.

Tomorrow would be OK as long as I didn't have to face Josh and Joe *together*.

TEN

I felt a lot better when I woke up on Sunday, and ready to face almost anything. All my talking to myself had worked and I decided that, however much I wished it was otherwise, Josh had merely been thanking me in his own way for finding Kate and that nothing the slightest bit significant had happened between me and Joe. That was until I opened the curtains and saw the two brothers standing together in the yard, two tall dark figures, Josh taller and slightly stooped, Joe more upright and solid. Like a coward I drew the curtains again and dived back into bed. I could hear them talking, their voices strangely similar, but I couldn't hear what they were saying. Any moment now, I thought, they are going to come in, together, and then what will I *do*?

But they didn't come in. I waited, expectantly, but noises in our house went on the same as usual and noises in the yard and the Rowlinsons' house stopped altogether. In the end curiosity got the better of me. I dressed and went downstairs. Viv and the boys were having breakfast. Scrappy was in her corner still, but looking slightly better. Everything was completely quiet and normal. The boys grunted at me through their Sugar Puffs. Viv looked up from the Sunday papers and said 'Hi. Help yourself to breakfast, love.'

I looked hard at everyone. Was all this normality fake? No. It was genuine. The drama was over everywhere apart from in my head. Soon Ollie was hobbling around complaining about his sore ankle. Ned was playing on Tom's Gameboy. Tom wasn't complaining – he wanted me to do things with him. Viv was clearing up. Nobody seemed the slightest bit bothered or interested in what the Rowlinsons were doing.

And so it went on all day. I phoned Mum and Dad from the house phone as, for some reason, my mobile never had a signal up here. They said they'd heard from Michelle and that she was having a fantastic time and had a terrific tan. Mum said she'd seen some of my friends around and that they'd asked after me. There was a card from Maddy. It all seemed so far removed from life up here. I tried ringing Hannah, but her dad said she was still away. Pity. I would have appreciated Hannah's opinions on my present situation.

I gathered that the Rowlinsons were all out for the day – they didn't often get the chance to do things as a family. But I didn't dare ask any more. No one mentioned them, let alone in connection with me. It struck me that of course they just didn't *know*. No one had seen me with Josh or even considered that anything might be going on. They all knew I'd fancied him for ever. Dumpy old Charlotte being in love with Josh was just part of the holiday fortnight. And as for Joe – something happening between the two of us would never have occurred to anyone, least of all me. I caught myself blushing at that moment. I blushed deeper when Viv appeared to read my thoughts and asked the boys if they had any ideas about Joe's birthday, and did any of them want to go shopping with her on Tuesday. Then she asked me what I was like at cake-making because she was lousy. Did I feel up to making a cake for Joe? Should it be a chocolate cake?

And so it went on. A nice calm day. That night, as I was walking back into the kitchen after hanging up some washing, someone waved to me from the Rowlinsons' window. I waved back. I never saw who it was.

On Monday morning Tom and I were helping Viv in the

kitchen when my worst nightmare came true. Josh and Joe came in *together*. Joe smiled at me briefly from under his fringe and quickly asked Viv where Ollie was. He wanted to show him something up by the weir and could he get there on crutches?

As Viv was answering him Josh came up to me, held out his arms in a theatrical way and said, 'Charlotte. Gissa a kiss. I've missed you.' He proceeded to wrap his arms around me and kiss me fulsomely on the lips. 'Lovely girl. Viv, I'm going to take her away from all this. All work and no play makes Charlotte a dull girl!' I was too flabbergasted to interject, but I caught a glimpse of Joe disappearing in search of Ollie, and of Tom's disgusted face before he followed Joe.

Viv appeared to take this new development in her stride and, scarcely batting an eyelid, said, 'Of course. Go and enjoy yourself, Cinderella. See you at lunchtime!'

Josh grabbed my hand and led me off down towards the river. It sounds romantic, but actually I wanted to go to the loo and if I had been expecting a romantic encounter I would have shaved my legs. And I certainly wouldn't have worn jeans that didn't do up properly because they were too tight round the waist. So I followed slightly reluctantly. But Josh was sprightly, full of the joys of spring. He practically danced down the path. To be honest, I was so shocked by this turn of events that I just followed him.

He led me to a sheltered corner of the field that ran alongside the river – in the opposite direction from the weir, I was glad to see. It was a warm, sunny spot, well hidden from the path. Well hidden from anything, in fact. I tried not to panic. Josh took off his jacket and laid it on the grass. He sat down on it and patted a place next to him. When I hesitated he reached up and grabbed my hand and pulled me down beside him. I sat rather stiffly, but he put his arm around me and bent his head to kiss me again, skilfully (I realised) lying me on my back as he did so. He carried on kissing me and leant the whole weight of his chest on mine – no way could I escape.

I thought I was doing OK, but next time he drew breath he whispered, 'Relax, Charlotte, relax. I'm not going to hurt you. Move your arms. Put them round my neck.' I realised that I'd been holding my hands together protectively over my chest. It hadn't been very comfortable, but with Josh's weight I hadn't been able to move them. Gingerly I put my arms around his neck. We were so close, it was scary. Here I was lying in a field with the boy of my dreams. His face was pressing on mine and he was kissing me. I had my arms around his neck and I was running my hands through his hair. He had his hands . . . Hang on, he had his hands pushing up under my T-shirt, and I wasn't sure that I wanted him to. This wasn't simply prudishness (I tried to tell myself) – I was worried he might grab my spare tyre by mistake. I'd had groping sessions with boys at parties before now, and they usually took slightly longer to get to this stage. And I wanted to enjoy the kissing bit for the moment. What's more, I still wanted to go to the loo and I was more than ever aware of my stubbly legs and . . . *I didn't want this right now*! I hadn't had any say in the matter.

'Josh. Please. No,' I said, and tried to sit up.

'What's the matter?' he mumbled, and tried to push me down again.

'Josh – I – I – *I want to go to the toilet*!'

The spell was broken. Josh moved off me and sat up. But as he did, I was aware of two familiar figures crossing the end of the field at a point where they could have seen us. One of them was on crutches. Oh my God. They disappeared from my view as I took in Josh's outraged face. 'What's the matter with you, Charlotte?'

'Josh—' I felt rather weepy – 'Josh, I just don't feel quite ready, for . . . for all this.'

'For God's sake, Charlotte. I'm not going to rape you. Just a bit of fooling around. Don't you like fooling around?'

I did, but I didn't know how to say so without him pouncing on me again, and I was still desperate for the loo.

'Josh. I know this isn't very romantic, but I'm going into the bushes over there for a pee. And then I'll come back and then I'll talk sensibly. OK?' Josh grunted and I dived self-consciously into the farthest, thickest bushes I could find. When I returned, he was looking thoughtful.

'Charl, I thought this was what you wanted. I – All the others are always telling me how you – and I feel—'

This wasn't getting anywhere. 'It is, Josh. It is what I wanted. But I'm four years younger than you and I'm inexperienced and, well – I'm just a bit scared of you. I never know what you really think.' I looked at him. It was the closest thing to an honest conversation we'd ever had. He stayed sitting on the grass. He smoothed his trousers down and wouldn't look at me. I saw the cynical Josh kick in.

'Run along home, little girl,' he said, narrowing his eyes. 'The old man *vants to be alone,*' and he lay on his jacket with his back to me.

I made my way back to the house, praying that I wouldn't bump into anyone. Viv was in the kitchen. She looked at my rumpled clothes but didn't refer to them. 'Lunch in half an hour,' she said. 'You can shell these peas.' I sat down at the kitchen table with them. I couldn't think of a thing to say. Viv hummed to herself and carefully didn't ask me anything. The door opened. Joe put his head round, took one look at me and hastily withdrew. Scrappy heaved a doggy sigh.

Tom came in. 'Don't like real peas,' he complained and also went out again.

Ollie creaked in, winked at me salaciously and sat down. He spoke to Viv. 'Me and Joe want to go and work on the raft this afternoon, Mum. Will you take us over to the boathouse? I can work on it sitting down, but I'm getting around quite well now. Aren't I, Charl?'

I carried on furiously podding peas.

'We could take Tom. Though he's in a foul mood at the moment. Dunno why. But we might cheer him up. You won't want to be coming with us *younger* boys, now, will you, Charl?'

I said nothing. I couldn't bear the thought that Joe must have seen me with Josh. Just when I'd been trying to push him off me. How must it have looked? 'I'm not feeling too good, Viv,' I said. 'In fact I feel a bit sick.' (I did.) 'I'm going to go and lie down. Don't worry about lunch for me,' and I ran upstairs to hide in my room. I knew I was hiding, and I wasn't proud of myself. It was just that Josh's behaviour first thing this morning had been so unexpected. There was me telling myself that him kissing me in the yard had all been a horrible mistake and then he'd done completely the opposite to what I'd forecast. Then all that snogging business in the field. I wasn't ready. I wasn't prepared. Had I really been a complete wet? Some of it had been quite nice. What could Josh think of me? Josh, Josh. The love of my life. Perhaps I could try again. I do like fooling around, though I prefer it in the dark. Aagh. I just didn't know.

Viv called upstairs to say that she was taking the boys off to the boathouse, that Ned was next door with Kate and could I let the vet in when she called round later on. I lay in bed reading to take my mind off things. I was reading *Pride and Prejudice*. Lovely Jane Austen (I've seen nearly all of them on video), all romantic where no one even so much as kisses. How much simpler life must have been in those days. There was a ring at the doorbell.

I thought it must be the vet, but it wasn't, it was Josh. At the front door. He looked embarrassed.

'Josh! Why have you come to the front door?'

'Because I knew you wouldn't answer the back door.'

'What do you want?' Somehow he had wrong-footed me all over again.

'I want you to come to the cinema with me tonight.'

'What?' Oops. That sounded rather rude. I said it more politely. 'What?'

'There's a film I want to see, and it would be more fun to go with someone. And I want to apologise for jumping you this morning.'

I looked at him with my mouth open. 'What?' I said again.

'Charlotte, don't make me say all that again. Please, pretty please, will you come out to the cinema with me tonight, for pity's sake!'

'You mean, go *out* with you?'

'Yes, Charlotte, go out to the cinema with me.'

I supposed that would be all right. 'All right,' I said.

'Good,' he said. 'That's settled then. I'll wait in my car down on the road at eight. OK?'

'OK,' I said. He squeezed my hands quickly and went away, leaving me standing, still gawping, on the front doorstep to face the vet.

Scrappy was on the mend. This was good because it meant that she wasn't going to die. But it was bad because it meant she was getting some of her energy back and couldn't be penned up all the time. It meant we had to start worrying about her getting into trouble again. I asked the vet if she thought we might be able to retrain her.

'It's worth a try,' she said. 'And if anyone can do it, your lad next door probably can. I can't believe he's only fifteen – he acted as well as any adult over this business.'

'He's fourteen,' I said. 'Nearly fourteen.'

I left the others having supper when I heard Josh tooting in the lane. Tom was still in a bad mood, which was very unlike him.

'I'm going out to the cinema,' I said. 'I'll be back about eleven,' and scarpered. As I went out I could hear Tom saying 'It's not *fair*! Charlotte was going to play with *me* tonight. And we were going to start planning our Warriors tactics . . .'

I got into the car and Josh leaned over to give me a kiss. (Blimey, I thought, this is like a real couple already.) 'Let's go,' he said. 'We must leave some time to park.'

The film was a 15. There wasn't a problem about me getting in. But there was quite a lot of sex in it. And it's one thing giggling with my friends in Sophie's loft, but quite another watching it with Josh. He had his hand on my thigh, and squeezed rather tightly when things got steamy. And he was very keen on snogging in the boring bits, which meant I lost track of the plot and the people behind us started to mutter. I was still having to work to convince myself that this was what I wanted. It was just so strange after all these years of hero-worshipping Josh. Now I 'had' him it didn't seem quite right. And to make things more complicated, Josh took me straight home afterwards, kissed me on the cheek and left me on the doorstep.

I went in. Viv had gone to bed. Ollie and Joe were watching television. They had Scrappy up on the sofa with them and Joe was stroking her. I said 'Hi'. Ollie grinned at me and waved one of his crutches. Joe attempted a smile – and failed. He got up suddenly and Scrappy landed awkwardly. Joe patted her and shot off home, leaving me to help Scrappy into the kitchen and Ollie up the stairs.

ELEVEN

I woke up early on Tuesday morning. I was glad because it gave me time to think – and boy, did I need to think. What hit me first was that although I should have been delirious with happiness, I wasn't.

The main problem, quite apart from my mixed-up emotions, was the way my altered relationship with Josh upset the balance of my relationships with everyone else. Perhaps that's what happens when you grow up. I was overcome with that terrible scary feeling you get when you think that nothing will ever be the same again. It was one thing me fancying Josh and the boys all teasing me about it, but quite another when I went from their junior camp into his senior one. I had suddenly become a Girl – with a capital letter – overnight. I should have been glad that it forced them to look at me differently, but I wasn't, especially as I still felt like the same old Charlotte. Perhaps it was wrong that Ollie liked to tease me about Josh. Perhaps it was wrong that Ned and Tom loved me unconditionally like a big sister. Perhaps it was wrong that part of Josh's role was to be horrible to me and make me blush. But it had always been like that. Before. And now it wasn't.

I tried to analyse my feelings for Josh. He was gorgeous, he was sexy – but he was no longer unattainable. He was still enigmatic, he still frightened me, but he seemed to *want* to be with me. I couldn't understand why. I was only me, Charlotte. I had a sneaky suspicion, which I tried to quell, that it was because I was the only Girl around. After all, last year Josh had fancied my sister.

I was so confused, and there was no one I could talk to about it. I reminded myself firmly that I was totally in love with Josh and always had been, but I must admit, I wasn't altogether convinced.

Meanwhile, it was Joe's birthday tomorrow and there were presents to buy, a party to prepare and a cake to bake. Tom needed my attention – he'd missed out lately – and we did need to plan our Water Warriors tactics. And I needed to think about Michelle arriving and what we would all want to do once she was here. If only I could put the whole

Josh thing on hold. I hoped he wasn't going to be too demanding.

I went down to breakfast. The first thing I noticed was an absence of dog. 'Where's Scrappy?' I asked, shocked.

Viv answered. 'When I came down this morning she was all floppy and panting, trying to move but not able to. So I called the vet. She was here about an hour ago. She was worried about Scrappy's leg rather than the shot wound and thought that she'd better X-ray it so she's taken her to the surgery. She's got her under observation today and if necessary she'll operate tomorrow. I feel guilty, but it's a relief not having a dog underfoot right now.'

I thought Tom was going to add something at that point, but it became obvious that Tom simply wasn't talking to me. Ned was off with Kate somewhere and while I ate my toast Ollie and Viv were deep in discussion about Joe's birthday. Viv turned to me. 'Do you still want to make Joe's cake?' she asked me.

'Why ever not?' I retorted rather too quickly.

'I just thought you might have other things to do today,' she said vaguely.

'Like snogging with Joe's brother,' said Ollie under his breath.

'Of course I'll do Joe's cake,' I said, trying to ignore everything that they were implying. 'What sort do you think he'll want, Ollie? Chocolate?'

Just then Josh came in, with Joe trailing behind. Josh came up behind me and put his arms round my waist. 'Well, what's on the agenda for us today, pretty girl?'

Tom made puking noises and dashed out of the kitchen. Ollie caught Joe's eye and, when he thought I couldn't see him, pointed his fingers down his throat. I pulled away from Josh. 'We're organising tomorrow and I'm making the birthday cake. What sort do you want, Joe?' I said to the shadowy figure hanging around outside the kitchen door.

'Oi, Joe, come in here when the lady's talking to you,'

called Josh. Joe came in past Ollie, who muttered, 'That's no lady . . .'

'You really don't have to make me a cake, Charlotte,' said Joe, looking at his feet and shuffling like a small boy. 'I don't usually have one.'

'Yeah. Surely we've all got better things to do,' leered Josh.

This was awful. 'I've said I'll make a cake, OK?' I said. 'Joe – ' I forced him to look me in the eye – 'I want to make you a birthday cake. Now what sort do you want?'

Joe flashed me one of his intense looks before glancing down again, his cheeks flushed, and answering, 'Thanks. Chocolate.'

Josh jeered. 'Chocky cake for diddums, then, Charlotte. Smarties on it, Joe? Do you want it in any particular shape, little bro?' He turned to me. 'So when do you spare a lecherous old man some of your time?'

Ollie swung past us to the door and went out with Joe. I didn't know where. Viv, who'd been loading the dishwasher with her back to me up until now looked round, an eyebrow raised. I felt wretched. Josh was doing this all wrong.

'Well, I'm going to the supermarket quite soon,' said Viv. 'I can buy the ingredients, or you can come with me and choose them yourself.'

'You buy them, Viv,' said Josh, before I could answer.

'And we've still got some organising to do,' Viv continued.

'I really don't see why you're making such a fuss about Joe's birthday,' said Josh, beginning to sound petulant. I could see that Viv was fed up with him, but it was me she spoke to. I could hear the irritation in her voice.

'I don't mind what you do this morning, Charl, but I'm going to need you here this afternoon when I take Ollie to the hospital for a check-up. And we must set aside a couple of hours for tomorrow's preparation. It's up to you, of course. Just let me know before I go in half an hour what your plans are.'

I wanted Josh to go away and give me time to sort myself out. I wished he wouldn't come over so early. It had disrupted yesterday and it looked like disrupting today as well. I found myself feeling guilty for not wanting to be with him. I said to him as tactfully as I could, 'Josh could you just give me a few minutes to sort myself out?'

'In other words, "Bog off, Josh." OK, but I'll be back in half an hour too.'

Viv watched as Josh left, but she didn't say anything. What on earth was happening? I even felt awkward with Viv now. Then she spoke. 'I won't interfere, Charlotte. But just don't let the boys – any of them, not even the younger ones – put pressure on you. OK? Take your time, is my advice. See you in a bit!' And I was left in the kitchen on my own.

The kettle was hot, so I made myself some coffee. There was a notepad and pencil on the table where Viv had been making a shopping list. I turned to a fresh page and picked up the pencil. I divided the page into six, the number of days left of the holiday. It seemed extraordinary that the end was already in sight, even though so much had happened. Today was Tuesday. Tomorrow, Wednesday, was the Water Warriors party. Thursday was blank. And on Friday evening, Michelle arrived! I wondered what on earth Michelle would make of Josh and me as an item! I couldn't see it somehow. I forced myself to think about the day ahead. Maybe Viv could buy the cake things and I could spend some time with Josh. Why not? It was what I wanted, wasn't it? Well, wasn't it? I wondered what Josh had in mind.

I went and shaved my legs and spent quite a while in the loo.

'So what's the plan?' asked Viv when I went down.

'Can you get cocoa and cooking chocolate and fondant

icing for me? I want to make a cake like Joe and Ollie's raft, Viv. What do you think would be best? Chocolate flakes? No – Twixes. Can you get me about £3 worth? I'll pay you back. And some of that icing you can write with. And some candles.' I wanted Joe's cake to be good.

'Fine,' said Viv. 'What about a present?'

'I just can't decide what he'd like. Joe's someone you feel you have to get exactly the right present for, isn't he?'

Viv laughed. 'I shouldn't try too hard. I'm sure this amazing cake will be good enough.' Ollie hobbled in. 'What do you think would be a good present for Joe from Charlotte, Ol?' For reply, Ollie gave a disgusting laugh.

Viv raised her eyes to heaven. 'See you later, Charl.'

Josh called for me and we set off for a walk. He didn't hold my hand or put his arm round my shoulder – we walked separately, he determinedly and me tagging along after him. I thought maybe he was annoyed with me. Why could I never tell what he was thinking?

'Is everything all right?' I asked.

'Yes. Why shouldn't it be?'

'You just seem – a bit—'

'A bit what?'

'A bit, well, in a hurry.'

I saw where Josh was heading. There was an old barn where hay used to be stored. We'd played there a lot one year as kids. It seemed as if more fooling around was about to take place. It seemed as if Josh was calling all the shots.

Josh reached for my hand and led me inside the rickety barn door. There were holes above the rafters where birds hopped about and a little light filtered in, but otherwise it was dim, like a church. He shut the door and leant against it, pulling me to him. I leant my head against his chest. It felt comfortable and I would have liked to stay like that for a while, but soon he was pushing my face up with his to kiss me. He held me very tightly, too tightly, and ran his hands up and down my back, up and down, feverishly. Like a four-legged creature he tried to steer us towards the bales of hay. I was shuffling along backwards and it would have been funny if it hadn't all felt so urgent. We literally fell on to the hay bales. I wanted Josh to talk to me, but he was breathing heavily and starting to fumble with the buttons on my shirt. 'Josh – please, let me talk . . .'

'Oh no, here we go again. Talk, talk. Charlotte, you're supposed to be enjoying yourself. You are here, in a wonderful hay barn with me, the cool, fit bloke of your dreams, remember?'

'I know. I'm sorry, Josh. I just – it just – doesn't feel right. I know I've been in love with you for ages, but I don't – I'm not sure that I really *love* you.'

'I don't believe this! What's love got to do with it? What's love, if it comes to that? I *fancy* you, Charlotte. You've grown up and I fancy you. Doesn't that mean anything to you?'

I looked at him. No. I could hardly believe the stark truth myself, but after an eternity of longing for Josh to notice me, fancy me, it didn't really mean anything. I thought it would have done, but right now it didn't. I was alone with Josh in a hay barn – and I wanted to be a million miles away. I wanted him to *love* me, but I didn't know how to tell him. So I let him persuade me to lie down, and I let him have a certain amount of his wicked way with me. And I hated myself.

Josh looked at his watch. 'Hey! Home time!' he said cheerfully. I stood up. I was covered in hay. 'Brush yourself down, gorgeous. We don't want everyone knowing where we've been.' I smiled weakly.

Josh was trying to be nice, I realised. And I also realised that I didn't really like him any more. I felt gutted.

We went in at our separate doors. Viv was on the point of setting off to the hospital with Ollie. 'I've put all the cake stuff out,' she said. 'The little ones are full of plans for tomorrow – I hope it's not all too frenetic for you. Bye! See you later.'

'Charlotte! Can we help you make the cake? Please?' said Kate.

'Can I lick the bowl?' begged Ned.

Tom sat and scowled.

'I want to make some drawings before I begin,' I told them. 'It's going to be a raft like the one Joe and Ollie have built. But I haven't worked it out exactly yet and I need to do that first.'

I sat down at the kitchen table with Ned and Kate on either side of me. Tom sat at the far end. He wasn't talking yet, but at least he was still there. I tried to catch his eye and smile at him. I wanted to say, Don't be jealous, Tom. I love you just the same. This is another bit of Charlotte that you don't know and don't need to know. And anyway, right now, I don't think there's much to be jealous of. But I didn't say it of course, and if I had, Josh's appearance almost immediately would have seemed very odd. Josh squeezed in between me and Kate, an arm round each of us. Kate didn't like it. She decided to test him out.

'Josh, you haven't forgotten that you're my partner in Water Warriors tomorrow, have you?'

Josh has never taken Water Warriors as seriously as the others, and he had in fact forgotten his promise to Kate. He chose this moment, the wrong moment, to be flippant. 'Don't you think I ought to be my girlfriend's partner, Kate?'

Kate's eyes blazed and she beat Josh on the chest with her fists. 'But, Josh, you promised! You *promised* you'd be my partner. And we're a big and a little. You couldn't possibly go with Charlotte because then you'd be two bigs and that wouldn't be fair. And anyway, who would I go with then?'

Josh tried to fend off the rain of blows, but Kate was beside herself. She was crying now. 'It's not fair, it's not fair.

Why do you have to go and spoil everything?' and ran out of the room.

Suddenly Tom was beside me, white-faced and angry. 'It's Charlotte who's spoiled everything. We were all right before you came, Charlotte. Even Scrappy was all right before you came. And though you might not remember, you were going to be *my* partner tomorrow. But I don't want to be your partner now, not ever. In fact I hate you. I hate Josh and I hate you even more.' Tom's voice cracked. 'And you've upset Kate, so she'll probably run away again and it'll be all your fault. Come on, Ned, let's not stay here. Let's go and play next door.' And they left too.

'I'd better go after Kate,' said Josh. 'Well, the apple cart has been well and truly upset. I'll see you later.'

I was on my own in the kitchen again. Tom's outburst had been the last straw. Dear, loyal Tom, my champion. What had I done?

I started on the chocolate cakes, good, mindless work, that helped me forget the mess I was in. I shoved the tins of chocolate mixture in the oven and began moulding two little figures of Joe and Ollie to go on the raft. I coloured some of the icing as near to flesh colour as I could get. It looked pink – a good match for Ollie, but not for Joe. I thought about the lovely golden tan colour of his skin. I added a drop of green and a drop of yellow to the pink. It was getting there. Then I did some red and some black for their swimming shorts before playing with the colours for their hair. I used yellow with a little brown for Ollie, and then brown for Joe. I added the yellow to Joe's in fine streaks, just like the gloss on his hair when the sun shone on it.

I sat back. The cakes were beginning to smell good. I looked at my handiwork and felt really pleased with it. And then I remembered what had gone before.

I thought of the way everything had gone so wrong. Everyone was so upset, and all for nothing. I didn't love

Josh. It was unbelievable, but I didn't. Nor did I want the others to think I did. The awfulness of it all washed over me. I could feel the lump in my throat and my eyes brimming. The cakes were ready. I got them out and put them on racks and then sat down again. The tears were coming down so fast I couldn't see any more. I laid my head on my arms and cried my heart out.

I didn't hear the tap on the door or see Joe coming in. I wasn't aware of anything until I felt a tissue being pushed at me. I looked up into Joe's concerned face.

'Here, have another tissue. You look hideous.'

'Thanks a bunch.'

'Good, I made you smile.'

Joe pulled up a chair. He looked at what I'd been making.

'You weren't supposed to see that until tomorrow.'

He picked up the little Joe figure. 'Is this me?' He laughed incredulously and put it down.

I sniffed. 'Where are the others?'

'All out.'

I relaxed slightly.

'What's the matter, Charlotte? You can talk to me if you want.'

I grinned wanly. 'That doesn't really seem fair.'

'I'm not blind, Charl, and I do know my brother. I know how difficult he finds it to be consistent with people. I love him too, you know, but he's still a weirdo. Now, tell me about it. Talk to Uncle Joe.'

Who was this amazingly mature person? He was being so sweet, I just started to cry all over again.

'Try,' he said. 'You've got half an hour before anyone comes back. I know, I checked.'

'Well,' I began. And then I found myself telling him everything. Well, almost everything. There were some details I omitted, but somehow I managed to say that I was no longer in love with his brother. I told him how worried I was that everyone hated me and that holidays here would never be the same again. Then he stopped me. He held my shoulders.

'Charlotte, no one *hates* you – it's because they all *love* you that this has happened. Don't you see?' He gave me his intense Joe gaze. (Why is it that boys always seem to be blessed with the longest, darkest lashes?) 'But you must talk to Josh and put him straight. I don't approve of girls who lead guys on,' he said sanctimoniously. 'In his funny old way, Josh must be fond of you and he also has his pride, misplaced though it is sometimes. You must be careful not to hurt his pride.'

I heard a car approaching. 'Promise me you'll talk to him tonight,' said Joe. 'I don't like seeing you so miserable.' He touched my cheek as he left. I felt as if I'd been scorched.

TWELVE

I went back to making the cake. Gradually, the others drifted in. The younger ones had been watching a film on TV next door, which was why Joe was able to predict how long they'd be. Josh had gone into town to get a birthday present. The mood had changed. Obviously Josh had mollified Kate a little and Ned wasn't taking sides. Tom came in behind Ollie and Viv. The cake was more or less finished, and I have to say it did look good.

'Wow!' said Ollie as he came in. 'That looks good enough to eat! Look at this, Tom. Cousin Charlotte is good on the pie front isn't she?'

'The cake's OK,' said Tom guardedly.

'I've still got to add the writing and the candles, but then it's finished. Can we work out our tactics after supper, Tom?' I asked.

He looked at me. 'Maybe,' was all he would say. But somehow I thought he might come round.

*

Because I was already in cooking mode I offered to get supper. I made a lasagne, which was everybody's favourite. Isn't it funny how the right food can put everybody in a better mood (especially guys, it seems)? I felt more in control now. Joe had given me the courage to do what I knew was right. So while the lasagne was in the oven I went and knocked next door. Louise let me in. 'I've come to see Josh,' I said, feeling braver than I felt, and hoping that neither Joe nor Kate would suddenly appear. Louise called Josh. 'Hi, Josh,' I said when he came downstairs, and before he could say anything – 'Could we go to the pub later, about half nine?'

Josh didn't want to talk in front of Louise. 'Fine,' he said. 'I'll meet you in the lane at nine-fifteen.'

'OK, see you then,' I said and left quickly, with Louise's words 'Isn't she a bit young for the pub?' just audible. And anyway, I'm not, I thought.

Supper with Viv and the boys was such a cheerful affair that I felt much better, even though I was nervous, about meeting Josh later. Tom saw that I really hadn't changed as much as he'd feared. Afterwards he came and sat by me. Without looking at me he linked his little finger in mine and said, 'Friends again?'

'Of course,' I said. 'Come on, Tom, let's go up to your room and make our plans. You know I've bagged the inflatable dinghy for us, don't you?'

'That means we're slow, but hard to tip up,' said Tom. 'OK, I've got some paper and something to write with. Let's go.'

By nine o'clock Tom and I had our strategy all worked out and we were good friends again. I noticed that he wasn't as cuddly as usual, but I suppose that figured – he's always been so tuned in to my feelings. I said goodnight to him and went downstairs.

I told Viv I was going to the pub with Josh, and I told her

not to worry. This drink was all about me going at my own pace. 'Well, good luck,' said Viv as I slipped out of the door. I needed it.

I got into the car with Josh. He leant over and kissed me affectionately. He'd washed his hair and he smelt of after-shave. This was going to be difficult. But I had made my promise to Joe. 'Don't hurt Josh's pride,' I reminded myself over and over. The pub was long and low with a log fire, even in summer. Josh bought me my usual Coke and a soft drink for himself. He was very conscientious about not drinking and driving.

We sat down by the fire with our drinks. 'All right, then, Charlotte,' he said. 'What's this all about?' He was tapping his foot nervously. 'Come on. You haven't brought me here just to be sociable.'

I had my opening. 'Josh, will you just hear me out before you say anything?'

'I won't promise, but I'll try.'

(Don't hurt his pride. Don't hurt his pride.) 'Ever since I can remember, you've been my hero.'

'—Got a bit sullied, have I?'

'Josh, please. You said you'd listen.' I had to keep going. 'And I got used to having you as my hero, whatever you said to me or did. It was easy really, because hero-worship is sort of two-dimensional – you never have to examine your real feelings about someone, or their real feelings about you, for that matter. You were just this distant, unattain-able guy.'

'So you don't like what you see close up?'

'Josh, shut up. I didn't say that. On this holiday I've got to know you so much better—'

'—I'll say!'

'Josh! I never even knew about your family before. I hadn't noticed how brilliant you were with Kate. I didn't know you had a gentle side. And then, just as I was getting to know these things, we—'

Josh gave me a lopsided grin. 'We what?'

'Well, suddenly we were having a relationship. And it was all too fast – and—' I grabbed his hand and took a deep breath. 'Josh, I don't want us to carry on.'

Josh pulled his hand away. 'Why on earth not? What's the matter with me?'

(Don't hurt his pride.) 'Nothing's the matter with you. It's me. I can't handle it. I'm new to relationships, especially with blokes as old as you. It might be different if I could concentrate on it, but I can't because of all the other distractions here. Perhaps if it was just you and me, in a different situation. No little cousins. No injured dogs. No aunts.'

Josh regarded me quizzically. 'You're a serious little thing, aren't you?'

'So? There's nothing wrong with that is there?'

'No, no. And in fact when you were so good about finding Kate, I felt seriously grateful to you. No, more than that. I wanted to let you know how much I liked you for it. And then, well, there you were. A girl. On the spot. I liked you and I thought we could have some fun in this godforsaken place. I thought you'd enjoy it too. Michelle did.'

'*What?*'

'Yeah. Michelle and I had a bit of a thing last year. It didn't seem to involve everybody else like it has with you.'

'You had a thing going with my sister last year?' I was incredulous. Michelle was a sneaky cow. We all just thought that Josh fancied her.

'It was nothing, Charl. Just a bit of fun, like I said.'

I was speechless. My thoughts were in a complete whirl. So was Josh more serious about me than about Michelle or was he still just playing games? Honestly, the more I got to know this guy, the more I wished I didn't. And yet his admission seemed to offer a way out.

'Look, Josh. You may pretend that you don't have feelings, but you don't fool me. I can't work out what you think about me, about us. But I do care about you, as a person rather than as a hero, and I don't want to hurt your feelings. I just don't want our relationship to go any further and mess up the other things that are important to me. Perhaps, since Michelle's coming, it would be better to stop anyway.'

Josh looked at his watch and got up to go. He held out his hand to me. 'OK. Come on then. Whatever you want.'

We went out to the car. It was a clear night with a sky full of stars. We stood looking up at them for a few minutes. Josh held my hand, his fingers entwined with mine. Then he hugged me in his usual tight Josh-ish way, before pushing me away slightly and resting his arms over my shoulders. He looked down at me and smiled. 'Pity,' he said ruefully, brushing my hair off my face with a sigh, 'you're a lovely squeeze,' and gave me a final, lingering, tender kiss. I could feel my knees buckling and my resolve weakening. But it was too late. My holiday romance was over almost before it had begun. Maybe, when it came to reporting back to the others, I'd pretend it had never happened at all. I'd have to think about that.

'When did you say Michelle was coming?' Josh asked.

THIRTEEN

I woke up on the morning of Joe's birthday feeling brilliant. I was free again, free of Josh, and it hadn't been too traumatic. I didn't relish seeing him later on, but I felt I could handle it. Now I could enjoy the boathouse bonanza and the rest of the holiday. Even the weather was great.

Joe burst into our kitchen, very much the birthday boy, to claim his presents. Viv had found a cheap CD-ROM on fishing for him and the boys had bought him a water gun. Of course they had to try it out immediately. Everyone was wet before Viv shooed us out of the kitchen into the yard.

While Ollie was dousing his younger brothers I apologised to Joe for not having a present for him. 'Let me know what you want, Joe, and I'll get it for you tomorrow.'

'Seeing you happy again is quite a good present,' he said lightly, his attention on his new toy. He took his eyes off the water fight for a brief moment and flashed me a grin, adding – 'Don't worry, I'm sure I'll think of a better one before the end of today.'

The cars were packed with swimming gear, the lilo, the inflatable dinghy, an enormous picnic, crockery, cutlery, Thermoses, water carriers, rugs, folding chairs and over-excited children. Josh took Joe and Ollie, who were every bit as hysterical as the younger ones. We had Ned, Kate and Tom in the back. I sat in the front with the cake on my lap. John and Louise had even agreed to take the afternoon off work and were joining us after lunch.

We parked the cars by the gate and started carrying everything to the boathouse, quite a laborious business. Josh fell in with me as I carted a hamper down the path and he struggled with the lilo. 'OK?' he asked. I nodded. 'Me too,' he said. It was as if the last barrier to a terrific day had been lifted.

We set up the picnic bench. Tea was going to be the main meal, but Viv had brought pasties for lunch which we ate while making the preparations for the game. The inflatable dinghy needed blowing up and the other dinghies needed cleaning – I was doing that with Viv and Tom. Joe and Ollie – Ollie hopping about without his crutches – were putting the final touches to their raft. Josh was lighting the fire in the boathouse with the little ones looking on. He detailed them to pick up twigs for kindling – I was impressed by the way he managed to occupy them. He also kept them in order by having incredibly strict rules about the fire. Maybe I could like this guy again! But Josh with Kate, I reminded myself, was Josh at his best.

By the time the Rowlinson parents came on the scene, the various craft were lined up on the bank, tea was set, the fire in the boathouse was lit and we were all kitted out in our swimsuits and old trainers. It was actually a hot afternoon. John and Louise, determined to be good sports on this occasion, retired to the boathouse to change and soon joined us. It was amusing to see everyone lined up like that. I even couldn't help noticing that Josh looked rather white and puny compared with the others.

Joe, as VIP for the day, was given the job of blowing the starting whistle. We all got into our boats. Viv and Ned had the old wooden dinghy – and one paddle. The Rowlinsons had the fibreglass dinghy, also with one paddle. Josh and Kate were lying on their fronts across the lilo – you can't sink the lilo but they didn't look too stable. Kate looked very happy snuggling up to her big brother though, and you never knew what tricks Josh might pull out of the bag. He was an ace tipper. Tom and I had the inflatable dinghy – nice and comfortable, but no paddles. We had found a long stick to punt with, and we also paddled with our hands. Joe and Ollie looked very smug on their new raft, but it did have a tendency to spin around. They had also made themselves a punting pole.

We all paddled around for a bit. I saw Josh manoeuvre the lilo some distance from the bank, where it was too deep to wade. He said something to Kate and then slipped overboard and swam underwater towards the raft. I watched as he suddenly shot up and tipped the whole thing over. I was so busy watching that I didn't notice Viv and Ned coming up behind us, Viv paddling very efficiently. Ned leant over and pressed the side of our dinghy down so that it started to fill with water before they paddled off again. Meanwhile, Tom was urging me to head for the Rowlinsons, who, despite having a decent boat and a paddle, had barely left the bank.

Joe and Ollie quickly righted their raft. Joe had his water

gun which he squirted at Kate and Josh as Ollie paddled them into the fray. The battle was well under way.

'Come on, Charl, let's get Mum and Ned. I'm going to board their boat and steal their paddle.'

'All's fair in love and war,' I told him, and we headed towards the wooden dinghy.

Josh and Kate now turned their attentions to the Rowlinsons. They floated innocently towards them in their dinghy, which was still in shallow water. Josh wedged the lilo in some reeds and he and Kate both climbed out. Kate swims like a fish, so they made their way underwater to the side of the boat, then both stood up and leant on the side, tipping John and Louise spectacularly into the water. Louise shrieked a bit and then climbed out on to the bank. She was out of the game. John had to let Kate and Josh have his boat and made for the lilo on his own.

Tom carried out the move that we had planned the night before, stealing Viv and Ned's paddle almost before they knew what had hit them. Ned leant out of the dinghy to splash Tom's departing figure and tumbled overboard. He decided that he might be better off with Joe and Ollie and made for their raft.

And so it went on. Our winning manouevre many small battles later was all thanks to Tom. Army general in the making, that one. We swam underwater towards Joe and Ollie's raft. Josh with Kate on his back was also swimming quite slowly towards it. It was easy to see which side they were going to board and follow them below the surface. So as Kate climbed onto the raft – bravely, despite having a water gun trained on her, and as Josh tried to ease himself on board too, Tom and I were ready to pull the raft under from the same side. It worked a dream. The raft overturned and we had all five of them in the water – just like that!

The real battle was over, and Tom and I had definitely won, no one disputed it, but we all splashed around for a bit until Viv and John, forgotten until now, and possibly the official winners, cruised past in the wooden boat, paddling with their hands, and reminded us that we'd better come in for tea before we all turned blue.

As the only girls in the party, Kate and I were given the privilege of changing by the fire in the boathouse first. As Viv had said – rubbing down by the fire was a real luxury. Joe and Josh brought the boats in as we found our places round the table, leaving the chair at the head for Joe.

It's a cliché, but food never tastes so good as when you're really hungry and it's eaten in the open air. Viv had gone to town with quiches and pizza as well as sandwiches. There was ice-cream in the cool bag. And of course there was my chocolate birthday cake. John Rowlinson made us all wash out our tea mugs before making a little speech about a son to be proud of and pouring us some champagne. He had his own fisherman's cool bag clinking with the stuff. We lit the candles on Joe's cake and he duly blew them out after we'd sung Happy Birthday. He picked off the little figures I'd moulded and wrapped them carefully in kitchen paper before cutting the raft into slices. 'Good cake, Charl,' said Ollie. 'I said you were good on the pie front.'

'Yeah, good cake,' said Josh, though he was mostly taken up with marvelling at Kate's ability to smear chocolate buttercream all over her face.

'No one's ever made me such an excellent cake before,' added Joe between mouthfuls, and the adults all started talking at once to cover up the implications of this last remark and the absence of Joe's real mother from his birthday celebrations. They were also tucking into the champagne in a big way.

'Am I going to be the only sober driver this evening?' asked Josh.

'Nah,' said Viv lazily. 'A little snooze in the sunshine after this lot and we'll all be fine.'

I fancied a lie in the sun, too, especially when I didn't have too much embarrassing flesh on show. 'Mind if I lay my pallid body alongside yours?' asked Josh and winked at me as the grown-ups reacted in their various ways. Viv tried to catch my eye; Louise was tight-lipped and John, who didn't have a clue about any of it, muttered something about not crowding the young lady.

'Fine,' I said, winking back. 'As long as I don't have to apply the suntan lotion.' I stretched out like a cat on my towel, exercised, fed and now relaxed. Josh lay beside me and I sensed the band of heat that hovered between our bodies, but it didn't do anything to me now. I drifted into a doze, lulled by the distant sounds of the other kids racing around through the woods in a massive game of hide-and-seek.

I surfaced when I became aware of a totally different band of heat coming from a body stretched out on my other side – and this time it was thermo-nuclear heat! I opened my eyes a slit to check who it was and found I was looking into a brown-eyed gaze that seemed to swallow me up. 'Didn't want to wake the Sleeping Beauty. Mind if I lie here?' asked Joe, never shifting the gaze. I thought I'd better play the sleep trick.

'Course not, birthday boy,' I said drowsily, and rolled to face the other way. The electric charge was tangible. I swear I could feel every hair and curve of his body across the distance between us. I felt as if I was on fire. I hardly dared move in case our bodies inadvertently collided and caused an explosion. Meanwhile, on the other side, Josh's marmoreal figure rose and fell as he breathed gently in his sleep and had no effect on me whatsoever. What fickle creatures we are, eh? Does this particular roller coaster never grind to a halt?

You can't sunbathe for long in the Lake District. Soon there was a move to start packing up and take the younger children home to bed.

'We don't have to come now, do we?' said Ollie, nudging

Joe. 'There's still a fire in the boathouse – it's a pity to waste it.'

'I can drive the rest of us home,' said Josh.

The others left eventually and it became clear that Ollie's request wasn't altogether innocent. 'I nabbed a bottle of champagne,' he said. 'Let's go out on the raft one more time and then come back to the boathouse and drink it. It is a birthday celebration, after all.'

'I'm not sure I approve of this,' said Josh, and then when Ollie's face fell – 'Yes, let's!'

The raft accommodated the four of us very comfortably. Joe punted while the rest of us just sat and dabbled our hands in the water. I gradually noticed that a spirit of mischief was afoot among the boys. Josh and Ollie were exchanging glances behind my back. Was it possible that there was some unfinished Water Warriors business? Suddenly I was being lifted bodily and hurled into the water, fully clothed. I should have guessed. I thought I'd scare them, the rats. I swam out of sight under water for a bit. Then I surfaced, glugged and yelled and went under again. It worked a treat. Before you could say 'shark attack' Joe was striking out towards me in full lifesaver fashion. Mmm, this could be good, I thought. I waited until he was right by me and then grinned at him.

'Let me rescue you anyway,' said Joe. 'Birthday treat?' I wasn't complaining. We all reached the bank at about the same time. Josh and Ollie looked sheepish, especially when they saw I didn't have a change of clothes, and I stood there dripping and shivering.

'We've got towels,' said Joe.

'I've got a dry pair of shorts,' said Ollie.

They all sniggered for a bit.

'You can have my T-shirt,' said Joe. 'I've still got my shirt.'

'And my jersey,' said Josh.

'That's settled then,' said Joe, reaching for his T-shirt

from the raft. 'Go and change by the fire. We promise not to look.' And they all sniggered some more, rotten lot.

It was lovely in the boathouse. I peeled off my wet clothes, praying the boys wouldn't come in (they didn't). I dried myself off and pulled on Ollie's gi-normous shorts. Then I put on Joe's T-shirt. It smelt lovely – I was reminded of how wonderful his hair smelt when he'd brought Scrappy home. But they were knocking exaggeratedly on the door now and coming in. I put on Josh's jersey.

'Snug as a bug in a rug?' asked Ollie, and proceeded to work the top off the champagne. Josh didn't have any because he was driving. We three, I'm ashamed to say, got very giggly very quickly as we sat round the dying fire.

'It's been a good birthday,' said Joe, slurring his words on purpose.

'Marvellous,' said Ollie.

'Time for bed, said Zebedee,' said Josh. He gathered up the remaining things and gave them to us to carry to the Beetle. I stayed till last with Joe as he kicked the embers before putting a stone over them. 'You still haven't told me what you want for a present,' I said, as the last of the firelight flared in his face.

He stood over me for a second and started to reach out his hand. But he checked himself and looked down at me. 'There are a thousand things I could think of right now.' His voice came from the glowing shadows of the boathouse. 'But I don't think any of them would be appropriate for my brother's ex-girlfriend.'

Josh called us. Ollie sat in the front with him. I sat silently in the back with Joe and tried to keep my distance, too afraid of my feelings if I didn't.

On our return I had a brief moment with him. 'I've thought,' he said. 'Ollie was going to do a walk on the other side of Windermere with me on Friday, but he'd never make it with his ankle. Would you come instead – your presence as a present?'

Well, it wasn't quite what I'd expected, and long hikes aren't exactly my idea of fun. But when Joe treated me to another of his melting looks and my insides turned to water, I felt bound to say 'Yes.'

FOURTEEN

The day of the big walk dawned disappointingly grey, with rain a strong possibility, so there I was in a hideous blue cagoule over a sweatshirt over a T-shirt. I wore my jeans but had a pair of shorts in my backpack. The finishing touches were Viv's walking boots and some hairy socks. Had I been intending to seduce Joe (perish the thought), I couldn't have chosen a less likely outfit. Except, of course, that it matched his. His cagoule was orange, though. (Aaaagh!) I was extremely glad none of my friends could see me. Hannah might have sympathised but the appalling vision I presented would have had Maddy and Sophie rolling in the aisles.

We set off for the bus stop in silence. I felt strangely shy now that we were alone together. Joe was very formal, and pointed out sights and landmarks for me as the bus trundled along the road to the Windermere ferry. On the other side of the lake we stood for a few minutes, in our cagoules, while Joe solemnly consulted the map. I wanted to giggle, say something that would bring us back to being Joe and Charlotte wearing silly clothes, but I couldn't think of anything. Oh well. Give it time, I thought.

The weather improved as we climbed. It was hard going for a slob like me, though I could see how amazingly fit Joe was. It was no effort to him at all. He gallantly offered his hand when we climbed over stiles, but looked away as I jumped down if I took it. We finally made it to a ledge high above the lake. I was sweating like a pig. 'Do you want to stop for a drink?' he asked. 'I could do with one.'

We sat on a rock below a stand of trees. The sun came out, and the view over the lake to the surrounding fells was spectacular. I took off my cagoule and my sweatshirt and stuffed them in my backpack. Joe did the same. 'Phew, that's better,' he said, and, for the first time, smiled at me. He lay back and stretched out in the sun, the gold streaks in his hair just like the model I'd made, gold hairs glistening on his tanned muscular arms. I lay back too.

'Look at the clouds,' he said, pointing upwards. Piled white clouds cruised overhead. 'There's one that looks just like America on its side. Can you see it? That's north and that's south. And there's the West Indies.'

I have a pretty feeble imagination when it comes to clouds. 'That one looks like a sheep – no, two sheep – and a lamb . . .'

'And here comes Scrappy,' said Joe. It was true. The cloud looked like a fluffy white Scrappy bounding along (though the Scrappy we had fetched from the vet the night before could only limp on three legs). 'I could watch these clouds for hours,' he said. 'They change all the time.' He sat up. 'Epic scenery, eh? Though it's even better when we get out on the fells. You feel on top of your own world up there. Come on. We'd better keep moving. Long way to go yet,' and he hauled me to my feet.

He wasn't joking. The path led down through several more fields before we started to climb seriously again. I plodded along behind him and began to see the point of comfortable shoes and clothes you could take off. We didn't talk much. Joe was relaxed now, and no longer formal, but we needed our energy for walking. It was a very companionable silence, the rhythm of our stride broken only occasionally when Joe pointed out a hawk, hovering, or a rare wildflower, or a new peak as it rose up ahead of us.

As we got higher the scenery changed. There were rocks instead of trees, grey instead of green. Stretches of honey-smelling heather bordered the path and the grass became golden and springy underfoot. 'Another half hour,' said Joe. 'And then we *will* be on top of the world and we can have lunch.'

In all the years I've been coming here I've never done a walk like this. Can't think why. Probably because of Tom and Ned. 'I'm really glad you made me come on this walk, Joe. It's like heaven up here,' I said, when we finally flopped on to the ground.

Joe stopped in the middle of unpacking the lunch and looked at me. He drew a breath as if to say something, and then changed his mind. 'It *is* heaven,' he said. 'Especially today.' He left me to ponder that one while he busied himself with the food. Louise had done us what Joe called a fisherman's packed lunch. Viv and I slung things together any-old-how, but today everything came in watertight packages: savoury sandwiches, sweet sandwiches, apples, chocolate, fruitcake. 'Your cake's better,' said Joe.

After lunch we lay out under the sky. One or two walkers passed and greeted us, but mostly it was just us and the birds and the heather and the sun – bliss. Joe and I chatted lazily about this and that, nothing significant. Sometimes I turned my head towards him and found him looking at me and smiling as I spoke, but nothing more. I felt outrageously happy being on top of the world with him.

More clouds were starting to gather and build on the horizon when we stood up and shook the crumbs off our clothes. 'Better keep our stunning cagoules near the top,' said Joe. 'Looks like we might be needing them. Do you want to see where we are on the map?' He pointed out where we'd walked and how far we had to go to get back to Windermere. It didn't look far on the map, but I felt as though I had crossed continents.

We fell into our stride again as we trekked across the fell. The path started to drop and we made our way down through bushes and rocks, sheep occasionally straying in our way and bleating as they fled. Clouds started to cover the sun, but we were warm from walking, so we didn't mind. Sometimes the path was just scree and we slipped and slid, shrieking as we went. Other times the stream ran alongside and we splashed our hot faces. As we got lower, the shade of the mountains closed in on us and the mood felt different, less carefree. 'Pit stop,' said Joe. We found a rock to sit on and drank tea from the Thermos. He had cut his hand while we were sliding over the stones. I saw the blood as he handed me the mug. 'That looks painful. You should wash it next time we get to the stream.'

'Good old Charlotte. I love the way you're so motherly!'

I made as if to punch him. 'Gee, thanks. You really know how to make a girl feel good.'

'I mean it—' he ducked away. 'I do. I like the way you look after everyone – Ned, Kate, Scrappy, Viv.' He paused. 'Josh.'

'Well it's not something I'm proud of. I want to be – cool. Sexy. Not *motherly*!'

'Forget I said it. It was *meant* as a compliment.' Joe slung out the slops from his mug. 'Let's head on down and I'll wash my wounds.'

Soon after that it started to rain. We put on our cagoules and laughed at each other. We were still in high spirits when I slipped and fell in a gulley. Joe helped me up. I held on to his hand as we carried on walking. It was a strong, warm, dry hand. But without saying anything, Joe let go. I felt stupid.

He walked on silently. We reached the ferry, but the boat was still on the other side. I bought us each a drink and some crisps at the mobile café and sat down opposite Joe, on the wall in the rain. I couldn't think of anything to say.

'It's been a brilliant day,' he said after a while. 'Shame it's nearly over.'

'I know. I don't feel quite ready to face all the others yet. Let alone my sister! She's probably there already!'

All too soon the ferry reached our side, and before long

we were on the bus heading for home. It was still raining as we trudged down the lane to the house, cagoules on, hoods up. My time alone with Joe was so nearly at an end. I had to say something. At the bend in the lane I pulled him in, under a tree. I took a deep breath.

'Joe, just tell me – so I know it's not all in my fevered imagination – there have been so many times today when I felt – when I thought that you were going to, you know, do something or say something to me – but you always pulled back. Have I done anything wrong?'

Joe leaned against the wet bank and made me sit next to him in the rain. It streamed down our faces as he talked. 'OK. I'll tell you. Of course you haven't done anything wrong! But you know, all those years you fancied Josh – and everyone knew? Well, all that time, I was besotted with you, right? It was my secret. No one knew. I didn't want anyone to know. You seemed so pretty and so kind and I never thought you'd even notice me. And then, this year, the night when we were looking after Scrappy, it seemed like all my fantasies were coming true. When you hugged me, I was on cloud nine. But then, in the morning, everything was different. Suddenly you were going out with Josh. I couldn't believe it! I could see that you weren't even happy – it was so unfair.'

I was going to say something about Josh but Joe carried on. 'If we got together after all this time, it might be like you and Josh. I don't know if *I* could handle it. And what if it all went horribly wrong? Three days ago, you were still going out with my brother. How can I be sure you won't want him back? He's older. He's better looking!'

Rain was clinging to those fabulous eyelashes. I took his cold, wet hands and held them both in mine. I looked up at him. 'I won't hurt you Joe. I promise. I really wish I hadn't had that thing with Josh. It was all so stupid. But I can't bear for us never to be alone together again. It was too nice, too special.'

'It was, wasn't it?' He grinned at me and then, quickly, so fleetingly I barely knew it had happened, placed a gentle, rainwashed kiss on my lips. I was still registering the aftershock when he stood up and walked on down the lane.

I followed, just a little more hopeful than before, to where I knew Michelle would be waiting.

FIFTEEN

'Bottie!' There was a tremendous squeal as we were washed up, dripping, in Viv's kitchen. (Maybe I haven't mentioned my sister's charming pet name for me.)

Michelle was about to hug me, but she stood back abruptly. 'Ugh! You're all wet! What have you been doing?'

Viv stepped in before I even had a chance to say hello. 'Go and get out of your wet things immediately, you two. Joe – Louise's been fretting so you'd better get on home. Come over later if you want – Josh is. Charlotte, I've put your washed jeans and T-shirts in the airing cupboard – so you can change into something warm. Michelle can help me serve the supper.'

I hadn't realised quite how wet I was, but I certainly didn't feel cold as I climbed the stairs. Joe was gone before I'd said goodbye and there was a vision in the kitchen that was my sister. As I had stood there making puddles in my cagoule and sopping wet jeans and walking boots, Michelle had most definitely taken centre stage in her white strappy top and extremely short cut-off jeans. Her skin was a deep tan and her hair was bleached white-blonde. Her make-up was carefully applied, I noticed, and quantities of silver bangles jangled on her wrist, taking the attention slightly, but only slightly, away from the little ring and chain that perched in her pierced navel, glinting among the expanse of smooth brown skin. I was already missing the blissful fortnight I'd had with no competition. But it was a long time since I'd seen her, and I was dying to hear all about Corfu, so I changed quickly into my dry clothes and ran down for supper.

'We'll start again, shall we,' laughed Michelle, giving me a sisterly hug. 'Wow! You look so healthy! All bright-eyed and bushy-tailed – you make me feel like some kind of sleaze!' She looked over to Ollie. 'And why didn't anyone text me to warn me what a hunk cousin Ollie has become?'

Ollie blushed prettily and said something like 'I don't think "anyone" has noticed,' before being interrupted by Michelle asking how soon Josh was coming over. (Ha! I thought. Little does she know what I know . . .)

'We are going down to the weir after supper, aren't we?'

'Of course,' we all told her.

'Because I've got so much to squeeze into so little time. Viv reckons we should go into town for the market tomorrow morning, Charl, and perhaps somewhere touristy and lakesy in the afternoon. And then, as it's our last night, I'm pushing for a barbecue at the boathouse in the evening. What do you think? Do you think the Rowlinsons would come too? We can have a family picnic on Sunday before we go. That way I think we'll have just about covered everything.'

Phew! I'd forgotten what a whirlwind Michelle was. I always knew we were travelling in different lanes.

After supper she replaced her shorts with tracksuit bottoms in deference to the brambles and wouldn't sit still until she could hear Josh and Joe's voices in the courtyard. They were preceded by Kate, who burst into the kitchen where we were, saying, 'Come on, everyone. We're all going down to the weir!'

'*We're* all going to the *weir*! *We're* all going to the *weir*!' sang Ned.

'And *Scrappy*'s going to the weir, too,' said Viv. 'On a lead. Can you cope, Charlotte?'

'Maybe I should take her,' said Michelle. 'Charlotte's not always very good with dogs, are you, Charl?'

'I think you'll find that Charlotte is extremely good with this particular dog!' said Viv. 'Charl, I can't believe we haven't had a moment to tell Michelle why Scrappy has a bandage on her leg!'

'Silly old girl,' said Michelle. 'Did she fall down a rabbit hole then?' Josh came in at that moment. 'Josh!' Michelle coloured. 'Hi!' And she moved as if to throw her arms round him and go 'Mwah'.

But Josh stayed put. 'Hi, Michelle.' (He was embarrassed, and so he should be.) He nodded to me. 'Are we off then?'

'Yes, yes, let's go,' said Michelle. We were all outside before she noticed Joe. 'Hey! And isn't Ollie's little friend growing up too! You'd better watch out, Josh. You'll have serious competition soon!' Joe lowered his eyes demurely, but managed to give me a quick smile before pairing off with Ollie.

Michelle followed with a slightly nonplussed Josh. Kate and Ned scampered along after them, leaving me with Tom and Scrappy dragging on her lead. Tom held my hand (and I'd thought he might never do that again) and said, 'Isn't it great having Michelle here? It feels just like old times again.'

As on my first night, the rain had cleared to give a beautiful fresh evening. I felt almost as though I was being given a fresh chance at the holiday. It was as if the episode with Josh had never happened. And Joe was my secret. I knew better now than to make my feelings public.

Unlike Michelle. She was all over Josh. Or would have been if he had let her. I could see her working at it even from a distance. She flashed white and tan and jangly silver as she swayed along. From time to time I also caught her voice drifting over to where Tom and I were hauling Scrappy out of the brambles. 'Well, Josh, I hope my little sister hasn't been giving you too much trouble this year when I wasn't here to protect you! . . .' And, 'Any chance of you and me slipping off to the pub tonight when all the younger ones are out of the way? I've got used to having a rum and Coke at sundown.' I wondered when Josh would put her straight about what had really happened. I assumed he would. I assumed *someone* would, though I thought it probably wouldn't be me.

But when Michelle came into our room later that night – having persuaded Josh to take her to the pub – I realised that perhaps no one had said anything. She was obviously ruffled. 'Charl,' she whispered loudly. 'Are you awake?'

'Mmm?' I answered sleepily. I wasn't sure I wanted to hear what she had to say.

'How d'you find old loverboy Josh this year?'

'Fine,' I said warily.

'Well, I suppose he never really talks to you properly anyway. Too embarrassed probably – you making your cow eyes at him – but with me, well, he's usually very friendly.'

(*Very* friendly by all accounts, Michelle.) I chose to let her rattle on.

'But, there we were in the pub, me all bronzed and irresistible, open to offers, you know how it is, and well, he just didn't seem to fall for it. Weird, because all the time we were in Corfu I couldn't keep the lads away. But Josh – well. And he is very attractive these days. I can see why you had a thing about him – I mean even *I* quite fancy him now. But he really wasn't interested. I tried to find out if he had a girlfriend on the quiet but he wouldn't tell me. Kept making jokes and saying sarky things, you know the way he does . . .'

I most certainly did. But I wasn't letting on.

'Still, I might work on him. What do you think, Charl? You don't mind? I mean, I know you're madly in love with him and everything, but he is more my type, isn't he?'

I kept quiet. In fact I pretended to be asleep, though

inside, I have to admit, a small and rather unsisterly satisfaction was taking hold.

Saturday! Our last full day. I couldn't believe it. I so much wanted a bit more time with Joe on his own, but I had no way of telling whether or not I would get it, especially with Michelle here.

She was slightly calmer over breakfast, and I finally managed to hear about Corfu, though of course it was a fairly predictable saga of divine men falling head over heels in love with her. (I'd forgotten just how self-centred she was.) And we managed to tell her about the various dramas that had befallen Ollie and Scrappy. But still no one let on about me and Josh. I even began to wonder if anything *had* happened. Perhaps no one wanted to be the one to tell Michelle. Ollie, now very much in favour, wanted to stay there. For Tom it was all too painful and anyway best forgotten. And as far as the little ones were concerned, it all happened centuries ago. I thought once or twice Viv might have said something, but perhaps she reckoned that Michelle should hear it from me, if anyone.

We went to the market. It was good fun being with Michelle. She's impossible to ignore and she struck up conversations with people wherever we went. I was glad we'd gone into town, too. I hadn't been in as often as usual this year and there were all the usual places to visit – the river, the museum and art gallery for coffee, and the busy Saturday market – particularly good for jewellery and for fabric. We sifted through the silver rings and earrings. Michelle was looking at ear studs and new bits and pieces for her navel when I came across a tray of friendship bracelets. They had some made of plaited leather with initials tooled on to them. I decided to buy one with a J for Joe. I chose one that looked the right size. I could just picture it on his tanned wrist. After all, I never did give him a birthday present. I paid for it quickly while Michelle was trying on rings and shoved the bag in my pocket. I prayed I'd find a moment to give it to him.

We chose to go to Beatrix Potter's House for the afternoon. We crossed Windermere on the ferry with a million other tourists. Tom and Ned loved looking at the familiar pictures. Ollie was rarely far from Michelle's side, nodding agreement with everything she said. Viv caught my eye from time to time, and even said at some point, 'Thank God my adolescent days are over – how ghastly to be such a slave to rampant hormones. Not that I begrudge Ollie a little attention . . .' On the way home we had to wait for the ferry at the same little mobile café I'd stopped at with Joe. We'd both felt sad there before – only yesterday! – and today I felt a terrible pang at the separation that was to come. And still I didn't really know how he felt about me. I put my hand in my pocket and stroked the bracelet. Even if we didn't get a chance to be alone, I would still give it to him before we left.

Michelle, as you've probably gathered, usually gets her way. The barbecue was on and the Rowlinsons junior were coming. In fact they had already gone on ahead when we got home. There was a note stuck to the door that said, in childish handwriting: GONE TO BOATHOUSE – PLEASE BRING KETCHUP AND SWIMMERS. The boys raced around looking for towels. Michelle grabbed her minuscule bikini, 'Though I doubt you'll get me into the freezing lake, not after the warm sea I've been swimming in,' she said.

I doubted very much that I'd be swimming either – a sunny day is one thing, a cool evening is another. But I hunted around for my swimsuit to put on under my clothes, just in case. I found it, a soggy bundle wrapped in an even soggier towel. Damn. That left my bikini. It had stayed in its bag until now. It would do for swimming in the dark, so long as I didn't have to stand next to Michelle. I put it on under my jeans and T-shirt and packed the last towel from the airing cupboard.

The others, including Scrappy, were piling into the Volvo. 'Have you all got something warm to wear after swimming? You might need something more, Michelle,' Viv regarded Michelle's midriff. 'Gets nippy around these parts in the evening. Not like Corfu!'

Michelle ran back up to our room to fetch a sweatshirt. She climbed back into the car with a sly expression on her face. 'Planning to give this to someone, Bots?' she asked me, holding out a brown paper bag. It must have fallen from my jeans pocket when I changed. 'I really think you should give Josh a break,' she added under her breath, and then, seeing the boys looking at her, changed the subject. 'Is Scrappy allowed in the water?'

I tucked the bag and its contents into my pocket again and heaved a sigh of relief. At least the others hadn't seen the bracelet. If Joe wore it they wouldn't know I'd given it to him. And Michelle obviously thought I still had eyes only for Josh. Best to keep it that way.

'I don't see why Scrappy shouldn't have a swim,' Viv was answering. 'She does love a quick dip, as long as you make sure she doesn't get too cold.'

We'd reached the lake. Viv waved us off. 'Have a good time! I'll be back for the little ones at eight. Look after them. Bye!'

The Rowlinsons had been busy. Joe and Kate had lit a fire in the boathouse and Josh had a proper barbecue going outside. The burgers and sausages were laid out ready to cook and Louise had sent along some rice and salads and even some marshmallows for us to cook at the end. Michelle instantly offered to be Josh's assistant. Ollie went to help Joe with the fire in the boathouse and Muggins suddenly seemed to be in charge of the younger children and the dog. What a lot of difference the arrival of one sister can make!

Tom, Ned and Kate were determined to swim. They stripped off to their swimsuits before I had time to persuade them to reconsider. In fact it wasn't particularly cold yet. I launched the wooden dinghy with both paddles and climbed into it. That way I could supervise the kids in the water without getting wet. Soon the three of them, and Scrappy, were swimming. There were a few shrieks as warm bodies became immersed in cold water, but it wasn't as icy as the mountain water. They threw a ball for Scrappy, who swam to fetch it. She swam strongly and was less lame in the water than out of it. After a while I shouted to Ollie and Joe to call her in. 'Can you dry her off – keep her warm?'

'Use my towel,' said Michelle. 'I *won't* be going in the water.'

'Won't you?' said Josh, with one of his leers. 'That's a shame.' I could see Michelle wavering ever so slightly. But then he said. 'Don't think I'll be going in either, somehow. You need to be under ten years old not to feel the cold.'

Ollie hopped over to get Michelle's towel. She pulled it out of her bag, scattering the two halves of her bikini as she did so. Ollie picked them up reverently and handed them to her. Clearly he, too, thought it was a pity she wouldn't be swimming. 'I think my ankle's probably playing up too much for me to go in,' he told her, and went to help Joe rub Scrappy down in the boathouse.

'The first burgers are just about ready,' called Michelle. 'Any takers?' The little ones splashed to the bank. I rowed in after them, and shooed them into the boathouse to change. Tom and Kate were fine, but Ned was blue and shivering. I wrapped him in his towel and sat him on my lap to rub him down by the fire. Joe was on his way out. He looked over at Ned cocooned in his big towel. 'Oh Ned, what a nice *kind* cousin you've got!' he said. I stuck my tongue out at him and he skipped out. Oh dear. *How* was I ever going to get him on his own?

We all sat round the table to eat. I ended up between Josh and Tom. Michelle squeezed in on the other side of Josh and Ollie manoeuvred himself to be next to Michelle. 'Ooh, got yourself a fan there, Michelle,' said Josh, enjoying the blushes that spread over Ollie's face.

'Unlike *you*, of course, I don't think,' Michelle flashed back, still angry with Josh for being impervious to her charms. 'You have fans who buy you secret presents . . .'

I inhaled sharply, only to be rescued from a surprising quarter. ''Course I buy him secret presents,' said Kate stoutly. 'I buy them with secret money from secret shops, so no one knows about them.' I saw Ollie start to relax and enjoy the show.

'And I buy secret presents, too,' said Ned, not to be outdone.

'No you don't,' said Tom – and the awkward moment had passed by. 'Anyway,' Tom carried on. 'It's our last night all together, which I think is really sad.'

I put my arm round him. 'I think it's sad, too, Tom,' I said, feeling my voice about to wobble. I buried my face in his damp hair.

'Oy, don't do that!' said Tom, wriggling away. 'That's soppy! Can I have another sausage, Josh?'

Kids! Don't you love 'em?

There was a toot from the road. 'Is it eight already?' said Josh. Viv had arrived to take the little ones home.

But Tom wasn't budging. 'Pleeease let me stay,' he whined. 'I had to go early last time and I didn't want to. And it's our last night. Pleeease.'

Viv looked at us. 'What do you think? Can Tom stay?'

Well, as long as Michelle and Josh and Ollie were still around, I frankly didn't care who else stayed or went. 'I'll look after you, Tom,' I said. 'But you could take Scrappy, Viv. She's worn out.'

'OK. Come on then, Ned and Kate and Scrappy. I've got ice-cream for pudding at home for you two.' They went without too much trouble, even Scrappy, who didn't have the prospect of ice-cream for pudding.

'Can we go out in the boat?' Tom asked me, as soon as they'd gone.

'Yeah, you two go out on the boat,' said Michelle. 'I've got this card game for four people that I want to play with the boys.' Honestly, I could throttle my sister sometimes.

Tom and I went out on the lake. The sun was setting and it was beautiful. And romantic. I heard laughter coming from the boathouse. In fact I was glad I wasn't there with the others. I felt that it was dangerous to be around Michelle when at any moment she could discover the truth about me and Josh, or inadvertently expose how I felt about Joe. And anyway, Tom, despite not wanting to be soppy, was slightly luxuriating in the sadness of our last evening. I said he always picked up on my moods. So we rowed around the lake, one oar each, the colours of the sunset dripping from them as they lifted from the water. The sun dipped below the horizon. My time with Joe was running out.

There was a call from the boathouse. 'Time to go home!' shouted Michelle. 'There's this thing on TV that we don't want to miss!' Tom and I rowed in and beached the boat. Joe and Ollie had packed up the rest of the stuff (while Michelle had continued to flirt with Josh, I presume). Ollie was looking disgruntled, but he still hung around Michelle. Poor Ol. I forgave him all his taunting in the past. I really felt for him, though I couldn't admire his taste. Had I been this transparent with Josh?

We carted everything to Josh's Beetle and loaded what we could in the boot. Josh looked at us all. He looked at Tom. Tom was extra. 'I can just about squeeze five of us in with all this junk, but I can't fit six. Joe, little bro, can you stay behind to clear up the last bits and pieces? I'll come back for you after the programme.'

'That's a bit unfair. He'll miss—' Ollie started saying, when somehow I found the strength to intervene.

'I'll stay with him,' I said smoothly. 'I've missed the last two episodes, so I don't care if I miss another. The fire needs to be kicked out and the boat put back in the boathouse anyway – and that's a job for two.'

'Are you sure, Charl?' asked Ollie, looking relieved.

'Always the helpful girl, my sister,' said Michelle, getting into the car. Ollie scrambled in after her. 'Come on, Josh, or we won't make it. See you later, you two. We'll pick you up in about an hour then.'

An hour. I had an hour.

We went back to the boathouse with our bags. 'Fancy another go on the lake?' asked Joe, as the others drove off. 'It's ace out there when it's getting dark.'

That suited me. Joe sat opposite me to row. We pulled out into the middle of the lake. The colours on the water were less spectacular now, subtler. Joe shipped the oars and the wooden boat rocked and drifted, blissfully. He squeezed my knees between his. 'Fancy a swim?' I hesitated. It looked cold. 'Come on, it's great swimming at night. Ollie and I do it often.' He looked at me. 'Got a swimsuit on?' I nodded. 'That's OK then. Ol and I go skinny-dipping but I don't think I know you well enough for that – yet!' I swooned at the very thought of it.

This was it then. My bikini was going to get its big moment. I took off my T-shirt and jeans at great speed and slipped over the side of the dinghy. Joe followed. The water was cold, but silky and wonderful, like the tarn had been. The sun had gone down, but a huge harvest moon was rising. Joe swam round me in circles. He disappeared under water and came up right in front of me. We trod water together, ripples spreading in the moonlight. He reached for my hands under water and pulled me towards him. 'If I hold you,' he said, 'we'll sink.'

'I don't mind.'

'Have you ever tried kissing underwater?'

'No, but I'm willing to try!' He put his arms round me and his lips on mine, and down we went.

We spluttered, laughing, to the surface seconds later. It was impossible!

'Again?' said Joe. It was one of the best games I've ever played.

Too soon Joe said, 'We'd better go in. I've lost track of the time. Chuck me the rope from the front of the boat. We can tow it in.'

We hauled the boat ashore and into the boathouse. The fire was still going. Our shadows were huge on the stone walls. Joe wrapped himself in his huge towel and stood by the fire to warm himself. I shivered, feeling self-conscious in my bikini, and delved into my bag for my towel. I pulled it out – Oh no!

'What's wrong?' asked Joe.

The last towel from the airing cupboard was the size of a tea towel. I held it up. 'This!' I said.

'Come here,' said Joe, 'Share mine,' and he opened his arms to draw me inside. He held me close and kissed me at last as we stood there by the fire in our wet swimming things, enveloped in his towel. I was completely intoxicated by the smell of the lake and the feel of his cold wet skin. After a while I pulled away to look up at his face. He smiled at me, and then all of a sudden his eyes filled with tears. 'I don't want you to go tomorrow,' he said hoarsely.

'Now you've started me off,' I said, and I was in tears too. 'I'm going to miss you as well. Come on, Joe, don't cry. It's our last night. Let's be cheerful. Please?' I picked up my little towel to dab at his tears. 'This is about all it's good for!' He gave a violent shiver. 'Let's stick some clothes on. Here,' I rubbed his beautiful brown back and his chest (gasp) and passed him his shirt, 'put this on.'

I pulled on my big sweatshirt while he put his shirt on. He gave me a wobbly smile. 'Thanks – "Mum"!' I made to hit him but he hugged me to him again. Something in his top pocket dug into my shoulder. 'Ouch! What have you got in there?'

'You'll never guess.' He pulled out the little figure from the top of his cake. 'Close to my heart, you see!'

'Daft thing! Oh, I nearly forgot. I've got you a present.'

'Me? I thought it was Josh you bought secret presents for!'

'No, that was Michelle getting it wrong.'

'She's a bit of a pain, your big sister, isn't she? Bit like my big brother really. They deserve each other.'

I pulled the little paper bag from my pocket and handed it to Joe. He unwrapped the bracelet. 'Tie it on for me.' He kept his eyes on mine while I tied it round his tanned wrist. It looked as good as I'd imagined – as far as I could tell by the light of the fire.

'Michelle saw it when it fell out of my pocket. She thought the J was for Josh.'

'One-track mind, that girl. You don't mind keeping us a secret, do you?'

One day I'd want to tell the world how I felt, but I didn't mind now, not while it was all so new. But then again, I was going home tomorrow, so nothing really mattered.

'You've gone all quiet. You don't mind, do you?'

I sniffed, and leant against him. I couldn't speak.

'Charl? I thought we were being cheerful.'

'What are we going to do, Joe?' I wailed. 'I've just found you, and now I'm going away.'

He stroked my wet hair. 'Don't think about that. I'm not, not any more. It doesn't get you anywhere. Tomorrow's another day, and all that. Everything changes, anyway. Who knows, you might meet someone else as soon as you get back. Things'll be different here, too. Josh will go. Ollie and I will go back to school. Kate starts in the juniors. Dad even talks about moving house. We don't know what's going to happen next, Charl.' He looked at his watch. 'And we've got precisely ten minutes before my brother comes to pick us up. So let's make the most of it.'

Wow. We did.

It was John who arrived to fetch us. We were listening out for the distinctive sound of Josh's Beetle, so we never heard John's car purring to a halt. We didn't know he was there until we heard someone approaching on foot. We sprang apart and busied ourselves gathering up the last bits and pieces and went to meet him.

'Well done, you two,' he said. 'Very noble of you.'

We got to the car. John opened the passenger door for me. I sat in the front. Joe sat in the back. 'Josh was going to fetch you. But it seems that he and Michelle had a bit of a spat. Had to sort it out in the pub.' John turned on the car radio. He wasn't one for chat. I felt Joe's hand come round the side of the seat. I reached back and held it tight. We sat like that all the way home, silent and holding hands in secret. I gritted my teeth at the thought of having to say goodbye. How could I ever do it?

John drove as far as his garage and told us to walk up to the house while he parked. As soon as we got round the corner to the windowless side of the house Joe grabbed me round the waist and pulled me to him. We kissed each other fiercely. I didn't want to let him go. We heard John shut the garage door. Joe stood back and gently traced the lines of my face with his finger. 'I love you, Charlotte,' he whispered, and suddenly crouched down as John approached. 'We saw a toad, Dad. There, I think it's waddled off now.'

John laughed indulgently. 'That's my boy! I'm sure the young lady's not interested in *toads*, Joe! Come on you two. Let's get you both into bed. You're off tomorrow, aren't you, Charlotte? I've said I'll try and get them home in time to say goodbye. No peace if I didn't. My little Kate's going to miss you, you know. She's loved having a nice big girl to play with.' Luckily I couldn't catch Joe's eye right then, but he tripped and fell against me, accidentally on purpose.

'Ooops, sorry!' he said, frantically clutching my hand and looking into my eyes for the last time. 'See you tomorrow, then.' And that was it. We both went in our separate doors.

'Hi!' Viv's voice came from the other room. 'I'm on the phone, Charl. The boys are in bed and Michelle's out with Josh. Have a bath, if you want. There's plenty of hot water!' Phew. I was able to scamper up to the bathroom and lock the door. I looked at my face in the mirror. Definitely flushed. Thank God I hadn't had to walk in on Viv, or Ollie, or Michelle. I could just soak in a nice smelly bath instead. I lay in the water and thought of Joe. I tried to fix the memories. I was going to have to live off them for a long time.

Later I popped my head round the door to say goodnight to Viv and then fell into bed. It had been a long day.

SIXTEEN

'Charl! Charl! Charlotte, wake up! I want to talk to you!' Michelle was shaking me awake. Quite roughly. 'Why the hell didn't you tell me you'd had a thing with Josh?'

I tried to get my brain into gear. What was all this? It was after midnight. 'I might as well say why the hell didn't you tell me *you'd* had a thing with Josh.' That silenced her for all of two seconds.

'But *you*! I mean, I've made such a fool of myself.'

'That's hardly my fault. So who did tell you?'

'It was Ollie, when the programme was over. I got a bit fed up with him moping around all the time, so I said something like – "You're great, Ollie, but don't you think there's a bit of a generation gap here?" and he suddenly came out with all this stuff. "Didn't put Josh off Charlotte, did it?" sort of thing. And then Josh got all flustered, and said, "Not quite the same thing, Ol." And Ollie said, "No, even bigger generation gap." So I go, "Will someone tell me what's been going on? Charl's been drooling over Josh since time immemorial – so what's new?" *"I'll* tell you what's new," says Ol. "No, Ollie, if you don't mind," says Josh. "I think I'll tell Michelle what's new – and what's now old. OK?" Ollie was really upset and stormed out – as dramatically as he could on one leg – saying, "Well, you'd just better tell her everything, because if you don't, I will!" and slammed the door.'

Oops, I thought. And, poor Ol. He must have been sore.

'So Josh bundled me into the car and off we went to the pub. In fact we went to two pubs. The first one was that lovely old one with the big fireplace. We went in there, and I'd just got settled by the fire, when Josh said, 'Sorry – this pub doesn't feel right,' and off we drove to the one we went to last night. He obviously wasn't going to say anything until we'd both sat down, so I just waited. And then he told me, Miss Bottie, that what Ollie had been referring to was the fact that the two of you had had quite a little scene going – cinemas, pubs, and quite a bit else besides. And that it was all quite public. Everyone *knew*! Except me, of course.' She glared at me.

'It was all over by the time you got here,' I said.

'So I gather. What came over you? Josh too hot to handle?'

I was about to say yes, but then I thought – why should I go into detail? It's none of her business. So I just said, 'It didn't work out, that's all.'

'*Josh* thought it was working out fine. *Josh* is really upset that it's all over. You've really quite hurt him.'

That stung. 'That's just not true. Josh was really understanding. He told me that he was all right about it. In fact, he was looking forward to you coming, and the two of you carrying on where you left off last year.' I thought I'd throw that in.

'As if,' she said, rather sorrowfully. I looked at her. She was really cut up. She sat on my bed with her tan and her sunstreaked hair and her enviable figure, and wanted to punish me for what I did with Josh.

'I don't know what you expect me to do about it,' I said.

'Well, you might at least apologise for not telling me.'

'If it makes you feel better. But honestly, I just assumed someone else would. I wasn't exactly proud of the whole business, and it did seem to upset just about everyone. You obviously had the right idea last year, doing it on the sly.'

'Thing was,' she said glumly, 'I would have been quite happy to go public. It was Josh who wasn't. He didn't want to upset *you*. And that was last year. He's really fond of you, Charlotte. But he says he just did everything wrong.'

What was Josh playing at now? The sympathy card to woo Michelle? I didn't know. I didn't want to know. I knew where my true affections lay. 'He's a complicated guy, Michelle. But I'm fond of him too.'

'Maybe you should let him know that. Did you give him the bracelet?'

Big change of subject needed! 'Do you mind if I go back to sleep now? Josh is all yours, as far as I'm concerned, apart from the fact that we're going on a family picnic tomorrow and then going home, so you'll see him for all of two minutes before we leave.'

She started to get into her nightclothes. 'Actually we might be seeing more of him if he gets the grades he wants. He's got a provisional place at UCL. Be good, wouldn't it, having Josh around to do things with? My friends would be dead jealous. You have to admit, he's a very fit bloke.'

Things were changing already. Just like Joe had said.

''Night,' I said. My real secret was safe. I could go to sleep again.

*

So. That's about everything really. We had our picnic the next day. The sun shone. We all swam. Scrappy stayed on a lead. (Joe is definitely going to train her, by the way. Viv, who I'm sure knows a lot more than she lets on, said that she thought Joe would need something to keep him busy when we'd all gone.) Michelle was particularly nice to Ollie. I could just see him blossom. It made me feel very old.

Michelle and I packed and then, just as we were leaving, all the Rowlinsons lined up to say goodbye. Kate leapt into my arms, saying 'Don't go! Don't go!' but both the boys were very restrained. Joe allowed himself to be 'Mwah-ed' by Michelle while Josh managed to squeeze me tightly and say quietly, 'I think I'll miss you more than you'll miss me,' and then, more loudly, 'You might be seeing more of me than you bargained for if I get into UCL – keep your fingers crossed!' And then he turned his attention to Michelle. But I wasn't looking, because I was saying goodbye to Joe, and I was trying not to let anyone see that I was fighting tears. He held me round my waist under my T-shirt and whispered in my ear – instead of going 'Mwah' – 'I'm putting a note in your pocket. Read it later.' And then he was gone. He just turned and ran into the house. Our family got into Viv's Volvo and drove to the station.

The train was hot and crowded. Luckily Michelle and I had reserved seats. I was having trouble keeping my face under control. 'Just going to the loo,' I told Michelle, as the train got under way. Of course there was a queue for the loo, but I didn't trust myself to read Joe's message until there was a locked door between me and the rest of the world. At last I got in. I let the tears come as I unfolded the little piece of paper. On it was a beautiful drawing of a toad and the words written around it in a circle were:

Remember what I said before we met this fella.
You are the sweetest, kindest, sexiest,

loveliest girl in the world.
Me and Mr Toad both think so.
All my love, Joe.
P.S. Please don't change too much.

OK, so I did something really corny. I stuffed the note down my bra. Yes, next to my heart.

The picture had made me smile. I splashed my face with cold water, took a deep breath and went back down the swaying train to my seat.

EPILOGUE

The rest of the holidays were pretty boring. I slept in late, shopped, went to the lido, spent time with Hannah. I filled her in on most of what had happened, but I didn't feel ready to tell her absolutely everything about Joe. He was still my secret and I wanted to enjoy him alone.

All too soon it was the end of the holidays. The evenings were crisp and the mornings were dewy. Michelle's results were OK. Josh's were good enough to make him our neighbour – well, bring him closer, come October anyway. The end-of-holiday sleepover was at Hannah's because Sophie's family had only just got back. Hannah had surprised us by really wanting to have it there. What's more, having threatened not to give anything away, she was full of it. After all, her new boyfriend lived quite near, and looked as if he was going to be around for some time.

Maddy and Sophie rolled up together. There's nothing like seeing those two for all my old insecurities to return. Maddy of course looked gorgeous, though I couldn't help noticing that her make-up was almost too carefully applied, as if to cover something up. The glow wasn't all good health and suntan. Sophie, on the other hand, wore the shortest shorts possible, showing her long brown legs off to perfect advantage. Her hair had gone lighter in the sun and her face – was this possible – had a slightly softer, less angular look than I was used to. Hey, what had happened there, then? Perhaps she had finally discovered what it was like to fall in love with someone, rather than having them all fall in love with her.

Preliminaries over, we settled down to exchange our stories. 'Come on, Charlotte. What about the lovely Josh? Did he fall at your feet?' asked Sophie.

I gave Hannah a warning look. 'Well, I suppose you could say that,' I said. And I told them all about Josh.

'And you didn't want to carry on?' asked Maddy, wide-eyed. 'A hunk like that? And him preferring you to Michelle. You must have been mad.'

'He's starting university near here next month,' I told them.

'What? Oh, introduce me, please!' Perhaps Maddy's holiday hadn't been as romantic as everyone else's. I would have to wait to find out.

'I think his younger brother sounded rather nice,' said Sophie thoughtfully.

Hannah cut in protectively. 'My turn now.' She smiled back at me. My secret was safe for a while longer.

Sophie

ONE

Here we go again. Mum: Have you packed yet, Sophie? Me: Yeah. Mum: Have you left your room tidy? Me (lying): Yeah. Mum: Have you cleaned out your hamster? Me (knowing I can't get away with this): OK, OK, I'll clean her out . . . And so it goes on, Mum and Dad taking it in turns to get frantic until we're ready for off. I suppose I am looking forward to it really.

I still feel uncomfortable about Ben. Shouldn't do really; he is horribly immature. I don't know what he thinks I could see in him. I rang Hannah to talk about him, but there isn't much to say – except that he makes me feel bad. And I don't think she would understand – Hannah's great, but she hasn't had much experience with boys. I hope for her sake that the boys on her music course are more interesting than the sad loser we saw in Boots.

We always get up early the morning we go away. Traditionally Danny and I just fall into the car in our nightclothes and sleeping bags and carry on sleeping until we get to the boat. We used to dress inside our sleeping bags, but since we both wear T-shirts to sleep in these days it's just a question of adding shorts. It isn't as if the people on the boat are worth dressing up for. Travelling seems to take for ever: five hours of fruit machines on the ferry and another five hours in a hot car driving on the wrong side of the road. One day my parents will think of some other way to get a suntan, something shocking like a package tour to Greece.

As soon as we're in France it's, 'Look, Sophie – a *chien*!'

'Yes, Mother, it's a dog. Wow.'

Or, 'Look, Sophie, a cathedral/river/horses,' or whatever.

'Mother, I'm not a kid. I don't have to have things pointed out for me.'

Ma looks crestfallen. Oh dear. I suppose it's because *she* gets excited by these things. Danny's almost as bad. '*Ball trap!*' he reads; and then cackles. He does this every year. Even I know that *ball trap* is clay-pigeon shooting. He reads all the signposts in a Eurotrash accent. Every single one. Give me strength.

I know we're getting close when Mum just can't help starting up again – 'Look, Sophie – sunflowers!' Admittedly there are great fields of the things, all busy turning their little faces to follow the sun, but – you know – see one field of sunflowers and you've seen them all. Mum doesn't seem to realise this. Every year she marvels all over again.

Dad concentrates on the driving, but even he seems to find France perennially wondrous. He positively encourages Danny. I can't understand how they manage to be so cheerful. I'm tired, hot, stiff, bored silly and bursting for a decent loo – *not* a hole in the ground, like the ones you find in roadside cafés.

At last we peel off the motorway. Ma and Pa squabble over the navigation of the last few turnings – perhaps they get tired too – and finally we're there, hauling up the road to the campsite and the *manoir* that goes with it. We park on the main drag, and pile out to book ourselves in and find our courier.

It's strange, this part. The campsite is humming – kids on bikes, people in swimsuits, olds playing *boules*, teenagers drifting about. All the activity takes place on a road that goes across the top. There's a bar, a shop, loos, showers, washing-up places, the office, table tennis, bike sheds, swimming-pool, all down this single highway. And that's where it all happens, with human traffic constantly passing backwards and forwards along it.

Like about a third of the people here, we're camping with a company called Suncampers. They provide the tent and all the camping gear. It means you get the buzz of being under canvas – if you like that sort of thing, and the parents obviously do – without the hassle of carting all the stuff around. It's not even particularly cheap – you only have to look at all the posh cars to see the types who can afford it, but my ever-so-slightly Bohemian family seem to gain comfort from the fact that they're slumming it in a tent, rather than renting a gross *caravilla*. Ho-hum. Personally, I usually try to make friends with someone in a caravilla as soon as possible. Better than a tent when it rains, I find.

Suncampers have their own couriers to meet and greet, usually gap-year kids and students. Quite funky sometimes. Certainly tanned and fit from spending all summer on a bicycle. I fell in love with a courier at this very campsite when I was about eight – only to be hopelessly disillusioned when I discovered that he had a girlfriend. To this day I can remember seeing them together for the first time – somewhere near the table tennis tables as I recall. I was grumpy for days – Mum and Dad still tease me about it!

We trooped over to the big green-and-yellow tent that served as the Suncampers' office. There were posters and notices on a board outside and chairs and a brochure-covered table inside. We went in. Mum and Dad sat down. Danny and I hung around looking at the posters.

There were three couriers, two of them women. It took them a while to notice us because they were having a heated discussion about an awkward family who had just left. They spoke in English, so it was hard to pretend we hadn't overheard. My father coughed loudly and they all turned round together. One girl was the wholesome, friendly type, the other was the small bossy sort. The guy was the courier of your dreams – lean, tanned, short hair, white teeth. Very fit. He looked French, but he introduced himself in perfect public-school English. 'Hullo. I'm Jacy. You must be the Morris family. Sign in here with Coralie before I take you over to Reception, and then you can follow me to your tent.'

Mum was obviously about to tell him that we'd done this

for ever and knew the ropes, but I could see that she was charmed, and simply thanked him. Dad was already signing things for the lovely Coralie, with Danny close behind. I was left eyeballing the weaselly girl, who wore a badge with the name Sonia. I couldn't think of anything to say, so went with Mum back to the car to get our passports for Reception. And then it was time to get back into the hot car and crawl along in low gear after Jacy on his bike.

'La Grange', as this campsite is called, is spread out over a large area. Parts of it are in a wood, others are on a slope that leads down to a lake, and there is the most recent *prairie* (say it with a French accent), which is like a little suburbia of green-and-yellow Suncampers' tents. The trees between the pitches haven't had a chance to grow yet, so I really hoped we'd be in the old, wooded bit, where you have shade and some privacy. I breathed a sigh of relief when Jacy's bike squealed to a halt and he hopped off at a pitch on the edge of the trees and unzipped the front of our huge tent, set up the sun umbrella over the table and righted the chairs that were leaning against it. He did this with a wonderful cat-like grace which had Mum and me mesmerised. Well, me anyhow.

So. Here was our home for the next two weeks. It had three bedrooms and a kitchen and a bit for sitting in if the weather was bad. The shower block and loos weren't too far away – nor were the bar, the shop, the restaurant and the swimming-pool. Good weather was almost guaranteed. Jacy swung back on to his bike and cycled off with a wave. I sat down in the car again. Mum gave a contented sigh. 'Isn't this great, Soph?'

Danny had been investigating the tent. 'I've chosen my pit. Coming for a walk round then, Soph? See if anything's changed?' Dan's amazing. We've been to this campsite God knows how many times and he can still get excited by a new *boules* pitch or an extra flume in the swimming pool.

'You go, Dan,' I said. 'I think I'll have a shower and sort my stuff out.'

'Suit yourself,' he said, but he looked a bit disappointed.

'Hire a bike if you want, Dan,' said Dad. 'Then you can chase the girls around!'

'Da-ad,' said Dan.

I humped my bag into my 'bedroom' and glumly contemplated the thought of two weeks under canvas with my un-cool brother, batty mum, and a dad who doesn't seem to realise that he stopped being God's gift to women at least twenty years ago.

Dan drew up with a screech and a skid outside our pitch – his campsite bike had very dodgy brakes. 'How long till supper?'

Mum, Dad and I had all showered and changed. Mum and Dad were transformed and raring to go. Even I felt a little less uncomfortable. I wore jeans to cover my white legs (well, white compared with people who hadn't just arrived) and a gauzy top with long sleeves. Another tradition – arrived at after years of Mum trying to cook for fractious children when she was knackered herself – is that we eat in the campsite crêperie the night we arrive. La Grange has quite a cool crêperie and tonight it was almost empty.

I had been quietly taking in the talent as we walked down the main drag, but most of the kids were small, and very probably Dutch – with white-blonde hair and brown legs. I peered into the bar as we went past, but that was pretty empty too.

'Did you see anyone our age on your travels, Dan?'

'Oh yes,' he said, as if it went without question. 'Loads. Looks quite lively.'

'Where've they all gone, then?'

'I dunno. Probably took one look at the gorgeous Sophie Morris and knew they couldn't compete, so they crawled away to die.'

'Thanks, Dan. So where are all the guys?'

'Fainted.'

'God you're so funny. There must be somewhere they all go in the evenings.' I didn't like not knowing, didn't like the thought of a scene that I wasn't part of.

'Don't worry,' said Dan. 'I'll sniff it out for us – no problem.'

'I'm not that bothered,' I said. 'It's always the same bunch of losers. Or *French*.'

'Heaven forbid that they should be French,' muttered Dad under his breath, but I chose not to hear him.

'You're so snooty, Sophie,' said Dan.

'Just because you *like* sad people,' I said, 'doesn't mean that I'm going to get thrilled about them.'

Then the waitress arrived with the menus.

I don't know why I felt quite so vehement or why the prospect of the fortnight ahead filled me with such gloom. Perhaps it had to do with me and my friends promising to have holiday romances. Fat chance I stood if I couldn't even meet anyone! More probably it had something to do with the scene I'd left behind and all the business with Ben Southwell. I quite enjoy the sense of power I get when blokes fancy me, I suppose, but I hate it when they go all soppy and start talking about being *in love* with me. Nothing puts me off so quickly.

Brother Danny is the other problem, though he wouldn't know what I was talking about. He's so darned straight and honest and friendly and upfront – but he's never been the slightest bit cool. He doesn't care what trainers he wears or if his T-shirts have holes in them. He even likes classical music, for God's sake, and Abba! He just says, 'I like it.' If I say, 'But only sad people like X – whatever,' he just looks at me with that infuriating 'what's-the-big-deal' look of his. He's like Mum, really, easily pleased. And this year, now he's sixteen, things have changed a bit. He's still straight old Dan, but with his new haircut he's actually quite good-looking. Even Maddy's started batting her eyelashes at him. That's another thing. My friends, who used to commiserate about the awfulness of having an older brother who is grandma's pet, teacher's pet, etc., are now starting to insinuate that I'm *lucky* to have an older brother! A different older brother, maybe, but *Dan*!'

'OK, sweetheart?' Dad hates me being silent. 'Pizza up to scratch?'

'Fine,' I said.

'Another Coke? Dan? We'll have another beer each, won't we, *chérie*?' He beckoned to the waitress and ordered more drinks for us all. She said, *'Bien sûr, Monsieur, tout de suite,'* and sashayed off in that way that French women have.

'Wow,' said Dad, the old lech. Mum slapped him on the wrist and smiled indulgently.

'In your dreams,' she said.

'Mine, too,' said Dan wistfully.

'Never mind, bro,' I said.

The waitress reappeared. She looked like *'L'Arlésienne'* (I've been doing Van Gogh in art), all raven tresses and black eyes with a perfect olive tanned skin. *'Merci,'* said Dan as she passed him his Coke, and was rewarded with a wonderful slow, full-lipped, white-toothed, sensuous smile.

'Concentrate on your food, chaps,' said Mum, catching my eye.

We all fell into bed shortly after our meal. It was only half-past ten our time, but eleven-thirty French time, and we had been up since four-thirty. Needless to say, the lively bits of the campsite were still humming – as if to taunt me.

Two

'Soph? Wake up, Soph. Dan's fetched the croissants and there's peaches for breakfast too.' I don't know why Mum gets so worked up. We have croissants from Tesco.

I grunted. 'It's too early.'

'Eleven o'clock French time.'

'That's ten o'clock my time. Too early.'

Dan's voice. 'Come on, Sophie. We can have a swim before it gets too crowded.'

Even less reason to get up. Half an hour later Mum unzipped my door. 'Mu-um!'

'Come on, love. I want to put the breakfast stuff away, and Dad will eat your croissant if you don't claim it.'

'Oh all right.' I stumbled out into the extremely bright morning in my knickers and T-shirt and slumped into the chair nearest the hedge.

'Croissant. Eat.' Mum handed it to me and proceeded to wipe the table around me. I crammed it into my mouth, all flaky crumbs and buttery grease, as Danny squealed round the corner into our pitch on his bike. Except it wasn't Dan. It was Jacy.

'Hi, Mrs Morris! I've just come to check that everything's working and OK.'

Oh no. Not when I'm looking like this. I decided to stay sitting. He couldn't know I was in yesterday's knickers. Bits of my croissant had fallen on to the ground by the hedge. Suddenly I saw a tiny fieldmouse shoot out of the hedge and grab a large crumb. Now I don't mind small animals – I have a hamster after all – but this one scuttled so fast, I screamed and leapt up from my chair. 'Eeek!'

Mum and Jacy looked at me. 'What's up, Soph?'

I felt very stupid. 'A mouse,' I said lamely, tugging at my

T-shirt and not knowing where to put myself as I stood there, white-legged.

'It's only a fieldmouse,' said Mum, smiling at Jacy.

Jacy looked at me coolly. 'It's when you have bare feet,' he said. 'You're afraid they're going to run right up your legs.'

'I'm going to wash,' I said, and dived into the tent. It was bad enough standing there half-dressed, but the way Jacy looked at me, I felt as if I hadn't got any clothes on at all. I could hear Mum and Jacy in the kitchen bit of the tent. The cooker was different from last time and we hadn't quite sussed it out. I prayed that they wouldn't get any closer. They went outside again and Jacy got on his bike. 'There's not a lot we can do about fieldmice,' I heard him saying, and winced, 'but let me know if there are any other problems. *Au revoir*!'

Pretentious berk, I comforted myself.

By the time I was washed and dressed, and possibly ready for a swim, Dan was back from the swimming-pool. 'It's getting really crowded now,' he said. 'Can't move for armbands and rubber rings. Fancy a walk down to the lake, Soph? That's where it all happens, apparently, this year.'

Last year it had all happened round the football pitch for Dan. And me, really, but I'd only been thirteen then. I'd tagged along with a Dutch girl and we'd ridden bikes and swum and played crazy golf. I hadn't been aware of a 'scene'. This year I felt different. And I wouldn't have been seen dead playing football.

'OK,' I said. I suppose we had to start somewhere, though I'd actually quite felt like a swim.

'Go on, darling,' said Mum. 'You know you'll start enjoying yourself once you've made some chums.'

Chums! Good old Mum.

'That's my girl,' said Dad from where he was sitting in the

car (go round any campsite and you'll find half the men sitting in their cars). 'Go and sort out the talent.'

Talent! Good old Dad.

Dan and I set off down the path that led through the woods, past the manoir and the tennis courts and down to the field by the lake. It was cool and green and the dust that we scuffed up as we walked shimmered in the shafts of sunlight that filtered through the leaves high above. After the trees the field seemed like a bright square with an even brighter strip of lake beyond it. There were a few kids out on the lake in pedaloes and some wrinklies fishing, but otherwise the place was almost deserted.

I raised an eyebrow at Dan. 'Happening, huh?'

'Well, it's humming with wildlife!' he said. It was true. The birds and the crickets made one hell of a racket. But no teenagers. We came to a heap of burned logs and ashes. 'Someone said something about bonfires,' he said.

'Looks like boy scout stuff to me,' I said. 'But you'd be more likely to have fires at night, wouldn't you?'

'Yeah. The people I heard it from were French, so I expect I got it wrong.'

'You were hanging around with *French* people?'

'We are in France.'

'Yes, but—'

'I want to improve my French.'

'Creep.'

'There is also this vision in an orange bikini, on a bike.'

'I haven't seen it. Gone off the waitress already then?'

'Bit old for me. Anyway, someone said she had one of the French couriers in tow.'

'You have been busy, listening.'

'Best way to learn.'

Lunch was bread and cheese and salad and wine. Simple fare, you might think. Yes, but not if you'd heard the parents raving over it. 'Wow – such cheap wine . . .

*Gor*geous cheese . . . *Pe*rfect bread – *noth*ing like it in England.' Tomatoes, 'Mwah!'

It was very hot after lunch. Dan disappeared on his bike and I was alone again. I really wanted a swim. I even saw a whole troop of teenagers – they did exist! – making their way to the pool, but I certainly wasn't going on my own.

'I'll sunbathe,' I told my parents, who were dozing in the sun – Mum had slipped her swimsuit straps down and Dad was snoring already. I slapped on the Factor 15 and stretched out on the sun lounger. I could at least start on the tan.

As I dozed off I heard the squealing brakes again and looked up, expecting Dan. I was wrong. 'Hi, Sophie!' said Jacy. 'It's OK, it's not you I'm after!' (Shame.) 'I'm checking out next door. You'll be getting neighbours this afternoon.' He disappeared into the empty tent on the other side of the hedge. I could hear him fossicking about in the fridge and banging the squeaky beds. Neighbours, eh? We already had Dutch neighbours on one side. Probably some family with a million screaming kids. That's what we usually get.

I was half asleep when they arrived. I heard Jacy's bike first, and then a clattery car. Lots of car doors banged. I rolled over on to my front so that I could peer at them. Their mum got out first, from the driving seat of an ancient clapped-out estate car. A pair of boys aged about eleven bundled out after her – twins, I guessed – and rampaged around after Jacy. I was so taken up with watching Jacy's lithe, tanned body in action that I was unprepared for more members of the family. Two older kids emerged, teenagers – a lumpy boy and a drippy-looking girl. 'Come on, Emma,' said the boy. 'Mam needs us.'

'OK,' said Emma. They had broad Geordie accents. There didn't appear to be a dad.

Isn't that just typical? The first time we ever get kids our age and they're a couple of unintelligible retards. I heard Jacy talking to their mum. 'The children's courier will be over in the morning. There's plenty of organised activities for the younger ones.'

'What about the teenagers?'

Jacy laughed. 'Ah,' he said. 'Don't worry about them, Mrs Robson. You'll find that the less organisation they have, the better!' And he swung off on his bike.

I picked up a magazine and turned on to my back again. But I couldn't believe what I was hearing. 'You have a rest, like, Mam.' It was the girl. 'Mark and the boys are goin' a unload and I'm doin' the supper.' (Comedy Geordie accent here.) Their mum protested, but not much.

'Go on then, lads,' she said. 'Get to it!' So. Byker Grove comes to La Grange. I could have stayed home and watched the telly. I decided to make myself invisible before they tried to get friendly, and went inside the tent to catch up on my diary. At least I can say what I like there without anyone telling me I'm a snob/intolerant/narrow-minded,etc.

Dan came back – big smile on his face, big ice-cream in one hand. He threw his bike down. For once I felt quite glad to see him. But he spotted the newcomers and went over to talk to them instead.

'Hi,' he said. 'I'm Dan. Long journey?'

'You could say that,' said Mark. 'A day to come down south from Newcastle. Overnight ferry and then driving through France today. We're shattered! And our mam's never driven in France before. Bit hairy on the roundabouts, eh, Mam? I'm Mark by the way, an this is ma sister, Emma.'

'Hi,' said Emma. 'Is there anything for the likes of us to do on this site, then?'

'Come to the bar with us later,' said Dan. 'That seems to be where the evening starts. You should meet my sister. She's about the same age as you. See ya.'

He came on to our pitch. 'Weren't asleep, were you?' he shouted noisily at the parents, waking them up. 'Where's Sophie then?' He saw me inside the tent.

'Dan!' I hissed. 'Why did you have to go and be all friendly to them? They're practically wearing shell suits, for God's sake! We'll never get rid of them now!'

Dan looked at me uncomprehendingly. 'Why should we want to?' he said.

We were about to eat supper when Mark came over. 'Hey, Dan lad, care for a game of footie, like, after supper? The game starts at seven-thirty. Emma's playin'. Does your sister want-a come?' He looked at me. No. I did not want to play football.

'Sounds good to me,' said Dan. 'Coming to watch, Sophie?'

'I might,' I said.

'We'll come and watch,' said Mum.

'Sounds like a fun evening to me,' I told her, but the sarcasm seemed to be lost on all of them.

I decided to roll up just as they finished so that I could at least go to the bar with Dan and maybe, just maybe, find some decent company. I couldn't stand the thought of being thrown together with drippy Emma. She'd set off wearing boys' football shorts and rubbish trainers. The *Aire des Jeux* (games area) was opposite the swimming-pool, behind the couriers' tents. It was a perfect evening and people sat watching on the bank as the players hurtled around the pitch. I found Mum and Dad. 'Dan's team are the ones without shirts,' said Dad. 'They had to put all the lasses in the other team – more's the pity!'

'Da-ad!'

'Young Emma's not a bad player, either.'

'No doubt,' I said, getting caught up in the game, in spite of myself. No one knew anyone else's name, so they simply shouted, 'Man on!' and 'Oy, mate, over here!' or *'Ici! Ici!'* It was a scramble, but clearly everyone was having a good time.

Emma scored a goal. The decider, what's more, so her and Mark's team – the shirts – were the winners. I even felt a slight twinge of jealousy as they came off. 'Big game next week,' said Dan to Dad. 'France v. England. The couriers are organising it.'

'Which team will our courier play for, then?' asked Emma. I knew she was daft.

I finally caught up with the 'scene' that night in the back room of the bar. And of course it had to include Emma and Mark. I discovered that Mark was sixteen and Emma fifteen. There were about twenty of us, mostly a bit older than me, though I know I look sixteen. Dan was right in there, but I didn't really know what to say to these weirdos. Things perked up briefly when Jacy poked his head round the corner. He seemed to be looking for someone. Me? (Well, you never know.) Surely not. But he caught my eye. 'Hi, Sophie!' And then, 'Hi, Emma!' What a letdown. Jacy obviously had an eye for the girls, but Emma, I realised with horror, had eyes only for Dan. When the others said they were going down to the lake I decided it was definitely time for bed.

THREE

By the second morning La Grange starts to work its magic on you, however stressed-out you've been up until then. I poked my nose out of the tent. It was the misty start to a glorious day that's standard here, and it made me feel eleven years old again. I pulled on a pair of shorts and some trainers, grabbed a twenty-euro note from where Dad had emptied his pockets the night before and set off on a round-the-camp route for the shop on Dan's bike. I pedalled like a kid, feeling the wind in my hair. Only a few people were about this early: one or two joggers and swimmers, dads with tiny children who'd been awake for hours. The bike ploughed satisfyingly through the sandy track, sending little stones skittering in my wake. The manoir loomed, gorgeous through the haze, silvery dew coating the hydrangeas and red hot pokers in the formal garden at the front. I scrunched to a halt by the shop and flung the bike down.

Huge crates of baguettes and croissants were piled up by the door – they smelt out of this world. I loaded up with Orangina and peaches and baguettes and waited in the queue to pay. Only when Jacy came in with wet hair and swimming shorts, with a towel round his shoulders and looking like an aftershave ad did I realise that I had bird's-nest hair, sleep in my eyes and a terrible T-shirt – and that I cared. I pretended I hadn't seen him and stuttered out my halting request for '*Quatre croissants au beurre, s'il vous plaît*' in my best shopping French.

Jacy was picking out the ripest peaches with his back to me. He turned round as I waited for my change and called out across the crowded little shop in totally brilliant French, '*Bonjour, Sophie! Tu achètes le petit déjeuner, hein?*' And then, 'What a good girl!' As I scuttled out into the morning sunshine, his sexy grin scorched, like the bright sun, on to my retinas.

I took great pleasure in waking up the others when I got back to the tent. The Dutch family were off to the showers in single file, perfect blonde mother with perfect tiny blonde daughters, father with comedy moustache carrying baby and leading little boy, all brown legs and good humour. Yuk. The Geordie twins were bent over their table, absorbed in twin-type activities, but there was no sign of Emma or Mark.

'Bog off, Sophie,' was all the gratitude I got from my brother. But Mum and Dad emerged tousled and smiling.

'Ooh! Peaches! Lovely, darling,' said Mum.

'I'll get some coffee on,' said Dad, and went to wash out the coffee pot.

'Did you hear Dan coming back last night?' asked Mum.

'No. Why?'

'Well, it was some terrible hour. I was quite worried. But I knew the two from next door were out too, so I wasn't as anxious as I might have been. I had a word with their mum. She said they were always up half the night in the holidays.'

'Probably doing community singing round the camp fire,' I said.

'Probably,' said Mum.

Dad came back. 'Thought we'd go to the supermarket this afternoon, Soph. Want to come?'

Now I'm a sucker for shopping, wherever it is. I like French supermarkets. And with the parents in a good mood there's often the opportunity to slip in the odd garment or bit of make-up, not to mention chocolate and other goodies. 'Yes, I'll come.'

'Good. Dan's keen. He wants to get a torch. We might check out the town, too. Eat out, even.'

'Don't get carried away, Dad.'

'I think I'll go and have a wash,' I said when I'd eaten what I wanted.

'I suppose we'll let you off the washing up, since you went to the shop,' said Mum.

'I should hope so too,' I said and gathered up everything I needed for a long session in the shower.

Dan still wasn't up when I got back. Next door the twins were batting a ball about and their mum was telling them to get off to the swimming-pool, otherwise they'd wake their big brother and sister. Oo-er. It *had* been a late night. Still, I didn't see why I should hang about all morning waiting for Dan. I went into the tent and banged on his canvas door. I unzipped and zipped the zip a few times. 'Move your lazy ass!'

'Bog off, Sophie!' There. He was at it again. I wasn't having this.

I put my head into his pit. 'Wakey, wakey! You know you want to get up and come swimming with me. I'll even let you have breakfast first. Mmmm, lovely croissants. Come on, Dan!' I was getting impatient.

'Leave the poor lad alone!' That was Dad.

'Yes. Leave me alone.' I felt a major sulk coming on. This wasn't like Dan. I really didn't want to have to do things by myself.

'Come and buy some postcards with me,' said Mum. 'They sell them in the *Accueil* – the reception bit by the bar.' She gave me a nudge. 'I just saw that dishy courier going in.' Oh great. I went with her, though, just for something to do. Fortunately Jacy wasn't there any more to see me doing things with-my-mum, but I had the sweaty palms and dry throat anyway. Mum laughed when we got in, and said in an embarrassing stage whisper, 'It's Dan I should have brought. Look who's on the desk.' I studied the postcards carefully for some minutes before turning around and seeing the waitress from the crêperie.

She smiled at Mum, ''Allo. 'Ow can I 'elp?'

'Well, well!' said Mum, laughing. 'How did you guess we were English?' and then struggled to speak in appalling French. I gave Mum the postcards I had chosen and legged it back to the tent.

And ran slap-bang into Jacy again. Literally, this time. 'Whoa there!' he said, gently levering me out of my headbutt. 'Throw yourself at me whenever you like, Sophie, but let me savour the anticipation next time!' I looked up at those laughing eyes and down again where he held my wrists. I was speechless. 'See ya!' he said, letting me go and tapping me lightly on the shoulder as he swung into the *Accueil*. I was shell-shocked. Was that a come-on or what? The guy seemed to be everywhere. He was practically following me around. I walked on in a daze to our tent.

Dan sat at the table in his swimming trunks, hunched over a croissant. He looked terrible.

'So it was a good night then?'

'Brilliant,' he said, between mouthfuls. 'Get us some Orangina, Soph.'

'Say please.'

'Please. I didn't get to bed till after two!'

'A swim will do you good then. Oh come on, Dan. I haven't had a swim yet this holiday.'

'Who's fault is that? I'll come anyway, but just be gentle with me.'

I don't need to tell you that this is not typical Dan. But he's stubborn, our Dan, and I didn't want to upset him, not when I needed his company so badly.

'I suppose you won't let me go on my bike?'

'No. Walk with me. I don't want to go on my own.'

'OK, wimp.' We fetched towels and set off for the pool. The road across the top was heaving with parents and young children. Not a teen in sight, though given the early hour I shouldn't have been surprised. I assumed some of them would be bagging poolside places in the sun by now. I was right, but they weren't English teenagers. They were French. And one of them was the most stunning girl I have ever seen. She was wearing an orange bikini. It showed off her tan – so deep it was almost black – and voluptuous curves to perfection. She had beautifully cut brown hair that looked light and shiny compared to her skin, and green cat's eyes. So this was the vision in the orange bikini. I turned to Dan to say, yes, for once I see what you mean (and I hadn't even seen her on a bicycle), but Dan hadn't hung around for his embarrassment to show. He had dived into the pool.

The pool was otherwise occupied by kids having fun. And I mean kids. Screaming, splashing, divebombing, hand-standing, snorkelling kids. Three years ago and I would have loved it. Now – it was hell. I couldn't even swim a length without bumping into several million of them. And I wasn't going to sunbathe. Not next to that French pussycat.

From the safety of the pool Dan waved at the French girls. *'Bonjour, Francine! Bonjour, Suzette!'* he carolled.

'Hi, Danny!' they replied, giving cute little waves.

'Suzette?' I asked him. 'As in crêpes?'

The French girls thought he was showing off for them. I might as well not have existed. 'Danny!' they called, leaping to their feet as all the dads' heads turned as one, and jumped into the water beside him, giggling. I watched. I'd agreed with Danny when he'd said they were out of his league, but they didn't seem to think he was out of theirs. There didn't seem to be much for me to do. I really didn't want to join in their ridiculous splashing games and watch my brother making an idiot of himself as he improved his French.

'I'm getting out, Dan!' I called. 'Too crowded!'

'See you later then!' he said from the water. He clearly didn't need my company half as much as I needed his. *'A bientôt!'*

I was starting to feel really sorry for myself as I slunk back to the tent. The day was heating up. I glanced towards the Suncampers' office. It was quiet. Sonia was sitting outside, reading, glasses resting on her pointy little nose. Nor did my temper improve when I saw Mark and Emma chatting with Mum.

'Hi, Sophie!' said Emma. 'Like your bikini!' Shame I couldn't say the same about hers.

'Hi, Sophie!' said Mark. But he was all red and flustered and quickly went back to their tent, followed hotfoot by his sister. I fetched my book and the suntan lotion and dragged a sun lounger into the sun. There might not be anyone on this campsite worth talking to but at least I would go home with a tan. Now would have been a good time for Jacy to appear and ask if everything was OK. I kidded myself for a while that he might, arranging myself languorously on the lounger. He seemed to turn up everywhere else – why not here, and now? I'm sure I could convince him of my superior charms, given half a chance. Dream on, Sophie. Yeah, dream on!

Dan got back as we were about to start lunch. He'd caught the sun and looked, well – happy. 'You could have sunbathed by the pool, Soph,' he said. I didn't tell him why I hadn't. It's not like me to feel outclassed, even if she was French, and probably thick as two short planks. And probably a tart too.

'Bread, cheese and salad for firsts,' said Mum.

'And fruity little French tarts for afters,' said Dad. I couldn't have put it better myself.

The car was like an oven. Dan opened all the windows and the roof and waved at people as we drove off the site. I felt as though we were on different holidays. 'We're being followed by a vision in an orange bikini on a bicycle,' said Dad, looking rather too long in his rear-view mirror.

'That'll be Suzette,' I said.

'Ha! As in crêpes?' said Dad waggishly. I was about to put him down when I remembered I'd made the very same quip.

The supermarket was on the edge of the seaside town. Mum and Dad had the inevitable squabble about the importance or otherwise of parking in the shade. Then we went into air-conditioned shopping heaven. French supermarkets are huge and brilliant. They have CDs and stationery and clothes and shoes and crockery and bikes as well as food and cheap booze (cause for barely contained parental joy). We spent a happy couple of hours wandering up and down the aisles. I persuaded Mum to buy me a top and some flip-flops. Mum spent ages hovering over the Le Creuset. Dan lost himself first among the CDs and then the camping gear. Dad drifted from the cheeses to mustards to sausages in an ecstasy of bliss. We finally met up at the checkout. I'd managed to chuck in a few more things, like underwear and chocolate, and felt at peace with France and the world. It was only when I thought for a moment that our good-looking, tanned cashier was Jacy that I realised with a jolt that he hadn't popped into my mind for at least two hours. But what does it mean when you think you see someone wherever you go?

We piled the shopping into the car and drove to the beach. It was a very French beach – civilised, with a small car park, lots of families with grannies and toddlers, people with big picnics in coolboxes, couples playing that silly game with little bats and a ball. Old men paddled, middle-aged women sunbathed without their tops on. Well, that was fairly gross, but in other ways it felt comfortable. If I had to be seen out with my family then I was glad it was a family beach.

It was quite good to be away from the campsite. I felt that social pressures were beginning to build up. I went for a paddle and thought about it all. It was annoying that Dan had made friends first, even though they were mostly people I wouldn't be seen dead with – like lumpy Mark and drippy Emma, and some of the others at the football match, or foreign like Francine and Suzette. Certainly none of the boys were anything to write home about, except of course, Jacy. There I was thinking about him again. Jacy makes the other boys look like kids. He's so fit. With a body like his he shouldn't be allowed to go around in swimming gear. And his voice, with that public school accent that makes him sound so confident. He *is* confident. He positively oozes confidence. And charm. But he's got a cute smile. And he seems to like me. I thought about the times I'd caught him eyeing me up. Not to mention 'throw yourself at me whenever you like'. I mean, I'm used to people fancying me, but it's rare for me to fancy them too. And he doesn't seem to have a girlfriend. It certainly isn't Coralie – though she is pretty gorgeous. Or Sonia? Unlikely. And that's the sum of British talent in his age group. Which leaves the field open for more youthful contenders – like me. I'm sure I could handle it. It's about time I had a proper mature boyfriend. Not an immature idiot like Ben Southwell.

At that moment a lightbulb seemed to switch on over my head. PROJECT! I did a little dance in the waves. Suddenly everything looked better. It was a challenge. *Jacy* was my challenge, my holiday romance! I was halfway there already, I was sure. I just had to impress him a bit. Show him how sophisticated I was. He probably thought I was sixteen anyway. A small aeroplane flew over the bay, trailing a banner. *'Bonnes vacances!'* it said. Thank you, I thought. Don't mind if I do.

I jogged back, swooshing my feet through the shallows. I ran like a Baywatch babe. I ran like the wind . . . It's all right – help is on its way! The others had made a pitch under our green-and-yellow Suncampers' umbrella, so they were easy to spot. Dad and Dan were delving into the coolbox. Mum was behind the umbrella chatting someone up. You can't take her anywhere! Still in Baywatch mode I dived under the umbrella and grabbed at Danny. 'Don't worry, little boy! I'll rescue you!'

Dan swatted at me. 'Oy! Pamela! Lay off!' He shoved me into the sand and ran his cold can of Coke up my back.

'Aaaagh!' I squealed and wriggled away, tipping the umbrella on to its side. There was Mum, looking down at us crossly.

'Kids!' she said, to Jacy – what was *he* doing here? (And what does it mean when you really *do* see someone wherever you go?) – 'Don't you love 'em?'

It was not easy to regain my composure, I can tell you. 'Hi, Sophie,' said Jacy, with *that* look again. I sat up demurely. 'It's my day off – but can I get away from my job? My fault for coming to the nearest beach. I should know better than to get close to a green umbrella!' It was OK. He was laughing. 'I'm telling your mum the best place to eat round here. And that's easy enough because I'll probably be going there myself later.' He turned to face the road into town. 'It's on the main road along the beach, just before you get to the apartment blocks. There's loads of restaurants but this one is called Hotel de Plage – I think. Blue-and-white awning, tables outside. Looks ordinary but the food is excellent, especially the *fruits de mer.*' He pronounced it 'fwee de mare'. 'You haven't lived till you've eaten their *fruits de mer.*' He turned to go. 'Might see you later on then. I've got things to do in town now. Bye!' And he was off up the steps to the road.

'That was a spot of luck,' said Dad. 'It will be nice to go somewhere other than a pizzeria. Get a real taste of France. You kids are old enough for that now, of course. You wouldn't have let us a couple of years ago, it was pizzas or nothing in those days.'

I really enjoyed myself on that beach. I was buoyed up by 'Project Jacy', but for the time being he was conveniently in the town. With the prospect of a grown-up boyfriend it was as if I had permission to be a kid again. Danny was on good form and we mucked about in the waves for ages. We looked in rock pools and even – don't tell anyone – built a bit of a city in the sand. We attracted quite a gathering of *enfants* and Dan was directing them in his best French to find shells and seaweed or fetch buckets of water. Whenever we got too hot we just went in the sea again, slapped on more suntan lotion and carried on. The afternoon flew by. I couldn't believe it when Dad said it was after half-past seven and that he, for one, could eat a *cheval*.

My stomach gave a lurch. I should have been hungry too, but I actually felt slightly nervous at the thought of bumping into Jacy again. I had to remind myself that I probably had the upper hand here, as long as I stayed cool – and sophisticated. As far as I could see, being too young was my only problem.

The restaurant was within walking distance. We all felt slightly dazed from our afternoon in the sun. We decided to sit out on the street so we could watch the world going by (and I wanted to look out for Jacy).

We ordered drinks and the waiter brought us the menus. Dan put his down very quickly and said, 'I'll have the pizza.'

'Oh Dan!' said Mum. 'I thought you were going to be adventurous. I'm going to try the fish baked in cider. It's so fresh here.'

Dad was positively groaning with anticipation. 'Amazing. The French just *have* it, don't they? I'm completely spoilt for choice here. Some sort of fish is the obvious thing to go for. Ah! Crab soufflé! That sounds good. I'll go for that. And what about you, Sophie?'

Well of course I wanted the pizza too, but as I read down the menu the words *fruits de mer* leapt out at me. *That's* what Jacy had been recommending. Fruits of the sea. Even my French could cope with that. Sounded OK. 'I'll have the *plateau de fruits de mer*, please, Dad.'

'Ooh, sweetheart,' said Mum. 'Are you sure?'

''Course I'm sure, Mum. I'm growing out of pizza, like you said. Have to try new things sometimes, don't you?'

'Well done, Sophie,' said Dad approvingly. 'Don't put her off, Sal. We should be encouraging her.' Mum smiled as the waiter came to take our order. Dan was smirking, but I don't know why. He'll still be eating pizzas when he goes out for business lunches.

'I wonder what's been going on at the campsite this afternoon,' said Dan as we waited for our food. 'I told them all I'd go down the pool this afternoon.'

'All of them, eh, Dan? I don't know how any of them will survive without your scintillating company, let alone the lovely Emma.'

'Don't knock Emma,' said Dan shortly.

'Sorr-*y*. Didn't know you cared.'

'They're people, Emma and Mark.'

'Oh, sorry. I hadn't realised.'

We didn't get any further. 'Look, you two,' said Mum. 'Our food's coming.'

Dan was served his pizza with a flourish. A second waiter came along with Mum's fish and Dad's crab soufflé. 'Don't mind me,' I said. 'Go ahead and start.' Secretly I was pleased that mine hadn't come. There was still a chance that Jacy might turn up and see me eating sophisticated *fruits de mer*. I kept thinking I could see him coming our way, but then there were quite a few dark-haired guys with tanned skin and white T-shirts around.

Dan was halfway through his pizza when our waiter appeared carrying an enormous plate. Could this be what I had ordered? He put it down in front of me with a smile. 'Bon appetit, Ma'mselle.'

Oh . . . my . . . God.

This plate had eyes and feelers. It had disgusting globby things and jellyish things. It had shells and legs.

And there was Jacy sitting down a few tables away, with Sonia.

Jacy saw us and waved. Then he turned back to Sonia. She said something to him and he looked up again. Looked straight at me. He was trying to say something without shouting across the other tables. I tried to make out what it was he was saying. Then I realised. It was 'Bon appetit!'

So that was it. I was going to have to eat the things. All around us other people were tackling hideous platefuls. I watched them carefully. I copied them. Gloop went an oyster. I shuddered as it went down. Eughh. Glop went a mussel. It tasted of seawater. Snap, crack, scoop, went the half-lobster – that wasn't so bad, actually. I tore off lots of bread, ate it and ploughed on. Dan finished his pizza and looked on admiringly, his mouth open. 'Well done, Sophie!' said Dad. 'Tackled like a native!'

'Are you sure you can manage all that, darling?' Mum was looking anxious. She'd nearly finished her fish. 'What a dark horse you are. I had no idea you liked seafood.' I didn't answer. I was concentrating too hard on getting the revolting stuff out of its shells and down my throat. I kept refilling my glass with water and washing it down. Every now and then I caught a glimpse of Jacy over the way. His head bobbed around as he talked to Sonia. I saw them ordering but no food seemed to appear.

I was nearly there. I had to be. Mum, Dad and Dan had finished ages ago. Dad and Dan were deep in discussion about the exchange rate and Mum was happily getting off her face on white wine. Maybe I didn't have to finish it. Maybe it would be cooler to leave a bit – as if it was no big deal. I decided to let myself off the last few and sat back with a sigh. I looked up to see Sonia's and Jacy's meals arriving. They were having pizza.

I started to feel queasy on the way back in the car. The sick feeling didn't go away. It got worse. 'Dad! Stop the car! I'm going to be sick!'

Mum looked over at me. 'Oh my goodness, Giles! She's gone green!' Dad pulled over as soon as he could. I only just got out in time. I threw up. Copiously.

Mum put me to bed as soon as we got back to the campsite. I felt terrible. Hot and achey as well as queasy. My head was pounding and my legs felt leaden. I felt shivery as well as burning. Mum's a good nurse, she didn't panic. She found me a bottle of cold mineral water and wiped my forehead with a flannel. Dad flapped about. 'Do you think she needs a doctor? Do you think we should ask the couriers? Do you think it was all that seafood? Perhaps it's food poisoning!'

'She'll be fine. I don't think it's just the meal. I think she had too much sun. Anyway, we know that two of the couriers aren't even here.' I didn't really want Jacy to know I had thrown up my sophisticated meal but I was past caring. I wanted everyone to go away and leave me to die in peace. But not even my body would allow me to do that. I was up and down most of the night, staggering to the toilet block. How I wished we were in a caravilla with its own loo. How I wished that somehow the divine Jacy would come and make me better.

FOUR

I slept quite late in the morning. I could tell when I woke up that it was very bright outside, and the campsite noises were mostly of cars starting up as people left for the beach. I turned away from the light and let the day come at me gently. I no longer felt sick. My skin felt hot and dry and I ached a bit, but apart from that I felt more or less like a human being.

There's not much you can do in a tent without being heard. My bed obviously creaked enough to let Mum know that I was awake. The zip of my compartment opened and her head appeared. 'How are you feeling this morning, sweetheart?'

'Bit better.'

'Would you like me to bring you a drink?'

'It's OK, Mum. I can get up. I need to go to the loo anyhow.' I started to get out of bed. It was harder than I thought. My burnt bits felt really stiff. Down came the zip.

'Let me help you.' I staggered into the open. Boy, was that sun bright. 'Sunglasses, that's what you need.' Mum plucked hers off her nose and put them on mine. The relief was instant. Her bathrobe was on the chair and she wrapped it over my T-shirt and knickers and walked me to the toilet block. I looked at the ground. Mostly I felt too lousy to care, but I wasn't totally keen on meeting people looking like this. I should add that Mum's bathrobe is extremely ancient, pink towelling and hideous and that her sunglasses look like something Edna Everage would wear.

When we got back she hustled me into the living room bit of the tent and pulled the gingham curtains across the plastic windows, but not before I saw Emma, Mark, the twins, a twin-aged friend and a large teenage girl all lined up looking at me. And not before my eagle eye spotted the designer label on the large girl's jeans. I'd have to be more than ill for an Earl jeans label to escape my notice. Danny, as my brother, felt permitted to say, 'Now there's a sight for sore eyes,' much to everyone's amusement.

'Yeah, hilarious,' I grumbled as Mum sat me down in front of a sliced peach and a glass of mineral water. I could *hear* them laughing.

Dan came in. 'Just going over to Becky's, Mum.'

'Will you be back for lunch?'

'Probably.'

'Dan!' I called back. 'Is Becky the one in the Earl jeans?'

'I dunno,' said Dan. 'She's the one out there if that's what you mean. See ya!'

Fancy not noticing jeans as classy as that. Even if she was quite fat. Good taste, though. She might be worth getting to know. I turned my attention to my peach – as far as Mum would let me. '*Every*one's been asking after you,' she said. 'Mark was very concerned – and their mum. And that nice Dutch family next door. And the couriers, they all asked after you. Even Jesse.'

Jesse? 'Jacy, Mum, as in Jaycee.' Hmm. How did Jacy know? Was I pleased at his concern? Anyway, it was sunstroke, Mum said, so nothing to do with eating seafood.

'I think you'd better stay under cover today.' Mum went on. 'We can bring one of the sunbeds in for you to lie on.'

'But, Mum,' I protested. 'I'll die of boredom! I can't even use my mobile over here.'

'No you won't. You've got your Diskman and your novels. You could write some postcards.'

'That will be scintillating.'

'We want you to get better. Perhaps Daniel will bring some of his friends to visit you.'

'That will *really* make me feel better.' Though, of course, if *Jacy* came to visit me I might start to revive a little . . . I got dressed, just in case I did have visitors. Mum fussed about to make me comfortable. Then she got to the point of her fussing. 'Dad really wants to go to the market in La Roche this morning. I'll stay behind and look after you if you want, but if you're really feeling much better, we'd only be an hour or so—'

'Go to market, Mum. I'll be fine,' – especially without you fussing over me.

'Emma and Mark's mum has offered to pop in from time to time, see if you need anything . . .'

'Mum – go!'

I was on my own. I tried reading. It made my eyes tired. I lay down and listened to my Diskman for a bit. In the abscence of texting, I thought about postcards. I could send one to Hannah – not that there was much to say. I don't think she'd be very interested in hearing about Jacy, and not a lot else has happened to me. I delved around in my bag. Good, it was there – my DIARY. That would pass a bit of time. It's one of those big hardback exercise books. Some days I write masses in it. And I decorate the pages, do fancy lettering, stick stuff in. I pulled it out and turned through it. There was the page I'd scribbled recently but the last thing I'd stuck in before that were some photos of the sleepover. There was Hannah without her glasses and trying make-up on. It was quite an improvement. Charlotte stuffing her face – as usual. Maddy, suffering from red-eye in this picture. And there was one we'd set up of us all dancing about. I looked quite good in that one, though I say it myself. I'd shoved in the note from Ben Southwell. Not sure why. Aagh. *Fresh* page, I think. Perhaps I'll write about Jacy. I wrote in pencil. Then I could rub it out if it got too embarrassing.

Let me describe Jacy, the only good thing about this terrible holiday. He's quite tall and incredibly fit with short dark hair and a terrific tan. He's got hairy legs and arms but not a hairy chest. His skin's a beautiful colour. He's got quite a good 6-pack and he looks amazing. The best thing about him is his eyes, though all his face is OK – good cheekbones. His eyes are hazel and shiny sometimes, and melty other times with very black eyelashes. He has this way of looking at you that's so sexy. I've heard Mum describing someone as having 'bedroom eyes', and I think that probably describes him perfectly. Definitely a 'man', though I think he's probably only about 18 or 19.

What else? Oh yes. Probably the sexiest thing of all (so far!) is his voice. Kind of deep and soft with this slightly public-school accent – the sort Mum likes and I usually don't like (intolerant as I am) – but it makes him seem very self-assured (is that the right word? – sure of himself, anyway). Could almost be smarmy, but somehow with him it isn't. And he seems to have quite a good sense of humour.

Someone was coming. My God – it was Jacy. I could hear him talking to the Dutch kids. They were saying 'Jacy! Jacy! You want to play football?' and he was saying, 'Later, later!' and laughing. There was someone with him.

Damn! It was drippy Mark.

I heard Jacy say goodbye and walk off. But Mark – aagh, *Mark* – came on to our pitch. 'Er – Sophie?' He said it quite quietly, in case I was asleep, I suppose, but it was ridiculous considering how loudly the Dutch kids had been yelling. 'Er – Sophie? Me mam said as how I were to see how you were doin'?' He came round the corner to where he could see me.

Should I pretend to be asleep or not? Too late. 'Oh. There you are. Do you want anythin', Sophie? I've brought a bottle of nice cold water.' He came in to the tent – *not* that I invited him. And he sat down. At the table. I hastily shut my diary, but not before he said, 'Ma sister keeps a diary an' all.'

There wasn't an answer to that, and he'd dried up all of a sudden. Nothing was said for a few moments and then, 'Do you want anythin', Sophie? I've brought a bottle of nice cold water.' Change the record, Mark. 'I'm goin' a get an ice-cream, right. D'ya want one?' Actually, an ice-cream sounded fab at that moment. And if Mark was prepared to get one I wasn't going to refuse.

'OK.'

'D'ya want an ice-cream?'

'Yes, that's what I said.' We had a bit of a language problem here.

He looked stunned. Then blushed. Then smiled a slow grin. Uh-oh! 'You really want me a get you an ice-cream?'

'YES!' . . . Perhaps he was waiting for me to say please. 'Yes please, Mark. A vanilla one would be champion.' Did I really say *champion*? Well, you have to speak the lingo to get results.

'Right. Like, right.' And he tottered off. What had happened to the guy? I mean, I know he's not up to much, but he seemed to have lost his marbles completely.

I picked up my diary and wrote.

Now let me describe Mark. Mark is fair and pasty and spotty. He is large and gawky. His skin is kind of pink and pudgy. His fingers are like sausages. Someone should buy him a shaving kit. His armpits niff. And I expect his trainers do too. His eyes are blue. On a scale of one to ten for sex appeal he rates minus five. What else can I say? Oh yes. Personality. What personality? Mark suffers from complete lack of personality, as does his sister Emma. Also lack of taste, humour, etc.

*

He was coming back – running, even. He shot into the tent before I had time to close my diary, but it wasn't him, it was two of them, one on each side of me, one accidentally knocking my diary onto the ground, the other thrusting an ice-cream at me. 'Ooh, ma sister writes a diary, an' all,' said one twin.

'Oy,' I bellowed, twisting over to shut the diary.

'Mark would have brought ya the ice-cream,' said one.

'But he got detained, like,' said the other.

'By Becky!' said the first one.

'*Big* Becky,' said the second – and they both cracked up and ran off to their tent, leaving me with a dripping ice-cream and feeling slightly confused. That's twins for you.

I decided to put the diary under the table before anyone else saw it. But visiting hours weren't over yet. It was Mark, again. 'Did ya like ya ice-cream, like?'

'Yeah, thanks,' I said not terribly graciously. I wanted him to go away.

'Did ya like ya ice-cream, like?' he asked again with an asinine grin. Oh please God, no. Not this repetition stuff again.

I was about to say, 'Yeah, cheers, thanks a lot,' when he said something different.

'Becky's comin' by. She wants a meet ya.'

Becky filled the doorway of the tent. As a silhouette she was large. Not just tall but loads of puppy fat and big hair. 'Hi!' she said. She had a surprisingly light voice. Quite posh. 'I just *had* to meet the girl who was Dan's sister, not to mention Mark's next-door neighbour!' She sat down at the table with me. 'You coming or going, Mark? Think you'd better keep an eye on those kids, don't you?'

'Ah!' said Mark and went to their tent. I could hear him repeating the 'Ah!' as he went.

'Real sweetheart, Mark. You seem to render him speechless, though. I've known him for two days now and I've never seen him so lost for words! You've got fairer hair than your brother, haven't you? Bet it's natural. Mine isn't.'

'It gets bleached in the sun,' I said.

'Why haven't I seen you before? Don't you get on with your brother, or something? You're really lucky having Emma and Mark next door. It's all little kids round us. Like my little brother. He's a complete pain, though it's much better now he's discovered Tweedledum and Tweedledee over there. I'd much rather have an older brother. Especially one like Dan. He's cool.'

'Danny? Cool?' It was beyond belief that this girl in her Earl jeans and her DKNY top (I now noticed) could think that Danny was cool.

'Yeah. And he said straightaway that he thought you and I would be into the same things!'

He was more observant than I gave him credit for. 'Where's your tent?'

'Miles away. Out on the prairie. It's a caravilla, actually. Suncampers' though, same as you. Hey, have you got the same sexy courier as we have, Jacy?'

I kicked my diary right under the table. 'I think so,' I said cautiously.

'He's gorgeous, don't you think? You're probably used to gorgeous guys though. I can't believe you're only fourteen. I'm nearly sixteen, though I don't look it, do I? Probably because I go to a girls' school. They try to stop us growing up by putting us in a hideous uniform. We don't really get to meet boys. My parents say I can go clubbing when I'm sixteen, but my dad's ever so protective. He thinks we're really safe here – all good clean fun sort of thing.'

'I know. And he's probably right. Pity, isn't it?'

'Do you know, he even went up to the girl on the bar, pointed me out and said – "That one is still fifteen. If I find out she's been served alcohol, I'll know who to blame." Luckily, she's French and didn't know what he was on about!'

Mum and Dad's car drew up at that point, followed by the tell-tale squeal of brakes that heralded Dan's arrival. Becky looked at her Storm watch and said, 'I'd better drag my little bro back home for lunch. Pity it's so far. I'm even contemplating hiring a bike. Wish I had my horse!'

'Hi, Becky!' said Dan, as if he'd known her all her life. 'Pool this afternoon?'

'Of course!' she replied. 'Pool in the afternoon. Bar in the evening. Bonfire down at the lake tonight. See you later!'

'Thought you two would get on,' Danny said to me, breaking off half a French loaf from the shopping and gnawing at it. 'Don't suppose you'll be coming swimming, will you?'

I started to say Possibly, but Mum interrupted. 'Certainly not. I might let you out again in the cool of the evening, but you're not going out in the full sun today.' She and Dad put lunch on the table inside the tent and we all sat down to it. 'It's unbelievably hot out there right now, isn't it, Dan? In fact you'd better take care down at the pool this afternoon. Apparently Mark got a bit burnt yesterday.' Dan didn't answer. I felt unreasonably irritable at him. I realised how great it would be to have a girl my own age to natter to. I could have kicked myself at completely missing the simplicity of the 'scene' that Becky described. I'd been in the wrong place every time. Unlike Dan.

'I don't think I want to be there anyway,' I said nastily. 'It's bad enough being caught in the cutesy crossfire from French bimbos, but the vision of Mark with a sunburnt torso might just make me feel ill all over again.'

'Shh!' said Dan. 'You seem to forget these walls are canvas. They can hear every word we say, you know.'

'Ah! But can they understand it?'

Dan turned on me. He spoke in a hoarse whisper. 'I do not understand you, Sophie Morris. You are just *such* a snob. They (he pointed next door) are perfectly OK people, really friendly, and all you can do is rubbish them because *you* have a problem understanding their cool accent. As for (and he mouthed "Mark") – well, he's actually taken in by the Sophie Morris mystique, says he's never met a girl quite like you before. I think he should count himself lucky. He's probably never met anyone who's been so unpleasant to him.'

I couldn't for the life of me see why Dan was so worked up. 'But he's such a cretin, Dan. He kept coming in here and bothering me this morning, with water and ice-cream and stuff.'

'Oh dear,' said Mum. 'I thought their mother was going to pop in. I didn't mean her to ask the children.'

Dan spoke before I could add anything. 'Mark wanted to, Mum. He's OK. He felt really sorry for Sophie because he'd got sunburnt too and knew how it felt. He spent ages deciding what to take her. We were all in the bar before lunch. It was Jacy who suggested the mineral water from the fridge. I expect that makes it OK now, does it, Sophie?'

Well, it certainly made it a bit better. Fancy Jacy thinking about what would be best for me.

'Well, Sophie, does it?' Dan wanted an answer. I couldn't think of one. If he couldn't see that Jacy's attentions were more welcome to me than Mark's, then he needed his head examining.

I tried to think of something smart to say. 'Just because you fancy Mark's sister doesn't mean I have to fancy Mark.' It wasn't smart, because Dan's sensitive about that sort of thing and it just made him angry.

'You're a pain in the bum, Sophie. I've a good mind to tell – (and he nodded next door again) what an ungrateful witch you are. Might just tell Jacy as well.'

'Children, children!' said Dad. 'If you can't say anything nice then don't say anything at all.'

'Sit in the shade this afternoon, Sophie. Then maybe you can join the others in the evening. I don't want you to miss out on any of the fun.' Good old Mum. There was me having a huge row with Dan that was about to ruin the whole awful holiday and she hadn't caught on at all. But she did make Dan do the washing up.

Dan still wasn't speaking to me when he set off to the pool. There were shady spots outside the tent now, so I buried my diary deep in my bag, found a novel and my Diskman and dragged a sunbed as far from the hedge we shared with next-door as possible. I was a tiny bit worried that they might have overheard us at lunchtime, but I can't say I really cared. Mum and Dad were having a snooze after their morning's exertions. Sleep seems to come very easily on these occasions. It wasn't long before I dropped off too.

'Hi, Sophie!' It was Becky. She and Emma had arrived on bicycles. They were both in bikinis. Quite a contrast. Emma is small and neat with (I have to admit) a good figure. Becky is the opposite. Her copious flesh was not a pretty sight, but the bikini was something to die for. It must have cost at least £80. 'See you later, Emma!' Becky called after her. 'Have a good tennis lesson!' She leant her bike against a tree and came over. 'You awake, Sophie? Do you want to come down to the lake?'

'I have to stay in the shade,' I said.

'Plenty of shade down there. I got too hot by the pool, and I don't like to keep jumping in the water because this bikini goes transparent. Your mum would let you, wouldn't she?'

'That's all right. I just won't ask. I'll come. I'm going stir-crazy anyway, and I feel OK now.'

'I'll leave my bike here then. We can spy on Emma's tennis lesson on the way down.'

I pulled on a top and some shorts. As a concession to Mum I wore a baseball cap as well. I even scribbled a note which I weighted down with a stone. 'Gone to sit in shade somewhere else with Becky.' We set off through the woods, the same way I'd been with Dan on our first day. Not many people were around. A few on bicycles. A group of kids on ponies. Far off we caught glimpses of Coralie and Sonia with a line of singing junior Suncampers. We came to the gap in the hedge at the side of the manoir where there were three tennis courts. People were having coaching – they didn't seem to mind the heat of the day.

'That's what Emma's doing next,' said Becky. 'By the way, why don't you two like each other?'

'What?' I was taken aback. OK, I didn't like Emma, but only Dan knew that. Didn't he?

'She says you don't like her, but she doesn't really mind. She just thinks you're a bit snobby about northerners.' Becky said all this in her even-toned, light voice. I looked at her but it was obvious she wasn't being spiteful, just passing on information.

'I suppose I don't really know her,' I conceded.

'Yeah, that's what I said,' said Becky. 'After all, all the rest of us know each other pretty well now, but you've been ill, haven't you?'

I wanted to say that the rest of them couldn't really know each other that well – none of them had been here more than a few days – and that I'd only genuinely been out of action since last night, but I liked Becky and, I realised, I needed her. God knows what 'they' had all been saying about me when I wasn't there. I wasn't even sure that I could rely on Danny to take my side. It wasn't looking good. And it wasn't what I was used to. Best to change the subject.

'Who does the tennis coaching?'

'Oh, I don't know their names, but they are these fabulous French guys. French guys are *so* sexy, don't you think?'

Well, I couldn't really agree with her there. 'Have you ever done any riding here?'

'Oh yes.' Horses were definitely still very much on the agenda for Becky. 'I'm down for one on Friday. Hey, why don't you come too? Emma can't afford riding as well as tennis. Oh, go on, it would be brilliant.'

I didn't really want to be a substitute for Emma, but I did quite fancy a ride. Get away from my folks, from the campsite. 'I'll ask,' I said.

We wandered on down the path to the open field in front of the lake. Even with shades and a hat the bright square of light exploded into our faces as we emerged from the wood. 'Wow. It's a bit bright,' said Becky. 'Let's go along the edge of the wood in that direction. There's a stream that runs into the lake and we could sit on the bridge.' I followed her.

We sat on the bridge, dangling our feet in the water. It was blissful. 'Where are you from, Becky?' I assumed she was a home counties sort of person, what with a horse and everything, but you never know, do you?

'Just outside Chester.'

Oh God, where is Chester? I thought I wouldn't ask, given what people thought about me already. It might be in the north.

'*Hollyoaks* has really put us on the map!' she added.

I watch *Hollyoaks*, but I still don't know where Chester is.

'It's great for shopping,' she said. 'But of course we're not far from Liverpool and Manchester.'

Great. Clues. So it *is* in the north.

'What about you? You and Dan both speak like southerners.'

'London,' I said. I'd never considered myself as a 'southerner' before. 'But quite a long way out.'

'Wow!' She said it as if I came from Mars. 'Don't you just spend all your time wanting to buy things?'

The sun had moved around. The lake glittered invitingly. 'Shall we see if we can grab a pedalo?' I asked. 'It doesn't look so lethal out there any more.' We jumped down from the footbridge and made our way over to the little jetty where one of the pedaloes was beached. They were there for anyone to use.

'I rode one of these round with Mark for ages last night,'

said Becky as we climbed in. 'We were trying to ram Danny and Suzette, but they were too fast for us.'

'Do you mean my brother shared a pedalo with the orange bikini girl?' I asked, pedalling furiously.

'Suzette, yes! She won't leave him alone!' said Becky laughing. 'Emma's dead jealous. She thinks Dan's wonderful. Now I've nothing against blond blokes, but on the whole I think I go more for the lean, mean Mediterranean look. Not that anyone answering that description would look twice at me!' she said comfortably. And, silently, I had to agree with her. 'You, on the other hand, are totally drop-dead gorgeous. I bet you could find a fab French guy.'

'Not all that keen on the French,' I said.

'Have you got a boyfriend then?' she asked.

I didn't want to give much away. 'Sort of,' I said vaguely. We let our boat drift about.

Becky looked over to me. Her mind was obviously still on romance. 'Who do you fancy here then?'

'Oh, no one really. They all seem a bit young.'

'Well, what about the couriers? You must have noticed Jacy, our courier. I'm sure he *is* yours too. Now he would make the perfect boyfriend for you.'

'Do you think so?' I said, rather too quickly.

'Oh yes! Why didn't I think of it before! You kind of go together. You're all slim, blonde and beautiful and he's bronzed, dark and handsome – the perfect couple!' Becky was away. I didn't need to say anything. 'Now, how can we get you together? You must come to the bar more. He's always hanging around the bar. Ooh! Isn't this fun? I love matchmaking!' We pedalled the boat back to the jetty.

As we walked back to our tent my head was still swirling with angry thoughts about Danny. I wanted to hurl insults at him and our stupid neighbours. But then I remembered that they all went to the bar in the evenings and that the bar was also where Jacy hung out and that it was where I wanted to be. I was going to have to make my peace with

Dan, but that didn't mean I had to pretend to like big Mark and drippy Emma. I could manage without them.

FIVE

The afternoon had got hotter and hotter and more humid. Even now, with supper nearly over, it seemed unnaturally warm, like a bath, and airless. I'd tried to apologise to Dan without grovelling and blamed the fact that I'd been ill. He was still fairly cool, but I felt that we were no longer at war. Emma passed by with their washing up. She put her head round the corner. 'Hi, Dan! Coming up to the bar later?'

'I'll be there!' he said.

'Can I come up with you?' I asked tentatively.

'Suppose so,' he said. 'As long as you're not snotty with my friends.'

'I'm not snotty with Becky.'

'I didn't mean her.'

'And Becky's not snotty with anyone.'

'That's true. But you know what I mean.'

I thought it would be politic to grovel just a little at this point. 'Yes, Dan. I'll try to be friendly. But—'

'But nothing.'

'Yessir!'

'You seem much better, Sophie,' said Mum. 'Do you think you are?' I did. I felt recovered, just a bit stiff. My afternoon at the lake with Becky had cured me. Things were looking up.

The bar had a back room that was packed with teenagers. We bought our drinks from the French waitress and carried them through. Becky had saved a place for me. She had changed into a gorgeous Diesel shirt with her Earl jeans. She was wearing make-up too, though I thought she could do with some sorting out in that department. I'd put on a short white dress. I knew it suited me and it showed off my legs, since my tan was now coming along nicely. Emma was sitting next to Becky. She was making cow eyes at Dan again. Yuk. He plonked himself next to her, what's more. Her evening gear consisted of cyling shorts and a belly top. Mark wasn't with her, but there were various other people there who I had seen waving to Dan. It was definitely a British group. Francine and Suzette were chatting with the girl at the bar and the Dutch seemed to have their own thing going outside. And to think our parents all bring us here to mix with European youth!

I'd spotted Sonia and Coralie as we came in. They were sipping bright blue drinks that looked lethal. No Jacy though. 'I wonder where Jacy is,' whispered Becky, louder than I liked. 'He's not propping up the bar like he usually is.'

Luckily no one heard her, and I was able to pretend I hadn't either because some raucous lads were asking Dan to be introduced to his sister 'and her legs'. John and Steve were Liverpudlians. I couldn't understand a word they said, but I could tell they were funny. And what seemed to fuel their jokes more than anything was the way Becky and I spoke! They found everything we said hilarious, even simple words like 'bar' and 'chair' (try saying them with a Liverpool accent) creased them up. I could see we were in for a jolly evening.

This was more like it – Becky and me being chatted up by two admiring blokes. Well, I felt pretty confident that they admired me, anyway. I felt happier than I had done all holiday. They kept buying us drinks, too. After last night's little episode I thought I'd better stick to soft drinks, and Becky, despite her brave words, was actually still afraid of her Dad catching her boozing, so there was lots of ice and lemon clinking about. The lads were downing *demis* and getting noisier as the night wore on.

Outside, the air was hot and soupy. Inside, it was hot and

plain sticky. There was talk of going down to the lake, but it felt as though it was going to thunder any minute. I felt a bit dodgy and went for some fresh air – but there wasn't any. I stood at the open door of the bar. The front of the bar was full of adults. My parents were there with the Dutch neighbours and Mark and Emma's mum. Little children were threading their way between the tables. There was a general air of excitement. It really felt as if the sky was about to break open. And then, as I was standing by the door, it did. There was a tremendous flash of lightning that tore the sky in two, followed by great echoing rolls of thunder. People outside squealed and headed for the bar as great fat drops of rain started to fall. I was joined by the French barmaid. She peered anxiously through the rain, but pulled back as a large figure in long shorts and wet plimsolls splattered over the tarmac and ducked into the doorway, shaking drips everywhere like a dog.

It was Mark. Drippy Mark, even! 'It's OK, Hélène,' he said to the barmaid. 'Your feller's on his way. The lightning missed him too. An' I need a drink!' Seeing her incomprehension he made drinking motions with his hand and shooed her back towards the bar. She tittered and gave him her lovely smile. I have to admit, it was a different Mark. Then he turned and nearly fell over me. I saw the change come over his face. 'Oh. Sophie,' he stuttered. 'Oh. Sophie. I didn't see you there. Can I buy you a drink?'

'No thanks,' I said, and squeezed my way through to the back room again. The French girls had materialised and were sitting with Dan. Orange bikini, now in an orange top, was being particularly friendly. Emma was looking bootfaced and called to Mark that she'd help him with the drinks.

'Yes, please!' shouted Becky. 'Coke for me! With ice and lemon.'

Mark put his head round. 'Anyone else? Dan? Sophie – are you sure you don't want anything?'

'Quite sure, thanks,' I said. 'I told you already.' There was a short silence. Becky looked over at me as I sat down. 'I wish he'd leave me alone,' I said to her.

'Lad was only offering to buy you a drink,' said one of the Scousers, somewhat disapprovingly.

'Yes, well. You wouldn't understand,' I told him.

He put his hands up to show he was backing off. 'Good-looking girl like you. I expect blokes are always trying to chat you up.'

'It can get tiresome,' I said.

'Lucky old you,' said Becky. 'I wouldn't complain!'

I sat back. I could hear the thunder receding as the rain grew steadier, beating on the roof and slanting across the windows. I wondered where Jacy was. I flicked my hair back and stretched out my legs. Mark and Emma came in with the drinks and started handing them round. Then, would you believe it, Mark came and sat next to me! He was all squelchy from the rain and disgusting. Can't that guy take a hint? And what did he say? He said, 'Er, Sophie, are you sure you don't want a drink?'

'No, Mark. I do not want a drink.' I couldn't stand this klutz any longer. I got up, pushed past him and went to the loo.

When I came out I wasn't sure what to do. I hoped Dan hadn't heard me snapping at Mark. I knew Emma had, but then she had already decided I was a snob. I suddenly felt a bit unsure of Becky and the Liverpool lads. Was I really behaving badly? Did I care what they thought of me? I didn't mean to be unkind, but they obviously, Becky in particular, had no idea what it was like to be followed about. It happens to me all the time. Lovesick blokes. It's not as if they're any fun. Don't they realise how boring they are? If only Jacy would come in.

I looked towards the open doorway. The dark square was lit up for a moment by blue lightning, and, as if in answer to my prayer, there was Jacy. And what a vision he was! His wet T-shirt was plastered to his pecs and his hair was slick with rain. Water ran down his face as he smiled towards me at the bar. A gorgeous, warm, melting smile.

'Hi, Jacy!' I called. 'Do you want a drink?'

'I'll get it, thanks,' he said. 'I get an extra special discount, don't I, Hélène?' He winked at the French barmaid. 'I'll join you in the back bar in a minute.'

So. My decision was made for me. I made my way through the crush towards Becky. Mark was still sitting there, but he leapt to his feet clumsily as I approached. 'You'll be wantin' a sit down. Here.' I didn't wait to be asked twice this time.

'We've decided to give the lake a miss tonight,' said Becky.

'Hardly the weather for a bonfire!' added John. I noticed he and Becky were sitting so close that Becky was practically on his lap.

Jacy appeared. I could see his wet seal-head above a group of girls. So did Becky. She nudged me hard, nearly spilling Coke over my white dress as she shot her other hand in the air like an eager schoolgirl. 'Over here Jacy!' she called, and squeezed up even closer to John to make more room for me and, of course, Jacy. He was carrying one of those virulent blue drinks. My God, he really was going to sit with us, with me to be precise. He perched himself on the end of the bench, right next to me. He was still damp from the rain and steaming gently. Wow! So was I. He leant in to me and Becky. 'How are you doing, girls? No bonfire tonight, then?' (There's one right here, did you but know it, I felt like saying.) He took a sip of his drink. 'That's better.' He sat back. 'It's been a busy night. Campers don't like rain. It'll be sunny again tomorrow though. It always is after a thunderstorm. And the girls have gone back to take over for a bit, so I'm sort of off duty.' He drank the blue stuff thirstily.

I was intrigued. 'What's that drink called? It looks pretty powerful!'

'Oh, haven't you ever tried it? It's called Bleu Tropique. Here, have a swig – but go easy!' He wiped the rim of his glass rather engagingly and passed it over to me. I sniffed it cautiously. It smelt strong, like some of the cocktails Hannah and I once experimented with.

'Hey! That's nice!' It was a lot nicer than any of the other ice and lemon drinks I'd had that night.

'Would you like one? I'll get you one if you like.'

'I'd love one,' I said boldly, though he'd already slipped off to the bar, leaving me feeling surprisingly bereft without his damp warmth against me. There was movement amongst the others in the back bar and I prayed that Mark wouldn't take the place left by Jacy. I shifted over slightly to fill it myself and turned to Becky and John and Steve so that I shouldn't look as if I was on my own.

'You're doing OK there!' said Becky excitedly. 'Where's he gone?'

'To buy me a drink,' I said smugly.

'Must have more money than us then,' said Steve. 'I've run out now.'

'Still,' said John, nudging Steve, 'he does get that *special* discount at the bar . . .'

'Don't know what you're talking about,' said Steve, smiling broadly at Becky and me. 'I'm going back for my beauty sleep now. See you, guys. Don't get too drunk, Sophie!' And he edged out from the table, sitting on each of us as he went, accompanied by lots of squealing from Becky, who took the opportunity to get closer to John again.

Jacy was back with my Bleu Tropique. I looked up and saw that Dan and the French girls had disappeared and that Emma and Mark were now sitting together with a bunch of saddos. I think they were discussing exam results.

I already felt slightly lightheaded from my share of Jacy's first Bleu Tropique. I decided to take this one slowly. Now the crowd had thinned out a bit, Jacy sat opposite me. Becky and John moved apart a little too. Becky probably wanted a part of the Jacy action. I didn't mind. I didn't consider her to be competition exactly, and I wasn't quite ready to be alone with him.

Becky went in to bat for me. 'It's good that Sophie's recovered so quickly, isn't it?' she said to Jacy.

Uh-oh. I didn't want to be reminded that less than twenty-four hours ago I was throwing up *fruits de mer*. 'It was nothing,' I chimed in. 'I'm just more sensitive to the sun than I thought I was. It's not as if I burn. I just go brown.'

'That's why that white dress looks so gorgeous on you,' said Becky loyally. 'And it shows that your legs go up to your armpits.'

I didn't want her laying it on too thick, but I drank some more Bleu Tropique and found I didn't really care. It was great just to have Jacy there, admiring me. I opened my mouth to say something coolly dismissive but no real words came out. 'Hic!'

'Pardon you!' said John.

'Hic!' came out again.

Jacy looked concerned. 'Drink a bit more. Drink it slowly,' he said. I did. But it had no effect whatsoever on the hiccups. They just got worse. Becky was no help. She just dissolved into a heaving mass of giggles beside me.

'Girls, eh?' said John to Jacy. He pronounced it 'gairls'. Becky was throwing herself around now. 'Watch out! I'm getting a face full of your hair!' He pronounced it 'hurr'! But Becky had had it. Tears streamed down her face. Every time I went 'Hic!' she heaved her large body around. Her giggles were infectious. To me, at any rate. I started to giggle as well as hiccup. I kept trying to drink slowly from my glass, but it only seemed to make matters worse.

'What shall we do with 'em?' said Jacy to John, as Becky and I leant against each other helplessly.

'I'll get this one back to her caravilla,' said John. 'It's almost next door to mine. And you (yer jammy feller,' he added under his breath), 'had better do the honours with

Sophie.' He pulled Becky to her feet and guided her out through the main bar.

'Bye, Sophie,' she snorted. 'Don't do anything I wouldn't do!' she added as she and John swayed off into the night.

Jacy had a quick word with the girl at the bar while I tried to stop myself from falling over. Then he put his arm round me. 'Easy does it, Sophie.'

'Hic!' I replied.

'Ssh! Most people have gone to bed.'

Through my haze I felt flattered and a little anxious at the same time. Was Jacy making a move on me? Could I cope? The rain-washed air smelt of wet pine. The moon had risen above the trees. I concentrated on putting one foot in front of the other, all the time intensely aware of the warmth and strength of Jacy's arm.

'Here we are,' he said when we reached our tent. 'Home in one piece.'

'Thanks, Jacy.' I smiled up at him, staggering slightly as he gave me a little push towards the tent.

He reached out and ruffled my hair. 'All part of the service,' he said, and set off at a jog back to the bar.

I unzipped the tent as quietly as I could. I needn't have bothered with the stealth. Danny was sitting at the table with a cup of coffee. 'Hi!' he whispered. 'What have you been up to?'

'Jacy walked me back to the tent,' I said.

'Ooh-er.'

'He got me rather drunk,' I added, knowing that Dan would agree that that meant Jacy was seriously interested in me. I threw myself onto a camp chair, remembering with pleasure the strong arm around me and the affectionate hand in my hair.

'What on?'

'Don't tell Mum and Dad!'

'Your secret's safe with me! They're next door with Emma's mum, anyway.'

'That blue drink. Bleu Tropique, or whatever. I feel really merry.' I giggled. 'And it gave me the hiccups.'

Dan looked at me. I realised he had a condescending smile. 'Bleu Tropique has no alcohol in it whatsoever, Sophie. That's why the couriers drink it when they're on duty.'

SIX

'Dad, can I have the money to hire a bike?'

'I'm surprised you've managed so long without one. Here's the money. Bring me the change.'

'Great,' said Becky. 'Let's go and get one for you now.'

It was twelve noon and I hadn't been up long. I'd lain awake for a while thinking about Jacy and what last night meant, but I didn't come to any earth-shattering conclusions. I could still bring back the memory of the hairs on his warm arm around my shoulders and the surprise of his impulsive gesture when he ruffled my hair. But I preferred to forget the embarrassing 'effects' of the Bleu Tropique. Now at last the holiday seemed to be falling into place, thanks to Becky. And here she was, dragging me off to hire a bike.

She wheeled hers as we set off for the Accueil. As soon as we were out of earshot she said, 'Well?'

I looked at her.

'You tell me about Jacy before I tell you what a good kisser John is. Go on! What happened? You're so lucky! How romantic! I knew Jacy was perfect for you!'

'You – and John? You pulled?'

'Yes! We went and sat down by the lake for a bit. He's nice. I like him. But I told my dad you were with me, so you'll have to cover for me if he says anything. But go on! I want to hear about you two!'

I was tempted to fib a bit. But since last night seemed to be a stage on the way to true romance I decided to tell it how it was. After all, it had felt romantic at the time. 'Well, he did put his arm around me. He didn't seem to mind anyone seeing us. And then he walked me back to the tent—'

'And then?'

'He – er – he sort of ruffled my hair!'

'Wow! I'd give anything to have Jacy ruffle my hair!'

'Hey! What about John?'

'Oh, that's just a physical thing really. You and Jacy are far more exciting!' She whispered that because we had come to the Accueil. The French girl, Hélène, was on reception. I knew her English was hopeless but I just said 'Bike?' and made pratty bicycling motions. She giggled and Becky stepped in.

'*Elle veut louer une bicyclette pour* – how long, Sophie? – *dix jours.*'

'*Oui, bien. Ca sera trente euros, s'il vous plaît. Choisissez.*'

'Give me the hundred note,' said Becky. 'Here's thirty change. Come on, let's find you one that works! *Merci! Au revoir!*'

'Bye!' I muttered.

'Now we can check out the horses.' We cycled off together. Becky on a bike was quite a sight. She wore shorts which were definitely not a good idea and a sleeveless Nike top. She was all thighs and elbows and big hair. But it was a great way to whip up a breeze and keep cool in the midday sun. We pedalled along the road at the top, past the entrance to the manoir, the shop, the table tennis area and the pool to the far end where the stables were part of the old farm. We turned into a courtyard with a square of green in the middle shaded by four tall trees. Around the sides were stables with horses looking out over the doors. There was a slightly whiffy farmyard-in-the-sun smell and hens scratching about. A couple of dogs lay panting in the heat and a group of girls stood in the shade chatting.

I wouldn't have known where to begin, but Becky went straight up to the girls and sorted everything out in French. It was impressive, this side of Becky. I haven't met her parents yet but I imagine that she has a marvellously large and efficient mum.

'That's all fine,' she said, getting back on her bike. 'We just turn up here tomorrow morning at ten o'clock. They'll kit us out with hats and boots – and horses, I dare say – and off we'll all go. Back about five. Bring a packed lunch, plenty of water to drink and forty euros, and Bob's your uncle!'

She picked me up again after lunch on her way to the pool. Dan had gone on ahead with Emma and Mark. Becky wore her shorts over her bikini, but we were still treated to ample amounts of flesh on view. I don't mind swimming and sunbathing in a bikini but I'm not quite ready to put myself on show to the whole world. I was wondering vaguely where Jacy was today when he appeared from the bar as we cycled past. 'Hi, girls!' he said.

'Wow! Did you see the way he looked at you?' Becky practically swerved into me.

It seemed to be accepted that the teenagers colonised a square of grass by the fence at the end of the pool. There was quite a large group already there as we flung our bikes down. We spread out our towels and before long John and Steve joined us, along with three Kates, two Jamies, a Lauren, a Tristan and a Melanie. Steve and John had an amazing repartee going – very funny and very quick. I could never have joined in their rapid-fire jokes and one-liners – they were like stand-up comedians on the telly. At first I couldn't even work out what they were saying, but after a while I got used to them. The accent was all part and parcel of the humour. They were different from anyone I'd ever met before, but I liked them. Steve was the older and bolder of the two. John was his stooge. Most of their jokes were about themselves, too. They didn't mind drawing attention to their zits and their white bits, bits that needed shaving, unruly bits. Becky joined in sometimes. She made jokes about being fat and having periods. I couldn't believe it. She wasn't embarrassed about herself. She didn't mind talking to the boys about the bits of her that were less than perfect. And believe me, there were plenty of them. I mean, I'm happy with my looks. I could do with bigger boobs and better nails, but I couldn't joke about it.

'Hey, Sophie, you like the fellas, don't you?' Steve asked.

'Course she does,' said John. 'She likes us, doesn't she?'

'Well, we know Becky likes us,' said Steve, nudging John.

'I like you,' I said. 'I think you're funny.'

'Did you hear that, Steve?' said John. 'She thinks we're a bit of a "larf".' He took the mickey out of my accent.

'I heard,' said Steve. 'You've got a treat tonight, girls.' He addressed the Kates and Lauren and Melanie as well as us. 'Because the Irish are coming. We met them at the last campsite and a whole lot of them are coming on here today.'

'That should keep the couriers busy . . .' said John. (So that's why Jacy wasn't around much.)

'And if you think we talk funny,' said Steve, 'just wait till you hear them.'

'Would you like an ice-cream, like?' It was Mark. I tried to put the thought of 'ice-cream' before 'irritation' and smiled graciously.

'Yeah, we'd like ice-creams, Mark. Do you want a hand?' Becky didn't have the same problem as I do with Mark. 'Can you cope with *la belle Hélène* or do you want some language support?'

'Got some, thanks,' said Mark as Suzette appeared at his shoulder. She had a pencil and some paper.

'*Cassis pour moi,*' said Becky. 'Double.'

'And vanilla for me, please.'

'Chocolate,' said John.

'Rum and raisin for me,' said Steve.

'Pay me when we get back,' said Mark.

'Ah, this is the life, eh?' Steve rolled over luxuriously. 'That Suzette can bring me all the ice-cream she wants.' He sighed lasciviously.

'Steve!' Becky slapped him resoundingly. 'You just keep your lewd thoughts to yourself, OK? There are women present.'

'Just commenting on the local beauty, that's all,' said Steve, cowering.

'Yeah, Steve!' said John, putting an arm round Becky. 'Put a sock in it.'

I decided it was time for a swim. I couldn't keep up with all this backchat. I walked off to the pool and dived in. Steve followed me. I swam a few lengths crawl and then one in backstroke. The trouble with backstroke is that you can't see where you're going. I bumped into Steve at the shallow end. I stood up spluttering. 'Spit on me, would yer?' he laughed.

'Sorry!' I wiped my face with my hand.

'I know you're a bit too high and mighty for the likes of us, Ms Morris,' said Steve as I ducked my shoulders under water, 'but, you know, there's one of the Irish lads that you'll find impossible to resist. All the girls just love him. He's called Fergal.'

'Fergal!' I said, splashing him and diving out of reach. 'What sort of a name is that?'

At suppertime Becky and I cycled back to our tent together. Her brother and the twins came to meet us. They looked hot and excited. Two of the Dutch boys were with them. 'Jacy's been training us for the big match!' they said. 'He's brilliant. He played for his county when he was at school in England.'

'He's so cool!'

'He's brilliant in goal!'

'He can shoot too!'

'He scores every time!'

Emma was behind us with Mark and Dan. 'What a lot of fans Jacy has,' she said. I didn't like her tone.

I don't believe it! Drippy Emma actually thinks she stands a chance with Jacy herself. When Becky and I went into the bar after supper we found them poring over a sheet of paper together. She looked so guilty! They both stood up when we came in. Jacy folded the piece of paper and said, 'Don't worry, Emma. Whatever happens, we'll make it a night to remember.' Then he turned to us. 'Girls!' he said. 'Can I get any of you a drink before I go and sort out newcomers?'

Emma had disappeared. At least she knows when she's outclassed. 'You go and sort out newcomers,' said Becky. 'Then you'll have all the more time to spend with us later!' He skipped out with a wave and Becky grinned at me triumphantly. 'You didn't want another Bleu Tropique did you?'

The bar was unusually empty, but there was quite a commotion outside. Becky and I bought our drinks and sat up at the bar itself where we could watch what was going on. Several cars had just arrived and a large number of people had clambered out of them. They were stretching their legs and shaking their shoulders as people do after long journeys. Steve and John and some of the others were also in there somehow and the whole crowd started hugging and high-fiving with a large amount of noise and good humour. Campers carrying saucepans of *frites* stopped to look, bikes skidded to a halt, dogs yapped and there was a general carnival air. So this was the great event. The Irish had arrived. I scanned them surreptitiously for a gorgeous bloke and listened out for the name Fergal, but none of them caught my eye half as much as Jacy, who was also in among them, trying to find out who was going where. Now and then he cast mock despairing glances in our direction at the bar and I melted, memories of his hands in my hair making me come out in goosepimples all over.

The scene at the bar never really got going that night. Some of our friends came in to buy cans and bottles, but it was too nice an evening to be indoors, and it seemed that the bonfire at the lake was going to be the main attraction. People were drifting over there already.

Becky didn't want to go down yet. 'Wait a bit,' she said. 'Then we won't get roped into building the fire. Anyway, it's much better when it's darker.'

'That's fine by me,' I said, seeing Mark and Emma, my brother and the French girls heading in that direction. I was more than happy with my grandstand view of Jacy in action.

'I want to stop off at the caravilla on the way down,' said Becky. 'Cover myself in insect repellent and find something with long sleeves. I got bitten to pieces down there last night.'

She caught my eye. 'By mosquitoes! And I don't want a repeat performance.'

'Not any of it?'

She gave a rueful laugh. 'I'm not bothered,' she said. 'I don't mind if John wants to, but I shan't be heartbroken if he doesn't. I don't have much experience with blokes, but the one thing I do have experience of is of them going off me. It's probably because I'm fat. They don't want their friends to see them with me.'

'John didn't seem to mind this afternoon.'

'That was just mucking about.'

She was right. But how bleak. My problem was the opposite. Boys don't give up on me. They ring me late at night and tell me they love me, and they blame me and call me a bitch – and worse – for not reciprocating. Maybe that's bleak too. Why do we bother with boys at all when they always make our lives a misery one way or another? But then I caught a glimpse of Jacy sprinting past again and remembered precisely why. I'm not sure that I've ever felt like this about anyone before. I don't think I've ever met anyone so gorgeous. Oh Jacy.

'Enough of this!' said Becky. 'Let's go to the caravilla.'

The prairie at this time of night was like a comfortable suburban street. Blue smoke rose from the barbecues. Adults sat around with bottles of wine, chatting, reading, playing cards. Little children batted around in their night clothes. A game of *boules* was in progress – elderly Frenchmen in swimming shorts fought it out with a group of white-blonde young Dutch girls. It was idyllic in a way. Becky's caravilla was a long way down. I could see why she needed a bike. Her brother and the twins were sitting over a Gameboy and I recognised her father reading a paper at the table.

'Hi!' said Becky, stepping up into the caravilla. 'I've brought Sophie back, Mum.' I followed her and saw, not the large lady I'd been expecting, but an amazingly beautiful forty-something *slim* version of Becky. She looked like the sort of woman who spent a lot of time at the gym.

'Nice to meet you, Sophie,' said her mother. 'Are you on your way down to the lake?'

'Any crisps I can take, Mother, or chocolate?'

Her mum laughed indulgently. 'I was just the same at her age! You never stop eating, do you, Becks? Look in the cupboard, darling.'

Becky opened the fridge first, took out two Cokes and slid one across the table to me. 'Have this, Sophie, while I get the anti-mozzie stuff. Do you want to borrow a top?'

I certainly wanted to check out her wardrobe. 'OK.' She had a tiny little cabin to herself in the caravilla – with its own wardrobe. She threw open the door.

'Help yourself.'

Wow. It could have belonged to Eddie Monsoon! There were even some *Lacroix* jeans! I didn't know you could even buy them in a size 14! I picked out a flimsy top, another of her Kookai numbers, that I felt comfortable with. 'How about this one?'

'Whatever.'

'Thanks. It's gorgeous.'

'I'm sure Jacy will go for you in that!'

I wasn't so sure. It was lovely having Becky being so full of romantic ideas and egging me on, but I had a nagging little doubt, unfamiliar to me, that maybe Jacy wouldn't go for me in anything. I've never felt so insecure. I just needed another sign from him that he thought I was special.

SEVEN

We walked down to the lake in the twilight armed with a torch, a large bottle of Coke and loads of crisps. We both smelt strongly of insect repellent. It was more overpowering than Becky's Chanel and my Calvin Klein. Where the path through the woods opened out into the field by the lake we could see that the bonfire was already well under way, rosy flames competing with the sunset and its reflection. There were about thirty teenagers silhouetted against it. The crackle of burning wood, muted shrieks and giggles blending with the aggrieved honks and quacks of waterbirds drifted over to us. It was magic. Becky squeezed my shoulder. 'Good, eh?' We used our stuff to set up a little base of our own near the bonfire and sat down. 'This is just so perfect. All we need now is for Jacy to come down, row you into the middle of the lake, take you in his arms and SNOG you . . .'

She practically sang that bit. Thanks, Beck. It drew a crowd, too. 'Did somebody use the word "snog"?' It was

Steve with John (looking sheepish when he realised precisely who had used the word) and four more guys. 'I told the lads they had better meet the posh birds at the earliest opportunity,' he said.

'We're not posh!' Becky and I said in unison from where we sat.

'Well, you talk posh,' said John.

Becky and I made 'What, us?' expressions at each other. Then Steve pushed the four Irish lads forward to introduce themselves. They stood there looking embarrassed.

'Sit down,' said Becky. There was a large log near us and they perched on it in a row, like four hunched crows in their hooded tops.

'I'm Sean,' said the first one. (He really said 'Oi'm'.)

'I'm Peter,' said the next one, 'his brother.' (Brother rhymed with bother.)

'I'm Gus,' (he pronounced it 'Goss') said the one with the little beard. 'Their older cousin and superior in every way!'

Then they all turned to the one on the end, the one with the copper curls and eyes so blue you could drown in them, who said, 'And I'm Fergal Maguire. No relation.'

I didn't know people spoke like that for real outside *Father Ted*. I felt the bubble of a giggle rising up in me, but Becky dug me sharply in the ribs with her elbow. 'Hi,' she said. 'I'm Becky and this is Sophie. So where are you from?'

'Dublin,' (Doblin) they chorused.

'Oh wow!' said Becky. 'I just love your accents. I could listen to you all night.'

'You shall, my darling, you shall,' said Gus and took a swig of his beer. John suddenly appeared at Becky's side.

'Let's go on the lake – there's a couple of pedaloes free.'

'Brilliant idea!' said Gus. 'Come on, Steve, Peter, Sean!'

'There's only room for four,' said Steve. 'Take Fergal instead of me!'

'Don't worry about me,' said Fergal.

'You and Sophie come with us, Fergal,' said Becky.

'You can pretend it's Jacy,' she whispered to me, as the boys went ahead of us.

The boats were pretty mucky – I was glad I wasn't in a white dress tonight! Fergal was the perfect gentleman. 'Would you be wanting to sit on my sweatshirt?' he offered as we clambered on to the rocking boat.

I looked at him to see how serious he was. He had folded his lanky frame into the corner of the seat and was grinning shyly at me. 'I'll be fine, thanks.' I smiled back at him. He was cute.

Becky rocked the boat a lot as she sat herself at the pedals. 'Whoa there!' yelled John, trying to keep the thing level.

Becky yelped. 'I'm what you call ballast!' she laughed. 'A boat needs weight!'

John sat at his pedals and whooped. He enjoyed himself with Becky, I could see. He liked the person underneath the flesh, and I admired him for that. They gradually co-ordinated their efforts and moved us out on to the lake. The four boys on the other pedalo were doing far worse. For a start, they couldn't decide who was going to pedal, and nearly capsized the thing as they argued over who was to sit where.

'Would you look at them! That's the marvellous thing about you women,' said Fergal. 'You have a civilising influence, so you do.'

'Doesn't take long for the charm offensive to begin!' said John. 'Take no notice, girls, he can't help it!'

'I like it,' said Becky comfortably.

We were moving quite fast. I dabbled my hand in the shattered water and pretended Fergal was Jacy. I imagined it was just the two of us out there on the lake. The sky was inky blue with a sliver of a moon. In the distance the fire leapt and danced. People moved around like shadows at a distance. Jacy and I were removed from all of them. He stroked my hair. He moved closer, cupped my face in his hands and looked deep into my eyes with that melting gaze. Then we kissed.

CRRUNCH! 'We've been rammed! This is war!' It was John. 'Come on, Becky, *pedal*!'

Steve, Sean, Peter and Gus were like little boys, grinning and yelling, 'Tee-hee! Gotcher!' as we went spinning out of control.

But John and Becky were up to the challenge. They pedalled us out into the middle of the lake at amazing speed and lined themselves up to ram the others. 'Weyhey, I love it!' said Fergal. I was sad to let go of my daydream but this was a gas. I knew it was the sort of thing Jacy would have enjoyed too. I threw myself into yelling and splashing with the best of them. We all got soaked. I hope Becky's blouse wasn't ruined. At six-four to us we headed back for shore. A small crowd had built up there wanting their turn, including my brother and Emma and the French girls. (Why Emma, Dan, I thought, when you could have Suzette on a plate?)

We climbed out – Fergal offered his hand to help Becky and me down, would you believe – and ran over to the fire to warm up a bit. We clutched our bottles and cans and crisps and got as close to the flames as we dared. The boys were chucking things on the fire as boys will, so Becky and I moved to one side. 'I know he's not Jacy, but Fergal's a bit yummy, isn't he?' she said.

'That's the thing, though, he's not Jacy. Honestly Becky, I think I'm going mad! I can't think about anything else. I just wonder what he's doing, and whether he's thinking about me. I'm not interested in anybody else. Fergal's a bit young. And – ' I made sure she could see I wasn't too serious, ' – he *is* a ginge.'

Becky had seen that I wasn't serious, but for the first time in our friendship she looked at me witheringly, in a way that made me uncomfortable. 'Sophie Morris! Does *everyone* have to be perfect in Sophie-Morris-land? You'll be saying you don't like fat people next!'

'*You're* not fat!' I lied unconvincingly and braced myself for the weight of Becky's scorn.

'So that's OK, then.' She emptied her can of drink and crushed it vehemently.

I wanted to make amends. 'I'm *so* sorry Becky. I seem to be getting it wrong with everyone this holiday, and I really don't want to get it wrong with you. I know I must seem a bit superficial. Perhaps I am.'

She didn't rescue me.

'Well, I know I have been up until now. But I can see I've been immature—'

'Don't grovel, Soph. We're cool. But even fat people have feelings. Hey!' she broke off. 'Look over there! It's lover boy!'

I saw him at the end of the path from the woods, just a white T-shirt in the dark, but unmistakably lithe and *Jacy*. 'He's waving!' I said, delighted. We waved back. But someone else was waving from the water. Someone else was climbing out of a pedalo and running to pick up a torch. It was Emma who became a bobbing will o' the wisp of torchlight, moving through the dark to where Jacy stood, and Emma disappearing up the path to the campsite with him.

Becky grabbed me. '*No.* It's not how it seems. Emma and Jacy, no way. That was about something else, something to do with them in the bar earlier. I swear, Sophie, that those two do not have a thing going. But we must make a cunning plan for you, Sophs.'

'Do you still want to?' I felt crestfallen on two counts.

'*Course* I do. When we go riding tomorrow, that's what we'll do. We'll plot and plan and work something out. I still think you're so right for each other. It will be so romantic.'

'Am I forgiven, then?'

'What for?' said Becky, laughing at my forlorn expression.

The rest of the evening at the lake was great, despite the turmoil in my head. People drifted around. Some smoked, some drank, a few couples sneaked off, but for most of us it was just friendly and undemanding. Gus was one of the ones who drank and made a noise. Steve kept him company. Fergal sat in the glow of the fire, gently playing someone's guitar. He seemed to be playing more for himself than the crowd, but I could tell he was pretty good. When it was late, John came and found Becky. I didn't see her putting up a big fight when he persuaded her to go with him. I decided it was time to go back and felt relieved to see Dan and the French girls coming towards me on their way up. Mark was with them. 'Coming, Soph?' Dan reached down a hand to pull me to my feet and I felt ridiculously grateful that my big brother was being nice to me. Mark was speaking desperate Geordie French, which Francine and Suzette loved, so Dan and I led the way with the torch. 'Good down there, isn't it?' he said, not really wanting an answer.

Just before we reached our tent Francine and Suzette came out with a torrent of French that I couldn't understand, though I judged by those cutesy smiles that they wanted something. 'They want us to take them back, because we've got a torch,' said Mark.

'Oh yeah!' said Dan, laughing. 'OK, girls, we'll protect you against strangers in the night, won't we, Mark? See you later, Sophie.'

I could hear Dad snoring inside our tent. It was dark. I stumbled around, looking for the hurricane lamp. Suddenly there was someone standing there. I drew in my breath ready to scream, but he put a hand over my mouth.

It was Jacy! 'Don't scream,' he whispered. 'You'll wake everyone up! It's only me.'

'What are you doing here?' I asked.

'Oh, just hanging around waiting to catch the lovely Sophie Morris alone.' He laughed softly. 'Sorry if I frightened you. Bye!'

Was that the sign I'd been waiting for? I just didn't know.

EIGHT

'What do you think all that was about, then?' I asked. Becky, inelegant in the extreme on a bike, knew what she was doing when it came to sitting on a horse. I was already a bit uncomfortable, being chafed in places I didn't even know I had, and we'd only been going about twenty minutes. Twelve of us followed two leaders round the far side of the lake into pastures new. It was another beautiful, hot day, but a light breeze was going to make the heat bearable.

'Do you really think he was waiting for me, Becky?'

'I suppose we're going to have to come to terms with the fact that he'd been next door with Emma.'

'I just don't see it.'

'We don't know why he was with Emma. They're planning something for sure, but I can't even think what they might have in common. I mean what could "a night to remember" possibly be?'

'I don't care, as long as it's not a romance. Jacy wouldn't have such poor taste!'

'Emma's all right. I don't really see what you've got against her—'

'Her dress sense for a start!'

'But she fancies your brother, doesn't she?'

'I don't know any more. It's just that, whatever the reason, I refuse to believe that Jacy fancies her. OK, then, let's assume Jacy had come from there. But why did he say he was waiting to catch me alone?'

'Typical male, isn't it? To assume that you'd be on your own. I suppose he must know you like him, and because he's so sure of himself he couldn't imagine there being any competition.'

'But he's right. Nothing compares . . .'

Becky started singing, 'Nothing compares, no-*thing* compares with you . . .'

'Well, they don't. And I do like him, so why would he mess around? You don't think—' I was about to express my doubts when Becky cut in.

'I KNOW!' she shouted. 'THAT'S IT! You've got to pretend there *is* competition. It never fails to pique the male ego. That's what we've got to do, Sophie. Make him jealous.' Her horse sensed her excitement and started to canter about a bit. She reined him in.

'Do I want to make him jealous? What if it backfires on me? What if he's been having a thing with Emma all along and I never realised?'

'Of course you want to make him jealous! If he thinks you're interested in someone else he'll be there to stake his claim before you can say "Bleu Tropique".'

'I suppose it might move things on a bit. I've been here since Monday, and it's Friday now, so it's time something happened. Well, time a bit *more* happened. He did walk me back to the tent on Wednesday and he did surprise me last night. I keep thinking one thing is going to lead to another, but it never does.'

'That's because blokes are lazy, and if they don't have to try then they won't. I expect he just takes it for granted that you'll be there for him whenever he decides to make a move on you.'

'A bit how I felt about him, really.'

'Then perhaps THAT explains last night! Perhaps he was trying to make *you* jealous! He's probably waiting for you to make the first move!'

Becky had a point. And I desperately wanted to believe

her, even if my gut instinct was to be less convinced. Her explanation also made sense of his behaviour. It was so unlikely that he really was after Emma, but he'd made sure I saw them together.

'OK, Becky. So how do I go about making him jealous?'

'I'm working on it.' The two of us had fallen behind the other riders, so we thought we ought to catch up. We were trekking through the trees where it was beautifully cool. It was no hardship to canter after them – the horses' hooves thundered satisfyingly on the forest floor. We met up just before our route took us along a sunbeaten lane that wound its way between fields of sunflowers. The sun blazed down on us as we took to the road. The riders – people of all ages from nine to sixty – went quiet in the extreme heat. I looked at row upon row of sunflowers all turning their faces to the sun and I thought – *Jacy is my sun. I want to turn my face to him wherever he goes. When he isn't there I want to close my petals and sleep until he appears again. If he were to leave me now I know I would shrivel and die*. A poem started to form in my brain to the rhythm of the horses' motion, but it was only the last lines, *If you were to leave me now, I know I would shrivel and die,* that kept on repeating themselves.

At last we turned on to a bridle path that was shaded by tall oak trees. It was bordered by blackberry bushes, and we leant down to pick a few early ones. 'Let's stop for a minute,' said Becky. 'I need a drink of water.' She glugged down half a bottle, screwed on the cap and said, 'Right. I've thought of our plan. The main problem is, who do you make him jealous with? There's Mark, of course—'

'I think not, Becky, not even for getting Jacy.'

'Well, I could lend you John. Or there's Steve. He fancies you.'

'No way! Does he really?'

'John thinks so. Could you pretend to fancy him?'

'I don't think so. He's just not my type.'

'Nobody's asking him to be. Remember what this is in aid of!'

It was no good. I couldn't contemplate lowering my standards even as a ploy. I cast my mind over the boys I'd met in the last few days. One of the Jamies wasn't too bad. At least he was taller than me and had a good tan. And though Tristan was a bit of a boffin and wore a brace, I found his brain quite appealing. But they still didn't meet the Sophie Morris impeccable requirements.

Becky burst in on my ruminations. 'What about the Irish lads?'

'What about them?'

'They're nice.'

'They're Irish.'

'So what? Sean and Peter are quite good looking. And Gus is a laugh.'

'I can't understand a word they say. And Gus is too noisy.'

'There's always Fergal Maguire.'

'Why d'you say his whole name like that?'

'Because its such a wonderful romantic name. I think he's lovely.'

I kept quiet about the 'ginge' reservation. In fact it didn't really apply any more – I'd caught sight of Fergal outside the shop this morning and seen that the colour of his hair in daylight was the most extraordinary dark foxy red, the henna colour all my friends dyed their hair a couple of years ago.

'Maybe.'

'Go on, go on, go on!' she said in her best Irish.

'OK. And suppose I do use Fergal, how do I go about it?'

'This isn't something I've ever done myself, you understand. But from watching other people I think the idea is to give Jacy the eye all evening, and then, just when he's interested, you head for Fergal as if you'd been together all along.'

'If Jacy's interested, I'll want to go along with it. No, the best way to make someone jealous is to pretend you don't care but make sure they can see you with the other person, or be able to overhear you when you're talking about him. Fergal would have to be in on it. Otherwise he might react all wrong.'

'Sounds as though you're an expert. You don't need me!'

'Shut up!' I attempted to swat her – not easy on horseback. 'I'm so scared that it won't work. I'm really crazy about Jacy, Becky. I don't think I've ever felt like this before. I was so sure he'd want to go out with me – other guys always do. And he's so nice to me, he makes me feel special.' I couldn't tell even Becky just how much I was in love with Jacy. This was something even I wasn't used to. I mean, imagine wanting to write poetry about him! Me, wanting to be a sunflower! I'd definitely got it *bad*.

'Exactly. So what you need to do is to be all touchy-feely with Fergal so that Jacy can see what he's missing. I'm sure I'm right, so don't argue. We'll ask Fergal tonight. You can start in the bar. We'll make sure you're sitting next to Fergal and Jacy's bound to see you – he always comes into the bar at some point. I sometimes wonder if he's got something going with the girl behind the bar.'

'No. Hélène's got a French boyfriend somewhere. Suzette told my brother when we first arrived.'

'OK. So you're all chatty with Fergal in the bar where Jacy can see you. Couriers don't usually come down to the lake, so you can just be normal there. Then tomorrow there's Karaoke night. And the couriers organise it so they'll have to be there. We know Fergal can sing OK – you'll have to do something sloppy together, some old thing like *Especially for You*. They always have that one.'

'OK, OK! Don't go too fast. Let me get used to the idea. Anyway, it looks as though we're stopping for lunch.'

It was a relief in some ways to climb down off our horses. I felt as though I'd be stuck in that position for ever. This was obviously their usual stopping place because there was a rail for tethering them and a water trough. We were at the top of a hill with a view down over the way we had come. We could see the campsite in the distance with the lake and the forest and all the toy-sized green and yellow tents among the trees. It felt as though we were looking at the Earth from the moon – a whole little holiday world down there full of people going about their holiday business, cooking, swimming, playing, falling in love. I wondered what Jacy was doing at this moment. Probably something mundane like cleaning out tents. Jacy even managed to make pulling a cleaning cart full of Flash and disinfectant look glamorous and noble. There I was again, *turning my face to my sun.*

'Oy, you!' Becky intruded on my daydream. 'Mum's given me far too much food. Do you want a peach? Or a yoghurt? Or a bunch of grapes? Or some chocolate? Sometimes I think she wants me to be fat! Do you know, she says she was once like me, but it all fell off when she left school. So there's hope for me yet. I might be as skinny as you one day.' She laid into the chocolate.

When we had finished eating, the guides called us all together to look at the view and point out where we were going on the homeward trek. They spoke in French so it wasn't much use to me, or half of the other people on the ride. Becky translated some of it for me. I'm beginning to think I should work a bit harder at French at school. It's humiliating not being able to understand anything even though I've been learning for three years.

We packed up our bags and got back into the saddle. The horses were a bit grumpy at first, but then they realised we were on the way home and got into line. Becky and I were up at the front this time, me following her. The guides, two girls of about nineteen or twenty, were gossiping – in French of course. Naturally we didn't take much notice, but then the name Hélène kept cropping up. Becky concentrated on listening. She dropped back a bit to report. 'I can't quite catch what they're saying, but it's something to do with her boyfriend – how they never get any time together. It's not as if we've ever seen her with a man, is it? I'll see if I can find out who it is.' She moved closer again, but fell back soon after. 'They're not talking about her any more now. They've moved on to football – *"le football"*! Shame. I like eavesdropping when people think you can't understand what they're saying.' We trotted on. I was in front this time. I tried listening in. Becky was right. It was all *'le football'* – and that's boring even when you do understand.

We clattered into the campsite at about four. We could hear the shrieks coming from the pool as we rode past the far side of it. 'Don't you just long to dive into that cool water?' Becky asked.

'Swimsuits would be good,' I said. We walked rather agonisingly back to my tent. Mum, Dad and Dan were still out in the town.

'It's all right for you,' said Becky. 'I've got to cycle with a sore bum to my caravilla to get mine.'

'I'll wait for you,' I said. 'I want an ice-cream, so I'll change and then meet you at the bar.'

'OK. See you in about twenty minutes.' Becky struggled on to her bike and pedalled off wearily. I was tempted to spend the time jotting my poem in my diary but somehow the thought of a shower was even more appealing. It was lovely to smell of shampoo and body lotion rather than horse and sweat. I put a pair of shorts on over my bikini, pulled a comb through my hair – it was only going to get wet again – and wandered over to the bar for *une double – vanille et cassis, s'il vous plait.* No time like the present for improving one's French. GET A GRIP, SOPHIE! I reminded myself. Poetry and learning French? What was going on here? The words 'sad' and 'geek' came to mind. I pushed them away, smiled back at Hélène – she was laughing at my French really, but her gorgeous smile was irresistible – and attacked my ice-cream.

It was dark inside the bar. I was about to make my way into the bright sunlight outside when someone called me. 'Did you not see me over here, Sophie? We've been lookin' for people all afternoon, but we've not seen them. It's good to see you, so it is!'

Fergal.

'Hi, Fergal. I'm meant to be meeting Becky outside, but I suppose she'll see me when she comes in to buy an ice-cream.' I sat down at his table. 'Where are Gus and Peter and Sean?'

'They went back to the tent to play cards. We don't spend all our time together, you know. I wanted to find out where everyone else was.'

'I was like that when I arrived,' I told him kindly. After all, I was going to be asking him a BIG favour pretty soon. 'The way it works here – for teenagers like us, that is – is sleep in the morning, pool in the afternoon, bar after supper and lake after that. Most days, that is.'

'So what are you doing here now?'

'Becky and I went riding for the day. It was great.'

'Won't that be costing a lot?'

'My parents paid.'

'Oh,' he said. 'That's nice.'

There was a short silence. I sensed I'd said something slightly odd. 'That's what parents are for, isn't it?' I asked with a laugh.

'I wouldn't know. I don't have parents,' he said shortly.

'Oh God, I'm sorry. Have I put my foot in it?'

'No. My mother died when I was very little. She was just a girl when she had me, so my grandmother and grandfather are like parents to me. I don't know my father. I think he was a student at the University, but my mother never told and he never knew about me.'

My ice-cream was melting. I licked it round the edge to stop it dripping while I thought about the turn this conversation was taking. I felt it needed booting into the present. 'Who's brought you here?'

'Sean and Peter's mother and father. They're teachers. They often bring Gus – he comes from a very big family, and this year they offered to bring me too. Me and Peter have been mates since juniors. But we don't have to do everything together. I like to be on my own sometimes.'

Becky burst in at this point. 'My God! Sophie! Don't tell me you're chatting up an Irishman?'

'Why not?' I asked, aggrieved.

'Why shouldn't she chat up an Irishman?' said Fergal, his face lighting up with amusement.

'Sophie doesn't do Irish. Or French. Or Geordie. She just about manages Scouse though, don't you, Soph?'

I wasn't sure I liked this. 'I understood every word Fergal said,' I protested. Then I realised that this sounded worse than ever. They were laughing too loudly to hear me trying to make amends.

'See what I mean?' said Becky, guffawing.

'I obviously spoke very slowly and clearly!' said Fergal, but he gave me one of his nice grins.

'I'm trying to be better,' I said feebly.

'Good,' said Becky. 'Let's go for a swim. Coming, Fergal?'

'How could I refuse?' he said, untangling his limbs from the chair and table. 'It just so happens that I have my swimming stuff right here.'

'Becky!' I hissed. We were playing on the flume in the children's pool. Fergal had just gone down ahead of us. 'You're going to have to ask him. I don't know what to say.'

'Perhaps you won't need to say anything. He seems pretty keen already.'

'Exactly. I told you – he has to know what's going on or

he might not do what I want, and blow it. Please, Becky. Please say something for me.'

'I love it when you beg. OK. Don't worry. I'll ask him.'

'Tell him that Jacy and me are virtually going out – we just need a little help. But make sure he knows that I'm in love with Jacy. Exclusively. I really need him to know that. At least – I think I do. He has to be told I'm in love with Jacy, doesn't he, Becky?'

'Stop wittering and leave it to me. I'll get to the bar before you do tonight and corner him.'

'You won't let Jacy hear, will you?'

'What sort of idiot do you take me for?'

NINE

It all went very well. I don't know exactly what Becky said to Fergal, but I sat next to him in the bar, and when Jacy put his head round the corner I quickly looked adoringly at Fergal and squeezed a little closer to him. I caught Emma giving me some funny looks, and Mark some doleful ones, but they didn't bother me.

Down at the lake we just had a laugh. We really were singing round the campfire (note to self: DO NOT tell the folks back home about this one). Fergal borrowed Mark's guitar and got us all going. He has a great singing voice. That's going to be useful because singing has never been my strong point and I'll certainly need him to be confident if we're going in for the Karaoke. It felt as if we'd all been there for ever – me, Becky, John, Steve, the Irish contingent, my brother, Emma and Mark, the French girls, Tristan, Jamie and all the others who formed our group. I had to admit I was enjoying myself. Having a great holiday even. Except, of course, for Jacy.

I bumped into him this morning at the shop. I tried to

compose my face to look uninterested, but how could I, when he was in swimming gear, a towel round his neck and drops of water still running in a delicious line down the middle of his chest and clinging to his hair? At least this time I was presentable. I'd had a shower and was wearing shorts and a top that showed off my tan.

'Sophie! Hi! Sonia and Coralie made me buy breakfast today so they could have a bit of a lie-in before the Saturday rush begins. What brings you here so early?'

I couldn't sleep for thinking of you. You shine like the sun. Are you jealous yet? I don't know what to say. 'We needed – ' I looked into my basket. It contained two plastic bottles of semi-skimmed milk and some bubblegum – 'stuff.' Well done, Sophie. I looked at him helplessly.

'Fine. Good. Right – see you later, at the Karaoke tonight?'

'Yes, please.'

Oh *God*! He wasn't in*vit*ing me! He was just reminding me that it was on. Too late. He'd gone. I cycled back to the tent.

Becky was waiting for me – she was up earlier than usual too. 'Do you want to come to the beach with us?' She was panting – she'd obviously cycled fast. 'My brother's invited the twins and Mum and Dad said I could bring a friend. There's plenty of room in the Volvo.'

'I'd love to. I have to get away from this place. I've just done something so cringe-making! Let me give these to Mum and then I'll come.'

'We'll pick you up in about twenty minutes – no rush!'

'There is for me. I really want to do a disappearing act right now.'

'I'll make sure they don't hang about.'

Dan wasn't up yet. Dad and Mum were having coffee – hence the milk. (OK, so I was being a helpful little girl to my loving parents for a change, but I wasn't going to tell Jacy that.)

'Did I hear you were off to the beach, darling?' said Mum.

'If it's all right with you.'

'Of course it is. I don't know what Dan's up to, but I think he said something about football, so I imagine you're not interested.'

'No interest whatsoever, Mum.'

'Are you going to the Karaoke after supper?'

'We were thinking of it.'

'Jesse mentioned it to us – it seems it's for everyone, us oldies as well as you.'

'Jacy, Mum. Jacy.'

Becky's family rolled up in their Volvo. They tooted and the twins shot out from the tent next door, scattering beach towels, goggles and boogieboards in their wake. I followed rather more sedately. Becky's car had three rows of seats; her parents sat in the front, Becky and I sat right at the back facing the other way, and the three boys sat in the middle. That meant we could chat without being too bothered by their incessant football talk, interspersed only with awful songs and chants. 'My brother has nothing whatsoever in his mind apart from the match on Monday night,' said Becky.

'What match is that?' I asked.

'WHAT MATCH?' said all three boys, turning round together.

'That's what I asked,' I said, laughing at their incredulity.

'Only the England v. France match at the campsite,' said one of the twins.

'Haven't you seen the posters?' said the other.

'Can't say I've seen any posters,' said Becky mildly, and we carried on talking about my embarrassing encounter with Jacy.

'Mum said he told them about the Karaoke evening too,' I said.

'And did your mum say "Yes please" like you did?'

'It wouldn't surprise me! She fancies him too.'

'At least it means he'll definitely be there. Which gives our plan a better chance of working . . .'

A Karaoke night might sound naff to you, but all I can say is that, when it's with a group of friends and there isn't any alternative entertainment, it's actually pretty cool. Our lot went to the bar first and rolled up at the crêperie where the younger kids were already up on stage doing their stuff. It wasn't so much a stage as a raised platform with stairs at either side at one end of the room. There were French windows all the way along so we could hang around outside and still hear. It was mostly parents and younger children inside, but I remembered that most of the little ones were dragged off to bed at about ten. We found the list of songs. They were all old favourites with a few corny French songs thrown in, but we signed up as a group for 'YMCA' and 'Bohemian Rhapsody'. Tristan was being very organised at this point and telling us what to do. 'Male solo here – where's Fergal?' Fergal loped over. 'I'm putting you down for "When I Need You", Ferg. And there's some male/female duos here too.'

'Only too happy to oblige,' said Fergal. He looked down the list. 'You'll do one with me won't you, Sophie – something from *Grease*? That will be some craic!'

Now, if there's one film I have watched at least a hundred times, it's *Grease*. I know all the words off by heart. 'Which song?'

' "You're the One that I Want".' He grinned. 'We can do a bit of a dance as well.'

'I'm on.' I knew all the steps, too, so maybe my less-than-brilliant singing voice wouldn't be so apparent.

Coralie and a huge bunch of kids were doing one of those songs with loads of actions. Everyone was joining in, including us. I looked around for Jacy but he was nowhere to be seen. He'd better be there for my romantic duet with

Fergal, I thought. Singing in public is not something I take on lightly.

'YMCA' was the next song to come up. An extremely large group of us crowded on to the platform, so many that it wasn't possible for all of us to see the screen. You know 'YMCA' – all you really need to do is fling your arms about to make the letters at the right time, so I didn't really care about the screen. 'Young man . . .' the intro started. I could see Coralie and Sonia marshalling troops for the next song. It seemed to be a gathering of campsite staff. Surely Jacy would be among them? I peered at the far doors – there he was!

'Y–M–' I sang as loudly as I could and threw my arms into a Y. Oops. The intro was repeating. Damn. I should have known that. Everyone else was singing 'Young man' again – and those around me were starting to giggle.

'Now!' whispered Becky, with an exaggerated nudge. 'Y–M–C–A!' I was trying to concentrate, honest. I threw my arms out again, in Becky's face this time. By now everyone was laughing. We were a riot. We had everyone joining in. In fact the only people not joining in were the campsite workers, as they prepared to do their rendering of 'Summer Holiday'. They filed up the stairs on one side of the platform as we toppled down the other and fell outside to let our excitement subside. The others whizzed off to buy drinks but I wanted to watch 'Summer Holiday'. Jacy, Coralie and Sonia were on stage, but so were the campsite staff who worked in the bar, the restaurant and reception, the *guardien* and even the owners who lived in the manoir. Madame had a wonderful operatic voice. It was quite a line-up. They were brilliant and had the whole audience in stitches. After it, Madame gave a little thank-you-and-welcome speech which was also the cue for parents to take the little ones away. Jacy had disappeared again so I lost interest for a while. Fergal wanted to run through the *Grease* steps in a corner of the courtyard. Yes, we went all the way through the dancing part, skips, 'ooh ooh oohs', dirty dancing and all.

'Hey! You can dance!' he said as I strutted my Olivia Newton-John stuff. So could he! John Travolta eat your heart out, I thought, but I didn't say it. 'I hope you can manage to sing as we dance – I'm not sure I can do both.'

'It's the singing I'm not so sure of,' I told him. 'I know the words and the steps. I'm just not so confident about coming in on the right note.'

'Don't worry,' he said. 'It's only a laugh! I've got to go back in again now and make a fool of myself with "When I Need You".'

'I'll come back in and listen.'

'I'll sing it just for you then!'

Steady on, I thought, but then, what better way to make another guy jealous? I found myself in a crush with the gang – Becky and John, Steve and Gus. 'Hit them with it, Fergal!' yelled Gus as Fergal made himself comfortable with the mike and the intro started up. Fergal looked over in our direction, and then – he was really playing his part well – he fixed his gaze on me and began singing.

'Wow!' said Becky. 'He's fantastic!'

'I know,' I said. 'I almost wish he was doing it for real! *Someone* can't fail to be jealous!'

Becky looked at me blankly. Then understanding dawned. 'Oh! Yes! Jacy. Yes, I bet he'll wish he could sing like that.'

The roar of applause that came at that point was deafening, but my pleasure in the ruse was short-lived. Jacy was going on stage again. Jacy, Madame et Monsieur, Hélène and – *my parents*! Oh my God, what was going on? Dad had his arm round Hélène's waist and was grinning like a moron. Mum was in between Monsieur and Jacy and, likewise, grinning like a moron. *CRINGE!* Dan looked wildly over at me, eyes popping and eyebrows working overtime. 'I don't know!' I mouthed back at him as I saw him block his ears. That wasn't enough for me. I covered my eyes with my hands.

'Haw-hee-haw-heee-haw-haw-haw . . .!' It was a French song – 'La Vie en Rose'. Mum and Dad have never done anything as embarrassing as this before. Dad kept looking at Madame and squeezing Hélène's waist instead of looking at the screen so his words just sounded like a donkey braying. Mum was the opposite. She glued her eyes to the screen and stood stock-still, so the others all bumped into her as they swayed from side to side in true Gallic fashion. It was a nightmare. I wanted to die. What would Jacy think of someone with such idiots for parents?

Everyone else was laughing uproariously. How could they! I realised I was standing with one hand in front of my eyes and the other over my mouth when Fergal tugged at my arm. 'Come on. It's us next.' So there we were, going up on stage as the French songsters went down the other side to great cheers of approval. The audience thought they'd been *funny*! Clearly a case of alcohol-fogged judgement. Our lot gave Fergal and me a clap. I had the satisfaction of Jacy looking back at us as he made his way down into the audience and hearing someone shout 'Break a leg!' – though actually I think that was Mark. Still, they were on our side. I struck my funky-Sandy pose, and we were off.

'Sandy!'

'Tell me about it – stud.'

And then Fergal was John Travolta. He did those amazing hip waggles, screamed, fell down – everything.

'You'd better shape up . . .' There wasn't much stage but I managed to skip about. Then I had the inspiration to skip down one side of the stairs so I could skip up the other. It worked really well and Fergal seemed to anticipate what I was doing all the time.

'You're the one that I want! Ooh Ooh Ooh!'

I got up the stairs again for my next verse and Fergal managed to fall down them convincingly after he'd said

'Wow!' but we somehow managed to synthesise our dancing for the duet at the beginning of the long last chorus. It was going so well.

But then disaster struck. I danced down the stairs again – and toppled – right over into the audience. My ankle was agony. I clutched it and looked up at the stage. Fergal was carrying on. He was singing and dancing as if I was still there! He ran his hands up and down my imaginary body and kept his eyes on my imaginary face. People were transfixed. I tried to stand but my ankle was too painful. I sat down on the floor again. Mark was at my side. 'I saw you fall, Sophie. I saw you fall.' He put my arm round his neck and helped me up. 'I'll get you some first aid. I'll get you some first aid.' He hopped me over to Sonia and Coralie.

'Jacy's our first aid man,' said Coralie. 'He went back to be on duty at our tent while we were all here.'

'I think I've only sprained it,' I told her. 'But it really hurts.'

Mark said, 'Can you move your ankle? You're sure it's not broken?' I wiggled it around. It hurt, but at least I could do it.

'Jacy might have company,' said Coralie to Mark as this was going on. 'Make lots of noise as you approach.' I was in too much agony to wonder why lots of noise should be necessary. She turned to me, 'But he'll bind up your ankle for you, Sophie. He's a dab hand with a bandage.'

Mark helped me out as all my friends leapt on stage for the last song, 'Bohemian Rhapsody', led by Tristan. There was no way I could have joined them. Being this close to the odious Mark was almost more than I could handle, but to be honest, my ankle was killing me. I even felt a teensy bit grateful to him for helping me when all the others were in thrall to Fergal doing our duet singlehanded. But most important of all – I was on my way to Jacy!

If he said 'Are you all right (a' reet), like?' once, he said it a hundred times as we made our way along the road at the top to the couriers' tent. 'I thought you sang great, Sophie,' he said. 'I thought you sang great. You and Fergal are great together.'

I was going to butt in before he could repeat that statement, but we were right by the couriers' tent and I thought it wouldn't hurt if he said that nice and loudly. He did. 'You and Fergal are great together. Hello?' Jacy wasn't in the office bit, but he emerged from his 'inner' tent, a courier's only refuge, looking slightly less cool, calm and collected than usual. From singing with my mum, I expect!

'What's up?' he said. 'Oh hi, Mark. Hi, Sophie.'

'Sophie's sprained her ankle. Sophie's sprained her ankle.'

'So Sophie's sprained her ankle has she?' said Jacy, with a mischievous smile at me.

'Sonia and Coralie said you might be able to bind it up for me.' I didn't want him thinking it was my idea.

'OK,' he said. 'Now let's have a look. All good training for doing medicine next year.'

'I'm hoping to do that, too!' said Mark.

Well, well, well, who would have thought it, I found myself thinking, but most of me was concentrating on my foot in Jacy's hands. And that took some concentration. He twisted it gently in both directions. 'Does this hurt?'

'Yes!'

'Does this hurt?'

'Yes!'

'I think you're right. It is only sprained. If it was broken you wouldn't be able to move it.'

'That's what I said,' said Mark.

Jacy went to a cupboard with a big blue cross on it and took out a roll of bandage. 'Mark, could you just pour some cold water into that bowl? Thanks.'

'This might not be very professional Sophie, but I can probably do this best if you rest your leg across my knee.' If my ankle hadn't been so painful I would have been in heaven.

'Thanks, Jacy. You're being –' I tried to catch his eye '– amazing.' That wasn't quite what I meant to say, but it's certainly what I felt as my throbbing ankle was deftly bound in wonderful cool bandage.

'There. How's that?'

I stood up. I was able to stand up. Great, I'd be able to get back to the tent without Mark's help. Maybe, if I could get him to go, I might get a chance to thank Jacy properly . . . 'Great. It's much less painful. I can get back on my own now, Mark.' I looked meaningfully at him, hoping he'd take the hint and leave me alone with Jacy. He didn't. 'I'd like to thank Jacy, Mark.'

'Thanks, Jacy, man. Thanks.'

'I'd like to thank him. Personally.' I glared at him.

'Oh. Ah. I'll wait outside. I'll wait outside.' He shambled off.

Jacy looked at me, puzzled. 'No big deal, Sophie. It's all part of the job.' He cast a glance towards his 'inner' tent. 'I'll be catching up on my beauty sleep now.'

I stood there. I wanted to throw my arms round his neck and thank him for making me better. I wanted to say he could hold my feet and bind my ankles whenever he wanted. I wanted to tell him I loved him, that I was doing all that stuff with Fergal for show. I tried to look in his eyes. 'I—'

'–You ready, Sophie?' Mark put his big head round the tent. 'Ready?' The moment was lost. Quick as a flash I gave Jacy a peck on the cheek.

'You were wonderful, thanks.'

Outside I could barely contain my anger at Mark's ineptitude. 'Don't you know when to leave people on their own?' I hissed. 'Jacy and I wanted to be alone. For your information, we've been waiting a long time to be alone together.'

'I'm sorry. Sorry. I thought he – you—'

'Well you were wrong. Of course, someone like you

wouldn't understand the meaning of sexual attraction—' I felt thwarted and furious. Dim old Mark couldn't stop putting his foot in it. I didn't care what I said to him.

'Sophie,' he said mildly, 'I can see why all the girls fancy Jacy. I can see why. But you do know—'

'Nothing that *you* can tell me,' I said rudely. We had reached our tents. I was aware that people could hear us. 'Well thank you for your help. Goodnight, Mark,' I said as dismissively as possible. Mum and Dad were inside the tent. Dan was no doubt out and about, but I wasn't up to larking around the lake. I didn't want to have to do my act with Fergal again, not when there was no possibility of Jacy seeing us. I couldn't understand why I had messed up that opportunity so much. If only Mark hadn't been hanging around. Effing Mark. I could hear him now.

All cheerful. 'Hi, Mum! Hi, boys! That were all good fun, weren't it?' Funny how he didn't repeat himself with his family.

I sat down at the table and lit a couple of nightlights. I put my foot up on one of the chairs and remembered Jacy's firm touch. It was a while before I noticed a note tucked under Mum and Dad's wine bottle. It was a piece of folded paper with SOPHIE written on it. I opened it: this is what it said:

I feel a weird affection that I'm too shy to convey.
So I guess I'll just meditate in your direction, and be on my way!
Fergal
PS Where did you go?

It was just a verse from our song. Why had he bothered to write it out?

TEN

Mum was very solicitous in the morning. She unzipped my compartment. 'Poor old Sophie! You *are* in the wars! Let me have a look at your ankle. We were right the other end of the room and by the time I got to the stage I heard that Mark had taken you off to the couriers for first aid. I was waiting for you, but I'm afraid I fell asleep. You should have woken me.'

'I was OK. Jacy bandaged it for me.'

'Let me have a look.' The ankle was a bit swollen but not too bad. The cool bandage had obviously done the trick. 'I'd like to see you walking on it before I pass judgement. It's quite late, darling. Why don't you get up and have a shower? Dad and I want to go to a service in the village church and I'd like to know you're fit enough to leave behind.'

'Of course I am, Mum. But I might as well get up.' I wanted to be fully prepared for visitors. Fancy being crocked twice in one holiday! It really isn't like me. I quite liked the idea of reclining on a sun lounger in my bikini and holding court. I hobbled off to the shower block. It was still quite painful to walk, but I could tell that I was already on the mend.

I put my sarong on over my bikini and sat down for breakfast. 'Well,' said Mum, 'and what did you think of me and Dad last night? Stars, eh?'

I started to um and ah, the very thought of their little performance still bringing me out in goosepimples, but luckily she interrupted me. 'I thought Fergal was marvellous. And you too, darling. He carried on so bravely when you disappeared. A difficult decision, I should imagine – whether to stop and see how you were or carry on.'

I thought about Fergal. I'd been quite impressed with him carrying on too. It hadn't occurred to me that it might have been nicer of him to find out if I was all right. But then Fergal wasn't anything to me. I wasn't bothered. And there had been that strange note . . .

'Eat your croissant, darling.'

Dan stumbled out, blinking in the bright light. 'Morning all. You and Fergal were pretty cool last night, Sophie. Especially when you fell over. We all had a good laugh!'

'Thanks, brother.'

'Did you hurt yourself?'

'Yes, as a matter of fact. But Jacy did first aid on it, so it's not too bad.'

'Jacy? He'd make any girl feel better.'

Mum grinned over at Dad. 'Just as Hélène would make any man feel better, don't you think, Giles?'

Dad looked sheepish. 'Well, she's a very lovely girl.'

'Thank goodness that was our one and only Karaoke night,' said Dan. 'Go on, you two. Go to church and confess your sins! I've got yet another football practice. They're working us very hard for people who are meant to be relaxing.'

'One more thing before we go,' said Mum. 'We've been invited next door for a barbecue tonight, so don't go making any other plans.'

I anointed myself with suntan lotion and made myself comfortable on the sun lounger with a Diskman and a pile of postcards. I thought it was time I sent some. I wrote to Hannah first. I wanted to tell her about Jacy. She's my friend so I had to be honest – I just put, 'There is the most gorgeous good-looking courier here, and I think it's only a matter of time . . . I've made some good friends. Weather good. Hope your music thing goes well.' For Charlotte I just wrote, 'Hi, wish you were here.' Maddy's was more difficult. Maddy expects men to fall at her feet, and mine for that matter. So I fabricated just a bit. 'I'm having a holiday romance with the most gorgeous good-looking courier. Tell you all about it when I get home.' (None of these quite tallied with the more anguished truth that was reported in my diary, but hey! I had to keep my end up in the holiday romance stakes. They expected it of me.) That was all for the time being. Mum had put stamps on them earlier – they might even reach England before I did. I suddenly found myself thinking about Ben Southwell. For the first time in my life I had an inkling of what he'd been feeling. Perhaps I should send him a friendly postcard. After all, we were going to have to see each other when school began again. But it could keep. He was probably still on holiday himself. In France, what's more. I remembered reminding him that France was a big place when we discovered we were both coming here – especially as he was going south and I was going west. I'd been pretty foul to him.

'Sophie!' That accent was unmistakably Irish.

'Hi, Fergal!' I held up his note and waved it about. 'What was all this about?'

'I – I – er – I just wondered what had happened to you last night. One minute you were falling off the stage and next minute I couldn't see you anywhere. I didn't know whether or not to carry on but, you know, the Karaoke machine is so relentless, and I was caught up in it. I'm so sorry. I really should have checked you were OK but I didn't know what to do for the best. I wanted to apologise.' He was quite distressed.

'Don't worry. I was fine. Jacy did first aid on my ankle.' I gave him a knowing smile.

'Jacy? Is that a French courier?'

'No, silly. He's English. You *know* . . .'

But he wasn't listening. 'About the note. It wasn't meant to embarrass you. Forget it. Anyway, I came to say we're off to the beach all day, but see you tonight, OK?'

'Wait! Why should I have been embarrassed? They were just the words from the song, weren't they?'

'Well yes, almost.'

'And I'm afraid we're having a barbecue next door tonight, so we won't be coming to the bar.' I grimaced at him, to show how I felt about the barbecue, but he was still looking confused when Gus came down and said, 'Come on, lover boy. We haven't got all day. See you later, Sophie!' and dragged him off . . . JUST in time to cross paths with Jacy. This was more like it!

Jacy had his cart, but he left it up by the road. 'How's the ankle?' he called, though he stopped briefly and said to the two boys, 'Are you two coming to the football tomorrow?'

'Our problem is that we don't know whether to be English or French!' said Gus.

'*Your* problem!' laughed Jacy. 'No one minds, mate. It's just a matter of making up the numbers! Come if you can! Though I warn you, the English have been practising!' He came over.

I propped myself up on my elbows. Then I suddenly remembered the postcards and turned them picture-side up. I wondered if Fergal had spotted them. 'The ankle's fine, thanks to you,' I said with an enticing (I hoped) smile. But then I suddenly felt nervous about being alone with Jacy. I'd made a conscious decision to wear my bikini – the pale blue one that showed off my tan – but now I felt exposed.

'I see your singing partner came to enquire after your health before I could!'

'Fergal?' Now I was stuck. Should I play the jealousy game and say how natural it was for Fergal to visit me, or should I be truthful and convey that Fergal meant nothing to me, compared with him?

'Who else?' he said. 'What a voice! That guy could do it for money!' Ha! He was jealous already! I didn't have to play games. 'Now are you lying there looking beautiful because you can't walk or because you can't help it?'

Wow. What a lovely thing to say. I realised I was making Bambi eyes at him. He had another stab. 'Is your ankle still too painful to walk on? I can only do first aid, you see, I'm not qualified to follow it up. But we could get you to a doctor if it's bad.'

'Oh.' I twigged. He was here as a courier, not as a courtier.

I got to my feet and limped towards him. He held out his hand ready to support me when I reached him. I was tempted to stumble so he could pick me up – my knees felt weak enough. But then – interrupted again! It was ratty little Sonia with her cart. 'Come on, Jacy! Stop chatting up minors! We've got four caravillas to clean out by lunchtime and I'm not doing them on my own!' I'd never liked her.

Jacy gave me a rueful smile. 'Slave labour, that's all we are. But it seems to me that you're on the mend, Sophie. OK, Sonia, I'm coming.' He caught sight of my postcards on the ground. 'Do you want me to post these, since you're immobilised?' He bent down and picked them up.

'NO!' I shouted, terrified.

'Censored stuff, are they?' he said, still smiling. 'Don't worry, I won't read them,' and walked off to pull his cart alongside Sonia, my postcards in his back pocket.

I couldn't run after him. I lay back, sweating. I tried desperately to remember what I'd written. I hadn't put his name, had I? Mum and Dad always say that messages on postcards are public property – an excuse for reading ones addressed to me, I reckon – but this was different! I'd said 'a courier', hadn't I? And he was the only male courier. I know! I could pretend they were Dan's postcards. That was it. I'd get Dan to thank Jacy for posting *his* cards and to say he hoped he hadn't read them. My mind was racing. No. I couldn't do that. I'd signed them. I could pretend that I thought Fergal was a courier. A motorbike courier! I could ask Jacy if he knew that Fergal was a really good motorbike courier as well as a good singer. Nope. Oh where was Becky when I needed her? Of course, Jacy might be flattered! The postcard to Hannah wasn't so bad. But Maddy's! What had I said? 'I'm having a holiday romance with a gorgeous, good-looking courier'? Depends how you define romance, I suppose. Perhaps he wouldn't be able to read my writing. Perhaps he really wouldn't read them at all, like he promised. No. Everyone reads postcards. Aaaagh!

Mum, Dad and Dan all came back soon after, but nothing could really take my mind off the postcards. I had to admit, I would be totally mortified if Jacy read them. I couldn't convince myself that he would be flattered. All I could do was pray that he hadn't read them, or that he'd passed them on to someone else to post.

My prayers were answered, but not quite in the way I'd expected. Becky came over after lunch and I decided I was up for a swim, so I limped along to the pool beside her. We were walking past the couriers' tent when Sonia called me over. My heart sank. I'd told Becky about the postcards. 'Uh-oh,' she said. 'Tell her it's none of her business. Whatever it is.' And she hung back while I hobbled over to see what Sonia wanted.

She was looking more ratty and pointy-nosed than ever and her glasses had an evil glint. 'Just a word, Sophie,' she said. I felt as though I was at school. I saw that she had composed her face into a sympathetic expression. 'I know it's none of my business,' she began. (Too right, I thought.) 'But Jacy gave me your postcards to post. Now, I don't normally read postcards, and I honestly wasn't intending to read yours, but what you'd written sort of leapt out at me and I thought I ought to put you straight.' Oh my God, she'd seen the one I wrote to Maddy. I couldn't speak. 'The courier, Sophie, is already spoken for.'

'What?' I said, rudely. What was she on about? Why couldn't she speak English?

She gave a smug smile. 'He already has an attachment to –' she paused, '– another member of staff.' She lowered her eyes meaningfully. 'I just thought you should know. In case – you make a fool of yourself.' My God! She meant herself! She was telling me that Jacy was attached to her! As if! What was she playing at? 'Don't take it too hard,' she said with a patronising look. 'Just a friendly word of advice.' She retreated into the couriers' tent.

I stared after her for a minute before hobbling back to Becky in high dudgeon. 'The cow!' I said. 'I always knew she was a cow. As if she could make me believe that Jacy fancied her.'

'Excuse me?' said Becky. 'Calm down. Take some deep breaths and tell Aunty Becky everything.'

I told her.

'Who does she think she is? I always thought she was like a school prefect. And she shouldn't have read your postcard. What a witch. Ignore it, Sophie. Just be glad it wasn't Jacy who read it.'

'That's a point. At least he doesn't know. Though I wouldn't put it past her to tell him.'

'What, and let him know that someone a million times more beautiful than she is fancies him? No way. She'll want to keep him for herself. I don't think she'll tell him.'

'Thanks, Becky. You're great.'

'Fat, but great.'

'I'll ignore that. I'm learning a lot on this holiday.'

'I'll say.'

I tried to hit her, but for once she was too quick for me.

The Irish boys left a big hole in the swimming party. Perhaps it was because Gus was so noisy. My brother was there but Mark and Emma, embarrassingly, were shopping with their mum for the barbecue in the evening. Francine and

Suzette had Dan to themselves. They were doing wonders for his French – and his street cred! So we were more sedate than usual.

Becky wanted to know more about last night. She said how everyone was talking about Fergal's singing and dancing. I felt ever so slightly peeved that no one was talking about my singing and dancing. I thought I had been pretty good until I skipped off stage. But I had to keep my thoughts to myself with Dan and Becky around. I thought I'd just bask in some of Fergal's reflected glory – since he'd made a point of singing at me.

'Tell me about Jacy bandaging your ankle,' she said with a sigh. 'Lucky you.'

'He's going to medical school after the summer,' I said.

'So the boy has brains as well.'

'Apparently Mark is heading that way too,' I said cautiously. I was feeling a bit worried about Mark after last night.

'Oh I knew about Mark,' said Becky. 'He's something of a genius according to Emma.'

'Mark?'

'Oh yes. Straight "A"s.' She paused to let that one sink in. 'By the way, Fergal was really worried about you last night. He was in a real state about carrying on when you'd hurt yourself. How did you end up at the couriers' tent?'

This was a difficult one. 'That's the point. Mark took me, actually. Sonia and Coralie told him to.'

'Mark?'

'The very same. Anyway, Jacy bandaging my ankle was fabulous – all sort of firm but gentle.'

'Wow. He wouldn't have been like that with just anyone.'

'I wanted to, you know, like, *thank* him, properly, but Mark got in the way.'

'Jealous, probably!' She laughed. 'Mark being jealous! Now that's not what we planned, is it?'

'Talking of our plan – Becky, what exactly did you say to

Fergal? You did tell him that I was in love with Jacy, didn't you? And that my liking him was all a fake?'

'It's not *all* a fake, is it?'

'I like him OK, of course.'

'Only *like*?'

'Becky! Did you or did you not tell Fergal about my feelings for Jacy?'

She was still hedging. 'Trust me! He was very willing to pretend to like you. I'm hot. Come into the water and cool off.'

I was not looking forward to the barbecue. I didn't like Emma. I didn't like Mark. The twins were irritating and I didn't know their mum. When Dan and I got back from the pool we could smell the charcoal burning. The rest of my family were in the tent when Mark came over to say, twice, that they'd be ready in half an hour. He was all spruced up in a clean T-shirt and wearing aftershave. 'Whatever,' I said, feeling bored at the mere thought of it, and went into the tent to tell the others.

'Yes,' said Dan. 'We heard. And we heard your reply too. Now just be nice for once. It won't hurt you. They just want to be friends.'

'Oh yeah. Mark because he fancies me and Emma because she fancies you. And their mum because she probably fancies Dad.' I stuck my chin in the air defiantly.

Suddenly Mum was on my case. 'SOPHIE!' she roared, and it frightened me because she's usually very mild, my mum. She linked her arm in mine quite viciously and dragged me off down a path that leads to the washing lines. We walked in total silence. When we were out of earshot of everyone she laid into me – verbally, that is.

'Sophie Morris. You are behaving like a spoilt little brat. I don't know what's eating you these holidays but I'm not proud of you. You boss poor Becky around and you're foul to Mark. You're rude, snooty and, quite frankly, plain horrible some of the time. I haven't liked some of the things I've heard you saying to Danny one bit. Now, you're my daughter and luckily for you I get to love you however you behave. But other people won't. Other people notice, you know. If you're unpleasant to Mark it reflects back on you eventually. Some of those boys you fancy won't like you any better for acting like a bitch.'

'Mother! How dare you call me a bitch!' I felt my mouth trembling.

'I'm not calling you a bitch, darling, but you've been bitchy, there's no denying. I don't like to interfere, but I also don't like to see my precious daughter letting herself down. You owe it to yourself to be liked for who you are as well as how you look.'

I cried. 'I'm sorry, Mum, I just get so fed up with droopy blokes.'

'That's not a good enough excuse I'm afraid, Sophie. I'm not about to lay a guilt trip on you, but you must realise that that family is not having an easy time at the moment.'

'Aren't they?'

'Has it escaped your notice that one member of their family is missing?'

'Well, no dad, but loads of families don't have dads.'

'And do you think that makes it any less hard for Mark and Emma? Not to mention their mum?'

'OK, OK. You said you wouldn't lay a guilt trip on me.'

'I just want you to look at the world around you a bit more.'

I rolled my eyes. 'Give me a break, Mum.'

Oh dear. I'd gone too far. 'SOPHIE!' she shrieked. And she carried on shrieking. 'OK. I'll play dirty too. You're sick of droopy blokes. Well, I'm sick of a droopy daughter. I don't know who you're mooning about after, and I don't care, but it strikes me that you need a taste of your own medicine. You don't deserve to have people falling in love with you, you really don't.' She looked unforgivingly at my tearful face. 'Right. I'm going back to that tent and I expect to see you there, looking nice, five minutes before we go next door. OK? Because if you can't behave yourself I can't enjoy myself, and we'll pack up and leave tomorrow. I mean it. So get your act together. Stop being so immature. And if you manage to do that you'll restore some of my respect for you and we can carry on as before.' She strode off.

I sank down on the grassy bank where she had left me. I couldn't stop crying. Mum had been shouting so loudly, people must have heard. The couriers were out and about at this time. Sonia might have heard. Or Jacy. Oh my God, what if Jacy had heard? Was I drooping about? I suppose I was, a bit. But to say I didn't deserve to have people fall in love with me – that was savage. Perhaps I simply didn't deserve Jacy? Was that it? I started crying all over again.

This wouldn't do. Mum, incidentally, is perfectly capable of carrying out her threats. I made a terrible fuss about going round to some family friends for lunch once and in the end Mum said she'd cancel them, even though we all knew that they would have made the meal and everything. She rang up and said she was very sorry but we weren't coming because Sophie was being so impossible. I was mortified for weeks because the daughter was a couple of years ahead of me at school and she told all her friends.

I tried to pull myself together. I wanted to tell myself that Mum had been unfair, but enough had happened on this holiday already to make me realise deep down that she wasn't. I do find it easy to despise people – Emma for her clothes, Mark for his looks, people who talk funny, fat people, ginger people. That word 'immature' stuck in my mind. Might someone despise *me* for being an immature person?

I looked at my watch. I had five minutes to get to the shower block, wash away my tears and show up at the tent. I ran (hobbled extremely fast would be a better description) for the shower block as if I had chronic diarrhoea so no one would stop me, and locked myself in a cubicle. I splashed cold water all over my face and through my hair for a couple of minutes. I looked in the mirror. I didn't look too bad. A bit like the romantic heroine in a film when her lover has just died. I smoothed back my hair into a topknot and headed for the tent. Mum was waiting for me. She didn't say anything but gave me a really big hug. I nearly cried again, but now wasn't the time. I was going to be NICE.

'Hello, everyone.' Mark and Emma's mum, Mary, had changed into what can only be called a 'frock'. Stop it Sophie, there I go already. Emma had put on tons of eye make-up – I say nothing, and even the twins had brushed their hair. OK, in my new caring mode I must give them names: Matt and Harry.

'Smells delicious,' said Dad. Actually, it did.

'It's bound to be,' said Mum. 'Mary's a cordon bleu cook.'

'Was,' said Mary. 'And cordon bleu isn't much use at a barbecue! Now, what's everyone going to drink? I'm assuming that your two will drink wine with us? We are in France after all. Or we've got some beers?'

I glared at Dan. 'On your life,' I whispered. I did not want him saying that I managed to get drunk on drinks without any alcohol. 'Coke would be fine for me,' I said with my sweetest smile.

'I wasn't offering drugs,' said Mary.

I looked at her, appalled.

'Joke!' she said. 'Sorry, Sophie. Fish a Coke out from the cool box, Mark. What about you Dan? A beer?'

'Great,' said Dan. 'Why don't you two give us booze?' he asked Mum and Dad.

'Because then there wouldn't be so much for us,' said Dad. 'Personally, I look forward to sharing a pint with you when you're eighteen, but we're not at home now, and when in Rome, you know.'

'All families do things differently,' said Mum.

I began to worry that we were being a bit rude. Mary was only being hospitable. But she didn't seem to mind at all. She was knocking back her gin and tonic pretty quickly in fact.

We filled our plates with food that was indeed excellent. Emma had made all sorts of salads and Mark was very efficient with the barbecue. The twins handed stuff round and Mary kept everyone's glasses filled. Well, she certainly kept her own full. By halfway through the meal Mum and Dad kept putting their hands over their glasses.

Emma, Mark and Dan were all quite easy with each other. I even felt a bit left out, sitting by Matt and Harry. They were eating with great gusto and talking loudly about, guess what, the football match. OK, Sophie, I thought, TALK to them about it.

'Right, you two. Now I know absolutely zilch about this football match tomorrow. Tell me all I need to know. One at a time.'

'Well,' said Harry. 'It's England v. France. And it's tomorrow night at seven p.m.'

'And Jacy's been coaching the England team.'

'But Emma's the captain.'

'And not all the English are English—'

'And not all the French are French—'

There are quite a few women playing—'

'And the French are wearing blue T-shirts—'

'And the English are wearing white ones.'

'And we're going to win!'

'Because Jacy and Emma are top!'

I blenched. They'd lost me some time ago but this statement brought me up with a jerk.

'So have the captain and the coach worked, er – *closely* together on this?'

'Oh yes. They've planned their team and their strategy, tactics, that sort of thing . . .'

So THAT was what Emma and Jacy had been up to. It was so simple. He didn't fancy her! He wasn't trying to make me jealous! Harry shrunk from my sudden interest. Matt leant over to him.

'Mum's at the bottle again, stop her.'

Harry got up and I saw him simply remove the bottle of wine from his mother's elbow and start offering it around. It was a practised move. 'More wine, anyone?'

'Well, why not?' said Dad, obviously aware of the situation and with a glance at Mum as if to say, I'll do this to help out but you'd better stay sober.

Mary got up to get the next course and promptly tripped over a guy rope. She swore roundly. 'Oops! Sorry, everyone.'

Quick as a flash Emma was at her side. 'Sit down and enjoy yourself, Mam. I'll serve it. Are the fruit kebabs done, Mark?'

'Yes. You just get bowls and cream and I'll deal with these.'

The fruit kebabs were gorgeous. I've rarely tasted anything so delicious. And that, added to my discovery that Emma and Jacy had only been planning football together, made me full of beneficence. 'They're amazing!' I said, and smiled at Mark. He smiled back, hugely, enormously, a never-ending smile. I held it. I saw all manner of mood changes and colour shifts pass through his grey-blue eyes. I thought, yes I really did: you poor bloke. Dad gone and your mum making a fool of herself and being the oldest and a family holiday and, OK, falling in love with me, and you have to hold it all together, all on your own. I was still feeling raw emotionally myself and tears started to prick at my eyes. I looked down. 'Really yummy,' I said.

'Thank you,' said Mark.

Mary was talking to my parents about sex. They were both pinned back in their seats, unsure whether to laugh or not. Mum did – she pretended that everything Mary said was enormously funny. Dad stood up. 'Mark, lad. Let's you and I have a game of pool. Dan can wash up. You've done enough.' I was aware, with a marvellously secure feeling, how Mum and Dad and Dan were coping with a tricky situation, just as Emma and Mark and the twins were. Nothing was said explicitly but all of them were sensitive to what was going on around them. I was impressed, and even a little humbled.

Possibly for the first time in my life I said, 'I'll help with the washing up!'

'We don't want to break up the rest of the party quite yet,' said Emma gently – she wasn't putting me down – looking over towards our mothers. 'I'm really sorry about this,' she whispered. 'It doesn't happen very often – well, not that often. I'm going to pack the boys off to the table tennis tables or somewhere, if that's OK with you. They seemed to have you rapt back there!'

'They were telling me about your football match tomorrow.'

'Blimey!' said Dan. 'I never thought I'd see the day!'

The twins were more than happy to leave us. 'Back by eleven, please,' said Emma to their departing backs.

'It's going to be a good match,' said Emma. 'Jacy's playing for us, but the Irish lads are playing for the French. Fergal's ace, apparently.'

'That will make up for Suzette, then,' said Dan. 'She's determined to play, and as we've got Emma and a couple of other girls Suzette thinks there should be at least three women on the French team.'

'Haven't you heard all this, Sophie?' said Emma.

'No. It's amazing what you block out when you're not interested. And as Becky isn't interested either we haven't a clue what's going on.'

'But you talk to Jacy, don't you?'

'Er, yes.' Was this a trick question?

'She thinks Jacy fancies her!' said Dan, suddenly getting his own back.

Emma laughed. 'I shouldn't think so!' she said. Then, 'Don't worry, Sophie, I won't let on!' And she and Danny laughed some more.

My good intentions went straight down the pan. 'You patronising cow!' I yelled and speed-hobbled past Mum, who was helping Mary out of her chair. I hurled myself into our tent, where I sobbed my heart out.

ELEVEN

'Mum says I've got to apologise for upsetting you. I was only teasing but she told me she heard what I said and that she can understand why you flew off the handle, especially after she'd just had a go at you. So, sorry. OK?'

'You can take a breath now.' It was a morning for apologies. Mary came and apologised for getting drunk. Dad apologised to Dan for getting him lumbered with the washing up. I felt I should probably apologise simply for being alive. But Mum decided it was a good day for a family outing. 'There's a cheese museum I simply have to see. I mean, can you imagine what might be in it? It's in a nice town with a market and some good places to eat. I thought we could go and check out this silly museum, wander round the market, have lunch, go to the beach and then get back in plenty of time for the match. What do you say?'

'I suppose so,' said Dan unenthusiastically. Mum glared at him. 'Yes, great,' he said. 'Whatever.'

The idea of getting right away from the campsite did seem appealing. I didn't want to see Emma, or Mark, or Sonia, or Fergal or even Jacy very much today. I even felt like giving Becky a rest. 'OK. Let's go. Let's go now.'

'Can I get dressed first, please?' Dad stood there in his

pyjamas looking dishevelled. His heroic drinking spree last night meant that he was rather the worse for wear. I went and sat in the car until they were all ready.

Mum drove and took charge of the day for all of us. It was a relief for me, and I suspect it was for Dan as well. We hadn't talked to each other properly for days.

The cheese museum was a hoot, all plastic cows and cardboard cheeses, but it was in a beautiful sleepy town with a river running through it. The market was sleepy too, but there was a basket of incredibly cute puppies on sale. Dan is as soppy about that sort of thing as I am, and we played with them for as long as we dared. 'I'll have that one and I'll call him Dylan,' said Dan.

'And I'll have that one and I'll call him Dougal,' I said.

'Sure you don't mean Fergal?'

'Enough! No more teasing, OK?'

'*Vous voulez acheter un petit chien*?' An old crone was approaching us.

'*Merci, non,*' said Dan and we had to leave them behind.

'I thought we'd go somewhere where they serve seafood for lunch,' said Dad solemnly.

'Dad!'

He ducked. 'Only joking!'

'We're going to a crêperie,' said Mum. 'Perfect for fastidious teenage children. And I'm going to have some of their cider and sleep it off on the beach before driving home.' The parents were being particularly kind. Last night's little episode had reminded them that we were lucky to be a four-square family and they wanted to make the most of it. Danny and I went for a walk along the beach after lunch. There were rockpools and hidden coves to explore. At one point we were forced to scramble up to the top of the cliff and found ourselves walking down towards a naturists' beach.

'I think not,' I said.

'We could stay and look a while,' said Dan wistfully.

'There is a word for people like you, Daniel Morris!'

'OK! OK! I didn't mean it.'

'For someone who gets an eyeful of Suzette every day I'm surprised you feel the need.'

'All blokes feel the need, Sophie. Haven't you learnt that much?'

This was near-the-knuckle talk from Dan. 'What's the problem? Suzette's obviously crazy about you!'

'Do you think so?'

'DAN! You ask if *I* haven't learnt that much! Yes! I'm telling you, as a female, Suzette fancies the pants off you. And so does Emma. And that's the truth, I'm not being snidey.'

Dan went quite pink. 'Really? Both of them?' We slid down to the beach again. 'Wow.'

'So are you going to do something about it?'

'Like what?'

'Oh Dan! Get off with one of them. I'd go for Suzette if I were you. She might teach you a thing or two.'

'But Emma – ' his voice softened, 'Emma's more real somehow.'

'Up to you, brother dear. I don't fancy either of them as a sister-in-law, but that's not my problem.' Dan was quiet for a while after that. Fancy not realising, when both of them made it so obvious.

He gave me a bashful grin. 'Well, we'll just have to see what happens, won't we now?'

'Just don't leave it too long, or we'll have gone home and you'll have missed your chance.'

Mum and Dad were asleep on the beach. Dad had his arm across Mum's back. 'Aaah,' I said and quoted, 'Old people can be so sweet!' (I've watched *Clueless* nearly as many times as *Grease*.)

Back at the campsite it was football mania. There were signs everywhere as we drove up the hill.

FOOTBALL CE SOIR
ANGLETERRE V. FRANCE

Somebody had found some French flags and some Union Jacks and there were little kids running around with them. 'I feel sorry for the Dutch and the Germans,' said Dad as we pulled up.

'They're fine,' said Dan. 'They can be either French or English for the evening. No one takes it that seriously.'

'Strikes me that some of you are taking it very seriously indeed,' said Mum. 'All those practices.'

'We want to win,' said Dan. 'Obviously. But since each side is such a mixture of nationalities, it's just our *team* that we want to win.'

'So no national pride allowed, then?' said Dad.

'No, none!' said Dan. 'Hey, Sophie, there's Becky!'

Becky was riding her bike in circles near the bar. She was wearing shorts and a top and a chiffon scarf round her neck. Dad tooted and she waved. She was waiting by our tent by the time I got out of the car. 'Come for a swim, Sophie,' she said. 'I want to hear all about the barbecue from hell! I asked Emma and Mark about it and Mark said it was great and Emma said it was ghastly and neither of them would say why.'

We went off to the pool. It was pleasantly empty. Most people were getting ready for the football in one way or another.

'Well?' she looked at me expectantly.

'Well. I had a row with my mum and my brother beforehand. And Emma and Mark's mum got horribly drunk. But the food was amazing. And – I sort of made my peace with Mark. We didn't say anything, I just felt I understood him a bit better.'

'Wow! Is this the Sophie Morris I know and love talking?'

'You don't have the monopoly on sympathy and niceness you know. Well, you do actually – but with your superb guidance I'm *learning*. See? I just felt sorry for the guy. No, not just sorry for him, that sounds patronising. I kind of felt I knew where he was coming from.'

'As I said, Wow.'

'Now, what about you and John?'

'We're cool.'

'I can't believe your dad hasn't noticed those lovebites on your neck.'

'I only take my scarf off to shower and swim, and since my dad doesn't accompany me on either occasion . . .'

'You mean he hasn't asked you why you're wearing a scarf in such hot weather?'

'I'll have you know this is a Gucci silk chiffon scarf.'

'Precisely!'

She splashed me. 'I've been spying on Sonia a bit. She and Jacy do seem to spend a lot of time together. She never seems to let him out of her sight!'

'Is she doing the football?'

'No. That's the only time she lets him go.'

'And then he's with *Emma*. I haven't told you this bit, have I? Jacy and Emma have been organising the football together. Jacy's the coach, Emma's the captain.'

'Oh! So that explains—'

'It does, except that Emma said—' I could hardly bring myself to tell even Becky about our exchange the night before.

'Go on,' said Becky.

'Well, it's part of what made last night so awful. Danny went and told Emma that I thought Jacy fancied me, and she said – she said, the cow, "I shouldn't think so," and then something incredibly condescending, like, "Don't worry, I won't let on."' (As if every word of what she said wasn't imprinted on my brain.)

'So she thinks Jacy fancies *her*!' Becky's eyes widened and her mouth dropped open.

'I suppose she must do. What makes these girls think they're doing me a favour by warning me off?'

'It's obvious. They both think he's more interested in them. As if he could be, with you as competition. Don't worry, sweetie-pie, you'll get there in the end. I'm surprised at Emma though. I thought she had her heart set on your brother.'

'I think she probably has, but that wouldn't stop her thinking Jacy liked *her*, would it?'

'Hey-ho! What a complicated web we weave! We'd better get back. Supper's early for us – Gregory does not want to miss a nano-second of the footie. But then neither do John, Steve, Gus, Fergal – or anyone else for that matter.'

It was hard not to get caught up in the big match. It was a perfect evening, like the first Monday night, and about a hundred people gathered on the raised bank by the football pitch to sit on the grass and watch. Becky and I knew practically all the younger people in the teams. Danny, Mark, John, Steve and two of the Jamies were all playing for the English, along with Emma and Jacy, of course, and two sad girls we'd never spoken to. Fergal and Gus were playing for the French. So were Suzette and Monsieur from the Manoir and the Dutch dad from next door. Suzette in football gear had to be seen to be believed. My dad certainly had a look of disbelief on his face.

Jacy was a joy to watch, he was so graceful. So, to give her credit, was Emma. She darted about more like a dancer – fancy footwork was definitely her forte. But the star of the match was Fergal. Now I don't know much about football, but it was obvious even to me that he was a brilliant player. He was everywhere, always in the place where he was needed, his tall figure and his extraordinary coloured hair making him easy to follow. He seemed to have control of his whole team, even though he'd only just joined them. '*Ici! Ici!*' And he'd be in the exact spot for them to get the ball to him easily so that he could score. At half-time it was two-one to the French. And very disgruntled the English team were, too.

The teams got into two huddles, a blue one (the French) and a white one (the English) to discuss their second-half tactics.

'Life won't be worth living in my family if the French win,' said Becky.

'Well Dan's very determined that it's only for fun,' I said. 'Have you any idea what's going to happen afterwards?'

'Party on the pitch I gather. The bar staff are setting up over there already. You know, it's true what the riding people were saying about Hélène. She never seems to get any time off.'

'I know. She was at the crêperie the night we arrived, the Accueil most mornings and the bar every night since. I think the couriers only get one day off a week, too. Jacy was off last Tuesday. Of course, he was with Sonia then, in the evening. They were having a pizza together when I had my seafood fiasco.'

'But you don't really believe they're an item do you?'

'No. No more than I think he and Emma are. But I do get the feeling there's something else I should know.'

'Well, banish it from your mind instantly. I've got my heart set on getting you two together now. I've been here a week and I've never actually seen him even *touch* a girl other than you.'

'To date that includes fending me off when I bumped into him, seeing me back to my tent when I thought I was drunk, putting his hands over my eyes to say boo and bandaging my ankle. It's hardly what you'd call conclusive evidence.'

'Courage, dear-heart! You forgot to mention *ruffling your hair*! And he bandaged your ankle very sexily. You told me so yourself.'

'Compared with what you and John obviously get up to, it's not a lot.'

'Me and John are different. Though he is getting a bit more romantic. He said today that he'd miss me when the holiday is over.'

'Oh, that's sweet.'

'I don't know if I'll miss him or not. I like his jokes. But you and Jacy were just meant to be. So hang on in there. Ooh. They're starting again.'

We lay on our fronts, propped up on our elbows. I plucked at pieces of grass and found some juicy bits to chew. The light was beginning to fade as the match progressed. I drank in the sight of Jacy running, running, exhorting the others, punching the air, cheering. I could have watched him for ever and ever. I wanted them to win. I wanted to give him a triumphal hug.

But the French were doing well. Fergal scored two more goals. Each time, Suzette threw herself at him, true footballer fashion. Much ruffling of hair going on there. Even from this distance Fergal looked as if he was going to suffocate and die happy. Hmmm. Fergal and Suzette. How did I feel about that? Wasn't Suzette meant to like Dan? And wasn't Fergal meant to like me? No. Don't be greedy Sophie. It would solve Dan's problem. And it was Jacy I wanted, not Fergal. Fergal and Suzette was good. Really it was.

'Looks like Fergal's found himself an admirer,' commented Becky. 'Maybe he'll get over you. You'll both just have to pretend a little harder, won't you?' She sounded relieved.

'Uh-huh.' I supposed we would.

Jacy scored. Emma scored. Four-three to the French.

Fergal just missed a goal. Corner. To John. Who scored! Wow! Becky leapt to her feet. 'Wooohooooohoooweyhey! Yo, JOHN!' Four-all. It was getting exciting. We were all on our feet.

Both teams were messing about. Only five minutes to go.

Please don't let it be a draw. Suddenly Emma was weaving her way from one end of the pitch to the other. The ball was all hers. Mark was ready to take it. With sisterly intuition she slipped it to him. I saw Mark gather himself up and, would you believe it, another GOAL for the English! The crowd was going mad.

Two minutes to go and there was Fergal, determined to be there to the end. He motioned Suzette into place and readied himself to pass the ball to her. The English were so sure of victory they hardly noticed. The goalie was looking the other way. Suzette was concentrating. Fergal gave her the ball. She swung her leg back – and then – she buckled! She missed the ball completely, landing on the ground at the same time as the whistle went. Oh dear! How *humiliating* for her.

The English had won. But only just. If only Fergal had taken the shot himself. But he'd wanted to give Suzette, who really was French, a chance.

'What a guy,' said Becky with a sigh. 'The rest of the team will be furious with him, except they won't dare, because it was all down to him anyway. And it was a good result. Our team would have been gutted if they'd lost after all their practice. Now, excuse me while I go and hug my man.' It's amazing what a goal does to a girl.

It was a brilliant night. *Everyone* was hugging and kissing each other! I tolerated a sweaty bear hug from Mark and an even sweatier one from Jacy. But then so did all the other girls in the vicinity. Somehow it didn't matter. The good humour was palpable. It was an excellent day for international relations.

It was definitely a family occasion. Having the grown-ups and little kids around made it less fun in some ways, but more relaxed in others. People were so nice to each other. Even Emma, though she was high as a kite on her success, came over to me and said she was sorry she upset me the other night and I said I was sorry I had mouthed off at her and what a brilliant match, etc., etc. Fergal was hugged to death by everyone, male and female, as he made his way over to our group. 'Well played, man!' he said to Emma, who took it as a compliment. He sat down next to me, near Gus and Steve and John and Becky. 'Did you enjoy the match then?'

'Impossible not to,' I said, trying to see where Jacy was. He was over by the bar hitting the beer.

Fergal lay back on the bank. 'I'm completely knackered. I'm out of training.'

'Me too,' said all the other boys in unison.

'I'm not going to last out much longer,' said John apologetically to Becky.

'That's OK,' said Becky. 'I think you're all heroes – and heroines,' she said as Danny and Mark came over with Emma and Suzette.

'Hi, guys,' said Dan as they sat down.

'Ooh, *in*teresting,' said Becky to me under her breath. 'Suzette coming over to see Fergal.'

'More interesting than you think,' I whispered. 'Danny's only just found out that both Emma and Suzette fancy him – if she still does now, of course – and he doesn't know which one to go for!'

'It has to be Emma. Doesn't it?' Becky whispered back.

But Emma was turning to go away again. 'I just want to catch Jacy before he gets completely out of it,' she said.

'I thought couriers didn't get drunk on duty,' I said.

'They don't. But he's off duty until Wednesday now, so I expect he's about to make the most of it!'

'Shower for me and bed, I reckon,' said Dan.

'Me too,' said Mark.

'*Et tu, Suzette*?' said Dan. '*Es tu fatiguée*?'

Suzette smiled wickedly. '*Oui*, but I like to shower too!' she said. All five boys keeled over.

Danny looked over at me. 'OK, Suzette,' he said. 'I'll escort you to the shower block.'

'Me too,' said Gus and Steve.

'They're mad,' said Fergal.

'I agree,' said John. 'Come on, Becky. How about you escorting me to the shower block?'

'OK,' said Becky.

Fergal stood up. 'See you tomorrow, Sophie,' he said. 'I'll escort you, Mark, if you'll escort me.'

'You'll be OK?' said Mark to me as I sat there on my own. And then, 'Here comes Emma. You two can go back together.'

And there was me, raring to go. What a letdown. Jacy on a bender and everyone else too tired even to talk. And what did I get? I got Emma. Still, it had been fun. Emma came up. 'Where've all the others gone? I couldn't get any sense out of Jacy so I gave up.'

'Off to have showers.'

'Yeah, I could do with one myself. I'm finished.'

'You were very good,' I said.

'Thanks. We do girls' football at school. We often beat the boys. I'm going to be captain next term.' She looked at me with pride. 'Even though I'm the youngest.'

'I'm impressed,' I said. It wasn't altogether a lie. I had been impressed by her playing. We walked past the crêperie and the bar together and stood briefly in the light before plunging down the dark path that led to our tents.

'Er – did Dan go off with Suzette just now?' She looked at me anxiously. Ha! the POWER. But I suddenly saw in that troubled look some of the shadows that had crossed Mark's eyes the night before.

'Him and ten million others. Anyway Suzette seems to have the hots for Fergal now, didn't you notice?'

'No,' she said. 'Can't say I did.' We'd reached our tents. Her mum was there, asleep on a sunbed in the dark, an empty wine bottle by her side. She'd missed the match.

'Emma,' I said.

'Yes?'

'My brother likes you, you know.'

She stopped in her tracks. 'Really?'

'Yup. Have a nice shower! Goodnight.'

TWELVE

Apart from the tedious man two tents away who called his office every day on the dot of nine on his mobile, giving useless instructions to people who were clearly getting on fine without him, all was quiet long into the morning. Even the little Dutch kids filed off to the shower block later than usual. I lay dozing, remembering bits about last night and smiling to myself. Dan had come back with Mark, not long after me. They had whispered together for a while, but Dan had fallen straight into bed and I'd not had the energy to get up and talk to him.

I thought it was time I updated my diary. I hauled it out of my bag. If Jacy wasn't going to be around today in person I could spend time with him on paper. A lot had happened since I last wrote, so I tried to remember a bit about each day. Then I looked back at what I'd written about Jacy and Mark before. My feelings about Jacy hadn't altered, though my opinion of Mark had undergone a U-turn.

Jacy

Jacy is as gorgeous as ever. The sight of him playing football last night will last me for a long time, not to mention a sweaty clinch with him after the match. He's very strong. Strong hands too. He even has nice-smelling sweat. Sonia seems to want him for herself, and I thought Emma did too. They both warned me off him for no good reason. I'm getting desperate – might have to resort to desperate measures. I just know he'll be wonderful. I'm still worried about being too young for him. Perhaps I'll have to let him know that I love him so much I'm prepared to go further with him. I think I would – for him. I mean, it's all right if you love someone, isn't it? I can't believe I'm so confused. It must be the real thing! I hope no one reads this.

Mark
I could still never fancy him in a million years, but I don't think he's awful any more. I don't even mind Emma so much. Their dad has left them and their mum has a drink problem, though she's nice otherwise. For the record, he does have a personality and a sense of humour, and even his blue eyes have a certain appeal.

Fergal
I ought to put in a bit about Fergal because he's helping me to get Jacy. I've never met anyone remotely like Fergal before. He has dark red curls and his eyes have clear blue irises without any darker lines round them like Ms O'Reirdan at school. He's tall but not too skinny and good at fooball and dancing. Oh yes, and he has a terrific voice. Suzette seems to fancy him, so he'll be the envy of most of the boys. He's nice too, and quite deep, and now I'm used to it I like his Irish accent.

I did a little list of couples and potential couples:

Becky *John*
Emma *Dan*
Suzette *Fergal*
Me *Jacy*

with lots of question marks and hearts around it. That was enough. Time to get up.

'So what was it like having a shower with Suzette?' I asked Danny over breakfast. Dad looked up sharply from his *Sud-Ouest* newspaper.

'Pardon me? You had a shower with Suzette?'

'Hardly likely, Dad. They have male and female shower blocks in case you hadn't noticed. But we did shout over the walls quite a bit, yes. And we did throw Fergal's shorts over to her and she threw her top over to us. Which left Fergal in his underpants and her in her bra. But we're broadminded. It's not as if we don't spend most of the day wearing less.'

'Well, I really don't know what young people are coming to these days,' said Dad.

'Hypocrite!' said Dan good-naturedly. 'And you a teenager in the Sixties and Seventies. You all had love-ins in the nude didn't you?'

'Sadly, no,' said Dad. 'Not in Welwyn Garden City anyway.'

'Anyway,' said Dan to me, 'that's what happened in the showers. We all thought Fergal and Suzette needed a little encouragement.'

'And did it work?'

'Suzette was keen, but Fergal wouldn't go for it.'

'Strange lad,' said Dad, behind his newspaper again.

'Well, she is a bit of a bimbo.'

'Oy, sexist!' Mum chimed in. 'Just because she's stunning.'

'She's stunning, but she's stupid.'

'Oh well,' said Mum. 'I suppose I should be glad that a son of mine heeds brains over beauty.'

I was relieved about that. I was dreading Dan making a major play for Suzette after what I'd said to Emma.

It was a strange, hazy day. Sea mists, Mum said. It felt like the aftermath of something. Dan was thoughtful. Emma and Mark next door were having subdued conversations with their mum. Becky didn't appear, as she usually did. We couldn't even hear Gus singing or shouting his way round the campsite as on other days. There was a tennis tournament in the afternoon. Emma was playing, but no one else we knew.

After lunch I biked over to Becky's. Her mum told me that she was with John and Steve. I found her there. She and John were in the caravilla making coffee in apparent domestic bliss. Steve leapt up as soon as I came in. 'Sophie! Rescue me from these lovebirds! Tell me you'll come swimming.'

'Hi!' said Becky. 'I don't want to come swimming because I've got my period.'

John wore a self-consciously grown-up expression as she imparted this news but Steve said, 'You didn't have to share that with us, you know.'

'Why on earth not?' said Becky. 'You might as well know that I'm not just being boring. What's the point in pretending I've got better things to do?'

Steve cowered. 'All right. Sorry. But you're OK – to swim – are you, Sophie?'

'That's why I'm here. The campsite's dead today. Where are the Irish lads?'

'We'll go and see, shall we?' said Steve.

The Irish encampment was almost down by the lake. I hadn't been there before. They had one big tent and three little pup tents. Gus was still sleeping, apparently – at two o'clock in the afternoon. Peter and Sean were seated companionably round a table with their parents, listening to cricket on the radio. Fergal was sitting cross-legged in the entrance of his tent, writing.

'Say you've come to offer to fetch ice-creams for us!' said Sean.

'Sean!' his mum reprimanded him. 'You're so lazy!'

'But I don't want to miss the match!'

'I didn't know it was on,' said Steve. 'Can I stay and listen with you?'

'I'll get ice-creams,' I said. 'I've nothing better to do. Though I haven't got any money.'

Their dad said, 'I'm ashamed of you all, but if you're offering, sweetheart, I'll pay for yours to be sure.' I took their orders and their money.

'Mango for me,' said Fergal. 'And I'd love to come with you, but I'm wanting to finish this while it's in me head.'

'I'll help you,' said Peter. 'You might not manage to carry eight and I've lost interest in the match.'

Peter and I set off walking together to the bar. 'What was Fergal writing?' I asked him.

'Who knows?' said Peter. 'Fergal's always writing things. Has done as long as I've known him. Might be a poem' (he pronounced it poyim) 'or a song or a letter or anything really. Might be a fairy-story. You never can tell with me old pal Fergal Maguire.'

'Quite a talented bloke, Fergal, isn't he?' I said.

'And that's an understatement! I've lived in his shadow most of me life. I ought to be envious of the guy, but you see, he's not competitive like that. It's just the way he is. And he's always had this air of tragedy surrounding him, you know, because of his mother dying and all, so he can be good at things and people don't hate him for it. Quite the opposite. The girls love him.'

'I haven't noticed him taking advantage of all this adulation.'

'Well, no. He's picky. Bit of a romantic. Still believes in love and all that.'

'You sound very cynical.'

'Me? No. Just practical. I just fancy Cameron Diaz and Marilyn Monroe, Suzette and Sophie, and know they wouldn't look twice at me even if they could. So I'll take what I can when it comes my way. High expectations in love make people very unhappy, don't you think?'

'I'll think about that one, Peter. Now are you going to ask Hélène in French or am I? Or shall we just point?'

We went into the sudden darkness of the bar. There was a harassed dad with a crowd of tinies round the ice-cream cabinet. He struggled to get his order out in French and the girl serving him said, 'So, zat is two vanillas, two strawberries, one blackcurrant and mango and one chocolate and pistache. Zat will be eight euros please.' It wasn't Hélène. I couldn't imagine Hélène saying all that in English.

I gave the new girl our order and asked, 'Where's Helene today? Has she finally got the day off to see her boyfriend?' It was nosy I know, but the place seemed strangely empty without Hélène smouldering behind the bar. I didn't like to think of her as Cinderella, all work and no play.

She looked up from her task of pressing perfect *boules* of ice-cream into cones. 'Oh yes, Hélène is wiz her boyfriend today, so I work! Here we are. Zat will be nine euros, *s'il vous plait.'*

Cut to happy boys eating dripping ices. Cut again to the pool, a late and lazy afternoon, people drifting to join us, including Emma, who had not done well at tennis, and Danny commiserating and attentive. Including Suzette who, in the face of Fergal's lack of enthusiasm had, to her surprise – and his – unleashed a superabundance of it on Steve. Cut right past the huddle in the bar without Hélène, or Jacy for that matter, and to the bonfire. A mellow bonfire, built and tended by Mark. It seems as if we've done this every night of our lives. We're sitting round the fire, John and Becky, Steve and Suzette, Dan and Emma, me, Fergal and a guitar. The others are here too: Francine, Gus, Sean and Peter, the Jamies, the Kates, Tristan. We're all singing kiddie songs, like 'Yellow Submarine' and 'Nellie the Elephant'. The sky clears for the first time today and we lie on our backs gazing at the enormity of the universe laid out up there. The fire burbles and hisses whenever Mark chucks on another piece of wood. The moon, big and benign, rises slowly.

'There's the Plough,' said Steve, to impress Suzette.

'Everyone can see the Plough,' said Tristan, the Brain, 'but can you make out the three stars of Orion's belt? Follow them and you come to the Pole star. And that swathe of white stuff is the Milky Way – our galaxy – and, over there, that bright reddish one, that's Betelguese –'

'Eh, you've lost me, mate. Beetlejuice?' said Steve, making Suzette giggle. She had even more trouble understanding him than I did.

Fergal rolled on to his side to face me. 'The stars in the sky are the eyes of the angels looking down upon our souls, making sure we've done not'ing wrong.'

'What's that?'

'It's what my grandma told me when I was young. I used to think that my mum was up there.'

'Why shouldn't she be there?'

'Because, as Tristan says, we know what is there.'

'I prefer not to know everything like that. After all, no one's been there. They don't really know! I want to keep stars romantic.'

'But don't you love the way the stars make our lives seem so small and insignificant? If each one of those is a sun and maybe each one has its own planets and on each of those there are millions of life forms? We're just specks! Tiny specks that mean nothing!'

'I think that's scary. I don't want to be a tiny speck that means nothing.'

'Not now, not when you're happy, but when you're sad and the whole world seems a terrible miserable place, then it's good to know that we're no more than grains of sand.'

'You don't feel that right now, do you?'

He turned on to his back, with his knees bent and his hands behind his head. 'No,' he said, 'Right now I'm very content.'

'Me too, for the moment.' It had been a peaceful day without Jacy. I still looked for him everywhere and saw him everywhere, turning my face to his sun. I longed for that moment when we finally stopped running and he held me in his arms. I wished I was lying here with him instead of Fergal. The irony of lying by the glowing embers – not with him! Or looking at the stars – not with him! It almost made me want to weep. Tomorrow night, that would be my moment. At the disco – I was going to tell him how I felt. I wouldn't leave anything to chance this time.

Mark appeared with an armful of wood. 'It's getting chilly. It's getting chilly.' He threw it on the fire, making sparks fly up into the air.

'My back was getting damp,' said Becky.

'Ho-ho,' said Steve. 'I wish Suzette's was.'

Becky ignored him. John put his arm round her protectively and drew her towards him as they sat by the fire. 'More music, Fergal!' said Danny. I saw that he and Emma were sitting very close to one another, too. Emma was wearing his sweatshirt.

'It is getting nippy, isn't it?' I said to Fergal.

'Have my jacket,' he said, shrugging it off. 'It gets in the way when I play.' I put it on. It smelt of woodsmoke.

This wasn't a singsong any more. It was Fergal playing and singing alone. People were sitting with their arms round one another for warmth, in groups and pairs even if they weren't couples. Fergal said I could lean against him so I sat warming my back against his, his movements transmitted through my body as he played. It was very soothing. He had a nice back. I could feel his spine and the muscles across his shoulders. I could feel the vibrations of his voice on the low notes, and sometimes his hair on my neck where mine had parted. It was kind of sexy. I pretended he was Jacy.

'Anyone else want a turn?' Fergal held up his guitar.

'I will,' said Gus. 'Prove that Fergal Maguire is not the only Irishman round here who can sing. Give us your guitar, Fergal.' Fergal handed the guitar over to Gus, but quickly put out his other arm to stop me falling as he upset our perfectly balanced back-to-back arrangement. Gus started strumming. Mark fed the fire, and a hard core – about a dozen – of us lingered on.

I saw John and Becky, their soft, lovers' faces lit up by the firelight; Dan and Emma, serious – Dan had a tentative arm round her; Steve and Suzette, giggling, Steve barely believing his good fortune. Tristan had got together with one of the Kates and one of the Jamies was with the other one. Francine and some Dutch girls were cuddled up with Sean and Peter.

And there was me, with Fergal. We sat facing forwards, his jacket round both of us. I had my arms round my knees but he had his arm round my shoulders, ostensibly to keep me warm. I couldn't pretend that he wasn't fiddling with my hair, and I don't think it was to keep his hand warm. Apart from that we kept perfectly still, breathing in unison. It felt very private. No one else could possibly notice.

The fire was going down. Mark was singing along quietly with Gus. Fergal's fingers in my hair gently touched my ear. It was the most imperceptible of moves, but it was a move all the same. I looked at him questioningly.

He was gazing at me with those depthless blue eyes. 'You're very, very beautiful,' he said. 'Did you know, your hair shines out, even when it's dark? It's as though it's lit up with a thousand little fires and stars.'

'Fergal—' I began, but he leant forward and kissed my lips, once, just gently.

'I'm sorry,' he said, drawing back. 'I got carried away – ever so slightly. I hope you don't mind.'

I felt confused. For over a week I had wanted nothing more than to be kissed by Jacy. Imagined it. Felt it. But the kiss had come from Fergal. Fergal Maguire, who I had been sitting close to all evening, breathing with him, moving with him, feeling his warmth, the tickle of his hair, the smell of his clothes. Was this the moment to tell him that I felt nothing at all for him, everything for someone else? Was it even true?

The party was breaking up. Torchlight flashed across the

field as people made their way back to their tents. 'Here's your guitar, Fergal,' said Mark, as we stood up.

'Go for it, Fergal,' said Gus loudly, punching him on the shoulder and walking on. We stood by the embers, the last to leave, no torch. I shivered.

'It's going to be very dark in the woods. I'll walk you back, Sophie,' said Fergal.

'Thank you,' I said, and slipped my arm round his waist. I don't know quite what I meant by the gesture. I wanted to let him know that I did like him, even though he already knew from Becky that I was in love with Jacy.

We made our way through the trees, stumbling and giggling a little, but we didn't speak. I kept my arm round his waist, feeling the sinewy strength of his tall frame as we walked.

As we came to our tent I spotted Dan giving Emma a peck on the cheek, but judging by the way they gazed longingly at each other before letting go their hands and going their separate ways, some understanding had been reached. My, how romance was in the air!

Fergal whispered, 'I'd like to kiss you again.'

I looked up at him and said, 'Well, yes, as long as you understand—' but I couldn't finish my sentence because he was kissing me and clasping me very tightly.

'It's my last day tomorrow,' he said, letting go of me, but holding both my hands in his. 'You're very lovely, Sophie. I don't expect you to fall for a fellow like me – but maybe, tomorrow night, you'll save me the last dance?' And he was off into the night before I could answer, or finish that sentence – 'as long as you understand that I'm in love with someone else.' It seemed that he'd never even been told.

THIRTEEN

'I've got a bone to pick with you.'

Becky waved goodbye to John before turning to me. 'Come again?'

'Becky, you never told Fergal anything, did you?'

She gave me a wobbly smile. 'What do you mean?'

'You were supposed to ask Fergal to pretend to fancy me so we could make Jacy jealous.'

'Well, he already did. Obviously still does! Nudge, nudge, wink, wink! Go on, Sophie, tell me what happened. Let's ride over to the horses, something to do.'

'Oh, OK.' I got on my bike and we cycled off together. But I wasn't letting her off the hook. 'Now listen. We agreed that you would tell Fergal that I was in love with Jacy and that we needed his help. I tried to get you to tell me precisely what you'd said to him, but you changed the subject, I seem to remember.'

'Lighten up, Sophie. You and Fergal were obviously getting along very well together last night. What's the problem?'

'The problem is that I assumed he knew there was someone else. And that we were just friends.'

'Is that how you behave with friends? I can't imagine you letting me kiss you as we snuggled up together by the fire!'

'Becky, don't be pervy! Anyway, I didn't think anybody saw that.'

'I'm your friend. I saw it.'

'Well, as I said. I thought he knew it didn't mean anything, because of my feelings for Jacy, but it all got embarrassing when I realised he didn't know. And that's your fault.'

'All right, so I didn't actually mention Jacy. I didn't think I'd need to. It suddenly seemed a juvenile thing to ask Fergal to do. He's quite an awesome guy. And he obviously fancied you anyway.'

'Do you mean you didn't say *any*thing?'

'Well, I said something, but not in so many words,' she muttered.

'BECKY!' I bellowed. 'Once and for all tell me what you said and didn't say, so I know where I stand. I don't believe this!'

Becky looked a little shamefaced. 'OK. Now don't shout at me, because you're not going to like this.'

'GO ON!'

'I said, don't shout. I went to Fergal all prepared to say what we'd agreed. I went to him, and at that very moment he was looking in your direction – all longingly. I was going to ask him to pretend to like you, but I saw that it wouldn't be necessary. And he's a cool guy, Fergal – like I said, it suddenly seemed very much the wrong thing to do at that precise moment. So then I thought, if he liked you anyway, there needn't be any pretending involved, so it would be much more realistic. So—' she faltered. 'So I didn't – er – say anything.'

'You didn't say anything at all?'

'Er – no. I lied.'

I stopped and got off my bike. 'HOW COULD YOU!' I screamed. 'So all the time Fergal must have thought I was going after him. Oh my God.'

Becky had stopped too. 'Well, I kind of thought that maybe you'd suit each other.'

'So – the other plan – have you been lying about that all along? All that "you and Jacy were meant for each other" stuff – were you just making it up? Just to please me? String me along? Poor little Sophie. Me and my ugly boyfriend are OK thank you very much but let's play at fantasy romance for her!'

Becky spoke very quietly. 'You shouldn't have said that, Sophie.'

I was too wound up to speak, though I knew I'd overstepped the mark.

She still spoke quietly, almost menacingly. 'I got cold feet. It didn't seem fair to "use" Fergal. But you don't seem to mind "using" people, do you?'

I knew I had to apologise. 'Becky!' She was getting on her bike again. 'Becky! I'm sorry!'

'Huh! Never thought I'd hear you say that!'

'Becky! Please!' Suddenly the tears welled up and I was crying. 'I'm sorry. I didn't mean to say anything so horrible. John isn't ugly. You know he isn't. I'm just – *jealous*!' And that was the truth. John and Becky had a lovely thing going. They were both lovely people. They had each other and I had no one.

'I just feel bad about leading Fergal on. It seemed all right if he knew. But now he's going to think—' I was crying again.

Becky, big, kind Becky, threw her bike down and put her arms round me. 'It's OK. I'm sorry I didn't level with you and I know you didn't mean it about John. Fergal's not stupid. Did he even try to find out if you had anyone else?'

'No. And I didn't ask him. We only kissed once – well, twice.'

'That's nothing! What are you worrying about? Tell you what. Let's spend today getting you ready for the disco. You look gorgeous anyway, but let's make you totally irresistible. I'll give you a makeover and do your hair and nails and stuff. And you can borrow some of my clothes if you like.'

I sniffed. 'Where's John gone today?'

'Their parents have taken them off in search of culture. Much against Steve's wishes. He's just discovered culture here! But they'll be back in time for the disco. And it's the

Irish guys' last night, isn't it? So we won't have to worry about Fergal after tomorrow anyway. Now cheer up. Operation Seduction is under way. Jacy will not know what has hit him! But let's say hello to the horses first.'

I was going to miss Becky when this holiday was over. 'Becky?'

'Are you going to shout at me or insult my boyfriend this time?'

'Becky, let's email to each other when we get home.'

'Won't you be too busy emailing Jacy at medical school?'

We called in at our tent. I grabbed a peach for lunch and told Mum where I was going.

'Eat more than that, darling!'

'Stop fussing, Mum.' I didn't feel the slightest bit hungry.

'She'll have supper with us later,' said Becky.

'I don't suppose you'll starve then,' said Mum. 'Drop by on your way to the disco, both of you. I want to see what you look like.'

'We'll look a million dollars!' said Becky. With Becky's wardrobe that probably wasn't far off the truth, but I wanted something tight-fitting as well, so I grabbed my white dress. Mum had just washed it. It was dazzlingly clean and sweet-smelling from drying in the sun and nice and clingy. And I was a lot browner than when I'd last worn it.

We cycled over to Becky's. I felt all fluttery and excited. Tonight was the night! I didn't want Jacy to see me until I was all dressed up. 'Try on clothes first,' said Becky, 'because that's what takes the longest. Then legs and armpits. Then you can have a face mask and maybe I'll give you a manicure. Then a shower, and I'll pluck your eyebrows while your hair's drying off. Then dress, then hair, nail varnish and make-up.' And we only had six hours.

'What am I going to s—'

'Don't talk!' said Becky, buffing my nails. 'You'll spoil the face mask!' I turned towards her. 'Don't move or those cucumber slices will fall off.'

I wanted to talk to Becky about what I should say to Jacy so that he was in no doubt about how I felt. I'd tried asking her before, but her line was that I was going to look so devastating that words would be unnecessary. One look and he'd be bewitched. I didn't want her advice exactly, just reassurance. I now had smooth-as-silk armpits and legs and my outfit for the evening hung over the chair in Becky's tiny room in the caravilla. I lay on her bed, my face plastered in goo with cucumber slices on my eyes while Becky filed my bitten nails into shape, ready for several coats of gold glittery nail varnish.

I was going to wear my white dress with one of her filmy tops. It was made of a beautiful opalescent material like a dragonfly's wings. She wouldn't let me wear my trainers with the white dress, as I normally did, but persuaded me to borrow a pair of her strappy high-heeled sandals. She also lent me a simple pale gold chain for my neck because she said it was the same colour as my hair.

'Five more minutes,' said Becky, 'and then you can talk. I'll go and get some drinks from the fridge for when you can move again.'

I took the cucumber slices off my eyes and sat up. 'Now go and wash that stuff off,' said Becky. 'There are loads of cotton wool balls by the basin.' Great. My face felt tingly and fresh, but that was probably because it wasn't covered in stuff any more. 'Lovely!' said Becky when I came back, though I couldn't see any difference myself. 'Have a drink and then you'd better get in the shower and wash your hair. It's already half-past four. Only three-and-a-half hours to go!'

'What do you think I—'

'We'll talk while I'm doing your nail varnish. Get in the shower and wash your hair now. There should be some conditioner in there too. Take your time. I'm going to sort out what I'm going to wear while you're in there.'

It was a cramped little shower in the caravilla, but at least the water was hot. Becky and her mum had a whole range of wonderful designer shower gels, body lotions, shampoos, conditioners. Not like the Boots stuff my mum buys. It was a real treat. I wrapped a towel round me and another one round my hair and went obediently to have my nails varnished while my hair dried off.

'What do you think of this outfit? Ta-da!' Becky did a twirl. She was wearing a beautifully cut black blouse with a deep neck that showed off her cleavage and the gorgeous Earl jeans that she'd been wearing the first time I saw her. She held her hair up in a topknot.

'Becky, you look lovely! Black really suits you and you look good with your hair scraped back like that.'

'No need to go over the top.'

'No, I mean it.'

'I suppose black does have a slimming effect.'

'Shut up. John will be bowled over. Let me do your nails when you've done mine, and I'll have a go at your hair for you too.'

Becky changed back into her shorts and top. 'Isn't this great? I wouldn't mind if we never even went to the disco. Getting ready is by far the best bit.'

'It is usually, but tonight is pretty important for me. You've got to help me, Becky! Do I just go up to him and say, "Take me – I'm yours"? What if I can't even get him to dance with me? What if he's all over Sonia?'

'What you want is a sort of "My place or yours?" line. Or "I hope you're feeling as hot as I am tonight." '

'Except that he'll just offer to open a window!'

'How about simply, "I want to make *lurve* to you, baby. We can go to my place if you like." '

'Because my place is a tiny compartment in a tent and my parents will be there.'

'Well, you know what I mean.'

'I think I'm just going to have to persuade him to dance with me first and hope it's a slow one. And then act all – seductive. You know, press up against him, nibble his earlobe sort of thing.'

'You'll have to go up to him and ask him to dance in a way that he can't refuse. Very straight, even – "I want to thank you for being a marvellous courier, so please dance this one with me—" '

'Oh yeah! Irresistible!' We both fell about laughing.

' "Young man! Let me clasp you to my bosom as a way of showing my appreciation for your superb ability as a courier!" Now keep your hand still or you'll muck this nail varnish up.'

It was a problem though. I'd never felt so unsure of myself. Such a big step, going from little meetings here and there to the in-your-face 'How about getting off with me?' question. Fine if he came on to me, but I wasn't sure I could pull it off if I had to do the asking. I'd never had to do it that way round before.

'It's gone six o'clock!'

'Aagh. I feel all nervous and clammy. I still don't feel like eating.'

'But we'd better eat before we dress up. Come on. I can smell cooking already. Here, put my dressing gown on.' Needless to say, I didn't eat a thing.

We teetered out at ten to eight. We both wore more make-up than usual and we'd put our hair up. Becky had done a really good job on mine. We had to walk rather than cycle, and even that was difficult with high heels. I'm not used to them, especially with a dodgy ankle. Mark and Emma were coming back with their washing-up as we got to our tent. Mark whistled. And then blushed.

'Is everyone dressing up for the disco, then?' asked Emma, taking us in.

'We're not *that* dressed up!' I said.

'We only spent the entire afternoon getting ready,' said Becky. 'But that was because we had fun doing it,' she added, catching my eye.

'I'd better change then,' said Emma. 'But I didn't bring anything glamorous.'

'I've got another dress like this, in pale blue,' I said. 'You can borrow it if you like. It would suit you.'

Emma flushed with pleasure. 'Could I really? I'd look after it.'

'Course. I'll get it.'

'Wow!' said my dad when he saw us. 'You two look stunning. I hope the young fellows appreciate it.'

I got out the blue dress and took it to Emma. Danny was sitting at their table. 'That will look pretty on you,' he said as Emma disappeared into the tent to put it on.

'Bless him,' said Becky. 'Come on, Sophie. Let's hit the bar first.'

It was still the other girl behind the bar. Becky and I drank Bleu Tropiques and waited for the boys. I was more nervous than I would have imagined possible. My thoughts had been so focused on Jacy all afternoon that I'd put Fergal and last night to the back of my mind. I wasn't prepared for my feelings when he came in. He was wearing a white T-shirt and jeans, nothing special, but I'd only ever seen him in baggy things and football gear before, so I was surprised at how fit he looked.

'Girls! Beer!' shouted Gus.

'Can I sit here?' Fergal asked tentatively.

I wasn't sure whether to say 'yes' and be accused of leading him on again, but I was saved by John saying, 'Sorry, mate, but this bit of glamour is mine,' as he slid in beside Becky. Then Steve sat next to John and Suzette sat next to Steve, so Fergal was stranded at the opposite end of the table from me. But Fergal wasn't really my concern.

When we all finally moved in a great crowd to the disco he caught up with me. 'Sophie, you look divine. Truly, like a goddess, all white and gold.' He looked me over. 'Even your skin is golden.' There was no answer to that. 'I've got a little poem for you. Save that last dance for me and you shall have it. And then I'll be bothering you no more. We'll be gone like the dew before you even open your beautiful eyes in the morning.' And he strode on because Peter was calling him.

Jacy was the first person I saw when we arrived at the crêperie, where the disco was being held. He wore a yellow shirt, so I couldn't miss him. He smiled and waved as we made our entrance. My stomach lurched. How was I going to carry this off? I just wanted him too badly.

I sat down to psych myself up and watched. There was plenty to look at. Our group swirled in and out of my vision. Danny and Emma. He was right – she did look pretty in the pale blue dress, and her face was lit up with happiness. John and Becky. He was still mesmerised by the black shirt. Steve and Suzette. Mark, Fergal. The couriers were all there. It had the feeling of a grand finale. I just HAD to do it.

I stood up. Jacy was across the floor from me. He had been dancing with Sonia but now she was talking to Coralie and he was on his own. I steadied myself and started to walk towards him. But damn. Fergal was right beside me. Fergal was intercepting me. I couldn't be doing with this, I'd lose my nerve.

'Sophie?'

'Not now, Fergal! Go away! Leave me alone! I have to talk to Jacy!' He looked puzzled. 'You don't understand! I'm in love with Jacy. I don't want you! Please!'

I was incoherent but Fergal got the message. 'I'm sorry,' he said, backing away. 'I didn't realise.' He looked at me, crushed, his eyes misty. I couldn't bear it. 'But—' He looked towards Jacy. 'Never mind, I'll go. I'll be away.'

I had to keep going. I went up to Jacy. My legs weren't working and those few steps seemed like a million miles.

'Hi, Sophie!' he said, cheerily, as if everything was normal.

I went right up to him, as close as I dared. I looked deep into his eyes. 'I am a sunflower,' I breathed, hotly.

'I beg your pardon?'

'I mean—' Oh God, he was smiling down at me, all shining eyes and sexy mouth. 'Dance me.'

The next record was a fast one but I wasn't going to be put off my stride now, oh no. I put my arms round Jacy's neck and moved my hips slowly from side to side, despite the fact that he was jigging about. I wished he'd keep still. I put my mouth to his ear. 'Jacy,' I whispered, 'I'm completely crazy.' He was trying to pull away. I didn't want him to pull away. I kept my arms locked about his neck.

'Sophie, are you all right?' My legs had turned to water. I knew I was losing it but I had to soldier on. It was my last chance.

'Kiss it to me,' I groaned, and fainted clean away.

When I came to, Jacy was crouching beside me, flapping a bit of paper as a fan. There was quite a crowd. Groggily I sat up and looked around at the circle of faces peering down. And then it happened. Suddenly, from being a blur, everything slid into focus. Hélène appeared from nowhere. She broke through the circle and knelt beside Jacy. She looked at me and she looked at him. 'Jean-Claude? *Qu'est-ce qui se passe, chéri?*' she asked.

'*C'est la jeune Sophie,*' he said. He spoke French like a native because he *was* a native. '*La pauvre enfant!*'

'The French courier,' I croaked, and passed out again.

FOURTEEN

I thought Jacy would have run a mile, but he didn't. He knelt down beside me and propped me up against him while Hélène got me a drink of water. Then together they walked me outside and sat me on a bench to get some fresh air. They talked to each other in French the whole time. Then Jacy asked gently, 'Would you like someone to be with you?'

'Becky,' I said. So Jacy left me with Hélène and went off to find Becky. I felt embarrassed to be with Hélène, but at least she hadn't come on the scene until after I fainted, so she hadn't seen me trying to get off with Jacy. I'm sure he'd told her something in French, but she wasn't holding it against me. Quite the reverse. She was incredibly kind, stroking my hair and offering me sips of water.

Jacy came back. But Becky wasn't with him. Mark was. 'I couldn't find Becky, but Mark offered to come and take you back to your tent. Will you be all right now?'

I couldn't look at Jacy. 'Yes. Thank you,' I said, feeling dreadful.

'Sophie?' Jacy crouched down beside me again, forcing me to look at him. 'There have obviously been some misunderstandings. I'm sorry. I'll come and see you tomorrow – OK?' I gave him a watery smile. 'That's better.' He stood up and gave Mark a friendly punch on the shoulder. 'Cheers, mate!' Spoken like a true Frenchman.

'Where did Becky get to?' I asked Mark.

'She and John weren't around. I saw what happened, Sophie, but I don't think anyone else did. Don't worry.'

Three sentences, all of them different. Was this a record? I was about to say something about him being able to jeer at me now, but I could see that he wasn't jeering.

'I tried a warn ya, Sophie.'

'Don't remind me, Mark. I was so rude to you then I'm surprised you're still speaking to me.'

'You've got a temper on you, I know. I've dealt with worse.'

'Can we go somewhere else, Mark? I don't want to see anyone. I was unspeakable to Fergal back there, too. So I've blown it with just about everybody really.'

'We could go and find Fergal.'

'No, I don't think so . . .'

'We c'n go and sit in a field near the horses if ya want.'

'Thanks. I don't want to go back to my tent or down to the lake. I'll just have to email the Irish boys.'

'I've got their addresses.'

We walked towards the stables. We could hear the horses chomping and rustling. We found some straw bales to sit on in the field.

'This is really nice of you, Mark.'

'It's OK. It's OK.'

'I feel such an idiot. I never twigged about Jacy and Hélène. I just assumed he was English. I never knew he was French.'

'It's understandable. He's both! He was brought up in France but his dad's English and wanted him to have an English education apparently.'

'But "J-C", Jean-Claude! It's so obvious. And I knew Hélène was going out with a French courier, but as far as I was concerned, Jacy was an English courier – and I never saw him with a girl. I probably wouldn't have looked twice at him if I'd known he was French!'

'No change there, then!'

'Actually, I have changed over this holiday, you know I have. And of course I would have looked at him – he's divine – I just wouldn't have fancied my chances. And certainly not against Hélène! Ooooh, Mark. I feel so-o-o stupid. I really was in love with him, you know. At least, I thought I was.

I've never had such gut-wrenching feelings about anyone before.'

'It hurts, doesn't it?'

'Yup.'

We sat in companionable silence for a while, both concerned with our own thoughts. Mark said, 'I want a tell you something complicated, Sophie. Complicated. Will ya hear me out?'

'OK.'

'It might embarrass you, but don't let it.'

'I could hardly be more embarrassed, could I?'

'I'm a big ugly bloke, me—'

'No you're n—'

'I said hear me out, and don't patronise me.'

'Sorry.'

'I'm big and clumsy and I don't have a particularly pretty face. Maybe I'll improve with age – that's what Emma says! But with girls I've always felt sure I was goin' a be rejected, so I sort of got round it by going for truly beautiful girls who I knew would put me down, like. I was going down the same road with you. You are very beautiful, as you well know, and, true to form, you were fairly unpleasant to me.'

'I know. Mark, I'm sorry.'

'No, wait. I haven't finished. Because since the barbecue you've behaved like a normal human being to me. A normal human being. We met on mutual territory. You knew I wasn't much to look at and I knew you could be a cow. But we've gone beyond that. We can stand to be with each other – and that's something new for me, Sophie. Something new. I'm in the company of a beautiful woman and she's not putting me down, making me feel like an ugly bloke. An ugly bloke.'

It was true. I didn't notice how he looked any more. I didn't notice how he spoke. I just saw the kindness and the hurt. He didn't notice how I looked any more either. It was as if I'd forfeited that when I was so bitchy to him. 'I don't see an ugly bloke at all, Mark. I see someone who is kind, with nice eyes.'

'Stop! Stop! You'll make me blush. I wasn't askin' for compliments.'

'And you saw someone who was unkind, with horrible, scornful eyes.'

'I didn't say that, Sophie. And I think we ought to stop this conversation. I was only trying a tell you that you've been good for me.'

Now this isn't going to turn into a fairy tale, Beauty and the Beast and all that. I didn't suddenly kiss him or anything. I still didn't fancy him, and he knew that. But some day, when his spots have cleared up and he's lost a bit of weight, both of which will happen, he'll be a brilliant boyfriend for someone – someone nicer than me. I suddenly felt incredibly tired, and hungry. 'Do you think the disco's over yet?'

'It's only ten o'clock. You can come back to our tent if you like. Mam will no doubt have passed out and the boys might be asleep too. We can go round the bottom if you want to avoid people.'

'I do. I don't really even want to see Becky. She hadn't put two and two together about Jacy and Hélène either.'

'Too immersed in her own affairs, probably. And it didn't affect her personally.'

'What about my brother and Emma? Did they know?'

'Well, of course they knew about Jacy and Hélène. Emma was referring to Hélène when she upset you so much. But they wouldn't have known that you were actually going to make a play for him.'

'I suppose only Becky knew that.'

'For anyone in the least bit observant it was probably common knowledge. Jacy spends half his time in the bar. They took yesterday off together. They sang together in the Karaoke.'

'With my parents, no less. Don't. It's all too humiliating.'

We walked up the other way to the tents. I could hear Mum and Dad talking, but they didn't see me. 'I'll go back when they've gone to bed.'

'Fine. What would you like to eat? I could knock you up a quick fried egg.'

'Perfect.' It was, too. That fried egg with French bread and butter was one of the nicest meals I've ever eaten. 'Just what the doctor ordered.'

'Maybe in ten years' time it will be!'

'I'd like to see you in ten years' time.'

'Let's not get carried away, now!'

'Perhaps my brother will marry your sister.'

'I wonder where they are?'

'I expect they'll all go down to the lake after the disco.'

'Are you quite sure you don't want to go?'

'Quite sure. I just want to hide away.'

'Would you mind if I went down there?'

'Of course not. If everyone's down there I can nip into the shower block without being seen and get into bed before Dan gets back. Mark, you won't tell people what happened to me, will you?'

'Now why would I do a thing like that? Plenty of people saw you when you'd fainted, but it was quite a crush back there and I think Fergal and me were the only ones who saw you when – you know. I'll just say it was too hot, and your ankle was hurting or something.'

'Tell Becky to come and see me in the morning – please?'

'You know I'm a pushover, me.'

I would have given him a kiss then for being such a lovely guy, but I was afraid he'd read too much into it. I promised myself I would before we went our separate ways, though. I so much wanted to make it up to him.

I fell asleep almost instantly – I was exhausted. But when I woke up the moon was shining brightly. It was still the middle of the night. I lay there, my brain totally alert, turning through everything that had happened. How could I have been so blind? So many little things fell into place once I was in possession of two simple facts: Jacy was French; Jacy was going out with Hélène. And it was as if, as soon as I'd seen them together and made the connection, I stopped being in love with him.

I had a lot to learn about love. If I'd really loved him, would I have accepted them being together quite so easily? There was no doubt my emotions had been in turmoil. The truth was, chasing Jacy had been a whole new experience for me. I was experiencing all those turbulent feelings for the first time. I had discovered, perhaps, a little of how Ben must have felt, or Mark, or even – and here I hardly wanted to admit the truth to myself because it made me feel so bad – Fergal.

I had behaved abominably to several people on this holiday, but to none of them more so than Fergal. I had toyed with his affections and used him. All right, I thought he knew he was part of a ploy, but that didn't excuse everything. That night by the bonfire – it had been wonderful being so close. If only . . . if only . . . And he was such a great guy – 'awesome' was Becky's word. I could have had him, but I'd let him slip away. I'd sent him away. He'd gone.

I found I was crying, for Jacy and for Fergal. I'd see Jacy in the morning, but he would be someone different – Jean-Claude, Frenchman, boyfriend of Hélène. I woudn't see Fergal in the morning. I'd never see him again. I sat up suddenly. Perhaps he hadn't gone yet. I'd never get him back but I could at least say sorry. I shone the torch on my watch – 3.30 a.m. They wouldn't have left yet! I quickly reached for a biro and a postcard and wrote: 'Fergal, please forgive me. I was blind. Email me.' And I put my address. I could put it under the windscreen wiper of their camper van.

I unzipped my compartment and climbed out into the night. The moon was huge and beautiful. It was completely quiet. I slipped into my flip-flops and made my way up to the main path that went past the Accueil. I was going to go down to their tents but then I realised that they would have to come this way when they left. I sat on the fence to wait for them, I didn't care how long for. And then I heard two cars, one of them the distinctive putt-putt of a VW van. They would have to stop and lift the chain that went across the road. I stood there clutching my postcard. They seemed to take for ever, crawling up through the wood, but at last the two cars reached the chain. It was Fergal who climbed out to unhitch it. 'Fergal!' I whispered. He looked over in my direction. I went to him and gave him the card. I thought he wasn't going to take it at first. But he did. He read it without looking at me. Then he contemplated me sorrowfully for a few moments. 'Ah, Sophie,' he said at last. 'We mustn't regret what could have been.' The others drove through and waited for him to put the chain back. Gus knocked on the window to hurry him up. 'But I left a little poem for you on your car. I wrote it for you.' He never said goodbye but quickly took my hand and kissed it before jumping into the van and putt-putting into the distance, leaving me, a solitary waving figure under the moon.

I sat on the fence again for a few minutes. I felt so bereft. It was as though a limb had been amputated, so acutely painful was my sense of loss. I went back to the tent. I saw the piece of paper under our windscreen wiper. When had he put it there? The moon was bright enough to read by. Here is Fergal's poem:

Eyes from Heaven

You shine
like a woman in love.

Truly
I feel
my way,
direct all my meditation

on you

Knowing, even as I do
that your love is not for me.

That other woman
I lost
in the moment of my birth
must have shone
as you do

Shone with love for me
if only for that moment.

But her light
has dwindled,
lies low,
overwinters, waiting to be rekindled
and blossom into
flames again

by a woman who burns
with love for me alone.

Oh, Fergal.

FIFTEEN

For the third time on this holiday I felt like an invalid. Certainly my heart ached. I still felt like an amputee. Danny knew I'd fainted but he was considerate enough not to pass on this information to Mum and Dad. Mark had been as good as his word – he hadn't told anyone, not even Emma, what I'd been doing when I keeled over.

Jacy was totally upfront about the whole affair. He came over and told Mum and Dad he wanted to talk to me about something, and then walked me over to the *Aire des Jeux* as if we were discussing a football match. He was very apologetic and said he was really really sorry if he'd led me on. It was just that, since he'd known from his files that I was fourteen before he even met me, and since there was no secret about his relationship with Hélène, it never occurred to him that I might take his jokes and teasing seriously. He said it would make him more careful in future and ended by saying – 'No hard feelings?' And I was able to answer truthfully – 'No, none.' Maybe I should have said I was sorry too, but I didn't think of that until later, and I didn't want to go any deeper or make it difficult to see him during our last few days. When we got back to our tent he double-checked with the parents that we'd be leaving on the Sunday and added that a family from our part of the world was stopping over on their way to the ferry on Friday night. He couldn't remember their names offhand, but their postcode was similar to ours.

Becky came over next. 'Come for a walk down to the lake,' she said, and tactfully asked no questions until we were on the path through the wood. 'I saw Jacy and Hélène together,' she said sympathetically. '*Why* didn't we make the connection earlier? It was so obvious!'

'I know,' I said. 'I couldn't believe I hadn't noticed. But it makes sense of everything, doesn't it?'

'Do you want to tell me what happened?' Becky asked. 'I know you fainted. Were you just nervous? I remembered you hadn't eaten all day.'

So I told her. I told her how I'd got into such a state that in the end I'd literally thrown myself at Jacy, and talked gibberish at him.

'What did you say?'

'Well, I got all confused. I'd thought of all these things to say to him, but they got mixed up.'

'Go on, what did you say first?'

'You'll never believe this.' Those first words had suddenly come back to me. 'Promise you won't laugh?'

'Why should I?' said Becky.

'All right. I said, "I am a sunflower." '

'You said *what*?' I knew the telltale signs – Becky was beginning to heave and had trouble keeping her face under control.

'You heard.'

'Aaaaa ha-ha!' Becky was away. ' "I am a sunflower!" You didn't, did you?' Her laughter was completely infectious.

By now even I was beginning to see the joke. 'I did! I said, "I am a sunflower!" ' I was going to explain to her about him being the sun, but I was too overcome with giggles. Becky doubled up and had to totter through the gap and sit down at the side of the empty tennis courts. I joined her, and together we rolled around on the grass, our eyes streaming, repeating over and over, when we could, 'I am a sunflower!'

'Becky, you are a tonic!' I told her when I had recovered temporarily. My gran used to say that about people and right now I knew just what she meant. I could so easily have spent the day feeling miserable. Trust Becky to make me see the funny side. The rest of what I'd said to Jacy was beginning to come back to me. 'Do you know what else I said to him? I was trying to say, "Dance with me", or "Kiss me", but I couldn't get the words out – so I ended up saying "Dance me!" ' We were off again.

It was wonderful to be able to laugh at it all. I don't think I've ever laughed at myself quite like that before. I didn't mention the Fergal stuff to Becky. That really wasn't funny. I put it away somewhere in my head to think about later.

'What shall we do today?' asked Becky. 'It's early for us.

Why don't we break the mould and do things differently for a change? I'm getting bored with the sleep/pool/bar/lake routine.'

'You mean, the sleep/pool/snog/bar/snog/lake/snog routine.'

'No, I don't mind the snogging bit! Dad's starting to ask a few too many questions, though. And I love being with John, but Steve and Suzette are beginning to get on my nerves.'

'Becky!' She'd said all this in her mild-mannered, light voice. 'We could go for a bike ride? Pick blackberries?'

'Brilliant!' she said, turning round to go back. 'We could go along the road to that place where we crossed with the horses. It's not far. I'll get Mum to do us a picnic.'

So that's what we did. It was almost as if the holiday had already ended. We went for a swim after supper instead of going to the bar and played *boules* with her parents until the light faded and then went to the bar where Becky's dad bought us Bleu Tropiques and my parents joined us along with Mary and our Dutch neighbours. We did sneak off a bit before they did so Becky could find John. As long as I didn't think about Fergal I was happy.

On Friday we played crazy golf in the morning and helped Coralie to organise a treasure hunt for the kids in the afternoon. But somehow after supper we drifted back to the bar. The others greeted us like old friends. I felt as though I'd been away. My brother and Emma were very much an item. Suzette and Steve, as Becky had said, were joined at the hip. They still couldn't understand a word the other said, but that didn't seem to bother them.

Jacy popped his head round the bar. 'Hi, Sophie!' he said, in precisely the same way as he always had done, you know – friendly, helpful, the good courier. 'Those new people I was telling you about. They're called Southwell. Mean anything to you?' I nearly fell off my seat.

'Do they have a son called Ben?'

Jacy looked at a sheet of paper he was holding. 'Benjamin, age fourteen – that one?'

I couldn't believe it. Of all the campsites, of all the families – Ben had to turn up here. I think the gods have it in for me. 'Yes, the very same.'

'So you know them! Shall I tell them you're here, or do you want to surprise them? They're in the Accueil at the moment – I'm about to take them to their tent. They're only here for one night.'

'Where is their tent?'

'Right down on the prairie.'

'Don't tell them. I'll go over there with Becky later. Thanks.'

'It's up to you. I won't say anything. Bye!'

'What's all this?' Becky had only half heard our conversation.

'Someone – a boy I know from home – has just arrived at this campsite.'

'Really? Let's go and see him. Is he good-looking?'

'Cool it, Becks.'

'Yeah, cool it, Becks,' said John and turned back to talk to Steve.

'It couldn't be worse. Something else to embarrass me. He's called Ben and we had this embarrassing scene at the end of term when he told me he was madly in love with me – and cried, and stuff.' I looked down. Now of course I felt ashamed of how unkindly I'd treated Ben, but him turning up here did seem particularly unfair.

'Jacy said they're only here for a night. It would be easy to avoid them altogether,' said Becky. She looked at John's back that was still turned on her. He hadn't been best pleased by us taking off these last two days. 'On the other hand, I bet he is good-looking if he thought he had a chance with you, and I'd like to meet him. Wouldn't it be great to see the look of surprise on his face? Oh come on –'

she was really getting into this now – 'we could take him down to the lake, show him what's what.'

'He's only here for one night.'

'All the more reason. Please?'

Maybe she was right. And I was going to have to face up to him next term. And I do like him – just not drooping around after me.

'OK. I've changed my mind. Let's go and find him.'

'Me and Sophie are just going to go and check out this old mate of hers,' said Becky to John. 'See you down at the bonfire?'

'Fine,' said John, and carried on talking.

'What's up with him?' I asked her as we set off for the prairie.

'Oh, I don't know. I think we both probably feel that this isn't going to go on after the holiday has finished, so what's the point?'

'But you live in Chester and he lives in Liverpool – they're quite close aren't they?'

'Ooh, you are learning! Yes, they are close but – not close enough.'

'Becky!'

'Oh, don't worry! We've had a good time. I expect we'll email for a bit, even meet up once or twice. But that's the good thing about a holiday romance, isn't it? It can end with the holiday.'

'Or the bad thing.'

'I'm a realist, me. I don't honestly think I'm going to end up marrying John! We've had fun and that's it. Now, show me this Ben! The people left that tent over there this morning.'

I approached cautiously. A family was unloading stuff from a car. 'Ben!' called the mother. 'Take this to Dad, would you?' The boy came out from the tent to the car. It was Ben.

'Wow!' said Becky from where we stood, mostly hidden by someone's four-wheel drive. 'You turned *him* down?'

Ben is my age but he's quite grown-up looking. He plays basketball for the school, so he's tall and fit. He had also acquired an astonishing tan, which we could judge for ourselves since he was wearing nothing but a pair of swimming shorts. He has mousey brown hair normally, but now it was bleached blond from the sun. Three weeks in the south of France had done that.

'Introduce me!' said Becky.

'Shh,' I said. I felt shy all of a sudden. 'Don't forget he probably hates my guts.'

'Nah!' said Becky, giggling. Ben looked over in our direction and I'm ashamed to say we both ducked down behind the four-wheeler.

'This is ridiculous!' I said. 'We can hardly show our faces now!'

'We'll just have to crawl away,' said Becky, and started to do just that.

We heard the mum saying, 'Thanks, Ben. Do you want to go and find some other young people now? Camilla can stay behind with us.' We stayed crouching to listen.

'I don't know,' said Ben. We couldn't see him. 'It's not the same without Rosie. And we're going home tomorrow.'

'Up to you, love. I just thought you might want to enjoy your last night before we go back to real life again.'

'Thanks for reminding me, Mum.'

'Well, you were in a bit of a state when we came away, darling,' she said.

'Becky!' I said, horrified. 'Help me!'

'Keep on crawling,' she whispered. 'We can go to our caravilla.' So we crawled, ignoring the curious glances we got from the other campers, and ran for the row of caravillas as soon as we could.

'Who is Rosie?' she asked as soon as we'd thrown ourselves on to the seat.

'I don't know. A girl he met on his last campsite, presumably.'

'And was he in a state before they went away because of you?'

'Yes.'

'Hmmm. I know what. I'm going to wander by and say hi. I'm going to ask where he's from. And when he tells me, I'm going to ask if he knows you by any chance. And then I'll bring him over to you. We've got to give the poor guy a good last night. Don't you think? You won't have to say much down at the lake, just let him mix in.'

'Oh all right then. I'll go back to the bar.'

'Tell John I've gone to the loo or something. What d'you bet me I can get Ben over in under ten minutes?'

'A Bleu Tropique.'

So that's how I came to spend my second-to-last evening with Ben Southwell. He was quite cool at first, but then we got more friendly as we sat by the bonfire. We went out in a pedalo and sat back to chat as we pedalled together.

'So how've you been?' he asked.

'Not so bad,' I said noncommittally. I mean, I wasn't about to say that I'd made a complete idiot of myself over a courier and behaved badly towards the most amazing guy I've ever met, was I?

'You're looking good,' he said. 'Have you had all the boys falling at your feet as usual?'

'You don't look so bad yourself,' I said back. 'And have you had all the girls falling at your feet?'

'Just one in particular,' he said, and a faraway look came into his eyes.

'Oh yes?'

'She's called Rosie. And don't worry, Sophie, I'm over you now. I'm sorry about all that stuff at the end of term. I was very messed up.'

I wasn't sure I wanted him to be so positive he was over me.

'Maybe next term will be different?' I said, smiling up at

him, thinking how fit he looked, and wondering why I hadn't noticed before.

'Of course it will. I'll have Rosie. She doesn't live that far away.'

'Oh.' I felt ridiculously disappointed.

'Now introduce me to these friends of yours. Becky seems a laugh. It's my last night away and I want to have FUN!'

Ben's family left early next morning. I couldn't believe it was our last day. I spent most of it exchanging phone numbers. As it was a Saturday lots of new families were arriving. I saw them peering out of their car windows as they drove up the hill, watching all the activity that went on along the top, the human traffic that passed back and forth along that road. The couriers were frantically busy. The whole place was humming.

Becky stayed with me all day. John had accused her of flirting with Ben, which of course she had been, so it seemed as if their relationship really would end with the holiday. I felt slightly disillusioned – they'd been so good together! Becky had her own cynical explanation. 'It was almost as if he was doing me a favour, going out with me. As soon as I stopped being grateful he was less interested.'

'Oh, Becky, that's not how it seemed to me. I think he really liked you. I think he was scared of you dumping him, so he decided to act cool first.'

'That's a very complicated explanation.'

'Trust me. I've been observing you. Enviously most of the time. And believe me, that guy really rates you. And he was right to think you'd be the first to get bored. Wasn't he?'

'I suppose that's true. OK, I'll be nice to him until we leave. It won't hurt, will it? After all, I'm going to be lonely when you go.'

Emma and Mark, John, Steve and Becky were all leaving on Monday, but it was most of our friends' last Saturday night. We decided to take over the crêperie, about fifteen of us, and have a meal together. Mum and Dad were very amused at such a sedate entertainment, but then they didn't see us dancing on the tables or any of the other things that went on.

My brother and Emma were glued to each other. Sweet lovers parting! You'd think they were married and he was going off to war or something! Mark and I had a laugh about our new in-law relationship.

'I still think that you and I will be the ones seeing each other in ten years, Mark, not them.'

'Aw, shucks!'

'No, really, Mark. I think you're great. You're really special to me.'

'I'm blushing!'

'Now I'm going to do this once and once only, so you'd better prepare yourself.'

'What? What?' He looked at me all wide-eyed.

'This—' I reached across the table and gave him a great big smacker on the lips.

'Yay!' Everyone cheered as Mark sat back looking stunned. It was the cue for everyone to start kissing each other – it was our last night after all, and we wandered back to the tents together in a big group, loath to separate and say our final goodbyes.

'What time are you leaving?' asked Becky from where she was wrapped around John.

'About half-past eight.'

'I'll get up specially to say goodbye then!' Our other friends said that they would too. It was nice to think we were so popular.

The car was packed. Mum and Dad were getting our passports and signing off at the Accueil. Danny and I were surrounded by a big crowd of bleary teenagers come to wave us off. Danny was awfully subdued when he finally said goodbye to Emma, and got in the car looking pink.

I was about to get in my side when Jacy appeared on his bicycle. 'Hi, Sophie,' he said. 'Now, I'm being the good courier wishing you a safe journey and hoping you had a happy holiday, but I also want to give you the address where Hélène and I will be in Paris next term. Why don't you give us a shout if you're in Paris? It would be good to catch up.' He gave my arm a little squeeze. Of course it was dead sexy, but he was being friendly and kind. 'I mean it,' he said. And I believed him. I believed that despite all my silly attempts to impress him he quite liked the person underneath. '*A bientôt*!' he said, and cycled off. I got into the car and waved like crazy to Becky and all my friends, particularly Mark, who had a big brotherly arm around his tearful little sister.

EPILOGUE

Mum couldn't get over how quiet Dan and I were on the way home. Barely any squabbling or complaining – a record. We went on the overnight ferry, so the whole journey took an age, but it was a necessary journey for me, bridging the gap between two worlds, a time to reflect. We arrived home while it was still early in the morning. Mum made us take our own bags in but let us off the unpacking and sent us up to bed like small children.

When I tottered downstairs in the afternoon Mum said that Hannah had rung to remind me about the sleepover tonight – it was going to be at her house. A good thing, considering the chaos here, though I was quite surprised. Hannah tends to stay as far away from home and her parents as possible. We usually have the sleepovers in my loft. The *sleepover!* I was hit with the full significance of this particular sleepover as I unpacked and sorted my things out. Our holiday romances! What on earth was I going to say? What if they'd all managed to have one – even Charlotte – and I hadn't? Especially after my postcards.

Stay cool, Sophie. Stay cool. I did *sort* of have a romance with Fergal. Well, we kissed. Twice. I *could* have had a romance with Fergal. But I blew that one, didn't I? Perhaps I should just merge the Fergal and Jacy stories? No one would know. Fergal and Jacy. Fergal – the stars. Jacy – the sun. I winced all over again at the memory of 'I am a sunflower . . .' But it made me giggle too. There was nothing for it. I was going to have to tell the truth about Jacy as one big joke. Play for laughs. Maybe the others would be pleasantly surprised by this not-quite-so-cool Sophie. I'd keep quiet about Fergal though. It's not an episode I'm proud of.

It would be great to see the others. Suddenly I couldn't wait. No friends like old friends, eh? I had a shower and washed my hair and then put on the clothes that showed off my tan to best advantage (of course).

As I stepped out into the street I was struck by how autumnal it seemed – especially for someone wearing short shorts. Hannah's house is just round the corner from mine. I looked up and saw Maddy about to cross the road. Brilliant! 'Maddy!' I screamed at her, and waved like a lunatic. She waved back and skipped alarmingly through the traffic to my side of the road.

It was so good to give Maddy a hug and be enveloped in her latest scent. We compared tans. Hers was pretty amazing considering she's been home a while. Still, we can't all go to Barbados.

Neither of us knew where to begin. Maddy told me that not only had Hannah got herself a boyfriend on her music course – she was *still going out with him*! Secretly I think we were both rather impressed. Charlotte hadn't told Maddy much about what happened in the Lake District, but she can be a quiet one. Then Maddy admitted that she had met someone gorgeous in Barbados, and I decided that I could certainly say in all honesty that I'd *met* someone gorgeous in France.

We rang on Hannah's doorbell. I was really longing to see her again. I expect that some time I'll probably tell her the whole story about Jacy and how it felt to be in love with someone who wasn't the slightest bit interested in me, for a change. One day I might tell her about Fergal too, and even about Ben Southwell. But not tonight.

Maddy

ONE

The whole holiday romance thing was my idea. Maybe it was a bit harsh, considering Charlotte's and Hannah's chances were practically zilch, but it certainly got them all talking at the sleepover. I was just *so* fed up with everything that was happening at home, and *so* looking forward to this holiday with Dad, that I wanted it to be totally perfect. And of course the perfect holiday means the perfect holiday romance.

My friends are great and I love them to bits, really I do, but I admit I sometimes feel envious of their nice little homes and their nice little families. Charlotte's mum even bakes cakes! My mum laughs about that sometimes when we're down to the pot noodles ag*ain*. She says I'm lucky to look the way I do, considering how badly she feeds me, but since I've inherited her skinny figure I'm not complaining!

We had the sleepover at Sophie's on the last night of term. Sophie's my mate at school. Bit of an ice queen, all tall and blonde and blue-eyed, but we like the same things. She's much more intellectual than I am, though not as bright as Hannah. Hannah's a boffin, in*cred*ibly clever, and she's absolutely brilliant at music too. She goes to a posh all-girls' school, so she's a bit backward socially, if you know what I mean. Charlotte's just plain shy. She could be really pretty if she lost some of her puppy fat. In fact she probably will lose it, because her sister was just the same, and you should see *her* now. Stunning! Charlotte definitely lives in her shadow.

Charlotte *sort* of started the romance idea, because she has the same holiday every year, poor cow, with her cousins in the Lake District. The only bright spot on that grey horizon seems to be a guy called Josh, who lives next door or something, and Charlotte has been madly in love with him for as long as I've known her. So we were talking about him and it made me think what a laugh it would be if we *all* decided to have a *real* holiday romance. No getting out of it, because we'd all have to report back at the end. I've been watching the video of *Pride and Prejudice* for the millionth time and I *still* fancy the guy who plays Mr Darcy, and I know that's the sort of guy I'm after. You know, a *man*, rather than a boy, or what passes for a boy at our school. Most of them are a complete waste of space. Ben Southwell's cute in an 'I'm so hard it hurts' sort of way, but we all know he's not hard at all really, though he is fit, and passionately in love with Sophie. I'm losing myself. Oh yes. I feel ready for a relationship with a man of the world. After all, I am almost fifteen.

I am going on *the* most fabulous holiday – with my dad, to *Barbados*! He's decided that he feels a bit sorry for me, what with Mum's latest, and anyway he's proud enough of me to go on holiday just him and me together. He's been to this place before and, although it's dead smart, it's apparently all super-friendly. He knows some people who'll be there already, and he's sure I'll meet up with loads of other spoilt brats just like me. As if! He really hasn't got a clue how Mum and me and my little sister live. He spends at least six months a year in America because he's a scriptwriter – he goes 'where the bucks are' as he puts it. It was Mum who blew it as far as he was concerned, and I sometimes feel as if he's never forgiven me either, not that I had anything to do with it. *I* wanted him to stay. But he's pretty gorgeous, my dad, even though he's middle-aged. I can't wait to have him all to myself for a bit and to be his little princess again, just like in the old days.

Of course, I didn't say all that to the others. It's exotic enough just to be going to Barbados. Especially when you compare it to Sophie camping in France and Hannah going on a music course. So I didn't want to go on about it too much. And after the video, the food, the thimblefuls of alcohol (I can't *wait* for that totally tropical banana daiquiri!) and giving each other makeovers – we made Hannah look amazing – we all went to sleep in our own little dream-worlds.

Mum goes around the whole time with a soppy smile on her face at the moment. She's permanently in a good mood, which is better than the permanent bad mood she was in six months ago, but I'm seriously beginning to think she's lost it. Eloise, that's my little sister, can't work out what's going on anyway, so she seems to be on another planet most of the time too. My family is bizarre, so I'd better explain it. Mum was married to my dad and they had me. When I was seven and in my first year at junior school – I remember it well because it's when I first met Sophie and Hannah and Charlotte – Mum fell in love with Gus. He converted Mum into a feminist, socialist, green, ageing hippy sort of person, all ready to find herself. Up till then she'd been perfectly happy to forgo the stage and stay at home looking after me, while Dad went off to work and earned the money. Dad left us, furious, which was just so horrible, and Gus moved in. Mum had Gus and I had no one. Then, the icing on the cake, baby Eloise was born. Gus was much nicer then. He adored Eloise and was even a bit more understanding about me. I was a helpful kid, and Mum started to treat me more like a friend than a daughter. Her short-lived comeback went for a burton with a new baby to look after, so she was thrilled with all the dance and drama stuff that I did on Saturday mornings.

Cut to about a year ago, when Mum met Roddy. Compared with Roddy, Gus was a dream. But Roddy is a fitness freak and Gus was starting to get pretty flabby round the edges. Probably the home brew and surfing the Internet till all hours that did it. Then Roddy, who is a neighbour, came to fix the computer, encouraged Mum to go jogging – and that was it. Gus was out at work, Eloise and I were at school and Mum was left to get it on with Roddy. Gus moved out after some awful rows. Eloise was traumatised. Roddy hasn't moved in, thank God, because he only lives round the corner, but I suspect it's really because he's mean and doesn't want Mum to rely on him for money. Mum gets the odd bit of work doing tacky advertisements or voice-overs, but she hardly earns anything. Gus sends money for Eloise and Dad has always paid maintenance for me, but there isn't much dosh around right now. I actually earn quite a bit helping out with the little ones at the dance and drama place so I have enough for a few little luxuries.

Barbados is going to be the *complete* opposite. Mum and Eloise are ever so jealous, but I can't help that. Eloise is going to stay with the grandparents for a bit, so at least she'll have a nice time there. Dad's going to come and collect me at eight o'clock on Saturday morning, so instead of doing my normal Friday-night thing of going out late and then staying over with a friend, I'm in my room and packing.

I didn't have a suitcase so Mum borrowed one off Roddy. He's the sort of man to have a whole set of suitcases, one in every size. It's plain dark green but Eloise has stuck on some glittery little stickers from her collection to make it easier to pick out on the carousel. She says she and her friends were talking about it in the playground. Six-year-olds are so sophisticated these days! Eloise is a wonderfully adoring little sister. She loves all my make-up and clothes, so she was right there packing with me as if I was a Barbie doll in need of all the right outfits.

'You'll need lots of bikinis,' she said. 'And lots of nice dresses to wear to discos. And some shorts. And a nice outfit for dining.' I gave her a hug. Eloise and I can't quite get to grips with the 'dining' concept.

'You will bring me a present, won't you?' she said, as I released her.

'You bet!' I told her. It wasn't as if Gus was ever likely to take her on a glamorous holiday. It's lucky for him his parents live somewhere as exciting as Southend for Eloise to visit.

She soon got bored watching me folding my underwear and started playing with my make-up. She put on some red lipstick and started jigging about. 'Do that dance with me, Maddy – the one they had on *Top of the Pops*?' She'd nearly worked it out on her own, amazing child, but I took her through it and we sang along as we did the steps. She watched, round-eyed, as I finished it off. I tried to do it just like the lead singer on TV. 'Co-ol!' said Eloise. 'That was *so* cool! Teach me the last bit, please!'

'Help me fold these things and then I will,' I said, being kind.

'Yuk, no! I'm not touching your smelly old knickers!' she said, and flounced out. Little sisters, eh? But I knew it was just because she was disappointed, and scared of me going away. I'm going to miss her too. I really, really love that kid.

She came back a few moments later with Mum. 'Oooh, you lucky thing,' said Mum, standing behind me and putting her arms round my neck. 'I wish I was going off on an exotic holiday. But not with Richard. And not the way I'm feeling. And someone needs to be with Eloise – don't they, sweetheart?' Eloise had come round to join in our hug. I forgot for a moment how cross I was about vile Roddy and woolly old Gus. I adore my beautiful Mum – I just wish she wasn't so fickle about men. I don't intend to be. I see what Eloise is going through, with Gus leaving. At least she won't have to put up with a new baby, like I did. But then the baby did turn into Eloise, didn't it? And I wouldn't be without *her* for the whole world! 'Give Lo-lo a goodnight story, would you?' said Mum. 'And I'll check your packing.'

'Thanks, Mum! Love you!' I said, giving her a kiss as Eloise tugged at my hand and pulled me towards her room.

Eloise snuggled down after I'd read her three stories and kissed every single one of her stuffed toys. Then she got up again and I took her through the last few steps of the dance, put her back into bed and kissed all the toys once more. Mum was zipping up my case when I went into my room. She got to her feet and stood with her hands resting in the small of her back. She straightened up when she saw me. 'There! I hope you've got enough of everything. Make Dad buy you things if you need them – he can afford it!' she said bitterly. 'Let's go down and have a cup of something and then you ought to get an early night.'

'Me?' I said. 'Not likely! I haven't watched Friday night TV for ages. I've got a lot of catching up to do.'

'In that case I might be in bed before you. I don't know why I'm so tired – but I'm exhausted for some reason.'

'Not seeing Roddy tonight, then, Mum?'

'No. I wanted to help you pack.'

'Well, you've done that. Come and watch telly with me instead.'

'Let's just do a final check of your journey bag. Camera?'

'Yes.'

'Passport?'

'Yes.'

'Book to read?'

'Lines for *West Side Story* to learn, yes.'

'When are the auditions?'

'As soon as we get back.' They're doing *West Side Story* at school next term, and if I don't get a part, I'll die. I'm OK on all the singing and dancing but it takes me a long time to learn lines. Oh, for the day when I can be in a movie and just do one short scene at a time! I was Tallulah in *Bugsy Malone* at primary school but Mum spent hours coaching me on the speaking part. She says she's just the same –

a good job she only has to say one or two words for her adverts! In the last one she just had to say, 'Mmmm! Soft!' Even I wouldn't find that too taxing! Songs are different – I don't have a problem with words when I'm singing them. Of course, I really want to be Maria . . .

'Sun lotion, Nurofen?'

'Yes, yes.'

'And what are you wearing for the journey?'

'These thin trousers and this top and these sandals.' I pointed to them laid out over my chair. 'And this jacket with all my important documents in the inside pocket.'

'That's my girl.'

'Let's watch telly. Tea or coffee? I'll make it.'

'Tea would be brilliant. I don't seem to fancy coffee at the moment.' She flopped down on the sofa with that daft smile on her face again.

Next morning Dad arrived at eight o'clock on the dot. He turned up on the doorstep looking all tanned and handsome and pleased with himself. 'Hi there, princess! You all ready then?' I threw my arms round him. I hadn't seen him for four months – we'd arranged all this by phone. Dad's a mobile-phone freak and likes to call up from all the weirdest places he can think of. ('Maddy – it's me. Guess where I'm calling from?'

'The toilet, Dad.'

'No,' etc. It's pretty childish if you ask me.)

Mum came to the door. Mum and Dad used to be really frosty with each other, and then they were very formal but now they act like friends. 'Have you got time to come in for coffee, or are you racing to catch the plane?' As Mum spoke, Eloise peeped round her, shyly. She used to know Dad as someone who was always angry with Mum (though never with her), so she's always unsure of herself when he turns up.

Dad crouched down to her level – 'Ello, Ello-ise!' he said

(Dad-type joke). But then he straightened up and looked at his watch and told Mum we ought to be getting going. So out of habit I went upstairs to the loo (before a journey) while they had a few words together, gave Lo-lo a final hug and told her to be good, came down for my case and followed Dad out to the flashy hire car he had for the journey to the airport (I hoped at least *one* of my friends might walk by at that moment, but of course it was too early for them). Then Mum kissed me goodbye and we were off, leaving Mum and Eloise to wave us into the distance.

'Excited?' Dad asked as we turned the corner and left them behind.

'Can't wait,' I told him. 'I can't believe today has really come, I've been looking forward to it for so long.'

'You won't be disappointed, I promise. So how's school been?' Absent fathers always feel they have to ask this.

'OK. I get by. Guess what – they're auditioning for *West Side Story* at the beginning of next term.'

'Maria, then, at the very least!'

'Glad we agree on that. I've got it with me to learn.'

'Good girl. Very dedicated. Though I want you to have a good holiday. Carefree. Forget about your troubles at home.'

Now, *I* can talk about it being bad at home, but at the end of the day, it's Mum I'm loyal to, and I don't want Dad jumping to conclusions. 'As long as we don't talk about Mum, Dad. Let's just say, of course I want a great holiday. And it will be, won't it?'

'It'll be great as long as this prat lets me get past him.' Dad concentrated on driving after that and we barely spoke again until we'd handed over the car at the airport. We flew a lot when it was Mum, Dad and me, but I've hardly even been to Heathrow since then, so I'd forgotten just how exciting it is. *So* many people from so many different countries all speaking different languages. Little kids charging about. Old people looking bewildered. Cool students. A whole group of American pensioners in yellow baseball caps. Dad grabbed a trolley and I kept close to him. He smiled at me. 'It's a long time since I've been accompanied by a girl who turns so many heads,' he said after a couple of guys whistled at me (I'm so used to it I don't notice any more). 'I can see I'm going to have to fight off the young men while we're away. Well, they'd better be afraid, very afraid, that's all I can say, when *my* daughter's virtue is at stake.'

'Gee, thanks, Dad.' So where has he been for the last two years whenever guys have come on to me? All those last-night after-show parties? My maths teacher? Robbie, my ex? Don't say it, Maddy, don't say it. We were queuing to check in and I didn't want an argument.

It didn't help when the guy at the check-in desk did a double-take at the date of birth in my passport. 'I had you down for seventeen at least,' he said with a charming smile and then pulled himself up short when he realised that the fierce-looking man behind me was my father. When we'd handed over our luggage, Dad and I had at least an hour to kill before our flight was called. We wandered round the shops and he bought me all sorts of bits in the Body Shop and *three* magazines. If Over-Protective Dad was the price I had to pay for Generous Dad then maybe it was worth it.

At last we were called and went through to the departure lounge. I remember waving my dad off so many times when I was little and wondering where he disappeared to. I'd imagined the departure lounge as a lounge in the sky with sofas made of clouds. But no. Just the usual seats and a duty-free shop. Oh wow! The perfume counter of my dreams and all at duty-free prices. 'I'm going to get a bottle of whisky,' said Dad. 'Do you want something smelly by Dior or someone?'

Do I! Something smelly by Chanel or Calvin Klein or Paul Smith would do me just fine. 'Are you sure Dad? I mean, I'd love just a little bottle of toilet water.'

'Fine. Choose what you want and bring it over.' I wandered up and down, squirting scent on my wrists. Aftershave too. How to choose? I've kept going on those little Calvin Klein testers you get handed out in the shopping mall recently, but a whole bottle! I went for the Chanel in the end.

Finally, finally it was time to board. It was all just so romantic – the whine of the engines, the bustle of people settling in their seats, doing up their seat belts, muffled voices. Dad had got me a window seat so I sat and watched all the last-minute stuff on the tarmac. I was just *so* excited – it was impossible to be cool.

And then we were taxiing along to the runway. I had a moment of sheer, delicious terror and then we were whizzing faster and faster down the runway and up, up. That awful moment when the plane seems to hang in the air before it straightens out and then a wonderful normality as the air hostesses do their stuff and the journey really seems to get under way. What a buzz! Who could need anything else!

It's a long haul to Barbados – eight and three-quarter hours. I felt I knew the people sitting around us pretty well by the end of it. There was an unforgettable family who were heading for the same hotel as us. I would have noticed them anyway because they were a good-looking couple with a little girl the same age as Lo-lo, called Bianca. Bianca's a stunning kid, apart from the fact that most of her hair has fallen out. In fact, I discovered, she's got leukaemia and this will almost certainly be their last family holiday. It's so sad and so unfair. She's a great kid. I read to her quite a bit – she had lots of the same books as Eloise, and I said it would be nice to do things with her once we're there, too. Give her parents a break. Dad kept saying, 'Don't get too involved,' but I wanted to.

One more thing about the journey. The film was a 15. Dad seems to forget that I will *be* fifteen in just over a month. A few bare breasts on show (no worse than the changing rooms at school) and he went frantic. 'Why on earth are they showing such rubbish? They ought to show a family film!' Which is ridiculous because he enjoys a good movie, and certainly wouldn't be happy with *The Lion King*, I know. It was quite funny – every time there was a faintly saucy bit he coughed a lot and said, 'I don't think you should be watching this, you know.' Does he really think I'm that innocent? Don't I have to put up with Mum and Roddy in the next room? – but that's hardly something I'd discuss with Dad. As I said, he doesn't have a *clue* how we live.

We ate and dozed and read and ate and chatted and dozed the strange, long day away. It felt like a lifetime before the captain's voice was telling us that we were coming in to land and we could see the edge of the island appearing through the clouds as we bumped down through them. And there was Barbados – small and green, encircled by a ring of white sand and turquoise sea. Wow.

Two

The first thing you notice about Barbados, apart from the warmth which hits you like the blast from a fan heater as soon as you get off the plane, is how like England it is! Our taxi from the airport was like a minibus with a lovely, smiley driver, and we drove for three-quarters of an hour down quite narrow lanes past English-looking churches and cricket pitches and golf courses and big old country houses. We went through one town but most of the time we had the sea to our left and hills to our right. They even drive on the left here! But the sky was a gorgeous blue with lots of little fluffy clouds and the flowers were all bright colours and the trees were palm trees. And the sea! That was pretty *un*-English! Dad was like a kid, he was so excited, and kept pointing things out to me. 'That's a sugar plantation over there! Look at the little wooden houses! That's where we will go down in a submarine! Look at the catamarans!' I caught myself wishing Mum and Eloise were with us, but then I was *so* glad that I was thousands of miles away from the odious Roddy.

It was getting pretty glitzy as we travelled up the west coast. Barbados is only 21 miles top to bottom. There's about ten miles of sandy beach with all those fabulous hotels and swimming pools and beach bars along it. My main impression was of great stretches of blue sky, blue sea and white sand, dotted about with colourful flowers and umbrellas and sails. Southend it isn't!

'We're coming up to our hotel now,' said Dad. I saw this beautiful old pink stone house surrounded by a cluster of buildings with tiled roofs, and two huge swimming pools. Posh, or what?

It was late afternoon/early evening Barbados time when we checked into the hotel. It was beautifully cool after the heat outside. I looked around the reception area for Bianca and her parents, but I suppose it had taken a while for them to sort out her wheelchair and things like that. Dad, with his tan and trendy shades, looked quite at home here, but *I* felt like something the cat brought in! I felt so scruffy, and as for my case with little glittery stickers all over it standing next to my scabby old schoolbag – well, I wished Roddy had been spared the trouble of lending it. I was glad when we were led away to our very own, completely wondrous two-bedroom suite (*suite*!) where I could dump my bags, throw open the French windows and gaze across the tropical gardens to the beach. It was almost like having our own apartment, with its own front door, a small sitting room with a balcony, and a bedroom off each side.

Dad definitely had the 'master' bedroom with its own

balcony, its own TV and a vast double bed. Mine was smaller with two single beds and my own 'en suite'. No balcony, but I wasn't complaining. I unpacked straight away and made it all cosy. I like to keep my room at home nice and tidy anyway and this was far too beautiful to mess up. The hotel had put vases of flowers around and the bathroom was full of all sorts of freebies. There was another TV in the sitting room and – get this – our own mini-bar. 'Hey, go easy on the mini-bar!' Dad said. 'The tap-water is perfectly drinkable. We don't want to run up unnecessary bills on the bottled stuff.'

'Do you mean I can't help myself to a pina colada, Dad?'

'Certainly not, my girl!' But he isn't really mean, my dad. 'Go on, have a Coke or something – since it's your first ever experience of a mini-bar – and some of those chocolate things if you want. I'm going to have a quick shower – and then we'll go and see what's what.'

'I'm ever so tired, Dad. Can't I just pig out on these things and sit in front of the TV for a bit?'

'Take a tip from an experienced traveller, love. Try and make it through to bed Barbados-time so that you don't wake up in the night and then you'll be fine. It's only four hours different – or is it five with summertime? Well, maybe you can go to bed at ten instead of eleven. Sit for a bit and then freshen up and change into one of your little dresses – we can hit the beach restaurant and watch the sunset. How does that sound?'

'Fab.' I put my feet up, punched the remote and found MTV.

'Come on, sweetheart. I want to see that sunset and drink that rum. What's taking you so long? Don't you look gorgeous enough already?' I was wearing my little O'Neill surfy dress and trainers – understated but sexy, I thought – and I was just putting the finishing touches to my make-up. I made kissy faces at myself in the mirror. 'Call me old-fashioned,' said Dad, 'but I didn't think fourteen-year-olds wore make-up.'

'Do fourteen-year-olds wear make-up, Dad! Is the Pope a whatsit – and do bears, you know, in the woods?'

'Sorry, sorry. I've obviously got a lot to learn. But do get a move on.'

I gave myself a last appraising look in the mirror. I've got quite a cat-like face and my eyes are a funny goldy colour – tawny, is how Mum describes them. My hair is annoyingly wavy, nearly shoulder-length and the same sort of colour. I describe myself as honey-blonde, but somehow I've inherited Dad's dark eyelashes and tanned skin. OK. Quick splash of the Chanel and we were off.

The restaurant was a short walk away through the tropical garden. It was dark and cool inside but the arches at the front were open on to a terrace bar that overlooked the beach and the setting sun. 'Let's go to the bar first,' said Dad, and led me past the tables to the terrace. I thought of Lo-lo and my 'dining outfit' – these people were *so* dressed up. My dress was new and so were my trainers – Dad broke in on my observations. 'Dressy lot, aren't they? But nothing beats a stunning girl simply dressed. I've got that heads-turning sensation again, last felt when I was first married to your mother!'

'I can't help it, Dad.'

'I know you can't – I'll just have to cope, won't I?' and he gave me his adorable worried bassett-hound look. He used to do that when he teased me and I told him off – '*Naughty* Daddy!' – when I was little.

'Have you seen anyone you know yet?' I asked him.

'Not yet. I think they're coming in a couple of days.' He looked away. 'Now, tell me what you want to drink and then I'll get us a couple of menus to peruse.' I perched myself on a bar stool and faced the sunset. I was totally confused about what time it was – hardly surprising since it felt like midnight but was in fact about seven, in which case it seemed far too early for the sun to be setting.

I mentioned this to Dad when he brought me my drink. Before he had time to answer, the guy sitting next to me started off about tropical sunsets. Then he held out his hand to Dad – 'Brian Hayter. Here for the golf, you know. You a golfer?'

'Richard Dumont. Well, yes, as a matter of fact,' said Dad.

'Does your wife play?' He looked at me. I felt a giggle starting.

Dad kept a straight face. 'My wife and I are separated. This is my daughter, Madeleine. She's fourteen.' Thanks, Dad. Make sure everybody knows.

'Sorry, old chap. They all look so grown-up these days. And my wife – well, you know, a little nip and tuck here, not to mention the hair colour stuff. Hard to tell the difference.'

We were soon given the opportunity to see what he meant when three women appeared. They were dressed similarly in little designer numbers, but the two daughters looked almost identical – one was brown-haired and horsy and the other red-haired and horsy. 'Girls!' said Brian. 'Madeleine, meet Cordelia and Flavia. Richard, this is my wife, Gina.' We all shook hands. Gina lit up a very long cigarette in a holder and proceeded to flirt with Dad.

'Not *the* Richard Dumont!' was her chat-up line. I must remember that.

The girls stood and talked to me. They held identical complicated drinks full of fruit and umbrellas and straws. 'I'm Flavia,' said the flame-haired one. 'People think we're twins, worse luck, but I'm older than she is.'

'It's not as if we even have the same colour hair!' said Cordelia. But you have identical noses and chins, I wanted to say, but, hey! Here were some people more or less my age. I was going to have to start somewhere.

'Have you been to Barbados before?' I asked them.

'Last four years. Same hotel,' said Flavia, yawning.

'You'll have to tell me what to do,' I said.

'Well, we ride and go to the races,' said Cordelia. Hardly surprising.

'And get sloshed!' said Flavia, with a whinnying laugh.

'Jonty does watersporty things,' said Cordelia. 'He's our little brother. A complete pain.' This was hardly encouraging.

Dad stood up. 'Maddy and I haven't eaten yet,' he told the Hayters. 'Would you excuse us if we go to the restaurant now?'

'Golly,' said Gina. 'You must be harry starvers. Let them go, Brian, you old bore. I'm sure we can all meet up again later, and girls, you'll be able to show Madeleine the ropes, won't you?'

I was really beginning to flag. Even the gorgeous food seemed like a huge effort. 'The golf's really good here,' said Dad. *Riveting*. I remembered why my friends try to spend as little time in public with their parents as possible.

'I don't know what Mum will say when I tell her you've taken up golf,' I teased him.

'It's a good game. I wouldn't mind a few rounds with old Brian over there one of these days. D'you fancy tagging along with old Flavi*ah* and Cordeli*ah*?' he put on a lah-di-dah voice.

'You know me, Dad. I'm not that fussy about the company. But don't you think they're a bit old for me? They "get sloshed" '! I mimicked Flavia's voice.

'Do they indeed? And they don't look half as glam as you do. How old do you think they are?'

'By my reckoning they're about fifteen and eighteen.'

But Dad was miles away. 'It must be expensive bringing a whole family here.'

'Something tells me they can afford it, Dad, don't you think?'

It was almost completely dark by the time we had finished eating. Dad was all for heading back to the bar, but my insides were swilling with Coke enough already, and I could really barely keep my eyes open. 'I'll come back to our rooms with you, sweetheart. You must forgive me, I'm not used to looking after a teenage daughter yet. I forget how young you are.'

'Just tired, Dad. I don't need looking after – honest. But I do need to sleep.' We were walking back through the tropical gardens. It was discreetly lit with lanterns and filled with an extraordinary chirping noise. 'What's that noise? It never seems to go away.'

'Tree frogs,' said Dad. 'You soon get used to them. They go on all night – rather fun, aren't they?'

There was another bar just off the reception foyer. I couldn't understand why anyone would want to have a drink with*out* a view of the bay when you could have a drink with one, but it was livelier right now than the one we'd left. Dad turned towards the bar where people were definitely gathering around one man. 'Gracious!' Dad nudged me. 'That's—'

But at the same time I was nearly knocked off my feet by a high-speed wheelchair with a little girl in it. 'Maddy!' she called. 'You're here in time to read me a bedtime story!' It was Bianca of course. She sounded just like Eloise.

'Hi, Bianca!' I crouched down to be at her level. 'Listen, I'm *really, really* tired right now, because I didn't get any sleep on the plane like you did. So will you let me off, just this one time?'

Bianca's mum chipped in. 'Poor Maddy, Bianca. Look, she's yawning! Don't worry, Maddy. She's getting quite spoilt by all this attention!'

'I don't really mind,' said Bianca. 'Night-night, Maddy!' She threw her arms round my neck and gave me a good night kiss.

'Does she always kiss strangers?' I asked her mum, laughing as I tried to break free.

'Usually,' she said, cheerfully.

I stood up and looked for Dad. I could see him hovering on the edge of the group gathered around an imposing blond guy with designer stubble and trendy specs, very good-looking in a rich and famous forty-something way. It was an incredible sight – really like bees round a honeypot (or wasps round a Coke can, in my experience). There was a distinct *buzz!* Dad looked round and I caught his eye. He beckoned me over, so I waved goodnight to Bianca and went to persuade Dad that I absolutely *had* to go to bed. He grabbed my arm and whispered in my ear – or shouted, rather, 'It's Oliver O'Neill!'

'*The* Oliver O'Neill?' Of course I had heard of him – he's only about the most famous film director there is. 'Don't you think the poor guy wants to get away from his adoring fans on holiday, Dad? Anyway, I want to go to *sleep*!'

'They're his friends,' said Dad. 'Some of them were here last year. He's the sort of guy who just loves an audience. And I think half of them are family. He pays for them to come here, I gather.'

'Ssh, Dad. I'm sure they don't want that broadcast!'

'Oh, all right, little Miss Bossy,' he said fondly, turning his back on the group. 'But I do know his son is here. He's got one of those ridiculous hippy names. Called after a tree. Linden – no, that's the daughter. Redwood, or something.' Now he was no longer drowned out by the people in the bar, his voice rang out.

'Did someone mention my name?' Oh my God. There, blocking our way, stood a drop-dead gorgeous, sun-tanned, sun-bleached teenage guy with an infectious smile and perfect Californian teeth. Totally unabashed, he reached out and shook Dad's hand. 'Hi! I'm Red O'Neill.' He grinned at me. 'O'Neill, as advertised on your dress!'

'Richard Dumont,' said Dad, quite used to this sort of friendly American courtesy, even from a teenager. 'And Maddy – who's suffering from jet-lag and about to be put to bed.' I smiled up under my lashes at this *divine* boy – around sixteen or seventeen, I'd say – and decided to look no further for my holiday romance.

THREE

My body clock told me it was practically lunch time when I woke up, but of course it was only half-past seven in the morning! I stayed in bed, listening to the waves breaking on the sand. I couldn't really believe I was finally in Barbados – I've been dreaming about it for *so* long. I lay there for about an hour, just thinking about the journey and the people in the hotel. I feel really involved with Bianca already, of course. And I'm curious about horsy old Flavia and Cordelia. Perhaps they're not so bad – and it would be good to have some other teenagers to muck about with.

And then of course, there's Red. Hmm. Perhaps he's already got a girlfriend, but I don't think so, somehow. There was a sort of jolt of electricity – of recognition – when we first saw one another. He seemed kind of *familiar*. About the right height, too. Nice mouth. Hunky – must do some kind of sport. Good cheekbones.

It was no good. I was *wide* awake. I just had to get up. I had a shower. It was lovely. All that free shower gel and shampoo. Checked myself out in my bikini. Fine, fine. One of the others – Hannah, or was it Charl? – once said that I had the sort of seamless body that never looked indecent, even when I had nothing on. I didn't know what she meant at first, but now I do, and I realise I'm lucky. Some girls seem to be made of all sorts of bits joined together, rather than all of a piece, especially if they tan unevenly. My skin goes a uniform golden brown, about the same colour as my hair and eyes. I'm not super-tall or top-heavy, or extra-anything, really. So, what I'm getting at, is that I don't feel embarrassed in any way when I'm wearing a bikini, just comfortable. I put some shorts and a blouse on over it.

I dried my hair and did my face – unblock those pores before I load on the Factor 15. I arranged my hair to cover my ears. They're my only major hang-up. They stick out more than I like. Just a subtle touch of make up and I was ready for my breakfast. There was juice in the mini-bar and fruit in the bowl, but I wanted real food. I went into our living room. No sign of Dad of course. I put my ear to his door. I could hear him snoring! Thank God we don't have to listen to that at home! I opened the French windows on to the balcony. There was the sea! I could see a few families – mostly with young kids, it has to be said – making their way towards the dining room. Perhaps Bianca's family would be there. Anyway, I was starving. There was some hotel notepaper and a pencil, so I left a note for Dad –

Morning Sleepyhead!
Gone to EAT.
See U later.
Maddy x x x x

I felt a bit peculiar going on my own, but I figured that I'd soon discover the crowd, and I certainly didn't intend doing everything with an aged parent. And it was fine. There was a huge breakfast table groaning with jugs of fruit juice and fresh fruit and rolls and yoghurts and croissants and pancakes and waffles, where everybody helped themselves. I poured some fruit juice, filled a bowl with chunks of pineapple and mango and peach and yoghurt, and surveyed the dining room, looking for somewhere to sit. There was no sign of Bianca and her parents, but to my surprise someone was waving from the terrace near the bar.

It was a girl with brown hair pulled up into a topknot and wearing a sundress. She was sitting with a boy of about fourteen. I walked some way towards them with my breakfast before I realised that it was Cordelia. Somehow she looked much more normal on her own and with her hair off her face – not all dolled up. The boy must be the brother – the 'pain'.

Cordelia pulled out a chair for me. 'Good! You're another early bird! I can't understand people who waste half the day in bed. Shove over, Jonty. Make room for – what was your name again? Call me Dilly, by the way. People only call me Cordelia when they're angry with me.'

I sat down. 'Maddy. Thanks, Dilly. Hi, Jonty. I just haven't got used to the time change yet. And it all seems so brilliant here. I can't wait to find out what's going on.'

'Depends what you're into,' said Jonty. 'The girls like riding, but I'm really into watersports – so there's masses to do here. Have you ever done any?'

'A bit of surfing,' I said casually. (I have, on a school journey to Dorset.) Anyway, dancers are quick learners at that sort of thing.

'Plenty of that here!' he said.

'Maddy won't want to go round with a fourteen-year-old!' said Dilly. I kept quiet on this one.

'Maybe Maddy's not like you!' said Jonty. 'If she likes watersports, she won't mind who she does it with. Anyway, there's an entire school cricket team down there every morning at the moment, and they're all fifteen.'

Dilly perked up. 'Really? Why didn't you tell me?'

'I don't tell you everything. Anyway, you and the Flavour aren't interested in what I tell you.'

'A *whole* cricket team, did you say?'

'Hardly likely to be half of one. They're from some day school in London.'

'That's where I'm from,' I said.

'Lucky you,' said Dilly. 'We live in the sticks. And go to boarding-school.'

'Not the *same* boarding-school!' said Jonty, as if it was out of the question that boys and girls should be educated together.

'London's cool,' I said, and decided not to talk about schools. 'So when do you start, Jonty?'

'Soon,' he said. 'Do you want to come?'

'Why not?' I said. 'I'll have to make contact with my dad first, though, so he knows where I am. Are you coming, Dilly?'

'Not today,' said Dilly. 'I'm stuck with Flavia. She's got plans. *When* she gets up. She fancies this bloke, so she wants to hang around the pool in case he goes down there. He's American. And good-looking.

'And won't be the slightest bit interested in our hideous sister,' said Jonty.

'Jonty!' said Dilly, suddenly loyal. 'But you're right,' she added, all loyalty instantly evaporating. 'Still, perhaps he'll be interested in me.'

'You're ugly, too!' said Jonty, and ducked. I thought he was pushing it a bit, but I don't have brothers, so I wouldn't know. Anyway, Dilly certainly isn't as plain as Flavia.

Dilly cuffed him and smiled at me. 'Told you he was a pain. Younger brothers are just so *rude*. No respect for their elders and betters.'

We all stood up. 'Meet you in the bar in half an hour,' said Jonty. 'You have to go on a banana boat even if we can't book you in for anything else.'

'He's right,' said Dilly wistfully. 'Wish I hadn't promised Flavia now. Never mind. See you later!'

I walked back through the tropical gardens to our rooms. The day was hotting up but there was quite a breeze rustling the leaves. I let myself in quietly, in case Dad was still sleeping. Far from it. As soon as I came through the door he *roared* at me – it gave me quite a shock – 'Where on *earth* have you been? I've been searching the rooms for you (yeah, Dad, all three of them)! How dare you just disappear like that?'

Deep breath. He probably has a hangover. I calmly pointed out my note and answered him really soothingly. 'I just went for breakfast, Dad. I've been awake for ages, and I was starving.'

'You went on your own?'

'Why not?'

'Well – how can I look after you if I don't know where you are?'

'I left you a note, Dad – and I'm not a kid any more. I do all sorts of things on my own, you know – go to school, go shopping, go out—'

'All right, all right. But I'm just not used to this.'

'As you said earlier, Dad.'

'Well, it's true. We'll have to come to some sort of arrangement.'

'Precisely. After all, you didn't feel the need to tell me exactly where you were last night, did you?'

'I was in the bar.'

'I wasn't to know that.'

'Well, it's different. I'm grown up.'

'Not that different, Dad.'

'But I want us to do things together.'

'Uh-huh. Like playing golf?'

'OK, sweetheart. I see what you're getting at. What shall we do today then?'

'Well, I'd sort of planned on going down to do water-sports with someone.'

'*Someone?*' He was shouting again.

'Calm down, Dad. With Jonty, the Hayters' son. It's all laid on by the hotel, all supervised. Why don't you come too?'

It clearly wasn't Dad's idea of fun. Trip round the bay maybe, but nothing too energetic. Mum would have been the opposite – she's willing to try anything. 'No, you go, darling, and I'll meet you back here at lunch time. You're sure you won't come to any harm? I thought I might sit by the pool this morning. See who's here, plan some outings . . .'

I packed a towel and sun lotion, found my shades and gave Dad a hug. 'Don't worry about me, Daddy. I'm only doing the same as you, really. I'm just more energetic. I'm sure I'll be quite safe with Jonty. See you at lunch time. Breakfast's brilliant, by the way. Oh, and can I have some money, in case I have to buy anything?'

Dad reached into his pocket for a few dollars. 'Here you are. Now, *lunch time*, OK?'

'Thanks, Daddy.' I gave him a hug. 'Love you!'

Poor old Dad. But he really has to learn that he can't go away for seven years and suddenly expect to boss me about when he chooses to come back into my life.

Jonty was waiting for me. He doesn't have the same horsy looks as his sisters and mother. He was a carbon copy – with hair – of his bland dad. 'Face like a smacked bottom,' as Sophie would put it – kind of squashed up and surprised-looking. He's OK though. I wouldn't want to introduce him to some of the lads at school, but no one was asking me to. 'I like your shades,' he said.

We wound our way down to the beach under the palms and past the vast swimming-pool. I hadn't realised just how enormous it was. It curved round several bends of the hotel, with shops and kiosks all down one side of it. Parts of it were almost hidden by brightly flowering bushes, and others were splashy with fountains and cascades. Some families were already out there under the sun umbrellas and there were plenty of children swimming. It seemed odd to me to have a pool when the sea was right there. I suppose it's all within the hotel grounds and it means people never need to go any further. What kind of people would choose that?

Jonty seemed to read my thoughts. 'I really like being down on the beach,' he said. 'We've been coming to this place for years, and I'm just bored with the hotel. Weyhey! Here comes a banana boat! You'll love this!'

When he'd first said 'banana boat', I'd thought he meant a traditional West Indian banana boat, for shipping bananas, but oh no! This was a boat *that looked like a banana*! A local guy brought it up on to the beach. People gathered around him.

'We won't get on this one,' said Jonty, 'but we'll be at the front of the queue for the next one. Just watch this time.'

'What about our clothes? Those people are wearing swimsuits.'

'You'll see why. Sorry. I forgot. Some of my mates are over there under that beach umbrella. Give me your bag and I'll get them to look after it. You stay here in the queue.' I stripped down to my bikini, bunged my stuff in my bag and watched Jonty make his way over to a group of boys – no doubt the cricket team. There were some girls with them too. 'If that's the cricket team,' I asked Jonty when he came back, 'who are the girls?'

'Sisters, and daughters of the staff, apparently. They're staying in chalets somewhere over there,' he said loftily and pointed into the distance. 'You haven't escaped their attention either. I'll have to introduce you after our ride. They have to be better company than my vile sisters!' But I wasn't really listening. I was watching the kids on the banana boat. They sat astride it and were towed off into the waves, curving round across the bay. Everyone fell off, but the water was so shallow they just stood up and tried to climb back on when it came past. Cool!

'It's coming back now,' said Jonty. 'Are you ready?'

'You bet!' We paid our money and climbed on. The water was warm and wonderful. The other kids were quite little – they made me wonder if it was something Bianca could manage if I helped her – and we were off. Aaagh! I fell off almost straight away! I stood up again and Jonty managed to haul me back on. I held on tighter this time, but then, just before the end, the driver did a particularly vicious U-turn and three of us tumbled into the sea. 'He always does that,' said Jonty. 'No point in getting back on.' We slooshed our way through the shallows back to the beach. He looked at his posh watersports watch. 'I've got wind-surfing in twenty minutes,' he said. 'Do you want to see if you can join in today or shall we sign you up for tomorrow?'

'I don't know, Jonty. Is there anywhere I can find out exactly what's on offer and then decide?'

'Of course,' said Jonty, gallantly. He is quite a sweetheart, I can tell. 'Tell you what. Come and meet this shower. They won't all be windsurfing.' We walked across the hot white sand to where the group were sprawled out together under beach umbrellas on sunbeds and towels.

'Hey, Jont!' called one of the boys. 'Where did you find this gorgeous creature?' (He was a smarmy one – I'd have to watch out for him.)

'This is Maddy,' said Jonty. 'She only got here yesterday, so we have to show her what's what – save her from my sisters.'

'Hi,' I said, and stood looking at them. There was indeed an entire cricket team from a London school, most of them leering at me in that embarrassed but friendly way boys have, as if each and every one of them is saying – *I'm* the one you ought to be interested in because *I'm* much fitter/cooler/more intelligent/better-endowed/richer/etc. than the others . . . At first glance none of them attracted me in *that* way – they were simply too gauche, but I'm always ready to be friends. The few girls were more interesting. They looked at me in that coolly appraising way *girls* have. Hmmm, OK so you're pretty, but you're probably a complete bitch without any brains and your hair's definitely dyed and you've almost certainly got tissues in your bra. You know the sort of thing. All except one. She stood up and came over to me. 'Hi, Maddy,' she said, her accent distinctly American. 'I'm Linden O'Neill. Red – my brother – told me about you.'

She was shorter than me, probably about my age, though she could have been a year younger or older. It was impossible to tell because she seemed so poised. 'Hi,' I said. 'I only *just* saw Red last night. I was dead on my feet!'

'Well, you made quite an impression!' she said. 'He told me all about this stunning English girl he'd just met.'

I smiled inwardly at this. It was good news, but right now I wanted to make friends with the crowd. Red could wait. Jonty was in a hurry to go windsurfing and several of the cricketers and their sisters were going too. I asked him where my towel and things were. 'Over here!' said Mr Smarm, waving. So I had to go over to him. Linden came with me. 'I'm Charles,' he said. 'You two could be sisters – did you know that?' Linden and I looked at each other and laughed.

'Well, we're not,' she said. 'Charles, give Maddy her stuff, you greaseball!' Charles pretended to look hurt as he handed over my bag. 'Now,' said Linden. 'We're going to sit as far away from him as possible,' and led me away with a backwards grin at Charles. 'He's OK,' she said. 'Just big-headed. With an ego that needs a few holes putting in it. I know he comes on strong to me because of my father being famous and everything, and I *so* don't like that!'

We sat down with the other girls. 'You must be very rich if you're in that hotel!' said one of the little ones.

'Shut up, Abby,' said another girl who must have been her older sister. 'Excuse her,' she said to me. 'We're only here because our dad's a teacher at the school which brought the cricket team and my mum can't stop going on about how much money everyone else must have. Why she can't just enjoy the perks of Dad's job I don't know. I certainly can. I'm Holly, by the way. Another tree, aren't I, Linden?'

I liked the look of Holly. She had long, dark, pre-Raphaelite hair and big bright eyes. 'I'm staying there with my dad,' I said. 'He and Mum are divorced. Mum and me and my little sister live in mortal terror of the gas bill and Dad comes on holiday to places like this.' I didn't want them getting the wrong impression. 'Not that *I'm* complaining.'

'Our hotel is something else, though, isn't it?' said Linden. 'They even tell you how to dress – "elegantly casual" is what it says in the brochure! Can you believe that? You know, there are some women there who change their bikinis three times a day, I swear. Oh yes, and not just their bikinis – the matching sarongs and headscarves as well.' She has a nice grin, like her brother's. 'We're on the single-dad guilt trip too – but that's been the story of our whole Hollywood little lives. That's why I like you British guys – you're just so down-to-earth and – normal!'

'Gee, thanks, Linden,' said Holly.

I suddenly felt the need to defend Dad. 'Dad wasn't the guilty party in my parents' divorce,' I told them. 'It was my mum who left him. Mum's great, though.' I wanted to defend her too. It was strange sharing all this stuff with people I barely knew.

'My mom's a saint,' said Linden. 'That's why Red and I aren't too *ab*normal I guess. She's always been there. But with a dad like ours – you'd have to be a saint.'

'What do you mean?' asked Holly. 'God, my family seems so *bor*ing!'

'Boring is good, trust me,' said Linden. 'Ever heard of the casting couch?' Holly and I nodded. 'It's where Dad spends his life when he's not actually directing, if you get my meaning. Not at all nice, and – before we go any further – let me say, keep out of his way! You might want a part in his teenage movie version of *West Side Story* – but believe me, you don't want it *that* much. He is *shame*less where women of any age are concerned, totally without morals. Amusing, clever, yes. But strictly for the grown-ups. I tell you, I don't let my friends near him.'

'That's awful!' said Holly, sounding very British and shocked. I could see Abby looking round-eyed next to her.

'*Hollywood*'s awful,' said Linden. She stood up abruptly.

I couldn't believe what I'd just heard. 'I'm auditioning for our school production of *West Side Story*!' I said. 'What a coincidence!'

'Our school's doing that this year, too,' said Holly. 'Not really coincidence – it's on the music syllabus.'

'Stick to school productions!' said Linden. 'Movies suck!'

Then Linden, Holly and Abby were looking at me. 'Banana boat?' said Holly.

'Come *on*,' said Abby, tugging at her arm. 'We won't get on it if we don't hurry!'

'Try and stop me,' I said, and followed them.

Linden and I walked back past the swimming-pool. Even from a distance we could see my dad and Brian Hayter at the poolside. Ma Hayter and the girls weren't far away. And there, crouched beside Flavia, was Red. Something clicked. Of course, Flavia's handsome American – Red. I even felt a pang of something. Jealousy?

'That girl!' said Linden. 'Now does she really think she stands a chance with my adorable brother? Jonty's OK, but her! Her hair's a fabulous colour but she looks kinda horsy. She's not even nice!' Linden looked at me. 'Uh-oh! She's not your friend is she?'

'I only got here yesterday,' I reminded her. 'And that's my dad with them.'

'That would explain Red, then,' said Linden. 'Probably asking your dad where you are. He doesn't waste time, my brother. Let's go and join them. I can't wait to see her face when you come along – or Red's for that matter. Hang on – watch this.' She delved into her bag for her mobile and tapped out a number. We could just hear another phone warbling in the distance and I saw Red reaching into the back pocket of his shorts. 'Red?' said Linden. 'Be prepared, brother dear. Guess who's coming to dinner!' She folded up the phone and grinned at me triumphantly. 'There!' she said. 'Didn't I say their faces would be a picture?'

FOUR

I don't know what Linden was on about. Red's face wasn't a picture at all. He put his mobile back in his pocket, stood up and waved to us. Flavia obviously didn't have a clue what was going on and simply looked over in our direction. Dilly leapt to her feet and came running to meet us. 'Hi, Maddy!' she called, as if we'd been friends for years. 'Wish I'd stayed on the beach with you. Flavia's been so boring. Wouldn't go *anywhere* in case Re—' she acknowledged Linden somewhat frostily – 'your brother showed up.'

'Don't blame me. I'm not his keeper,' said Linden and went ahead to join Red.

'Ugh,' said Dilly at Linden's departing back. 'She thinks she's so great, little Miss film-director's daughter. At least Red is *friendly*.' She laughed ruefully. 'That's the trouble. Even I know he's just being polite because he's got a nice personality, but Flavia's utterly convinced it's because he fancies her!'

Dad looked quite at home by the pool, well oiled, fat paperback and cold drink at his side – the burdens of caring for a teenage daughter can't have been weighing on him too heavily. Brian was obviously telling him things and Dad was nodding from time to time, probably, from what I know of him, not paying much attention. Gina Hayter unfolded herself from her sunbed as we approached. She might have had a horsy face but she had a sinewy suntanned body, unlike poor old Flavia who had fair skin to go with the red hair and had to wear a sarong and filmy top for protection.

'What frightfully good timing,' said Gina. 'We were trying to persuade your father down to a beach bar for lunch. We're meeting Jonty down there. Look, Richard,' she called, 'your daughter's turned up right on cue!'

'So hunger finally brought you to heel did it?' Dad asked me.

Give me a break, Dad. 'Not true, Dad. I said I'd be here at lunch time and here I am.'

'Ooh, beg pardon,' said Dad, smirking at Brian and Gina. I caught Red's eye in a 'parents, huh?' moment and had a sudden desire for the others to all disappear. What was he doing there, anyway?

'Well, it's super that you're here,' said Brian Hayter. 'Let's all go and have lunch together. I hope you and Linden will both come too, Redwood. I know Jonty wanted a word with you.'

Linden looked sulky, but Red actually said, 'Sure! Thank you, sir!' (Can you believe it?)

Gina said to the girls, 'Let's not bother to change' (can you believe *that*? Why should they want to change?), and we set off back the way we'd come to a beach bar under the palms. Bliss.

Jonty was there already, perched on a bar stool in his boardies, sipping a long fruity drink through a straw. His hair was wet and his legs were sandy. His towel was in a heap at his feet. He looked happy.

'God, Jont, you're *disgusting*!' said Flavia before sitting on the stool furthest away from him. 'Banana daiquiri please, Dad.'

Brian Hayter smiled jovially. 'Banana daiquiris for all the ladies then?'

Trust Dad to start. 'But they're alcoholic, aren't they, Brian?' I wasn't keen on him blabbing about my age right then, and I also fancied a straight fruit juice with loads of ice.

'Pineapple juice for me please,' I said quickly.

'BD for me,' said Dilly.

'G and T for me, darling,' said Gina, settling herself.

'And how about you two?' said Brian to Red and Linden. 'We're fine with fruit juice, sir, thanks,' said Redwood. He sat down with Jonty and Linden, so I joined them. Dilly hovered and came to rest by me, leaving the grown-ups to fill in the spaces between us and Flavia. Poor old Flavia had shot herself in the foot by dissociating herself from Jonty, because of course it was Jonty Red had been looking for all along.

'Hey, Red,' said Jonty. 'The windsurfing's ace, but here's the deal – if we go along later we can book into a trip to the east coast where the surf's more spectacular. I think we should check it out.'

'I already did,' said Red. 'Dad took me there a couple of years back, but if the club organises it that's cool. I'll come with you. What about you, Lin?'

'Maybe,' said Linden noncommittally.

'So have you all been here together before?' I asked.

'I was going to ask the same of you!' said Red. I had that smug feeling that he was trying to find a way of talking to me.

'I met Red windsurfing last year,' said Jonty. 'He's wicked at it. I'm just a beginner by comparison. And there was that other guy, Matt, from the hotel. He was the same age as me—'

'They were kinda like kid brothers,' said Red. 'But that was last year. You're catching up fast, man!' He threw a punch at Jonty.

'I wonder if Matt will show up this year?' said Jonty.

Linden joined in. 'I didn't like him much. I hope he doesn't.'

'That's only because he was better than you at everything,' said Red.

'No, not really. It was more because he wanted to be with you all the time and I felt left out. And I didn't like his mum. It was all "Poor old Matty-Matt – it's so nice for him to have *some*thing he's good at." '

Jonty laughed. ' "Poor old Matty-Matt" milked it for all it was worth, didn't he? He was fine away from his mum, though. My sisters took against her, too. They said she didn't like *girls*, full stop – too much competition!'

Linden clearly bore a grudge. 'It was all the silly little things, like, "Oh Linda, would you awfully mind if poor old Matty-Matt went on the banana boat instead of you this one time? It's just so nice for him to have Edward to be friends with." That was another thing, she insisted on calling us Linda and Edward. It used to make me mad. She just didn't care about anyone other than Matty-Matt.'

Dilly joined in with us now. 'He cheated at tennis. He always said it was out when we could *see* it was in! He had to win. And his mum just said "Poor old Matty-Matt! It's so nice for him to be good at tennis," as if the rest of his life was unbearable.'

'Probably was,' said Linden, 'with her for a mom!' Everybody laughed.

Brian brought us our drinks. 'Something seems to be amusing all of you,' he said as he handed them round.

'Just that boy Matt last year, Daddy,' said Dilly, 'and his awful mother. They were here for our first week. Do you remember?'

'Fine figure of a woman, if she's the one I'm thinking of,' said Brian. 'What was her name?'

'Who, darling?' Gina lit a cigarette and blew smoke rings.

'Matt's mum,' said Dilly.

'Oh!' said Gina, inhaling. 'Her!' She blew out more smoke, mostly through her nostrils. 'What *was* her name?'

Dad was in on this now. He smiled from Brian to Gina over his rum sour as they racked their brains.

'I know—' said Brian.

'It was—' said Gina –

'Fay!' they both said together. And for some reason the name made Dad splutter his drink all down his Hawaiian shirt.

'Mummy, are we going to eat, or what?' Flavia whined from her distant post.

'Oh yes,' said my dad. 'Food, food. What we all need is some food. Now, last year I became very partial to that barbecued fish. You should try it, Maddy.' So we all got on with ordering and eating our food. I could get used to this! I wanted to send an instant satellite video shot to Mum and Lo-lo, so they could share in the fun of being in this fabulous place by the blue, blue sea, in the cool shade of the palm trees, eating yummy food without caring how much it cost.

Food plus warmth makes me sleepy. Add to that a few hours of confused body clock and I suddenly felt I needed a siesta. I wanted to be somewhere dark and cool – like my room. 'Dad, do you mind if I go back to the hotel and have a bit of a rest?' I asked.

His face fell. 'I was looking forward to spending some time with you on the beach, sweetheart, or by the pool.'

'Not for long – just an hour or so. Anyway,' I suddenly realised the sun had gone in and clouds were piling up, 'it looks like rain!' That was surprising. Rain was the last thing I expected here. How wrong can you be?

'Oh, that's nothing,' he said. 'It'll all be over in ten minutes. But go on, darling. Have a rest if you need one. I'll come and get you in – what shall we say? One hour, two hours?'

'Make it two, Daddy. Gives me time for a shower as well.'

Red was suddenly at my side. 'I'll walk back with you, Maddy. I've got to pick up my stuff – thought I might bring the camcorder down.' Linden was talking to Jonty, and I got the feeling Red was hoping he could slip away without his sister noticing. He was being distinctly furtive.

We had only gone a short way when the first huge drops of rain began to fall. After all that heat it was blissful. 'Do you want to shelter?' Red asked, 'Or get wet?'

'Definitely get wet!' I told him.

'Let's go for it!' he shouted and pulled me into the middle of the tropical garden, turning his face up to the sky and holding out his arms. 'Woo-hoo!'

It was like a warm shower. I was soaked right through. Red put his arm through mine and we danced a silly little jig right there, and got a clap from some of the people sheltering under the trees. We gave them a bow.

The rain was easing up already. 'I feel as if I've known you a long time already,' said Red, 'but we haven't really had a chance to talk yet. Oh – and don't mind Lin.'

'What do you mean, "don't mind her"? I really like her.'

'Well, she comes on a bit strong sometimes, and she's a bit clingy round me – big brother, you know.'

'Well, I'm a big sister, so I do know.'

'She also, er, "expands" the truth sometimes. How can I say it? – just don't believe quite everything she says. It comes from being brought up in Tinseltown. We can't always tell the difference between reality and fantasy. Well, I like to think I can, but I'm not so sure about her. I don't want to be disloyal – we're real close – but I think I like you and I don't want you to be misled.'

'That's a very long speech from someone who looks half-drowned!'

'You don't look so great yourself! Actually – that's not the slightest bit true. You look fantastic – like some sort of mermaid.'

I blushed at the image. Not that I minded. He looked gorgeously hunky with his wet shirt clinging to his bronzed skin, and the rain making dark spots in his sunbleached hair. He shook himself like a dog before we went into the foyer. 'They don't like it if you're too casual here,' he said. 'Don't want us lowering the tone!'

'Maddy! You're all WET!' I knew that little voice. It was Bianca. She was in a swimsuit and her dad was carrying her. 'I'm going swimming, Maddy! Look – I've got armbands *and* a rubber ring!'

'Wow!' I said. 'Everybody had better get out of *your* way then!'

'Will you come swimming?' she asked.

'I'm just going for a rest, sweetheart,' I said. 'Perhaps by tomorrow we'll be in synch.'

'Don't worry, Maddy,' said her dad. He looked as sleepy as I felt.

'Tell you what, Bianca,' I'd had an idea. 'How about Mummy and Daddy having cocktails on their own tonight while I read you some bedtime stories? Would you like that?'

'Yes *please*!' said Bianca.

'Won't you be having cocktails of a sort yourself at that hour?' said her dad.

'Hardly!' I told him. 'But I know from my mum and my little sister that parents sometimes need a break from their children. And I like reading to Bianca – she reminds me of Eloise.'

'Well, that's very kind of you,' he said. 'Her bedtime's around 7.30.'

'See you then, Bianca!' I said. 'Have a good swim!'

I'd forgotten Red. 'What's the story there?' he asked. 'Why doesn't the kid have hair?'

I was already used to Bianca, but telling her story brought tears to my eyes. 'She's got leukaemia and she's dying,' I said. 'They've brought her here for a sort of perfect last family holiday. She's quite perky now, but she has to rest a lot. They're all so *brave*.'

'I think you need your rest,' said Red. 'You going to be around in the evening? Before your storytelling? I'm out on the water with Jonty this afternoon but how about we get together about six? Meet you at the beach bar?'

'I'm going to need a diary! But yes, fine. I imagine that's where everyone will be anyway, won't they?'

'As long as you're there, and I'm there, that's all I care about! See you later!' and he disappeared off to their suite.

I tottered along to ours. Wow. Red wasn't slow in coming forward! It was nice though. I felt flattered. I pulled the curtains and stretched out on my cool bed – and knew no more.

I was woken by a tap on the door and Dad popped his head round. 'Time to wake up, Sleeping Beauty. I'm going to fix you a lovely cool drink with lots of ice while you get up, have a shower or whatever. See you in ten minutes.'

'Mmmmm. Thanks Dad.' I struggled into consciousness.

I had a shower, dressed in dry clothes over a dry bikini and went to join Dad. He handed me my drink. 'What do you want to do now, darling?'

'I can't believe we've been here less than twenty-four hours. I feel I've done all sorts of things, met all sorts of people. It's incredible how much can happen in a short time isn't it? All I want to do for the rest of today is sit around, by the pool or on the beach I suppose. Have you any idea what the other kids are doing?'

'The Hayter girls went somewhere to find horses, I know that. And young Jonty went off with Red, closely followed by Red's sister. *Are* there any more?'

'On the beach this morning there were loads. A whole cricket team from Beale College in London – plus their families. There was a girl called Holly who was really nice. Still, I expect they're playing cricket!'

'Shall we just go down to the pool or the beach, then? Take something to read? I expect Brian and Gina are down by the pool. There's plenty of time for excursions.'

'A whole two weeks! This is so brilliant, Dad. Thank you

for taking a whole two weeks out of your busy schedule to spend just with little me.' I gave him a hug.

Dad hugged me back. 'Well,' he said. 'Everyone needs a holiday.'

'You don't seem to have met up with anyone you know yet, though.'

'Oh. No. Well. I expect some of them will turn up next week.'

'Any cool teenagers amongst them?'

'No,' he said quickly. 'Not this time. Huh. Well, we'll see won't we?'

'Some of the teenagers here already are quite cool. Well, one of them, anyway!' I laughed. I didn't mind Dad knowing I liked Red.

'If you're talking about Red, I noticed that he couldn't keep his eyes off you! Now, go easy, young lady.'

'Not my fault, Dad!'

'He seems a pleasant enough lad.'

'Not much competition so far. Unless you count the entire cricket team! And Red's dad, of course. He's pretty cool for an old guy.'

'A bit less of the old, thank you very much. He's only in his early forties – like I am.'

'I said he was cool.'

'Like me?'

I humoured him. 'Like you, Dad.'

Dad and I had a really nice companionable time down on the beach under a sun umbrella. You'd burn in ten minutes in the full sun. He read his paperback. I had *West Side Story* with me, but I didn't look at it much. I watched the Hobie Cats and the water-skiers and the banana boats out in the bay, though I was feeling far too slothful to want to go on anything right now. When either of us got too hot we went and cooled down in the sea. What a life! Red's dad and entourage were a little way off and I enjoyed watching them too. Oliver seemed to spend most of his time on the mobile. Obviously a workaholic. I remembered Linden's advice to steer clear of him – and then Red's warnings about Linden's attitude towards the truth. And then I saw a troop of boys and Holly running into the sea further down the beach and forgot about the O'Neills altogether.

'That's the cricket team, Dad,' I said, and pointed in their direction. 'I'm just going over to say hello to Holly. Back in a mo!' I ran over and called to Holly.

Holly waved. 'Hi, Maddy!' I caught up with her. 'The boys have just lost their match, so they're taking out their frustrations on the waves. And cooling down. It's really hot for them when they're playing. What have you been doing this afternoon?'

'Sleeping, mostly,' I said.

'What about Linden?'

'She went off with Jonty and her brother – windsurfing again I think.'

'Have you met her brother, Red? He looks like a film star.'

'Well, I suppose he is from Hollywood! Yes, I've met him. He seems a really nice guy. I'm meeting him at the beach bar soon.'

'Really? Lucky thing! Though I'm not surprised, looking like you do. I suppose he's not much older than us – sixteen or so?'

'It's hard to tell, isn't it? I can't work out how old Linden is either.'

'Oh she's fourteen, like us. I assume you're fourteen too?'

Girls your own age are the hardest ones to lie to about such matters. 'I'm fifteen next month,' I told her. 'But no one ever questions my fake ID!'

'OK,' she said. 'So if Charles or anyone asks, you're over sixteen?'

'Why not?' I said, and we both laughed. 'Where do you live? Beale College isn't that far from my house.' It turns out that she goes to a state school similar to mine. In fact our lads play them at football (but not cricket!). It's like having Hannah or Sophie here to stop me getting too carried away by all the high life.

'I've got to go,' she said. 'It's time to go back for supper with the boys. See you on the beach tomorrow morning perhaps?'

'Probably,' I said, and then saw that it was already six o'clock. 'I must dash off too – got a boy to meet in a bar.'

'Lucky cow!' Holly is *my* sort of friend.

I ran back to Dad. Brian Hayter had found him and they were discussing golf. Yawn. I grabbed my towel and my script. 'Dad, I said I'd meet Red at six – See you later?'

'What – yes – sorry, Brian – fine. So, see you for supper, Maddy?'

'Yup.'

I walked over to the beach bar. The first person I saw was Linden. Then Jonty. Red was buying drinks. He kept looking round – I suppose he was looking for me. 'I fancy a plain old Coke, please,' I said, ducking round him.

'Maddy! You're here.' His eyes lit up, gratifyingly. 'Good. Sure. Another Coke please. Too bad about the others being here – you were right.'

Linden and Jonty were both pleased to see me – I don't think they have much in common. I found myself looking at Linden slightly differently, which was a shame, because I want to like her. I *do* like her! She told me all about the windsurfing and how I should give it a try.

'It's brilliant,' said Jonty. 'Everyone should give it a try. You teach her, Red!'

'I'm only qualified to teach scuba diving. Beginners need proper grown-up instructors,' said Red. 'But it's all part of the hotel programme.'

'Perhaps Dilly would do it with me?' I asked Jonty.

'If Flavia will let her go. I'll ask her if you like.'

Red sat down next to me. I saw that he was left-handed,

which meant that his drinking arm rested beside mine, and every now and then the hairs on it brushed against my skin as he raised his glass or set it down. I pretended not to notice – I didn't think he was doing it on purpose, but you can never quite tell . . . It was nice, anyway – I wasn't going to move. I hardly got to speak to him though, because as soon as he sat down, Jonty demanded all his attention and Linden demanded all of mine.

'I'm sure you'd be good at windsurfing – and the other watersports. It's what our hotel's best for. Do you do any other sports? You look kinda fit.'

'I do a lot of dance-drama stuff and singing, so I have to be fit – and quick at learning, physically. I just haven't had the opportunities to do any of these water things. We usually bunk off games and gym at school. Girls' football isn't my idea of fun!'

'I guess I can imagine you doing all that dance stuff. You've got the right kind of figure. And you're pretty. Maybe you should talk to my father! NO! Don't even think about it. You know what I said before.'

'What are you telling Maddy about Dad, Linden?' Red was in there, quick as a flash.

'Only joking, Red. Guess what! Maddy's learning *West Side Story* for her school production!'

'Hey!' said Red. 'Did you know my father's doing a film version with young teenage stars – kinda like Zeffirelli's *Romeo and Juliet*?'

'Linden told me,' I said carefully. 'A school production's quite a big enough challenge for me!'

The sun was setting. It happens suddenly here – very dramatic. 'Check out that sunset!' said Red, *West Side Story* forgotten, thank goodness. 'Guys – I want to video that.' He reached down for the camcorder. 'Take your drinks down to the water – I'll shoot you all there. Go on, take off your sandals and leap about in the water – make some good silhouettes for me.' We did as we were told.

'Let's tango!' said Jonty – surprisingly, and swept me into a smart bit of Latin dancing. Well, I can just about do it, but *Jonty*! He led with all the turns and the straight arm movements down to a tee. He was really good! Especially considering we were dancing in the sea!

'Where did you learn that, Jonty?'

'Oh, my parents don't pay astronomical school fees for nothing, you know. *Turn*. We get to do ballroom dancing with the girls' school down the road once a week in year nine. *Head swivel*. And if a thing's worth doing, it's worth doing well – as Dad always says. *Lean together*. Actually, Mum and Dad made us all have lessons in the hols too – Flavia's ball is in the spring. *And again*.'

'I don't know what ya talking about, Jonty,' said Linden. 'But I'm impressed by the fancy footwork! And you, Maddy! You know they have a dance here in the hotel once a week. Not that anyone under twenty-five would be seen dead there!'

Red was scampering about with his camcorder. 'That was totally outta this world! Who'd a thought I could have found two kids to tango against the sunset for me. Wow! Not even Dad could manage that!'

'JONTY! Jonty! JONATHAN!' It was Flavia. 'Mother says to come and change for dinner. What *are* you doing?'

'Can you dance, too, Flavia?' Red asked. Flavia blushed like the sunset.

'Are you asking?' she said, looking down, coyly.

'Well, no, not exactly!' I could see Red wondering what he'd got himself into. 'We're just all so stunned by Jonty's prowess on the dance floor – especially as it's just the beach.'

'Well, we go to balls, you see,' said Flavia. As if that explained it. 'And though they're usually just a scrum, it pays to know what one's doing. Especially at our local hunt bash. And I'm having mine in the spring.'

So Flavia's a deb! I've never met a deb before. She realised that this wasn't an invitation from Red and quickly recovered herself. 'Do come on, Jonty. The parents are waiting.'

I looked at my watch. It was seven-fifteen. 'I'll have to come up with you,' I said. I looked apologetically at Red. 'Bianca! See you later, maybe!' and ran after Flavia, who was marching ahead with Jonty hopping along to keep up with her.

Bianca was all tucked up in bed surrounded by soft toys. There were some the hotel had donated as well as all the ones she could carry on the plane. On a shelf near her bed was a vast array of bottles and pots of pills and potions. Poor little mite. She looked pale and drained, but pleased to see me.

'She's had all her medication,' said her mum. 'We're very grateful, Maddy. The hotel does have a babysitting service, but we don't really want to leave her with strangers. And she likes you so much – don't you, darling? Here's our mobile number. We'll be back in forty-five minutes, but call us if there's a problem. We're not far away!' They went off and I sat on Bianca's bed.

'I've chosen my stories,' she said. 'They're all cheerful ones because I've been sad this evening.'

'Oh, Bianca,' I said. 'You don't want to be sad, not here.'

'I'm sad when Mummy and Daddy are sad. They're sad about me dying.'

'Bianca!' What on *earth* do you say in this situation?

'I don't mind dying. I love God, and I really want to meet Him, you see. But I love Mummy and Daddy, too.'

'And I love you, too, Bianca, because you remind me of my little sister, so I want to read you a lovely happy story to make you smile. What have you got for me? Ooh – *Winnie the Pooh*, that's nice.'

'Tigger's happy!'

'And *The Cat in the Hat*.'

'The cat makes me laugh. And one more . . .'

I thought three stories was about right. 'Have you got *The Snowman*? – that's Eloise's favourite. Only it's not very seasonal!'

'Of course I've got *The Snowman*. I think I might be able to walk on the air one day. Are you really going to read me three stories?'

'Yup. Are you sitting comfortably?' Kids! They wrench you one way and then the other – but I really wasn't prepared for the emotions that Bianca brought out in me. She fell asleep with a smile on her face when I finished *The Snowman*, but I was feeling pretty weepy by then. Read it for yourself and you'll see why. I splashed cold water on my face and dried it just before I heard the key in the lock.

'Perfect timing!' I whispered as they came in. 'She's just dropped off.'

'Was she OK?' asked her mum. 'She's had a lot of pain today.'

'Poor little scrap,' said her dad. 'But you know kids, they're so resilient, so brave. She ends up trying to cheer *us* up.'

'She chose cheerful stories for me to read.'

'Well, thanks. It was lovely to have a break.'

'I'm really happy to read to her most nights. And, another thing. Might she be able to cope with a banana boat ride if I hung on to her? I went on one this morning, and I thought how much Bianca would love it.'

'I don't know,' said her dad. 'Maybe on a good day. You might have to strap her to you, literally. But let's see. I wouldn't rule it out.'

'I'd better go.' I looked at my watch. It was already half-past eight. I hoped Dad would wait for me before eating.

FIVE

I woke up feeling that I had been here for ever. Dad and I both emerged from our rooms, showered and ready for action, at about the same time. He outlined our schedule for the day (has to have it all planned out, my dad) as we walked through the tropical gardens to breakfast. 'On Dilly's advice I booked you in for the watersports this afternoon. It's a scuba diving lesson if you want one. Some of the other kids are doing it, too. I might have a go myself one day – I never got round to it last year – but not today because I'm playing golf with Brian Hayter. Gina and Flavia will be out riding, I gather.'

We loaded our plates with luscious fruit – slices of mango and pineapple and papaya. 'And tonight there's something rather naff that Gina describes as "very touristy but frightful fun". They hold a beach barbecue at one of the hotels further round the bay. Steel band, limbo dancing for all-comers, good barbecue. Has to be done, I reckon, don't you?'

'We *are* tourists. I don't mind. I think it sounds cool. Will the others come?'

'Where you go, sweetheart, I'm sure others will follow. I don't know, but let's ask them.'

I spent the morning by the pool. Bianca was down there. She was having a good day. I towed her around the children's pool for ages and she was dead bossy – just like Lo-lo. Dilly and Jonty turned up around lunch time. They wanted to know if I was coming on the watersports course. 'And we're all going limbo dancing tonight,' said Jonty. 'Every year the parents pretend that it's far too common for us, but they absolutely love it.'

'It's Mum, mostly – there's this enormous guy in a grass skirt who helps you under the bar and we reckon Mum has the hots for him. She always goes back for more,' said Dilly. 'And guess what – Charles and the Beale College lot are all coming too. Holly told me.'

'Charles *and* the Beale College lot . . .' Jonty started mincing around. Dilly smacked him round the head. I'm glad I don't have brothers.

'Flavia's desperate for Red to come with us, so I suppose that means Linden too. Do you think we can persuade them?'

'I think Maddy could probably persuade Red to do most things,' said Jonty. I know he's not *my* brother, but I took the liberty of smacking him round the head *à la* Dilly.

'We'll see them this afternoon, won't we?' I said. 'Who exactly is doing what, watersportswise?'

'Jonty and I are both doing the scuba diving. I've got a feeling Linden might be too. She was keen when we were talking about it last night. So with you as well we can be two pairs.'

'Red doesn't need lessons, he's got an instructor's certificate already,' said Jonty. 'He dives with a camera – he's really interested in all that sea life stuff. I expect Linden's quite experienced too, though she might be like us – just the odd holiday lesson now and then that doesn't really add up to anything serious.'

At lunch Dad was all kitted out for golf. Not a pretty sight. Dilly and I set off for the beach together. We stood watching some people parascending – it looked completely brilliant, but quite scary, especially with all those maniac jetskiers zipping about. One of the jetskiers came back to the beach. It was Red. He saw us as he was beaching the jetski, and came over. 'Maddy! Hi! What are you two waiting for?'

'Scuba diving,' I told him.

'Linden's coming down for that too,' he said. 'You'll love it. There's so much to look at down there. I do it a lot.' He pointed out into the bay. 'That's your boat, so you won't have long to wait.'

Dilly had been waiting for him to draw breath before butting in. 'Red – might you and Linden be coming to the beach barbecue thing tonight? Maddy's coming, aren't you, Maddy?'

'Sure,' said Red, 'if it's open to anyone. When are you leaving?' he asked me.

'I don't know,' I said, 'but why don't we meet at the beach bar at six again?'

Jonty chose that moment to join us. 'Secret assignation or can we all come?'

'It's just so we can meet up with Red and Linden before going out tonight,' said Dilly.

'Huh! So you've been persuaded to join the limbo dancing team, have you?' he said to Red.

'No one mentioned limbo dancing!' said Red. 'But now I can't wait!' Linden was running towards us. 'Hi, Lin. You having a refresher course then?'

'Sure am,' said Linden. 'Hey, Red, take my mobile would you? I don't want it to get wet.' She threw it to him as our instructor came towards us, and Red set off up the beach to the hotel.

Linden, Jonty and Dilly were all very laid back about our scuba diving lesson – they'd done it before. I might skip gym at school, but I'm a good swimmer. Swimming was one of the things Dad and I used to do when he still lived with us, and it was also one of the things we used to do on Sundays when he took me out. Our instructor was gorgeous. He made me feel very safe as he checked out our swimming and diving experience. We wore our swimsuits – no need for wetsuits in this warm water. He told us a bit about scuba diving first – I mean, did *you* know that SCUBA stands for Self-Contained Underwater Breathing Apparatus?

Because I didn't! You have to do it in pairs, for safety, and you have signals that you make to each other about coming up, going down, and so on. I found I was concentrating very hard.

And then, we were off. We wore our oxygen packs on our backs and carried our flippers and goggles to walk out to the boat. We sailed out into the bay where the coral is, and then flippers, goggles and noseclips on – check breathing apparatus, and backwards over the side of the boat we went. I was paired with Linden. She certainly wouldn't have let me go with either of the others – but it was good because she knew what to do. It was FANTASTIC. It was like being in a completely different world. I felt transformed into a bubble-blowing sea creature, flitting about over the coral reef, part of an enormous and wonderfully choreographed water ballet – I practically had the soundtrack going through my brain.

There was a nasty moment when I was following Linden closely and looked around to see that we had lost the other two. I had a feeling our time was up and I tried to use my signals, but Linden didn't take any notice. In the end I propelled myself into her, working my flippers overtime, and grabbed her. She turned round, then, and we were back with the others quite quickly, and making for the surface. I could tell when we came up that we had worried the instructor, and he had a bit of a go at us. Linden pretended not to care, but I could see she was rattled. I tried to apologise without making it obvious that it had been Linden's fault, but I think he knew.

Overall it had been wonderful. I couldn't wait to do it again. A little thought crept into my mind that it would be fabulous to dive with Red. I stored it for the time being. Meanwhile, the others were comparing notes on all they had seen. 'We need Red here,' said Linden, as if she'd read my mind. 'He's brilliant on all this stuff. He knows the names of everything on the reef.'

I felt as if we'd been out for ages but it was only mid-afternoon. We stopped off at the beach bar for a drink. 'Where did you two go down there?' Dilly asked. 'I didn't think it would be possible to lose anyone in that short a time.'

'Probably Linden showing off, eh?' Jonty seemed to feel he could treat Linden as an honorary sister too.

'Just enjoying myself,' said Linden. 'I thought you guys could look after yourselves.'

'So what about Maddy?' said Dilly, aggrieved on my behalf. 'Bet you gave her a fright.'

'Maddy's cool,' said Linden. 'She didn't mind – did you, Maddy?'

I decided to laugh this one off. 'So what does everybody want to drink then?'

I chose to go back to my room for a bit. I wanted to flop around and then have a shower and the chance to do my make-up properly before we met up with Red again. The more time I spent away from him the more I looked forward to seeing him. I liked being with Linden because she was a connection, but there were things about Linden that were difficult. It was as if she *owned* her brother. I almost felt I had to stay in with her, because if she didn't like me she would certainly make it difficult to be with Red. And she was picky about the people she spent time with. Her father certainly wasn't one of them. And she didn't have much time for Dilly. She seemed comfortable with the cricketers – perhaps they were a good audience. Oooh, Maddy. Mentally I slapped my own wrist. It wouldn't do to start having bitchy thoughts about Linden.

I washed my hair in the shower and tried out the lovely aloe vera conditioner. Great believers in aloe vera, the Barbadians, it seems to me. They sell a gorgeous cool aloe vera sunscreen on the beach as well. I put on a green top and a short white skirt – I hoped I wouldn't have to change again for the barbecue. I couldn't tell if the Hayters would turn up wearing ballgowns.

I checked myself out in the mirror. The tan was coming along nicely and my hair was starting to streak. I had a tweak at the eyebrows – thinner eyebrows show off my eyelashes. They're so long they're sometimes a bit of a nuisance. I put on some foundation. The colour looked a bit at odds with my tan, but it covered up everything else, including a couple of spots I could see starting on my forehead. I blended two lots of eyeshadow, brown and gold, and then some very dark brown eyeliner and black mascara. I know you're not supposed to use black if you're a blonde, but since my eyelashes are black anyway I think it's OK. Then I found some blusher and put it on to make my cheekbones stand out. I sat back to admire the overall effect.

Aagh. No. Too much! I was only meeting the others for a drink. They might have just come out of the water. I grabbed the tissues and started to wipe it all off. When one half was wiped and the other was horribly over made-up the phone rang. Who would ring us? I went into our living room and picked it up. It was Linden on her mobile. 'Where are you, Maddy? It's six o'clock and everyone else is here, including your dad.' I hadn't realised it was that late.

'I'll be right over.' Help. I wiped all the make-up off, whacked on some lip gloss and squirted myself with the Hugo Boss. I was even beginning to feel nervous – and I liked it! ROMANCE! Red, here I come . . .

The barbecue starts quite early because it's a family do. We were going to walk along the beach. 'Is your dad coming?' I asked the O'Neills.

'No way!' said Linden, laughing scornfully. 'You won't find him mixing with the masses!'

Flavia looked offended. I could see she wanted to say that this wasn't the sort of thing they usually went to, but Red said, 'He's so lazy! If he doesn't need to set foot outside his hotel on holiday, then he won't! I've got the camcorder though – I'll be able to show him what he's missing!' He looked at me and Jonty. 'You two started it. I've decided to shoot as many sorts of dancing as I can. Dad approves. He's into dancing right now because of *West Side Story*.'

'What's all this? What have you and Jonty been getting up to now, Maddy?' said Dad, smiling indulgently. He clearly approved of my friendship with Jonty, us being the same age (not that Jonty knows) and everything.

'Oh, just a spot of tangoing on the beach,' said Jonty, enjoying himself.

Flavia said, 'Oh, Jonty! Why do you always have to be so em*bar*rassing?' She looked pained at the memory of Jonty shaming her family in front of Red.

Dad still looked puzzled. 'Jonty's ace at Latin dancing, Dad. Life is full of surprises, isn't it?' Jonty got up and did a twirl just as Brian and Gina Hayter appeared. Gina was wearing *slacks* (for limbo dancing, no doubt), I noticed, and a lot of make-up.

'Gina would insist on the dancing classes,' said Brian gruffly. 'But the boy does himself proud on the rugby field too.'

'So that's OK then,' said Dilly mischievously. 'Come on! The Beale College lot are getting there at six-thirty, Holly said so. And it will be so much more fun if we're all there together.'

We kicked off our shoes and walked along the beach to a hotel less than a mile away. I could see Red manoeuvring himself into position alongside me. For once Linden was more than a few metres away, talking about Charles from Beale College with Dilly. 'So how was the scuba diving?' Red asked as he fell in beside me. 'I've already heard about Linden being irresponsible from the instructor. She does actually know what she's doing and you weren't in any real danger, but I had a go at her myself. I told her I wouldn't tell Dad – he'd forbid her from going again and there'd be a helluva row – but I thought I might come along and go down with you next time. Did you like the fish? Did you see any angel fish?'

'It was brilliant,' I said. 'But I couldn't tell you what I did and didn't see. I can't tell fishy things apart.'

'You definitely need me then,' he told me, and smiled to himself when he realised what he'd just said. He looked down at me, to see if I'd realised too, as we walked along the edge of the sea in the evening light. A warm breeze ruffled his hair and the low sun cast long shadows of his striding figure. He looked like a Hollywood Viking – but Red was no actor: the warmth in his blue eyes was one hundred per cent real.

The barbecue was fun. We queued for our food and sat down at long tables on the beach. Red sat next to me and was very attentive. Flavia didn't like it, neither did Linden, but I decided that that was their problem. I liked it a lot. Not being alone meant that we talked about general things all the time, when really I wanted to get to know him better, but I reckoned there would be time for all that over the next two weeks. Holly came over to us and pointed out where their enormous party was sitting. We agreed to meet up for the limbo dancing. I could see Dilly peering over in their direction, trying to pick out smarmy Charles. She kept pulling out a make-up bag and retouching her lipstick in the mirror.

A steel band had been playing all along, but now the music was louder and a guy with a lovely deep voice told us over the PA that the limbo dancing competition was about to begin. Gina was one of the first to get up and go over to him. She even stubbed her cigarette out and put the holder away in her handbag. It shouldn't have been a surprise that she and Brian were good dancers, considering Jonty, but boy, did she love shimmying under the bar. I could see why. It was a real challenge – and for a few brief moments all eyes were on each competitor. Red's camcorder was on us too.

The first few rounds took ages. There were about a hundred people at the barbecue and at least fifty wanted a go at limbo dancing – in between jigging around to the steel band. It was a shame Red was videoing all the time, or we might have had a dance. Still, Jonty and the entire cricket team were willing partners. So, more embarrassingly, were Brian Hayter and Dad. The bar was getting lower. I knocked it off and went to stand by Red for a bit. 'Are you filming everyone as they go under?'

'No! I only press the button when I think it's interesting. But I don't want people to know when I'm focusing on them. Like you, for instance!'

'Red!'

'You're such a cool dancer! Over there too. It's a good job I have to take my eyes off you to film this!' Gina was going under the bar. She was pretty good. Stomach muscles like steel. She went back to where Dad was standing with Brian. As I watched, another couple came over and greeted them. They seemed to know Dad too.

'Were those people who are talking to my dad and the Hayters here last year, Red?' I asked him.

He turned the camcorder in their direction. 'Yes – at our hotel. They must be staying somewhere different this year.'

'I wonder what they're saying to Dad.'

'I'll zoom in on them if you like, and see if I can lip read. In fact, how about you try?'

'OK.' He showed me how to use it, taking the opportunity to push my hair off my face so I could look into it properly. Again I wanted all those people to disappear. But instead I focused on Dad and his cronies. The new couple greeted him fulsomely.

I didn't need to lip read – the woman had a booming voice. 'Richard!' she said. 'Are you here on your own, then?' At which point I would have expected Dad to shake his head and nod in my direction. But he didn't. He did look up and see me pointing a camcorder at him though, and turned his back on me. Then I heard a name I'd heard before: 'When's Fay arriving?' asked the woman, but I didn't hear Dad's answer because he was facing away from me.

'Curious,' I said, shaken for some reason, as I handed back the camcorder to Red.

'Why?'

'They were talking about Fay. Isn't that the infamous mother of Matty-Matt?'

'Yes. I think Meryl and Fay were at the hotel when we were last year, though your dad must have left before we arrived.'

'I realise that. I just had a horrible thought that maybe Dad didn't come here just for my sake. You know how you end up spying on your parents.'

'I've given up doing that with my dad, though Linden still watches him like a hawk. Forget it. I'm bored with the camcorder. Let's dance.'

So I danced with Red and forgot about Dad. It was very hot on the dance floor and the adults were all pretty drunk. We were all thrown together and it was brilliant. It wasn't couple dancing but Red grabbed me whenever I got pushed too far away. He had to lean close to make himself heard, and what with one thing and another we managed to find plenty of occasions for touching and bumping into each other. Every now and then I felt Flavia's or Linden's jealous eyes on me, though Linden was mostly busy with the cricket team and – apparently – enticing Charles away from poor old Dilly. Jonty seemed to be getting on very well with Holly. Only three days into the holiday and it was beginning to feel like one big happy family . . .

The family part of the barbecue was definitely over. The cricket team were led away and Flavia started rounding up Dilly (who was looking tearful) and Jonty (who was gazing longingly after the departing Holly). 'JONTY! Come ON!'

said Flavia, cuffing him. 'You're FAR too young to be interested in girls. HONESTLY!' Meanwhile, Gina had Dad transfixed with a smoke-ringed gaze from which he couldn't escape. Linden, having ruined Dilly's evening, now took it upon herself to comfort her, so Red and I were left to bring up the rear as we all walked back along the beach. We fell behind the others *almost* without realising it.

When they were safely out of sight around the curve of the bay Red stopped for a moment and leaned against a palm tree. The waves swished against the shore and the moon made a path over the sea. It was too romantic for words. 'Come here, Maddy,' he said, and held out both his hands to me. I moved towards him – and then two things happened simultaneously. His mobile rang and Dad came storming back to find us.

'Yes, Linden, I'm on my way,' said Red into his mobile, as Dad roared, 'Madeleine! I thought I'd lost you. Now stop loitering and come along at once!'

SIX

I barely spoke to Dad on the way back to the hotel. Red was all apologetic – 'I'm sorry, sir – we weren't far behind,' etc., etc. Dad had nodded grimly but practically dragged me back to our rooms, saying, 'Yes, well, it's late anyway.' When we got in I had a go at him, briefly, for behaving like the thought police, and couldn't I even have a bit of a holiday romance, or wasn't it *allowed*? It wasn't as if Red and I were even *doing* anything!

All he could say was that I was only fourteen and Red was seventeen and we didn't know him. I said I knew Red as well as he knew Brian Hayter, but that didn't stop *them* going off together, did it? I also reminded him that I was only a few weeks off fifteen and Red was only just seventeen. Then I detected Linden's hand in the affair because it all became a little clearer when Dad went on about us not knowing what *sort* of boy Red was. 'What do you mean, what *sort* of boy?' I asked him.

'Well, according to his sister, he's something of a . . .'

'Go on,' I said wearily, knowing that Linden would have deliberately put a spanner in the works.

' "Sex maniac" was the expression she used.'

'And you'd trust her judgement over mine?'

'I'm only trying to protect you, darling.'

'What from, exactly?'

'Oh, you know—'

'No I don't!' I yelled. 'You just don't want me to have any fun! You bring me on this brilliant holiday, expect me to look pretty and be grateful, but you just can't cope with a living, breathing teenage daughter. Look at me, Dad! I am a teenage girl! I happen to like teenage boys! It's *normal*!'

Dad looked at me sadly. 'I'm sorry, sweetheart. Give your silly old dad a hug.' I gave him a quick squeeze. I don't like hurting his feelings. 'I don't want to spoil your fun, Mads, I really don't. It's just that you're very young still.'

'Not that young, Dad. I watch television. I see movies. I hear the news. I go to a whacking great comprehensive school. You can't really protect me from the real world.'

'And that's what saddens me,' he said, pouring himself a drink and turning away.

'I'm off to bed now,' I said. 'See you in the morning, Daddy. Love you.'

'Love you too,' he said.

I woke up feeling cross. I'd forgiven Dad for last night in some ways, but he *had* interrupted me and Red. We'd been working up to that kiss all evening, and now I felt cheated. I tried to relive the moments just before. The anticipation had been delicious. I would just have to imagine the rest.

Damn Linden! She's really good company, but I don't think I should trust her farther than I can throw her.

I thought about the day ahead. There was some beginners' windsurfing on the afternoon watersports schedule. Dilly said she'd do it with me – there's no way Jonty and Linden can be classed as beginners! And before that, some serious sunbathing on the beach. I might see Holly and the cricketers there – I like them, they remind me of home. And of course I want to catch up with Red, too, but somehow I don't want to plan that – I just want it to *happen*. And then there's Bianca. When did my social life get to be so busy?

Dad and I went down to breakfast together. He seemed almost sheepish. 'I hardly like to say this after your comments last night,' he said, 'but Brian has asked me to drive over to a new 18-hole golf course with him this afternoon. Would you mind being left here?'

'But, Dad,' I teased, 'we hardly even *know* the man! Are you sure you should be leaving me? After all, I'm only fourteen . . .'

'Good gracious, child, you're nearly fifteen!'

'When it suits *you*, yes. But who'll look after me if I hurt myself windsurfing?'

Dad looked serious. 'Oh dear. You know, I hadn't really considered that. Perhaps I'd better ask Gina. I'm a pretty hopeless father, aren't I?'

'Shut up, Dad. I'm just making you suffer for last night. I'm not really likely to hurt myself – unless that sex maniac Red catches up with me, of course!'

'I'll be back in time for supper.'

'You'd better be!'

It was still early and the cricketers were playing cricket on the beach while it was more or less empty. Holly and Abby came running over as soon as they saw me. '*You* looked as though you were having a nice time last night!' said Holly.

'So did *you*,' I said. 'Jonty and Dilly are on their way down now, even as we speak . . .'

'What are you talking about?' asked Abby, who hadn't been to the barbecue. 'No one will tell me anything!'

Holly caught my eye and put her finger to her lips. 'It was a good barbecue,' I told Abby. 'We all really enjoyed the food.' Holly smiled gratefully, but then Jonty arrived and she started to blush.

'Hi,' said Jonty, at a loss for words – for the first time in his life, I imagine.

'Hi,' said Holly.

No prizes for scintillating conversation there.

Then Dilly caught up with them, running in the heat, her feet sinking into the sand. She sat down in the shade of a beach umbrella to draw breath. 'Jont, Mum says you must come riding with us this morning if you want to go surfing on the east coast tomorrow. Don't ask me why. I think she must miss you or something. And the O'Neills are all off somewhere this morning too – Bridgetown I think – so you won't miss out on Red. Though *you* will, Maddy!' She turned to me. 'I don't know what makes Linden tick. She wasn't content just with getting Charles away from me, she had to ruin your evening, too. I heard her freaking out your dad by telling him that her brother was a bit of a sex maniac! Red of all people! He's such a gentleman!'

'Ooh, what's all this?' asked Holly, her eyes nearly as wide as Abby's.

'Get Maddy to tell you,' said Jonty. 'I have to go, I'm afraid – see you later,' and he suddenly darted forward and gave Holly a peck on the cheek before heading back for the hotel with Dilly.

'*Lots* to talk about,' I said, as Holly put her hand up to touch her cheek where Jonty had kissed her, and we made ourselves very comfortable indeed on the sunbeds.

'Run away, Abby,' said Holly, not unkindly.

'Why can't I stay?'

'Big girls' talk. Now, go and find someone to play with – see if Mum's around.' With Abby dispatched, Holly settled in. I told her about my row with Dad. 'Trust Linden!' she said. 'Sometimes I think she's in love with her own brother! As for dads – mine throws a fit whenever he comes across one of my magazines. They seem to think that if we know what sex *is* we're going to run off and get pregnant – just like that! As if we mightn't be just a *teensy* bit choosy about who we do it with, or when? They never give us any credit do they?'

Dad came to say goodbye before he went off with Brian Hayter in search of the new golf course. Brian told me that Dilly would be back in time for the windsurfing and then they went off like two eager schoolboys and left me to have lunch on my own.

Dilly said I took to windsurfing like a duck to water, which seemed quite appropriate really. It was *brilliant* – I only fell in once. It's all a matter of balance – and I'm good at that. The sun was burning down – we really had to slap on the sunscreen before going out – but the sea and the breeze were cool. The instructor was very complimentary as well. It might just have been because he fancied me, but I'm much stronger (from all the dancing) than I look, so I think I surprised him. Oh dear – it's yet another thing I'm longing to do with Red. Now I know why he and Jonty love it so much – you just feel so free out there, you, the sea and the wind. Dilly says it's a bit like riding in a way, you're independent and in control, just you and the elements. What all teenagers need, with parents like ours!

As we walked back up the beach afterwards I saw a group of people waving to me from the deep shade of some palm trees. 'Come and meet Bianca!' I told Dilly. 'She must be feeling good today if they've brought her to the beach!'

'Maddy!' squealed Bianca. 'Mummy says I can go on a

banana boat with you and Daddy. I've been waiting *hours* for you to finish your lesson!' Imperious little madam. I looked at her dad.

'We've devised a sort of harness for her – so you can strap her to the front of your lifejacket. She'll be pushed backwards by the thrust of the boat anyway. I'll sit in front as well, so if we go over we three will go together. What do you think?'

'He's thought of nothing else since you first mentioned it,' said Bianca's mum. 'And she's so *desperate* to have a go – we decided it was worth a try.'

'Fine by me,' I said. 'And if Dilly – this is my friend Cordelia Hayter – comes too we can have one to ourselves.'

'I would go,' said Bianca's mum, 'but it scares the life out of me just watching! I've never been much of a swimmer.'

'Come *on*!' said Bianca. So off we went to find a banana boat. The boat hire guy found a special small lifejacket for Bianca and we strapped her on to my front with a modified set of child's reins. The little thing was positively *trembling* with excitement as we were pulled into the bay. The boatman was brilliant – and went in wide curves so we didn't fall in, but then Bianca kept saying, 'I want to do it properly!' so I made a decision. Usually someone sets a banana boat undulating like a snake to make it even harder to stay on. When the trip was nearly over I bounced up and down once or twice and then rolled off into the sea, taking Bianca with me. I'd towed her around the pool enough – I felt pretty sure I knew what she was capable of. And she *loved* it – she just bobbed about with me, yelling '*Look at me! Look at me!*' I wasn't even out of my depth, so I unhitched her and towed her along, just like in the pool.

'You had me worried there,' said her dad, when we were back sitting on the beach.

'Me too,' said her mum. 'I was convinced she was going to drown.'

'I *loved* it!' said Bianca. 'It's the best thing I've ever done in my *whole* life!'

'That's why you did it, isn't it?' said Cordelia when we were in the beach bar later.

'Yup,' I said. 'She was *desperate* for the real thing. Wouldn't you be if you didn't have long to live?' I felt the tears pricking still at what Bianca had said. 'Her parents treat her like porcelain and it's not what she wants.'

'They have to do what they think is right though, don't they?' said Dilly.

'I suppose that's the thing with parents,' I said, thinking of Dad.

Dilly and I wandered back up to the hotel. I wanted a shower after such an energetic afternoon. 'It's been peaceful without Linden, hasn't it?' she said.

'Don't you like her?'

'We're very different,' said Dilly diplomatically.

'She's good fun,' I said, defending her. After all, she was Red's sister.

'She's just always rude to me,' said Dilly. 'And I can't trust her. I mean, why did she say that about Red to your dad? Quite apart from her trying to get off with Charles last night. By the way, Flavia's terribly shocked – she takes herself and Red ever so seriously, when it's obvious he's nuts about you, but she can't cope with her little brother and sister fancying people. She complained all the way through our ride this morning!'

'Have you any idea when the O'Neills are coming back?'

'None whatsoever.'

'Have you ever met the great man?'

'I think we had dinner with them and some other people last year. Why?'

'What's he like?'

'No less normal than the other people here. I mean, he

is about the most famous film director in the world – as Linden never tires of telling me. I don't think he has much in common with Mum and Dad to be honest, but hardly anyone does, unless they happen to live in the identical corner of Warwickshire as we do, and since we own most of it there aren't many who fit that description.'

'I like your mum and dad. I've never met anyone like them before. Your mum reminds me of Penelope Keith!'

'They're OK. They don't fight or anything like that. It's just that they're out of the ark – time-frozen somewhere in the 1930s – long before they were born, even. That's what comes from generations of a family that has always lived in one corner of Warwickshire. Flavia's a great one for saying why change if you don't need to. And I suppose I am too, sometimes. But I do *not* want to be like Flavia!'

We'd come to the point where our ways parted. 'See you later,' said Dilly. 'Hope you find Red. I have to wait until the morning to see Charles. Holly told Jonty they'll be on the beach early because they're going on some outing to-morrow.'

'See you,' I said, and went to our rooms. It was very cool and peaceful. I grabbed a banana from the fruit bowl and opened the balcony windows. I ate the banana and looked out over the tropical garden and the pool to the sea. People were making their way back to the hotel. Loads of them change for dinner – you should see them, they look as if they're going to meet the Queen! I'm just so annoyed I forgot to pack my tiara! You know, I shouldn't be at all surprised if the Hayters really have them. I must ask Dilly some time. I've never met anyone as posh as her before, but she's just nice and normal underneath. I'm not so sure about Flavia though. Fancy owning a large part of Warwickshire and coming here every year. And skiing at Easter. And sometimes New York for Christmas – or the flat in Chelsea. Unbelievable. I can't wait to tell Mum and Eloise about them all. And fancy rubbing shoulders with

Oliver O'Neill! Mum would be gobsmacked. Talking of the O'Neills . . . I really wanted to see Red tonight – *alone.* For at least five minutes. I wondered if that would be possible?

I had a shower, washed my hair and changed into one of my little clubbing dresses – a shimmery strappy number in a soft rose colour that I know suits me, especially when I'm brown. I thought I'd look nice for dinner with Dad, to make up for our row last night. I know he's trying. And I'm still really touched by the fact that he's laid on this fabulous holiday just for me.

I dried my hair, made up and put on some jewellery that my ex gave me. He had surprisingly good taste and it all looks even better with a tan. I went down to wait in the bar for Dad, and had myself a little fruit cocktail (or FC as the Hayters would call it). The sun was setting on a perfect evening and the palm trees were waving in the gentle breeze. *Honest!* The brochures do not lie on this matter! I finished my drink but there was still no sign of Dad. I didn't see anyone I recognised. The Hayters must have gone somewhere else. Perhaps the O'Neills weren't back yet. I waited a bit longer. I wondered if he'd left a message for me in reception.

I went to the desk and the receptionist told me to look in our pigeon hole. There was a fax message there! It said DUMONT on it and our room number. I read it, but it was *for* Dad, not from him, from someone called F. Marchant. It said, 'Will Saturday ever come? Grantley Adams 5.00 p.m.' I reread it. God knows what it meant, work no doubt, but I didn't quite like the sound of it and I'm ashamed to say I crumpled it up and tossed it in the nearest bin. Dad's fault for not being here.

'Maddy!' I looked up, and there was Red. He must have just spotted me, because Linden and Oliver were walking on through reception. 'Did you eat dinner?' His eyes burnt into mine as he spoke – it was lovely. I was so pleased to see him.

'No. I'm waiting for my dad to get back from golf. I thought he'd be back hours ago. And I'm starving!'

'Right. Maddy, quick. Come with me.' He checked his back pocket. 'Mobile. Dollars.' He took my arm and hustled me out to the front of the hotel where a taxi was still ticking over. 'Good. This is the one that just dropped us.' He pushed me in and told the driver – 'Carambola please!' and then sat back and dialled the hotel. 'Hello? Message for Richard Dumont from his daughter: Gone to Carambola with Redwood. Home by eleven.' He laughed at my surprised face. 'I'm not Oliver O'Neill's son for nothing you know. I like to make things happen.' He started dialling another number. 'Hi, Dad. It's me, Red. Change of plan. I'm eating out. See ya around eleven.'

He looked at me appraisingly. 'You look stunning! Now listen. I have it on good authority that the golfing party got a little held up and won't be back at the hotel until nine at the earliest. I saw Jonty, you see.'

I felt breathless. 'What's the Carambola when it's at home? Should I be screaming? You know what Linden told my father—'

'Though I'm embarrassed to say it, yes, I do know what Linden told your father. Jonty also informed me of this. The Carambola is an extremely trendy place to eat, but the reason I want to go there is because it's the best place to watch the flying rays. Our taxi driver was telling us they were good tonight on our way back to the hotel. So you can scream if you want to, but I shouldn't bother because we're nearly there.' The taxi had climbed to quite a height and drew up outside a restaurant on a cliff terrace. We got out. Red paid the driver and asked him to come back at 10.30. *So* efficient! *So* unlike my previous boyfriends!

'Dad will be furious.'

'Well, he's no right to be. He was late and didn't tell you. He knows where you are. Forget it. Enjoy!' And he put his arm around my shoulders and steered me in.

We found a table that overlooked the sea. Red quickly ordered us the set menu and some mineral water, so we could stand up and follow where people were pointing. And there they were! Silver-backed in the twilight, giant rays broke through surface and flapped across the water. At first you saw nothing and then you saw one and then another and another – it was magic, like looking for stars in the evening sky.

'They are just so outta this world!' said Red with a happy sigh. 'And we can still see them if we sit down. Great. I last got to see them when I was too young to appreciate it, you know? And another time I pestered Dad to bring me here and we were too early. Linden was quite little and we had to go back. I was real angry.' He smiled at me. 'I hope you didn't mind me kidnapping you, Maddy. You looked so pretty standing there, and kinda forlorn, that I wanted to whisk you away. Especially after last night.' He took my hand in both of his. 'Later, huh?'

And then, guess what. His mobile rang! 'Linden, hi. Yes. Sure I know what I'm doing. Yeah, I woulda taken you, but it wasn't like that. Now you know where I am and who I'm with so you don't need to ring again. In fact – Linden? Linden, I'm switching off. Messages only, OK? Bye!'

Our food arrived. It was all beautifully arranged on the plate and the cold drinks came in an ice bucket. I still have to pinch myself (just above the inside of my knee where it really hurts) to believe all this and remind myself that I'll be back to pot noodles when it's all over. We were both ravenous and spent a while stuffing our faces.

Then Red turned to me and said, 'You know, I cannot believe I just did that – kidnapped you.'

'Feel free,' I said. 'Any time.'

'I just *so* did not want to miss the rays, and I kinda wanted to see them with you – and there you were.'

Hey! He wanted to share things with me, just like I wanted to share them with him!

'I'm really sorry about my dad last night. He thinks he's protecting me.'

'After what Linden said to him, I cannot say I'm surprised! You know, I guess *she* thinks she's protecting me and Dad, in her way, by scaring people off. Not that it works with Dad – it is not unknown for him to take advantage of his position. That's why my mom moved us a few blocks down. She is so totally different from him.'

'What does she do? Is she an actress, like my mum?'

'Mom? No way! She's a shrink! No shortage of work for her in Hollywood – though she's a child psych now. Ironic, considering Linden.'

'What do you mean?'

'Linden's so like Dad. Mom's real steady and sensible – ha! like me, I guess – and Dad's the opposite. A few years ago, when Lin was twelve or so, and cranky, she really hated Mom and moved in with Dad – a few blocks away. Mom didn't stop her, but it was a disaster. Dad had another girlfriend who did not want Lin around. So Lin came back, but for a while she'd only talk to Mom through me. Mom thought it wisest just to let her get through it. They're OK now, but Lin feels she has to keep tabs on me and Dad all day long. It's time she grew out of it – and got on with being a nice kid, you know?'

'I like her.'

'She's OK – but I think that says more about you than her. And I don't want to talk about Linden any more. I want to know more about this golden-eyed English girl with a face like an angel, who dances like a dream. Where have you been all my life, Maddy?'

'Living with my mum and little sister in a London suburb and going to the local comprehensive.'

'A what?'

'A big state school.'

'I can never work out your British education system. Don't you call private schools public schools or something?'

'This is not a private school – it's more like your high school. Twelve hundred kids.'

'So you're an English schoolgirl, huh? Do you get to wear a uniform?'

'Enough, Red! I'll start to think you're kinky! And no, we don't have a uniform – sorry to disillusion you!'

'And your dad? Has he remarried?'

'No, he hasn't married again. My mum left him for another bloke and they had my little sister.'

'What's your stepfather like then? Is he a nice "bloke"? (I love that word, "bloke"!)' Red laughed.

'Well, it's complicated you see. Mum left him, too, for another bloke that lives down the road. I don't like him much – the new one, Roddy.'

'Sheesh! Today's kids really suffer for their parents, don't they? I'm not complaining though. Mum's cool and so's Dad.'

'What's it like having such a famous dad?'

'People always ask that. Basically he's just my dad. For a while I was embarrassed about it but now I'm real proud of what he does. He's very dedicated and very focused. It gives me a real buzz to watch him in action. He loved those tango shots by the way.'

'You showed him?'

'Why not? They were fantastic! Jonty was such a shock, man! I took that guy for a total jerk when I first met him, but now – he is so cool. So British. Your genuine article.'

'They're seriously rich, the Hayters.'

'What the hell! So am I! We wouldn't be eating here if I wasn't. Does it bother you?'

'No, just makes me jealous. Since I am seriously poor.'

'And seriously, seriously beautiful.' He found my hand and stroked it. I still couldn't believe my luck – this amazing guy, who I fancy like hell, fancying me! I mean, it hardly *ever* happens that way, does it? And no Dad, and no Linden. 'What say we go outside and look at the view from there?' Red asked, fixing me with that piercing blue gaze. 'It's a while before our taxi arrives.'

I followed him outside. It was dark and quite steamy – clouds covered the moon and it felt as if it might rain. The tree frogs were very noisy. Red held my hand as we stood looking out over the black sea and then pulled me to him. 'Would you object if we carried on where we left off last night?' he said (ever the gentleman).

'I'd object far more if we didn't,' I said, and reached up to kiss him, feeling I'd explode if I didn't.

. . . And explode if I did. Red is *dynamite*. He's *really* really strong with broad shoulders and fabulous windsurfer's pecs. I didn't stand a chance! I had to lean back against a tree for support! I could have gone on kissing him for ever, in fact I would have done. But Red was whispering into my ear, first something about how it was a good thing we were in a public place or he wouldn't trust himself not to answer to Linden's description and then, 'Don't look now, but I think we've been rumbled. Your dad has turned up.'

This was ridiculous. *Just* as things were getting interesting. Red gave me a big sexy squeeze and then straightened out his clothes. 'Go to the bathroom and sort out your lovely face and your mussed-up hair,' he said. 'I'll go find your father and reassure him that all is well. We don't want to antagonise him.'

'It's just so frust*ra*ting!'

'At least we're agreed on that. Go *on*, or the sex maniac will attack again and your father will have real grounds for anxiety!'

I went to the ladies and looked at myself in the mirror. I was very flushed. I splashed cold water on my face. That was better. I took a deep breath. Wow. I'd have to watch myself with Red – it wasn't *him* I was worried about. A romance is one thing, but this is like a – a – *jugg*ernaut. What do you *do* when you like someone so much and they like you back? All I want is for us to curl up together out here on the cliff and stay all night. Oh well. It's not to be. I'll go quietly, Dad. This time.

SEVEN

To be fair to Dad, he'd come out to the Carambola partly because he felt guilty about getting back late, and partly because when he picked up my message they told him that I'd picked up an earlier one and he wanted to know what it was. 'I'm sure whoever it was will fax again, Dad – I honestly can't remember what it said. Anyone important would double-check, wouldn't they? Might it have been someone called Grantley Adams?' We'd said goodnight to Red (Dad even gave us a couple of minutes to ourselves while he paid the taxi driver) and Dad and I were in our rooms, having drinks from the mini bar.

'That's the name of the airport, airhead!' he said. He was going to say something else, but he stopped himself. 'Did you see the rays at the Carambola? I saw them last year – terrific sight, aren't they? Quite romantic, as I remember!' He gave me a quick smile. He really *is* trying! 'I must say, I find it rather endearing in the boy that he wanted to see them.'

'Red's really keen on wildlife. He does underwater filming according to Linden.' I said. 'Imagine growing up with all that sort of equipment there for the asking. It does seem unfair sometimes.'

'Talking of the Great Man – I get to meet him on Thursday. A couple of them are going to join me and Brian for golf.'

'Wow, Dad. Do you think he might offer you some scriptwriting?'

'Different league, darling. I'm not distinguished enough for him to know me by name.'

'Gina Hayter knew your name, didn't she though?'

'Ah, that was for a different reason. Now, since I'm your father, I think I should probably tell you to go to bed. But do what you like – as long as you stay up here. I'm whacked, so I'm hitting the sack.'

'I'll stay up for a bit. I just feel like looking at the sea. I love our rooms here, Daddy – just you and me. And you can relax tomorrow! Red and Jonty are going windsurfing on the east coast, so you won't have to worry about me one little bit. I intend to catch up with Holly and co. on the beach.'

I woke up early and lay there thinking about my lovely Red. He is *so* gorgeous looking and *so* kind and *so* sexy and so – *everything*. I really think I'm in love. I sort of want to be with him all the time but then again I don't mind *not* being with him if I know I *am* going to be with him later. I don't have that scary feeling you sometimes get that if you're not with your boyfriend all the time he's going to find someone else, or go off you or something.

I got up and dressed for a morning on the beach. I remembered what Dilly said about the cricketers being down there early, and hurried over for breakfast. Dilly was racing through hers on her own. 'Want to get down there before Linden,' she said. 'I don't think she knows they're going off later. You coming?'

I wrapped up some fruit in a paper napkin, grabbed a croissant, and followed her out. I'm sure it's not how civilised guests behave, but tough. Our speed was rewarded. There were the boys, and Holly, and no Linden. 'You're so lucky, Holly,' said Dilly, 'being with this lot all the time.'

'You wouldn't think so if it was you,' said Holly. 'Anyway, I could say the same about you being with Jonty all the time!'

'Hmm,' said Dilly, and they both laughed. Dilly, tanned, with her hair tied back, a discreet amount of gold jewellery and a *really* expensive bikini, looks less and less horsy than my first impression of her. And I like her. She's funny and she's self-aware. 'Now help me, you two,' she said. 'There's to be no escape for Charles!'

'I happen to know,' said Holly, 'that Charles is very susceptible to flattery. He doles it out so much himself that it comes as a shock when the compliments are aimed at him. So how about – er – "I really like your shades / boardies / sixpack / haircut / eyes . . . tan?" '

'But I like *all* of them,' said Dilly plaintively.

'Ask to borrow his goggles, or something,' I suggested. We had to get the girl to him somehow. 'Charles!' I called. Dilly shrank. 'Charles, come over here! Dilly wants to ask you something!'

'Mad*dy*!' Dilly hissed.

'Just think of something, anything,' said Holly, starting to giggle.

'What? What do you want?' Charles looked at us suspiciously. And then, bless him! – 'That's a cool bikini, Dilly,' he said.

Dilly opened her mouth, but no words came out. Charles sat down beside her, and in a flurry of sand and sunscreen bottles Holly got up and grabbed my arm so we could run off and leave them together. We raced to two empty sunbeds under a beach umbrella and collapsed on to them. 'Well done, us!' said Holly. 'They just needed that little extra push, didn't they?'

'I hope they get it on before Linden arrives,' I said. 'She's going to be at a loose end with Red and Jonty on the east coast, so it's only a matter of time before she finds us.'

'Don't forget we're all going off in an hour – to Harrison's caves – so Charles won't be here. Neither will I. You'll have her all to yourself!'

'That's OK really. If we go back to the pool, Dilly can keep the Flavour company and I can be with Linden.'

We looked over to Charles and Dilly. They were wandering down to the water together. 'Ooh, look!' squeaked Holly. 'They're going for a swim together! How sexy!' They disappeared into the waves and bobbed up again a few metres away, Charles in hot pursuit of Dilly. 'Lucky things,' said Holly. 'Why aren't Jonty and Red here – we ought to be frolicking in the sea with them, too!'

'At least we can indulge in girl-talk,' I said. 'That's almost as much fun as what they're doing.'

'Almost,' said Holly. 'Especially if you tell me in *great* detail all about last night.' So I told her about Red kidnapping me and going to the restaurant and watching the rays.

'And then?' she asked. 'Did you finally get to kiss him? I bet he's incredibly sexy! You can tell, just by looking at him. I mean, he's all fit and hunky – magazine stuff. Well? Did you?'

'*Yeah*,' I said.

'And?'

'He was a*ma*zing,' I said, and fell back in a pretend swoon on the sunbed.

'Maddy!' she said, pretending to be cross. 'Don't stop there! I mean, did you – *do* anything else? Or did you just kiss?'

'None of your business!' I said, and swatted her. 'But we were out on the cliff terrace with loads of other people! It was a public place.'

'Oh,' she said, disappointed. 'I'd like to be in a very *private* place with Jonty. And I was hoping you might be able to give me the benefit of your experience . . .'

'You have to go at your own pace,' I said, realising I sounded very *old*. 'And that's the problem, Holly – with Red. I've got this feeling that Red's and my pace is a bit too hot for comfort. I just *know* we both really fancy each other – it's not as if he's rushing me or anything. But I don't know whether we should try to keep the lid on it, or not. Especially with Dad and Linden on our case all the time.'

'Seems like circumstances are going to hold you back,

for the moment anyway. What with Red not here today, and Linden following you everywhere, not to mention your dad. My problem is getting to be with Jonty at all – the Beale boys' schedule is quite hectic, and he has stuff he wants to do with Red. I keep wondering if we'll be able to see each other when we get home. We might live in different worlds, but at least it's the same country!'

Dilly and Charles were coming up the beach hand in hand. 'Aaah!' said Holly, and nudged me. The other cricketers were beginning to get up and go. 'Looks like his time is up!' she said, getting to her feet. 'I don't suppose I'll see you until the morning again – but I shall want to know *everything* this time! And you, Dilly!' She turned to Dilly, who was rubbing herself down with a towel. Charles had gone to join the other boys. Dilly had a *big* smile on her face.

And not even the sight of Linden making her way towards us across the sand could wipe it off.

The three of us – me, Dilly and Linden – wandered back up to the pool. Dad was there, so were the remaining Hayters. Oliver O'Neill and his entourage were out in force, too. Dilly said, 'Catch you later,' with a meaningful look – she wasn't about to discuss Charles in front of Linden. I waved at Dad but dived into the pool with Linden. It's uncanny how like Red she looks. And that's the closest I'm going to get at the moment!

We climbed out and sat on the side with our legs dangling in the water. Linden, unaware that Dilly had finally snatched Charles (as if she honestly cared anyway), was all American good humour. We chatted the rest of the morning away – I was really interested to hear about her life because it was Red's life too.

We had lunch by the pool and afterwards Bianca's parents came down without her and joined us. They had left Bianca sleeping, with one of the hotel's nurses in charge. 'We can't expect you to be the only one that gives us a break!' said her dad. 'In fact she's still exhausted from yesterday. I can't tell you how thrilled she was. I don't think I've seen her so happy for ages – and that's thanks to you, Maddy.'

I offered to read to her tonight – people don't believe I really get a buzz out of it, but I do. After lunch Dad came windsurfing with Linden and me – he wasn't bad at all – and we spent the rest of the afternoon flopping about on the beach and dipping into the sea. It was all totally laid-back and relaxed – just how a holiday should be.

I went up for a shower and then went to read to Bianca before supper. 'Maddy!' she snuggled up against me. 'Will you tell me a story about Bianca and the banana boat tonight?'

'OK.' Her mum and dad joined in and helped me elaborate on the story. I felt pleased that I'd had the courage of my convictions and made it special for her. There wasn't any talk of dying or sadness tonight, though I suppose it hung over them all like a cloud the whole time. On the positive side, they were working hard to make happy memories for themselves. One day all this would be distilled into a small golden Bianca era, captured on film and video and in their heads. Concentrated.

I went out to find the others for supper, feeling elated but raw – a strange emotional combination. And there was Red, waiting for me! Ooooh! He caught me up in a wonderful hug – all warm and rugged and lovely aftershave smelling. 'I want to walk along the shore in the sunset with you,' he said. 'I've been thinking about it all day while I was out on the water. And when we've had some time alone together I'm happy to join the others, but not until then, you know?'

'That's fine by me,' I said, 'But how *do* we avoid the others?'

'Easy! We head out the front and round the side.'

We did just that, stopping to kiss every few moments. It felt so right – when Red held me it was as if we were two halves of the same person. We took our shoes off and walked along the edge of the waves in the sunset. Most people had gone up for dinner so we had the beach almost to ourselves. I thought of storing up memories and decided to fix this one in amber. Red held me at arms' length and smiled. 'I'm just so – happy!' he said simply, and then pulled me to him again, and we stood ankle-deep in the shallows. 'I know we only just met, but I never felt like this before about anyone.'

'Me too,' I mumbled into his shoulder. We kissed some more and clung to one another – I really didn't want to meet up with the others right then. I wished Red and I had somewhere to go, but we didn't. My dad was expecting me, and no doubt Linden would be calling Red on the mobile any minute now.

Bang on cue, his phone rang. 'Tell Dad I'll be there in a coupla minutes,' he said to her, no more.

'*C'est la vie*,' I said with a sigh. It was no bad thing to be leaving the sand – lots of little crabs were coming out and going about their business. Was *everything* conspiring against us?

'Tomorrow,' he said, 'I'm not going anywhere. And I know both our fathers are playing golf. How about we just lie out on towels all day? You oil my back and I'll oil yours? Cool off in the sea together?'

'Sounds perfect,' I said, and wondered why my voice wouldn't come out properly. He squeezed my hand and went off to where Linden was waving. I saw Dad coming in with the Hayters and went to join them.

And perfect is how the next day was. Red and I took the cushions off a couple of sunbeds and put them next to each other. We bought some cool aloe vera stuff off a guy on the beach and rubbed it into each others' backs – *very* sexy. Then when we got too hot we just went into the sea and cuddled underwater. That was *very* sexy too. I knew we were storing up trouble with Linden, but we ignored everyone for most of the day. The cricketers also had a free day, so Holly and Jonty were able to be together and so were Dilly and Charles. Something in the water, obviously! Flavia appeared once, to boss Jonty and Dilly about, but stalked off, furious, when she realised that they were ignoring her, and went to be with her mother.

Red told me all about himself – his childhood, his ambitions to make wildlife documentaries or set up a watersports school. I just loved everything about him. I couldn't bear to think about the holiday ever ending – so I decided not to.

I told him more about me and Mum, Eloise, Gus and Roddy, even my old friends Sophie, Hannah and Charlotte. He said he couldn't wait to come to England to meet them all – he's travelled a lot but never been to Britain. He had a lovely way of looking at me when I talked to him, and stroking my arm or my hand, my hair or my face, as if he never wanted to let go. We didn't bother to go up for lunch – in fact we fell asleep in the shade. I woke up to see Red so close, his eyelashes on his cheeks. I didn't want to move but Jonty broke the spell when he and Holly came by kicking sand on us and offering to bring us back some drinks. Then Red's phone rang. I answered it. It was Linden being dangerously nice – she'd bagged us some seats in the beach bar. I told her Red had fallen asleep and that we might see her later, but I could tell she wasn't pleased. I couldn't blame her really, but it had to be *her* problem, not mine.

Jonty and Holly came back with the drinks and Red sat up and rubbed his eyes. 'I need to cool off and wake up,' he said. 'Maybe we could go for a bit of a windsurf later on?'

Jonty looked enthusiastic, but Holly quickly said, 'You mean with Maddy, don't you, Red?'

'Definitely with Maddy,' said Red, smiling. 'I want to do *everything* with Maddy. You know?'

'Blimey,' said Jonty. 'Thank you for sharing that with us, Red, but you didn't have to.'

Holly cuffed him. 'You know that isn't what he meant, Jonty,' she said. 'I might have thought twice about you if I'd known you had such a dirty mind,' and she dragged him off, leaving me and Red to wander hand in hand down to the water.

We went windsurfing in the afternoon together, Red helping me to do it better than before – he was a really good teacher. 'I'm going to take you scuba diving one of these days,' he said. 'There's so much to see. We won't go very deep or anything, but I guess I just want to show it to you.' So that was something to look forward to.

We went back to our place under the beach umbrellas, and there was *Linden* lying out on one of the sunbeds. All good things have to come to an end, I suppose. Linden was being fine – it's just that she was *there*. Soon after, Jonty and Dilly joined us too.

We all went up to the hotel for showers. Linden was trailing behind Red and me, practically treading on our heels. We were about to go our separate ways when she came out with a Linden-special and said to her brother, 'Now don't go thinking you can sneak off to Maddy's rooms with her, Red, just because her father's away. I know he'd disapprove, wouldn't he, Maddy?'

'I never even considered it,' I said. I hadn't.

'Oh leave us alone, you're embarrassing us!' said Red. He looked uncomfortable.

'I'm off,' I said.

'So are we,' said Dilly. 'They won't be late back from golf, tonight. It's only just down the road a little way. See you all later!'

Dad came in soon after. I was drying my hair after my shower. 'That was terrific!' he said, throwing himself into a chair. 'Apart from the fact that I haven't seen much of my darling daughter!' He poured himself a drink.

'Well I had a lovely day, too!'

'Did you, sweetheart? Good. By the way, you've got a fan!'

'I know. Red.'

'No, I don't mean Red. Now don't let this go to your head – but it's none other than Oliver O'Neill.'

'In other words, Red's father – he approves of his son's girlfriend, does he?'

'I don't know that he's aware you're Red's girlfriend – but he's seen you dancing on video and he thinks you're – now, what was his word? *Sensational*! Yes, that's it. He asked me if I was the father of the *sensational* English girl! I shouldn't be surprised if he asks to see you before the holiday's over.'

'He's seen me already, Dad. What do you mean?'

'You know, *see* you. Casting. *West Side Story* and all that.'

'Oh, Dad, don't be a silly old proud dad. I mean, *do*, but don't go giving me ideas! The school production is quite enough of a challenge for me, thanks very much. And I know all about Oliver O'Neill and his casting couch.'

'What *do* you mean?' He realised what I meant. 'Oh *honestly*, Maddy! I'm sure Oliver's not like that. He's far too professional.'

'Well, whatever. I'm glad it gave you two something to talk about.'

'Now, I was thinking it was time you left the hotel and saw something of the island. How about you and I go off somewhere tomorrow?'

'This isn't a ploy to get me away from Red, is it, Dad?'

'No, not at all. You can bring your friends if you like. I just want to spend some time with *you*, before – before the holiday ends.' Dear old Dad. I suppose we haven't spent much time together so far.

'As long as I can see Red in the evening! Let's just go together, Daddy. You see, Dilly and Jonty will want to be with Charles and Holly if they possibly can, and Linden gets really narky when I'm with Red. I suppose it could just be Linden, but perhaps if she has a whole day with her brother all to herself she'll lay off a bit.'

'Whatever you think is best as far as your friends are concerned, but I thought we could go to Harrison's Caves. In fact, I expect the others have all been before anyway. I went last year and they are quite an experience.'

EIGHT

Red was *so* disappointed (it was very gratifying) when I said I was spending the day with my dad, but he agreed that I ought to see Harrison's Caves, and cheered up at the prospect of being together in the evening. 'Except—' he started.

'What is it?'

'Well, it was Linden's idea in the first place – after Jonty's Latin dancing display – that we should all go along to this swanky dinner dance in the hotel tonight that the olds are going to – you, me, Linden, Jonty, and I suppose the other Hayters. Whaddya say?'

'My father won't know what's come over me, wanting to go to something like that, but yes, OK. I'm on. I like dinner and I like any sort of dancing. *Especially* with you.'

'My feelings exactly. Any opportunity to hold you close in a dimly lit place – and on this occasion it will be sanctioned, you know? So long as you do not go smooching with anyone else.'

'Oh yeah, Red. *Who*, precisely?'

Dad and I caught the bus after breakfast. It was the first time I'd been away from the hotel other than when Red kidnapped me and took me out to the Carambola. Quite apart from anything else it was good to see real Barbadians, going about their business – not just a whole load of horribly spoilt white people getting burnt and getting drunk. OK, the holidaymakers aren't all like that, but it must look like it sometimes. Dad said I mustn't forget that Barbados needs its tourist trade, but I still feel uncomfortable with it. Politics isn't my thing, but getting under other people's skin is what acting is all about – so I can't help thinking that way.

Inland the island is quite flat and green. You forget about the sea and the sand. And then it started raining! It chucked it down, and the bus splashed its way along the narrow roads. People on bicycles were soaked through, though no one seemed to mind or be surprised. So most of my view of this wet world was accompanied by the rhythmic beat of the windscreen wipers. It made me feel melancholy, and reflective. I kept thinking about how this brilliant holiday would end and become a bright memory that contained Red like a glowing star, and about how it would be the same only a million times worse for Bianca's mum and dad. And then I thought about Mum and Lo-lo and our comparatively grey and struggling lives – most people's lives, in fact. And then I suddenly felt a rush of affection for Dad – after all, I only had *him* for this fortnight too. I clutched his arm and rubbed my head against his shoulder.

'Hey,' he said. 'What's all this?'

'Love you, Daddy. I suddenly felt all sad about us only having another week together – and how I won't see Red after we go home and—'

'Mid-holiday blues!' he said dismissively. 'You'll get over him. That's the thing about holiday romances.'

I pulled away from him. 'Thank you for your sympathy, Dad! I suppose you think I'll get over you, too?'

'No, darling. Let's not get confused here. I'm your father. Red's just a lad you've met on holiday.' Dad was being very unsentimental.

'Two men I love,' I said, and started looking out of the window at the rain again. I felt hurt.

Of course the sun came out after a while and I can't feel angry at Dad for long. He seemed preoccupied, as though he had problems of his own, so I decided not to make a big deal out of it. The bus turned to go downhill and we rolled under a big wrought iron arch that welcomed us to Harrison's Caves. 'This will be worth a hundred geography lessons,' said Dad, as we put on hard hats and climbed aboard the special train. I'm not altogether happy about confined spaces, but Dad said I would be far too interested to feel claustrophobic. He was right. It was *weird*. The train rumbled along and then we came out into what was like a vast underground palace, all on different levels, with waterfalls and cascades and lakes. It was cleverly lit up, but there were still dark shadows and all those pointy bits – sorry, stalagmites (mites grow UP) and stalactites (HOLD ON tight) – that looked like carvings in stone. We drove on and down and twisted round bends. It wasn't scary exactly, just eerie. I felt as though Dad and I were in another world – a fantasy world, like in *The Hobbit*, and that we might never leave it. He could be King and I'd be Princess and all these people would be our subjects, but we'd never get out and see our families or friends again – no Mum, but no vile Roddy either. No Red, but no annoying Linden. Weird thoughts in a weird place.

The rushing water was terribly noisy – it made your brain do funny things. The guide was giving us information about how the water carved all these shapes out of the limestone, and the amount of time it took for the pointy bits to build up. Everyone was oohing and aahing and flashing their cameras or rolling their camcorders. I felt stranger and stranger.

'*Amazing*, isn't it?' said Dad. 'Aren't you glad you came?'

'Yes, but it makes me feel *odd* being down here. Another planet altogether.'

'I know what you mean. As if the real world didn't exist. Sky and clouds are just something you made up.' It's obvious that Dad and I often think alike.

At last we emerged. We'd only covered a mile, but it seemed like a much longer journey. The heat and the bright light as we came out burst on to us like an explosion.

We went into the restaurant. 'I fancy a pizza, please, Dad. Something to make me feel real again. I feel so weird today – you and me on this tiny island thousands of miles from home. I don't quite know what's brought it on. Suddenly everything seems so – fragile.'

'Sit down, poppet – I'll go and get us some pizza. I'll be back in two shakes of a puppy's tail.' He was talking to me like a child and I found it reassuring. This oddness had to do with Red, I was fairly sure. I felt safe with *him* – I felt safer with him than my own dad. Why? I couldn't explain it. I felt tiny, so small, as if I was sitting in the palm of someone's hand.

Dad came back with the pizza. 'There! Good old pizza. That should feel like home. Perhaps you've been eating too much seafood or something else exotic. Are you feeling a bit better now?'

'Yeah, yeah. I'm fine really – I don't feel physically ill, just odd. Anyway, my strange mood has passed now. What do we do next?'

'Wander round here for a bit? Drive around in a bus and have tea somewhere?'

'Fine. You've heard about tonight, haven't you?'

'I gather you young ones might grace the dinner dance tonight with your presence. It's a good job I'm willing to pay for you. You do know it's *dead* posh – don't you? If I go I have to wear my DJ.'

'Cool. Does that mean Red and Jonty will have to, too?'

'Oh yes.'

'I'm sure I can borrow something from Dilly or the Flavour, or even Linden.'

'You'd make any dress look glamorous.'

'OK, Dad, I'll wear my little clubby number shall I?'

'Better stick to the dress code just in case they decide to impose an age limit too, though I think you'd be able to get away with most things. I can't see them turning you away.'

'So long as I have the long gloves? I forgot to pack them as well as the tiara – oh no! You'll have to take a photo of me, Dad, for Lo-lo.'

'Of course I will. I'll want one for myself, won't I?'

We seemed to bumble about on buses all afternoon, but it was fun. Some of the buses were really crowded, but Dad and I got a seat together again on the last leg of the journey back to the hotel. He leaned towards me and cleared his throat. 'Today wasn't an attempt to keep you away from Red, Maddy. You know that, don't you?'

'My decision entirely.'

'But—' he coughed again. 'You will watch yourself, won't you, darling?'

'Da-ad. Say what you *mean*!'

'Well, I know I've left you alone quite a bit—'

'That's been good for both of us.'

'Well, yes. But you wouldn't – wouldn't *abuse* the fact that I'm not around, would you? I mean, you and Red wouldn't slip upstairs . . .'

'Dad! I hadn't even thought of doing that. Well, not until Linden suddenly came up with it last night.'

'Ah.'

'Dad – did *she* put the idea in your head?'

'Well, she did just say something – not quite within earshot, I must admit.'

'Dad. Listen. Will you just see things from my point of view – just for a moment. OK? Now – Red and I have just met. We like each other very much. We're getting to know each other. We need time alone sometimes. It's all very new. I don't *know* where it's going! I don't *know* if it's going to last! I don't know *anything* yet! But what I can't stand is other people jumping to conclusions about what we're getting up to. It's none of your business – or Linden's! No wonder we need time alone.'

'Maddy! You know and I know that what we're talking about here is sex.'

'Precisely. Which is why it's no one's business but our own. Dad – we have been lectured at school, I talk to Mum, I read the advice in magazines! I am not ignorant. Red is not my first boyfriend. But give me credit, will you? These are *my* decisions. Some adult having sleazy thoughts about my private life is pretty disgusting really. I don't do it to you!'

'While you are still a minor, and very much a minor, it *is* my business! What would I tell your mother?'

'Oh, get off my case, will you, Dad? Treat me as a human being in my own right, not as just another one of *your* problems. Mum always says that every person and every relationship is different – you can't make the same rules for everyone. It's like speed limits. If there's no one around and you're on the motorway you go at 90, I know you do.'

'That's quite different. No one's going to get pregnant at 90 miles per hour.' He was deadly serious of course, but it made me giggle, and then he saw the funny side of it and we both managed to laugh as the bus pulled up near the hotel.

Dad and I went in search of the others and found them on the beach. Jonty, Red and half the cricket team were stripping off their T-shirts suggestively and waggling their shorts in Full-Monty fashion, while singing 'I believe in miracles' to a hysterical audience, including Bianca and her parents. My dad turned to Holly's dad – 'Kuh! Kids today, eh?'

I felt as though I had been away from Red for a week. 'I

missed you so much,' he said. 'I had all these horrible feelings about how it was going to be at the end of the holiday.'

'Me too,' I said. We were walking along the beach. 'Let's not spoil our time together, Red. We have to think of it a bit like Bianca's family – except that there's a possibility we *will* have a future.'

'Speaking of the little lady,' he said, 'she and I are as close as *that* now,' (he linked his little fingers). 'She was dancing for me on the beach and I videoed her. She played to the camera like a dream.'

'She must be feeling well today!'

'Her mom and dad said she was having a good day. And now – what about *my* dancing girl?' He put his arms around my waist and lifted me right off my feet.

'Glad to be back. It was interesting, and it was nice to be with my dad. But he got quite heavy – about us, actually – and that was a drag.'

'What do you mean, heavy about us?'

'Oh, never mind.' It was as if precisely what I'd been talking about with Dad was happening. Other people speculating about our relationship could tarnish it. 'I can't wait to see you in a tux, Red. Do you really own one?'

'Part of the famous film-director's family uniform. Linden has a glitzy dress or two as well.'

'I feel like Cinderella! I don't possess anything that glamorous. I'm going to have to ask Dilly or Flavia.'

'One of my father's friends will have something, I'm sure. There's one I like – Tricia – who must be about the same size as you. Probably why I like her! She has good taste. She'll be only too happy to do a favour for the Great Man's son.'

'Red!'

'There have to be some compensations! She'll be by the pool, I figure. Let's go find her.'

Tricia was sophisticated New York Chinese and slim as a whippet. I could see why Red liked her. She was cool and intelligent as well as being stunningly beautiful. And far from treating him like the Great Man's son, she acted like he was a friend of hers. 'Sure!' she said. 'Maddy, you're so pretty you'd look terrific in a dishcloth, but you're welcome to try some things on. D'you want to go choose something now? I was getting bored down here anyway.'

'Go on, Maddy,' said Red. 'I can't wait to see you.' He was all excited, like a kid. (I had a moment of thinking – look at us, Dad, Red is thrilled because I'm going to wear a gorgeous dress – allow us to be this innocent.)

My wardrobe in my hotel room was a vast empty space with a few little dresses and tops languishing on hangers at one end. Tricia's, on the other hand, was *bursting* with dresses, blouses, skirts, suits, trouser suits, tennis gear, aerobics gear and *ballgowns*. It was like Eloise's Barbie wardrobe. Plenty of 'dining outfits' here. 'Wow!' was all I could say.

Tricia started pulling hangers off the rail and laying dresses out on the bed. 'Your colouring's kinda golden,' she said. 'Hmmm. Now, green looks good on honey blondes. And so does red. How about this one?' It was divine – simple, with thin, thin straps and fitted like a corset at the waist. 'I'm sure it will fit. Try it.'

I went into her bathroom and climbed into the dress, then made an entrance into the bedroom, walking towards her long mirror. Tears sprang into my eyes when I saw my reflection – I realised it was a RED dress, a red dress for Red. And I've never felt so beautiful in all my life.

'My turn to say Wow,' said Tricia. 'In fact I have to sit down. Maddy, you look *gorgeous!* And Red, my favourite young guy in the world, will love it. Hey, you're *perfect* for each other.'

'Can I borrow it, then?'

'With pleasure, honey.'

Dad was straightening his bow tie when I went back to our rooms. 'Weyhey, Dad. You look cool!'

'Not so bad for an old guy, eh?'

'Not bad at all. But just wait until you see your little girl in this dress.'

'A princess, I'll be bound.'

'Will you wait for me, Dad, while I shower and change? I'd feel a bit shy going out all dressed up on my own.'

'Of course, I'd be delighted to escort you.'

I had a shower, shaved my legs and under my arms – you can't hide anything in a dress like that – washed my hair. I rubbed half a ton of body lotion into my skin, dried my hair, put on the dress and spent a while on my make-up. The lipstick was a problem – what colour lipstick do you wear with a red dress? I ended up just wearing loads of gloss. I sprayed on a bit of glitter and squirted scent on my neck and pulse points. 'Come on!' Dad was knocking on the door.

'OK, Dad, hold your horses.' Shoes were my last problem, but actually my strappy sandals looked fine. I stepped back to look at myself in the full length mirror. Yup, I could go to the Oscars with Red dressed like this.

'Ta-dum!' I threw open the door.

Dad looked at me long and hard. He coughed once or twice before he passed judgement. 'Your mother always looked beautiful in red – not many women do. You look absolutely fabulous, darling!'

'No kidding?'

'Absolutely no kidding.'

Red looked so handsome in his tux I practically fainted. His eyes were glistening – because he said *I* looked so stunning! But *everybody* did! Even the horsy old Hayters were in their element. Gina and Flavia were dripping with jewels as well. In fact Flavia with her hair up looked incredibly grand – she's well on the way to owning half of Warwickshire already (it's probably dangling from her ears and nestling in her cleavage at this very moment)! Dilly had the good taste to stick to something plain and gold . . .

Oliver O'Neill wore evening dress as if he wore it *every* evening and looked very film-starrish. He and his entourage had a table to themselves but Linden and Red sat with us. Linden is very pretty whatever she wears, but her dress was fussy – I felt more elegant in the simple red gown.

It was a brilliant evening. Red's not a bad dancer and I took a few turns with Jonty (for sheer class) and my Dad. I even had a dance with the Great Man. 'I hadn't realised the little tango dancer was the young lady who's turned my son to mush,' he said. 'But I can see why!' And he smiled down at me with all his smile lines crinkling. Red looks very like him, but more honest somehow. Oliver held me rather tightly to dance – I was glad to escape from him.

'Dad never dances with *me*,' said Linden. 'You should be flattered.'

Red and I managed to nip outside on our own for a bit. 'I'm taking pictures of you in my brain,' he said (when we came up for breath). 'No film could capture how you smell,' he sniffed at my shoulder, 'or the golden-brown softness of your skin,' he stroked my neck.

'You old romantic, Red.'

'No, I mean it, Maddy. I'm crazy about you. Sometimes it seems unbearable,' and his eyes really did fill with tears as he kissed me again. So did mine. I couldn't believe my luck. It all seemed too good to be true. We stayed out there for quite a while – at least until Linden discovered us.

'Come back in, you two,' she said. 'Don't abandon me to Flavia and Cordelia.'

'You've got Jonty to talk to,' I said. 'Think how jealous Holly must feel tonight!' But we went back in. A steel band had replaced the more conventional dance band and everyone was boogyin' on down, so we threw ourselves into it, collapsing back at our tables to cool off and have a drink. Linden was really quite drunk and Flavia, her hair starting to come down and her lipstick smeared, was getting frightfully sloshed. Dad was very merry and so were the Hayters. Gina had a bright glint in her steely gaze as she drew deeply on her cigarette in its holder. The music went all slow and smoochy. Red and I were about to get up and dance when Linden said, 'Hey, Maddy. You weren't here today so you won't know. Guess who's coming tomorrow?'

'How can I?' I said. 'I don't know anyone.'

'Come on,' said Red. 'Let's dance – it'll be over soon.'

'Well at least we're spared Matty-Matt, aren't we, Richard?' She looked at my *dad*. Since when has Linden been on 'Richard' terms with my dad?

'I – er – believe Fay Marchant is coming on her own,' said Dad.

'Maddy. Come and dance,' said Red urgently. 'Please.' So I was able to lose myself in Red and forget what Linden had said for several hours.

NINE

I woke quite late to hear Dad clattering around. It sounded as though he was tidying up and rearranging the furniture. I turned over and tried to get back into my dreamworld – a re-run of all the best bits of last night. But it was not to be. Dad knocked on my door. I grunted. He took that as a signal to come in.

'For heavens' sake, Maddy! It's nearly eleven o'clock!'

'So?'

'High time you were up, my girl.'

'Da-ad.'

'Things to do.'

'Dad. I'm on holiday. We had a late night last night.'

He stood up and looked around my room. The bright morning sun came in through the gaps and illuminated the make-up and tissues and cottonwool balls on my dressing table, the clothes I'd stepped out of on the floor, and the trail of towels, hairbrush, hairdryer from when I'd been getting ready. Nothing unusual.

'This room is a disgrace!'

'Calm down, Dad. I'll tidy it up. I always do.'

'They will have stopped serving breakfast hours ago.' He was like one of those horrid little wind-up toys. Natter natter natter.

'Dad! Sit down for a minute. I'm awake now – not that I want to be. What is all this about? Are we expecting visitors?'

Dad sat down. I had a sudden cold sensation. Something was wrong. There were things I didn't know. Phone messages. Half-finished sentences. 'Dad – is there something you haven't told me?'

'Nothing that need bother you, darling.'

'Well, it's sure as hell bothering *you*, so what is it?'

'All right. I'll come clean. My friend Fay is arriving today. I'm meeting her at the airport this afternoon.'

'What's this got to do with me getting up and tidying my room?'

'I – want – the rooms to look nice when she comes,' he said carefully.

'She doesn't need to look in my room, does she?'

He didn't answer straight away. I sat up in bed. I felt sick now. A realisation was dawning. 'Dad. I've twigged. That's it, isn't it? "Your friend Fay" is your *girl*friend! She's not coming to visit us – she's coming to *stay*!' I prayed that he would contradict me.

But he didn't. He wriggled and squirmed, but he didn't say it wasn't true. 'Well, yes. She'll stay, but it needn't affect you, darling.'

The crassness of those words. 'DAD! NEEDN'T AFFECT ME?'

He tried. 'Well, nothing will change. You'll still spend

time with me and with your friends. It'll be just the same, except that Fay – will – er – sleep here.'

I shook my head in disbelief. I felt like a maddened bull or something, shaking my head from side to side. I was sitting crosslegged on my bed now, and I found myself rocking backwards and forwards as I shook my head, thinking, 'NO! NO! NO! My special holiday with my dad. His little princess. These lovely rooms all to ourselves. It isn't all for me at all. How *could* he think nothing would change. How *could* he!' I started to cry.

'Maddy – sweetheart!'

'How *could* you, Dad! You made me believe this was all for *me*, and it wasn't. It was for her.'

'I wanted you to meet her,' he said lamely. 'She wants to meet you.' He put his arm round me, and tried to stop my shaking sobs. 'Please don't be so upset, Maddy. I wanted to come back here, see Fay again, and I wanted to have a holiday with you. Is that so terrible?'

I was too upset to answer. If he couldn't see that I felt betrayed by his not *telling* me, there wasn't much point in saying anything. I put my feet back under the bedclothes and curled up, snuffling. Dad tiptoed out and left me. My untidy room had ceased to be an issue.

Half an hour later Dad knocked on my door again and came in with a tray of fruit and rolls. 'I don't know what to say, darling. Just, please, give Fay a chance. Give your old dad a chance. OK?' He set down the tray and left again.

I picked up the phone by the bed. Red's mobile number was written on my hand. 'Red, I need you. Something awful's happened. Where are you? Down by the pool? I'll see you there in a few minutes.' I didn't bother to shower. I just took off all the make-up I should have removed last night, put on my bikini and shorts and ran out. I was red-eyed and I felt as if I'd been crying all night, but seeing Red would have to help a bit.

Red saw me approaching and came over in his swimming shorts to meet me. He gave me a slippery hug – 'Factor 10 hug, that is!' he said, to make me laugh. 'I'd just put it on.' I managed a feeble giggle. 'So what's happened? Nothing to do with Bianca I hope?'

'No. No. It's not that awful really. Well it is to *me*, but I suppose it could be worse.'

'Well?'

'It's this Fay woman. She turns out to be Dad's girlfriend. She's coming today and she's going to be sharing our rooms.'

'It *could* have been worse, then,' said Red, trying to lighten up. 'She could have brought Matty-Matt with her.' But he could see that I wasn't laughing – even the implications of a Matty-Matt were ghastly. They didn't bear thinking about. I tried not to remember the conversation the others had had about him in the beach bar. We sat by the pool. I had to cheer up because Dilly and Jonty were pleased to see me, and Linden was there too.

'Good dancing last night,' said Jonty.

'You looked fabulous in that red dress,' said Dilly.

It already seemed a lifetime ago.

'Flave has a terrible hangover this morning,' said Jonty, nodding in the direction of Flavia, who sat fully clothed in the shade wearing a turban and sunglasses and looking pained. On the table beside her were two bottles of water and several sorts of hangover cures.

'Linden is a bit the worse for wear, too,' said Red. 'She's more cranky than usual.'

'We're off to the beach now,' said Dilly. 'We're meeting Charles and Holly there. See you later!'

'Come in the water,' Red said to me. 'It will cool us off, and we can talk.' We slipped into the pool together and swam to the other side where it was empty.

'Perhaps I'm being selfish about Dad,' I said. 'But I'm hurt that he didn't tell me. No, it's more than that – I'm hurt, full stop.'

'I hate to see you unhappy,' said Red. 'It's not how I think of you.'

'No one can be sunshine and light all the time.'

'Of course not. I've seen you serious, just not unhappy. I've got a lot to learn about you.'

'And not long to do it!' I splashed him and dived underwater so he'd chase me, and we came up together, laughing.

'That's better,' he said. 'Forget about your dad while you're with me. Please?'

'I intend to,' I said, and swam off again, with him in hot pursuit.

I did intend to, but Linden came and sat with us when we climbed out of the pool and she seemed determined to keep the subject uppermost in my mind.

'So you get to meet the mother of Matty-Matt today? Wow!'

'I'm reserving judgement,' I told her.

'Well, as we all know, she just *adores* teenage girls!'

I wanted Linden to leave off. But she wouldn't. 'I kinda remembered that she and your father were an item,' she said.

Red said impatiently – 'How could you have done, Lin? Maddy's father wasn't staying here last year when we were. It was the Hayters.'

'Oh, something Dad said,' said Linden vaguely.

'Great,' I said crossly. 'So everyone except me knew that Fay was my dad's girlfriend. No doubt everyone except me knew that she was coming today.'

'Oh yes, I knew,' said Linden. I could have hit her. I jumped into the pool instead. She came after me. I climbed out and she followed me out. 'I don't know why you're upset,' she said. 'My dad has women staying with him all the time. And not always the same woman.'

'Well, my dad DOESN'T! OK?'

'Leave it out, Lin,' said Red. 'Can't you see that Maddy's upset?'

'I would be too if Fay was going to be *my* stepmother, I suppose,' said Linden.

I was ready to kill Linden. I went ice cold. 'Shut up, Linden. You don't know what you're talking about. Go away and leave us alone.'

She looked at me and she looked at Red. 'Beat it,' said Red. I would have said something far worse, but I didn't need to, because, eyes blazing, she turned on her heel and left.

I started to cry again. 'I'm sorry about Linden,' Red said. 'I told you she was cranky today.' He hugged me. 'Hey, look who's coming! This will cheer you up. Howdy, Bianca!'

Bianca was being carried down to the pool. She waved like crazy when she saw us. 'Maddy!' she called. 'Did you know that Red is *my* boyfriend now? I'm going to be a film star and marry him!'

'Puts it all into perspective, doesn't it?' Red whispered. 'Hi, girlfriend!' he said to Bianca. 'Coming for a swim then?'

Red was right. Bianca always puts everything into perspective. So although the word 'stepmother' was grinding away in my brain, we managed to spend the next hour very happily with Bianca before going to the beach bar for lunch.

Dad was there. He sat up at the bar amongst all the semi-clad holidaymakers dressed in a pressed shirt and trousers and cleanly shaven. He looked nervous. 'What do you two want to drink?' he asked as we came up to the bar. 'I'll get these while you sort out some food for yourselves. Here are some dollars, Mads.'

'Thanks, Dad. You're looking very smart! Not as smart as last night, of course.'

'I'm going to the airport in a taxi. Don't want to be too scruffy.' He waited for the drinks while we ordered food and came back to sit down. 'OK, I'm off now.' He kissed me goodbye as if he was leaving for ever. And I suppose, in a way, he was. Our holiday *a deux* was over. 'We'll all meet up for supper. Fay will need to settle in first, so – 7.30? In the dining room bar?'

'Red, did *you* know Fay was coming?'

'Yesterday Dad took Linden and me out to lunch with that woman who was talking to your dad at the barbecue – Meryl. She's a screenwriter he works with. She said something like, "Did you know Fay was coming tomorrow?" I went off to the mens' room at that point, but she must have said something about her and Richard – your dad – while I was away, because Linden picked up on it on the way home.'

'So you *had* heard!'

'You know Linden! She was the one going on about "Fay and Richard", oooh, poor old Maddy! I just assumed she was winding me up. She does it all the time. So yeah, I knew Fay was coming. I knew she had some connection with your dad. I did not know she was staying with you. There! Am I forgiven?'

'I just hate the thought of being the last to know.' We had reached the beach. I was trying not to think about Dad, but it was impossible. The thoughts just wouldn't go away. Holly and Jonty were there with Dilly and Charles.

'Wait here a minute!' said Red. 'I'm gonna fix us up a boat. I'll be back.'

'Ace idea! I'm coming too,' said Jonty, and ran after him.

'Hi, Maddy,' said Holly, giving me a girly hug. 'I feel as if I haven't seen you for ages. How was Harrison's Caves – and the posh dinner dance? I've heard all about *that*! Linden said you completely silenced everyone at one point because you looked so stunning and you're such an amazing dancer. She said her dad was all over you, wants to sign you up for his film.'

'*Holly!* You know not to believe a word Linden says! She

was blatantly winding you up because you weren't there with Jonty and she was!'

'Dilly said you looked fantastic too.'

'OK, so I borrowed a fabulous dress. It was *red*, Holly! Don't you think that's romantic? Red for Red? I was with him most of the evening – God he looks *gorgeous* in a tux. Can you imagine?'

'I can. And how did Jonty look?'

'As to the manner born. You'll have to get him to invite you to Flavia's ball!'

'Do you think he would?'

'Can you imagine that he *wouldn't*?'

'Oooh.' Holly went all starry-eyed.

'Linden's winding me up too, at the moment,' I said.

'Really? What about?'

Suddenly Holly was the best person in the world to be talking to. 'Have you got five minutes? An hour? A lifetime?'

'I haven't got anything else to do!'

'Well – you know how I was really excited about this holiday and being just with Dad and all that? Well, now it seems that some woman is going to be with us for the second week. His girlfriend. I didn't know he had one.'

'What? He never mentioned it?'

'Not once!'

'Bummer!'

'It is pretty poor, isn't it? And Linden somehow got to know because the woman, she's called Fay, has been here before – I think Dad might even have met her here – and the others all think she's awful. She's got this monster of a son called Matt.'

'Oh yes. I've heard stories about Matty-Matt. He was here with Jonty and Red last year wasn't he?' Then she opened her mouth and put her hands to her cheeks. 'Oh NO! She's THE MOTHER!'

'Thanks for that, Holly.'

'Eughh!'

'Precisely. And Linden goes on about how she wouldn't like to have Matty-Matt's mother for a *stepmother*!' I could feel my throat closing up and tears coming again.

Holly saw. 'Oh Maddy,' she said, and put an arm round me. 'It's not funny, is it?'

I snivelled. 'No. It's a nightmare.'

'Oh poor you.'

'Red's asked me to try and forget about it while I'm with him. But I can't forget it Holly, how can I? It's like Dad saying it needn't affect me! What are men made of?'

'They just don't like being troubled by women's emotions. It's nothing new.'

'Red's being really kind otherwise. And I don't want to spoil our time together.'

'You two are really perfect for each other, did you know?'

'You're the second person to say that. I think so too. Do you think I've met him too early in my life?'

'Oh no! You can marry him! I'm going to marry Jonty!'

'And be very rich?'

'And be *very* rich!'

Jonty came running up at that moment and announced that they had a boat for the six of us – Red was getting it ready. So we spent a really great afternoon on the water. Red knows how to sail like I know how to dance – he was lovely to watch. And, guess what – I really didn't think about Fay. Perhaps Dad was half right, at least. I *can* still spend time with these friends. They are almost as important to me as him now. And, sorry, Dad, but Red is more important to me now than *anyone*.

I changed for dinner. *I changed for dinner!* I felt as nervous as Dad about meeting this Fay. I waited for him in the bar. I had my *West Side Story* to pass the time. I sat over my fruit cocktail, reading '*Te adoro*, Anton.' Of course it's all about love and families and death. Right up my street these days. A man slipped on to the bar stool next to mine – 'Dad!' But it wasn't Dad, it was Oliver O'Neill.

'Drink?'

'I've got one thanks!' (Duh!)

He smiles his crinkly, blue-eyed, sun-tanned smile. He still has good teeth. He's like Red but not like Red – it's very odd. 'What are you reading, then?'

Aagh. *'West Side Story.'*

'A *script*!'

'Yes, it's because—'

'I only cast professionals, you know.'

'It's nothing to do—'

'Does Red know about this?'

And this is when Dad and Fay choose to roll up, followed by Red and Linden. Red is smiling sympathetically at me. Linden is doing a silly walk behind Fay. Oliver knocks back his drink, nods at Dad and Fay and herds his children away from the bar. Dad and Fay sit down with me.

'I think that's the lad who had to beat poor old Matty-Matt at everything last year,' said Fay, looking after the O'Neills. 'Doesn't he have some ridiculous name?' And she laughed with a snorting giggle.

Fay is too streaky blonde and too tanned. She has a face like a hamster and she wears too much make-up. I hate her on sight.

TEN

I said as little as possible during supper. I was aware of the O'Neills glancing in our direction from time to time. Dad and Fay were lingering over coffee when I excused myself and ran up to my room. Fay's scent lay on the air. Her jacket was thrown over the back of the sofa. I felt invaded. I ran to the phone in my room and phoned Red. 'Meet me out the front in five minutes,' I said, grabbed the dollars left over from lunch time, left a message for Dad and went down there to wait for Red, praying that he'd turn up without Linden.

He did. 'What's up?'

'Get me away from here. From her. Can we just go to a bar somewhere?'

'Sure. We can walk or take a taxi.'

'I've got some money.'

'OK. We'll take a taxi!' We drove towards Holetown and got out at a bar Red had been to with Oliver. 'They won't serve either of us with alcohol, you know.'

'I don't care. Coke is fine. I just need to get right away from that stupid woman.'

We paid the taxi driver and went into the bar. It was pleasantly uncrowded, with a couple of guys playing music in the corner. It was nice to be indoors for a change, *without* a sea view and without all the visible signs of luxury that I was beginning to take for granted. 'Do I detect signs of jealousy?' said Red, smiling at me.

'Of Fay getting attention from my dad, yes. But unless *you're* planning on paying her lots of attention, no!'

'Your sense of humour has returned, though. Welcome back!' He gave me a hug and a kiss right there at the bar, to cackles and wolf-whistles from some of the old guys there, before ordering a couple of Cokes.

'You want me put some rum in that?' asked the barman. More cackles.

'No, sir, we're fine, thanks,' and we went and sat down. 'Nice guy.' He leant back to admire me. 'Hey, you're looking pretty cool this evening!'

'I dressed up for dinner. Thought I ought to make the effort. Everything you all said about Fay was right, wasn't it? She's vile. I don't know what Dad sees in her.'

'They lose their good taste when they get older. My dad

had plenty when he married my mom, but he never seemed to find it again!'

'Same with my parents.'

'If your mom looked anything like you – your dad would have been real proud!'

'I can't tell. Most of the photos of her at my age are black and white, and she had long hair with a long fringe, so you can't really see her face. Though Dad keeps saying things like, "Your mother looked good in red."' We were sitting very close to each other on a plastic-covered bench. Red just kept looking at me as I spoke. Then he made me put my drink down so he could turn to face me and hold both my shoulders to kiss me. More cheers and cackles from the old guys.

'Thass one beautiful woman you got dere, maan!' 'You treat her right, maan.'

'I don't care if they're watching,' said Red. Then, 'Maybe I do. But what they're saying is true, you know? You're beautiful and I want to treat you right. Let's go outside, Maddy.' So to cries of delight and whistles we made our way out through the door. It was dark outside and there was an empty bench on the pavement where people walked by. We made ourselves at home on it.

'No Dad,' I said. 'And no Linden. But still nowhere to go.'

'Let's start walking,' said Red, 'and catch a bus back to the hotel. It's not that late yet.' So we set off walking in the dark, stopping all the time to hold one another and kiss. It was kind of exhilarating but desperate at the same time.

We reached a bus stop as a bus drew up, and it seemed silly not to get on it. 'Tomorrow,' said Red, 'I'm going to take you scuba diving. Did you know it's meant to be the sexiest sport there is?'

'No wonder Linden and I weren't suited!' I said. 'But yeah, Red, that would be brilliant. Anything to take me away from Dad and Fay!'

'Let's go in the morning then – give you an excuse to get away early.'

We were pulling up at the hotel. 'I wish we could be together until then,' I said. 'I don't want to go back to our rooms with *her* there.'

'You have to, Maddy,' said Red. 'Think of all the ructions if you didn't – not that any of my lot would notice if you came back with me.'

'Linden would,' I said.

'True. Anyway—' he kissed me goodnight in the foyer. 'See you at breakfast. OK? Breakfast – no later.'

'Yessir!'

I crept back to my room. I could hear Fay's awful snorting laugh from Dad's room. I shut my door hard so that they knew I was back and set my watch alarm to wake me in the morning. I dreamt of Red. I dreamt of us finding somewhere to be alone together. It was heaven, but when I woke I wasn't sure whether we'd had to die first to get there.

Dad and Fay weren't up when I went down for breakfast. I left another note after the one I'd written last night. 'GONE SCUBA DIVING. SEE U LATER, M xxx.'

Red was waiting for me. 'Let's get down there straight away. I've abandoned poor old Lin again – I just said I'd see her down at the beach – so we need to get going. I've got the underwater camera.' He patted the camera slung over his shoulder. He'd booked the boat, everything. He instructed me as carefully as the official instructor had – almost grimly.

'Now – we have to rely on each other down there. We can't call an ambulance if something goes wrong. We can't talk, so let's just run through those hand signals again.' And again – we went through them about five times. But I felt really safe with Red. It was comforting to know he was qualified. The boat took us out, and over the side we went, diving together. It was fabulous, the only two humans in a world of colourful fish, even a couple of small sharks. Scary! But Red had assured me they would leave us alone if we kept moving – and didn't cut ourselves. We swam side by side all over the coral reef – Adam and Eve in the octopus's garden! It was all so beautiful. When we came up I felt as though we'd shared the most incredible experience.

'Your life was in my hands!' said Red, easing himself out of his oxygen pack.

'And yours was in mine! It was wonderful, Red. Can we do it again?'

'Sure! We have to get our thrills where we can!'

'Red!'

'Well, I spent a lot of last night wishing you were with me, and realising that it was impossible.' He held my hands. 'Around three a.m. I found myself thinking that perhaps the only way to be together was to – sounds dramatic, I know – but, kill ourselves! Around 3.01 I got a grip – but sometimes I feel that desperate, you know?'

I knew.

Linden was waiting on the beach. She looked at us accusingly. 'Why didn't you say you were going scuba diving? I've been stuck here on my own. That's when I could escape from that terrible woman and your father, Maddy.' Here we go. 'They were real worried about you. She was going on at your father about how she wouldn't let Matty-Matt run that wild. And Dad wants us to meet him for lunch, Red. He wants to talk to you. About Maddy, I think. I expect la Fay has been moaning at him, too.'

'Surely not,' said Red. 'I'll go sort this out, Maddy. You come with me, Lin.' He pointed down the beach. 'I can see Holly over there! See you in the beach bar at 2.30 if we don't meet up before!' He said that looking over his shoulder. Linden was dragging him towards the pool and Oliver O'Neill.

Holly was alone. She sat on a towel, hugging her knees. 'You OK, Holly?'

'The Hayters have gone on a two-day cruise, did you know that?'

'No wonder Linden is bored. She says she doesn't like them, but she likes needling Dilly and she and Jonty get on OK. Well, I'm here now – and I'm very pleased you're here too.'

'How's it going?'

'If you mean with Dad's girlfriend – badly. Though I've managed to avoid her since supper last night.'

'How'd you manage that?'

'Red and I went out to a bar near Holetown last night and we went scuba diving this morning.'

'Bet that went down well!'

'Linden's already taken great delight in telling me how badly it went down. But I don't care. They're such hypocrites, adults, aren't they? They were far too interested in each other last night to know *when* I came in.'

'Aren't they just! Mum's starting to have a go at me about Jonty, now. Ever since I've been interested in boys she's said why don't I make friends with some of the *nice* boys at Dad's school. But now *Jonty's* too posh for her. "Oh I think you'll find you don't have much in common ultimately, dear." We can't win, can we?'

I love being with Holly.

'So how *is* the romance with Jonty?'

Holly rolled over on to her back. 'Oh he's so *cute*, Maddy. I'm not sure that he's ever been out with a girl before. And my experience isn't vast, so neither of us feels pressured by the other. We just have a *lovely* time. It's amazing what you can get away with under water, isn't it?'

'Holly! I'm shocked!'

'I don't believe *you're* shocked. I mean, you can see the *smoke* coming off you two. That's how Jonty put it. He said he could see you and Red "smouldering" whenever the other one was anywhere near. He told me to "look out for scorch marks"!'

I sighed. 'That's how it feels. Sometimes when we're together I imagine we're about to spontaneously combust! Tricky though. All the adults keep saying how *young* we are. As far as I can see, if you're in love you're in love. It feels the same whatever age you are. Look at Romeo and Juliet. Weren't they supposed to be thirteen and fourteen or something? We're fifteen – well, almost – and seventeen. Positively geriatric.'

'Not compared to your dad and Fay.'

'Don't remind me.'

Holly and I missed lunch, but then I had to go and meet Red, and she felt she ought to check in with her lot. I hoped I'd managed to miss Dad and Fay. I had indeed, because Red had a message from Dad saying they'd gone off to play golf (so Fay is the golfing inspiration). Oliver had gone too. Red looked serious.

'What's up, Red?'

'Maddy?' He swallowed. 'Just tell me. Going out with me has nothing to do with who my father is, does it?'

'What?' I'd never seen him like this before.

'I didn't know you'd asked him for an audition.'

'*What?*'

'He said you'd talked about it in the restaurant bar last night. You had a script and everything.'

'*What?*'

'And then Linden said—'

'*Hang on.* Hang on! *Linden said* . . . Since when have you believed what Linden says?'

'She said you'd told her you wanted a part in his film.' He looked at me anxiously.

'Red – I don't believe this. Do you really think I'd do a thing like that? That everything we've done together has been a pretence, just so that I could get in with your father?'

'It wouldn't be the first time it's happened.'

'RED!' I was horrified. Did he *really* think that?

'I'm sorry, Maddy.' He looked miserable. 'I didn't want to believe her.'

I grabbed his wrists. 'Listen to me.' I shook them up and down. 'I brought *West Side Story* to learn as my holiday reading because they are auditioning for the *school play* when term begins. Ask Dad, Holly, Dilly – anyone. No, don't ask them, *believe me*. I'm a good dancer and performer but I'm lousy at learning lines. I wouldn't *dream* of auditioning for an Oliver O'Neill film. Well – I might *dream* of it, but no more than that!'

Red looked mortified but relieved. 'Oh, thank God for that! I was so scared it might be true. That's Linden for you – at her worst! Twisting things. I just wish she wouldn't do it!'

'Red, how about spending this afternoon on the beach – just dipping in and out of the sea from time to time?'

'Fine.' He hadn't quite got over it yet. 'Maddy – there's more. You see, Dad thought he'd been a bit harsh with you yesterday, and he told me he thought you *might* have the right qualities after what he's seen of you on video . . .'

If I hadn't been so keen to get into the water, Oliver's words might have gone to my head. As it was, well, I didn't think about them again that afternoon.

I had to go back to my room. I needed a shower – and I had to get out of my bikini some time. I didn't want to go there. I hoped Dad and Fay were still playing golf but I couldn't be sure I wouldn't open the door and hear her ghastly laugh. They weren't there. I had the place to myself – I could see that they'd come back from golf and gone out again. Still her scent pervaded the whole suite. Her bits and pieces were everywhere – her camera, her book, her shoes, a pair of earrings. My room was the only place still my own, thank goodness. I sat down on the bed for a few moments, glad to be alone – even to be away from Red for a little while. I was appalled that he had entertained the idea *even for a second* that I might have wanted to be with him because of his dad. Some terrible insecurity lurking there. But then we're all full of insecurities, especially those of us whose parents have split up. One of the things about Holly and even Dilly is a sort of rock-solid stability that I envy. I mean, Mum has always been there for me, and it's obvious Red's mum has been for him, but somewhere, deep down, kids like us are always on the alert for something to go wrong. We can't help it. It's how we've survived.

Mum. I had a sudden urge to ring her. Did she know about Fay? Would she care or would she wish Dad well? I looked at my watch before picking up the phone. It would be five hours later there – midnight. Mum wouldn't mind. I dialled the code for the United Kingdom and then our number. The phone rang and rang and rang. Mum wasn't there. She hadn't even switched on the answer machine.

Dad and Fay were sitting at a table for three with an empty space. No Hayters. The O'Neills were part of a huge noisy group on the terrace. Linden saw me and waved, but dinner with our families seemed to be the way it was. I could see Red's back. I could tell even from this distance that he was charming Tricia. So. Dad and Fay, here I come. 'Sit down, love,' said Dad unnecessarily. 'We're just about to order.'

'Yes, sit down, dear,' said Fay, even more unnecessarily. I bit back the retorts that were ready to come out.

'I'll just have the soup, Dad. I'm not very hungry.' I looked around the room and realised that I hadn't seen Bianca all day. It was too late now. Bianca. Eloise. Mum. 'I tried ringing Mum at home, but she wasn't there, Dad.'

Fay pursed her lips – she obviously didn't like me mentioning Mum in front of her. 'Oh, she wouldn't be,' said Dad.

'How do you know?'

'She rang last night.'

'Why didn't you tell me?'

'You were out.' *Touché*. 'And anyway, she wanted to tell you something herself. She said she'd ring you again.'

'I had a great time scuba diving with Red, Dad.' I thought I'd better change the subject.

'Ah yes. Now I think we should talk about that, Maddy. Fay says you should only *ever* go out with a proper instructor.'

Fay had to stick her oar in. 'I did say to Richard that I certainly would never let my fourteen-year-old out of my sight. Especially not at night. And certainly *never, ever* in the water.' She sniffed and took a sip of her drink.

I looked daggers at Dad. 'Dad and I have our own way of dealing with things,' I said stiffly. 'And, for your information, Red *is* a qualified diving instructor – has been for over a year.'

We ate our meal in virtual silence after that. So when Dad suggested that we all went to the bar together and then up for an early night – together – I could only conclude that they wanted to keep an eye on me. I was seething with anger, but too upset to argue.

ELEVEN

Mum. Mum. I had to talk to Mum. I wanted to tell her all about Red and I wanted to tell her about Bianca and I wanted to tell her about Dad's *vile* girlfriend. I wanted to hear her voice. It was seven a.m. Barbados time. Broad daylight, birdsong and surf noise outside. All quiet in our suite, thank goodness. It was twelve noon in England. I dialled our number. It rang – in the hall at home – four times and then the answer machine. Even a recording of Mum's voice made me feel a little calmer. I left a message. 'Mum, please ring me back. I have to talk to you. Don't worry, no one's ill or anything. Love you, Mum. Love to Lo-lo.'

Then I settled down to wait. I padded around in my nightdress, helped myself to fruit and mineral water and turned on the TV, partly to drown out the noise of Dad and Fay waking up. The noise of the TV brought Dad out to the living room. Tee-hee. 'Bit early, isn't it? Are you going down for breakfast?'

'Sorry, Dad. I'm waiting for Mum to ring me back. I've left a message on her answer machine. So I'm not going anywhere.'

He considered the implications of this. 'Harrummphhh.' He tottered back to bed. I knew he wouldn't want me to have my phone conversation with Mum while Fay was around. I heard the shower going and getting-up noises and then a rather cross-looking Fay appeared. She'd found time to shovel on the make-up, but her eyes were all small and piggy from sleep still, and her cheeks were puffier than ever. Part of me was looking forward to describing her to Mum. Mum would sympathise.

'Morning, Fay!' I said brightly. 'You and Dad off for an early breakfast then?'

'Yes, we are as a matter of fact. I want to make the most of my time here. Life in the city is so stressful, especially as a single mother – I want to be fresh as a daisy when I get back to Matty-Matt.'

'Yes,' I said, 'Mum finds it stressful too.' That shut her up.

Dad appeared, his hair sticking up from rushing around. 'So what are your plans today, Maddy?'

'Nothing, until I hear from Mum. I want to know what she has to tell me. So I'm staying right here. You needn't worry about me. I've got plenty to eat and drink.'

They went to breakfast and came back but still no call from Mum. They were off for a quick round of golf followed by a few hours out on a boat which would include lunch. 'I was hoping you'd come on the boat trip with us,' said Dad unconvincingly.

'You'll enjoy yourselves much more without me,' I said.

'So are you just going to leave her here?' said Fay to Dad, as if I wasn't in the room. 'She might get up to anything, *anything* – and you wouldn't know! I wouldn't *dream* of leaving Matty-Matt on his own all day in a foreign country.'

'Dad trusts me,' I said through gritted teeth, 'Don't you, Dad? I'll be fine. Have a nice time. See you when I see you.'

'Really, Richard!' Fay just couldn't shut up. 'That's *far* too vague. I think Madeleine should be down at the pool when we return from our boat trip. Don't you, Richard?'

'I'm waiting for Mum to ring back,' I said. 'I'll see you later.'

Dad tried to pat my arm in a reassuring way, but I shook him off. Right now the two of them were welcome to each other. That dread word *stepmother* was beginning to haunt me again.

I enjoyed having the place to myself. I prowled around – even Dad's room, I'm afraid. I looked at Fay's things. They were all nasty. Her clothes, her shoes, her make-up – they were precisely the sort of things Mum and I avoided. Horrible fussy bows. Two-tone loafers. Bright blue eyeshadow. Eugghh. Hate. Hate. Hate. I watched some more TV and ate some more fruit and some chocolate from the minibar.

The phone rang. Mum! It wasn't Mum, it was Red. 'Maddy! I'm phoning from the pool. Your dad said you weren't coming out! You can't spend all morning in your rooms! I want to be with you! Come down for a swim at least. Please! Oh, yeah. Linden says to come down, too.'

'Red – I really want to, but I have to speak to my mum and I left a message for her to ring me back. I'm sure she'll ring soon, and then I'll be right down. Promise.' I did want to be with Red, especially after our misunderstanding last night.

'Come to the beach bar at lunch, whatever. Oh – Bianca's here. She wants to talk to you.'

'Maddy! Maddy! Red has been towing me round the pool and I'm going to marry him. Will you read to me tonight? I'm going to bed early because I've got to see the doctor tomorrow.'

''Course I will, sweetheart.'

'Here's Red again, Maddy. Byee!'

'See what happens as soon as your back is turned!'

'I'll be at the beach bar at lunch time then.'

As soon as I'd put the phone down on Red I missed his physical presence. It was as if I'd been holding something in my arms and then found I was only clutching the air. I wandered round the suite, willing Mum to ring. It would be afternoon at home by now. I picked up my *West Side Story* script and sat out on the balcony to learn it. I couldn't quite see the pool from there, but I imagined that I could hear Red laughing and Bianca squealing. I went through it and highlighted all Maria's lines.

It was lunch time, getting on for *six* o'clock at home. What was Mum up to? I rang again and left another message on the machine, giving myself an hour to have lunch with Red: 'Ring me after seven your time, Mum. I'll be waiting by the phone.' I had a quick shower, put on shorts and a bikini top and went out into the bright midday sunshine.

'Aaagh!' Red pounced on me. He'd been hiding in the shadows again.

'Just wanted you for two minutes *all* to myself, you know? Before we hit the full Hayter/O'Neill contingent waiting for us at the beach bar. The Hayters have just got back. I think they're all a bit curious about Fay.'

In the bar they were all waiting for me. 'You have to tell us everything!' said Linden.

'Any news of Matty-Matt?' said Jonty.

'Oh leave the poor girl alone,' said Dilly. 'It must be

bad enough without us all giving her the third degree. AND –' she moved closer to us and further away from the group that contained her parents, Flavia and a young man ' – I have to divulge the important news that *Flavia's* found herself a *chap*!' I peered over at him. He was very small with a lugubrious expression. 'He's exactly like a man, only smaller,' said Dilly.

'He's a *jockey*,' said Jonty, and then practically fell off his bar stool laughing. Red caught his eye, guffawed, and joined in and soon Dilly, Linden and I were all doubled up in hysterics as well.

'He's apparently a very famous jockey,' said Linden. 'Dad recognised him.'

'I can't wait to see when they stand up,' said Red.

'He was at the dinner dance,' said Dilly, 'but everyone was far too busy watching you two to notice them!'

'It was her necklace,' said Jonty, eyes streaming, 'the long one that—'

'We know, we know,' said Dilly.

'Well, it was at eye-level for him!'

We giggled all through lunch like naughty schoolchildren.

I looked at my watch. 'Two o'clock, Red. I have to go.'

'Oh, don't go!' said Red. 'Can't you just ring your mum on my mobile?' I was torn. It did seem a shame to waste even a second of my time with Red. But then Jonty and Linden were on either side of him.

'He said he'd go with *me*!' said Linden.

'Red, old fellow,' said Jonty, parodying himself. 'Did you or did you not undertake heretofore to come windsurfing with me this afternoon?'

Dilly joined in. 'Let Linden go with Red, Jonty. The Beale boys had a morning match today, so they might have made it to the beach by now.'

'What about me?' said Red. 'Do I get a say in this? I was just trying to persuade Maddy to stay out here in the sun with me instead of waiting in a dark hotel room for her mother to ring.'

'Dark hotel room, eh?' said Jonty. 'I can't understand you not wanting to wait *there* with her, mate!'

Red looked at me in mock despair.

'Go windsurfing with Linden,' I said. 'Then everybody's happy. Call me when you get back. Mum's bound to have rung by then. Cheerio! I'm off to learn some more lines.' I called after Jonty, 'Say hi to Holly for me! She'll be really pleased to see you!'

Three o'clock. Eight p.m. at home and still no Mum. Four o'clock. The phone rang. It was Red, back from windsurfing. 'This is *so* not the way to spend our precious few days together, Maddy. What are you doing up there?'

'Learning my lines for *West Side Story*. Mum hasn't rung me yet.'

'When does your dad get home?'

'Don't know exactly.'

'I'm coming up, Maddy. I'll test you on your lines or something. I'm walking as I speak. Hey! Look out from your balcony!'

He was just down below! 'Romeo, Romeo!' I started – and then, 'Hang on a second! Let's get the relevant version!' And then I sang the first two lines from *Tonight*.

'Wow!' Red scampered off, singing the same words a semitone up, and before I knew it there was a knock on the door.

I let him in. 'Red – I'll be in big trouble if my dad and Fay get back and find you here.'

'It strikes me you'll be in trouble with Fay whatever you do, so just relax, would you?' He sat down on one of the armchairs and helped himself to a passion fruit. 'Mmm! Passssshion fruit!' He slapped himself on the wrist and went into an English falsetto. 'Naughty, naughty boy! Passsssiion' (he hissed) 'is only for wizened *old* people in this suite, Richard. Matty-Matt does not know the meaning of the word "passion" and neither should you. I would *never* let Matty-Matt know that I indulged in such a thing. He might realise I was a hypocrite or something.'

I threw several cushions at him. 'Throw me your script instead,' he said. Then before I could do anything he leapt to his feet and chased me round the room, scattering more cushions and newspapers, two mangos and a spectacles case. He lunged at me and caught me up in some heavy-duty kissing. Impossible to resist. We toppled onto the sofa.

A phone rang. 'If that's Linden—'

But it was my phone. I went over to answer it. Red lay on the sofa with his feet dangling over the arm, hands behind his head.

'Mum! At last!' It was slightly weird hearing her voice in the middle of fooling around with Red.

'I'm sorry, darling – I've spent nearly the whole day at the hospital.'

'*Hospital!* Mum! Is Eloise all right?'

'Yes, yes. Everything's fine! Can't you guess what, darling? It was the antenatal clinic – I'm going to have another baby!'

'Whoa, Mum! Slow down! Say that again!'

'Well, I had to tell Eloise because of going to the hospital and everything. She's so excited. I thought you'd like to hear the news straight from the horse's mouth, so to speak, before Lo-lo told you!'

I didn't get it. Was this Vile Roddy's baby? Was I going to have to suffer more Vile Roddy as well as Vile Fay? 'It's you and *Roddy*, Mum, who are having this baby?'

'Of course, darling. He's very excited because it's his first.'

I found myself shaking my head from side to side again. Red looked up, anxiously. He'd got the gist of the news from my end of the conversation.

'Well, hey, Mum.' I couldn't do any better than that. Not the way I felt inside.

'What about your news, darling? Tell me quickly before I ring off – I'm paying for the call.'

'There isn't much, Mum. It's not really important – not like your news. I can tell you in person on Saturday. This is costing a bomb. Love you, Mum. Love to Lo-lo.' I put the phone down and found I was crying.

Red came over to comfort me. He made me sit on his lap and cradled me like a child, stroking my hair and handing me tissues that he pulled from the fancy box on the table. Some went on the floor.

Suddenly Dad and Fay were standing in the doorway. It didn't look good. Two very scantily clad teenagers on the floor, surrounded by scattered cushions and tissues and newspapers.

'Well *really*, Madeleine!' said Fay. 'What did I tell you, Richard?'

'Maddy – I'm very disappointed in both of you. I think you'd better go, Red. I'll be speaking to your father about this.'

Red didn't lose his temper. He just said quietly, 'I'd appreciate it if you spoke to your daughter first, sir,' and left.

'I'll leave you to it, Richard,' said Fay and went into the bedroom, no doubt to plaster after-sun on her horrible boiled-lobster sunburn. Her nose would peel tomorrow.

'Maddy?' Dad actually looked sympathetic. It didn't take a genius to see I'd been crying once we were face to face.

'It's *not* how it looks,' I said, sniffing. 'Just take my word for it. Please?' I looked at him pleadingly.

'Why the tears, sweetheart?' He held my shoulders and looked enquiringly into my face.

I leant my head against his still-Daddyish chest. 'Mum. Her news. She's only having another baby. With Roddy. It's happening all over again, Dad, and I don't think I can bear it. It was so awful with Lo-lo in the beginning. And Gus was bad enough but Roddy's loathsome. What if he moves in?' Fresh sobs shook my body.

'There, there,' said Dad. 'Sweetheart, I'm so, so sorry. You really don't deserve it. How we've both let you down! *My* poor baby!' He was pretty shaky too.

'Red came because he knew I was in a state.' That was near enough the truth. No point in confusing the issue.

'I can see that now. We jumped to conclusions too quickly, I guess. Let me go and put Fay straight. We don't want her thinking badly of you, do we?'

As if I cared. I found myself another tissue and picked up the ones that were strewn about the room. Red must have pulled out at least three for every one he gave to me. How dare they send him away like that. He was being so lovely. And he was so dignified.

I went into my room and called him up. 'Red?'

'Maddy! You OK?'

'I'm OK but I'm angry. You were so cool, Red. Anyway, Dad knows the truth and he's telling Fay.'

'Shouldn't you be reading to Bianca?'

'Oh my God! Yes! – Red, meet me after supper. Meet me by the children's pool. There won't be anyone there then. See you about 8.30?'

I splashed cold water on my face and put on a top and some long trousers. I knocked on Dad's door. 'Got to read to Bianca, Dad! See you at supper?'

Dad popped his head out. 'Yes, dear, fine. Fay's had a bit too much sun on the boat, so I don't think she'll be joining us.' Best news I'd had all day.

Bianca was already in bed. 'Can I have some *hospital* stories tonight, Maddy?'

Hospital stories are healthier in Bianca's case than happy stories. 'Sure. Have you got Zo-Zo?'

When I'd finished reading to her, Bianca said, 'Mummy and Daddy hate going to the hospital, but I quite like it. Everyone's always so nice to me. But I'm not sure that they will be so nice to me this time!'

'Bianca! Don't say that! Why on earth not?'

She beckoned me close and then whispered in my ear, 'Because I think I'm getting a bit better!'

'But that's great!'

'Mummy and Daddy don't believe me – but just wait and see when we get back tomorrow. Night night, Maddy. Sleep tight!' And she snuggled down under her covers.

Dad didn't say much over supper. I sensed that things weren't going very well with Fay, and knowing how antagonistic I was towards her he didn't want to discuss it with me. I didn't want to dwell on Mum particularly either, so we ate in companionable near-silence which made me feel as close to him as I had all holiday. I met Red by the pool and we climbed up above the road and sat looking at the stars for a couple of hours. A quiet end to an explosive day.

TWELVE

This is bizarre. Dad and Fay, Red and Linden, Jonty and me are all sitting on a bus going to Bridgetown for shopping and a trip in a submarine.

Fay woke up feeling just a tiny bit guilty, it seems, after blowing us out, and in great pain from overdoing it in the sun. Ha, ha, serves her right. Needless to say, her original tan was fake. So she decided to make today her shopping day and suggested to Dad that they take me and some friends on the submarine – Matty had loved it last year. They fixed it all up over an early breakfast and Dad woke me with a cup of tea and the news that I was to meet my friends in Reception in half an hour.

I wasn't altogether sure that I wanted to be organised like this, but there wasn't much to be done about it. I called up Red on his mobile. 'Isn't this weird?'

'Your dad said he was real sorry about yesterday, you know? And that they wanted to make amends. I've never done the submarine thing – could be cool. Linden's happy to be with us all – so! And I'm happy as long as I can sit next to you! See ya!'

The Hayters were all going to watch Flavia's jockey in action, but Jonty was more than happy to come with us instead. The Beale College lot were doing the same trip, so there was a slight possibility that he might see Holly in Bridgetown, too. All in all, my objections seemed pretty feeble, so I did my best to suppress them.

It started off fine. I enjoyed sitting close to Red as the bus joggled along. Dad and Fay were sitting in front of us, not saying much. Jonty and Linden were being extremely noisy behind us. Jonty is one of the few people Linden doesn't feel jealous of. They were playing Spot the Banana (you shout Banana! whenever you see one), which had them both in fits – there were plenty to be seen – growing, being sold, being eaten – but it got pretty raucous, as you can imagine.

It was funny being in a town with shops and car parks again. The sunshine seemed much harsher reflecting off metal and glass, so it was a relief to dive into air-conditioned shops. Jonty and Red reached their shopping-boredom threshold in about two minutes flat, so we split up – me and Linden, Dad and Fay, Jonty and Red. The boys went down to the beach to go out on jetskis. The rest of us went in search of presents and souvenirs. Linden and I looked round some of the department stores, but there was nothing suitable there, so we wandered down to the market stalls. It was hot and crowded but I soon found a lovely sarong for Mum and a perfect little bikini for Eloise. I bought some bracelets for my friends. When Linden was busy looking through some CDs I bought a ring for Red too. Soppy, I know.

We wound up at the harbour café that was our meeting place some time before the others. It wasn't very nice – brash and noisy. Linden and I sat down outside with our Cokes. The sun beat down on us and my head started to ache.

'I told Red it was a bad idea to go up to your room when your dad wasn't there,' said Linden, starting a wind-up out of the blue.

'He wasn't in *my* room, Linden.'

'Oh no? I heard that Fay hit the roof!'

'Linden – I don't want to talk about it. This whole trip is by way of apology! Let's change the subject.'

But Linden was just getting into her stride. 'So are you going to audition for my dad's film?'

'No way, Linden. I haven't got what it takes.'

'He thinks you have. He told Red to tell you to ring him if you're interested, but I bet Red won't pass that message on.'

Red hadn't passed that message on. 'Red doesn't think it's a good idea.'

'Well, he wouldn't, would he? He wants you for himself!' she said with a sly smile.

'Linden – what are you getting at?'

'Nothing!' she sang – and slurped noisily on her Coke, rattling the ice cubes. 'Do you want another one?'

'Yes please.' Anything to get her off my back. Anything to make this headache go away. Does Oliver O'Neill *really* think I've got what it takes? Why hasn't Red told me? I don't really want a part. Do I? How would I call Oliver? I suppose he's got a mobile too.

Linden came back. It was as if she'd read my mind – witch. 'If you do decide to call Dad, his number's easy to remember if you know Red's – we three are all one digit apart. I could call him now for you.'

'NO! Linden, let me make my own decisions.'

'Sor-ry.' She sat back, clicking her fingers and tapping her feet to an imaginary song. She looked around. 'Hey! Here come the boys. They do not look happy.'

'Phew! We've been ripped off,' said Jonty, kicking out a chair and flopping down on to it.

'They saw us coming,' said Red, leaning on my back and putting his arms round my neck. 'Shame, because the jet-skis were real *fun*!'

Jonty tossed a heap of small change on the table. 'Buy us a drink, someone. That's all I have left of my spending money. You buy me one, Red, it was your rotten idea.'

'OK, OK, man!' said Red, and went up to the bar.

'It was your idea, too, Jonty,' said Linden, leaping to Red's defence.

'It's being ripped off that annoys me,' said Jonty. 'They had us down as *tourists*.'

'We are,' I said. I didn't like his tone.

'Not like some of these people—' Jonty took off his shades and mopped his brow.

Red put down their drinks. 'Well – prepare to like tourists on the submarine. We won't be able to escape them down there!'

'Hey, everyone!' I said. We were all very tetchy. 'Lighten up!'

Then Dad and Fay arrived. Fay was red in the face. She wore her sunhat at a rakish angle which made her look slightly mad. Dad had sweat pouring down his face and neck.

'Well, we've got Matty-Matt's present sorted out, so *that's* all right.' He was playing to the gallery, I knew, and it was a bit embarrassing.

'What did you buy him, Fay?' I tried to sound interested. The others were smirking.

She was only too keen to show us. She pulled a horrendous pair of palm-tree patterned boxer shorts out of a bag. 'These!' she said proudly. 'And this!' A T-shirt with "I heart Barbados" on it. 'And this!' An inflatable banana.

'Banana!' shouted Jonty and Linden together, drawing attention to our little group.

'Well,' said Dad, 'it took us two whole hours to buy those.' Did I detect a note of sarcasm in his voice? 'And I need a drink.' He looked at Fay. 'Pina colada?'

Fay was determined to be difficult. 'Don't you think we should be ordering lunch, Richard?'

'This is a bar. They don't do lunch.'

Ooh dear. This was shaping up to be a tiff. I didn't think my headache could stand it.

'Dad,' I said, 'why don't we meet you at the submarine boat place? You two have your drinks and we'll sort ourselves out with burgers or something.'

'But shouldn't we all—' Fay's day out wasn't going the way she wanted.

'Good idea, Mads,' said Dad. 'Here's some money.' And he handed me a fistful of Barbados dollars. 'We're booked on the three o'clock submarine. See you there.'

'*Richard!*' we heard Fay saying as we left. 'Wasn't that rather a lot of money for burgers?'

'Rather you than me, Maddy,' said Linden.

'Shut up, Lin,' said Red.

And so it went on. We were all too hot. It felt thundery. I wanted to be just with Red but Linden was always there, needling.

The boat out to the submarine was a relief. It was shaded by a tarpaulin and the cool breeze on our faces was a treat. We passed a boat like ours coming back from the submarine, and before we knew it Jonty was standing up and waving his baseball hat. 'Holly! Holl-ee!' he cried. He sat down. ''Spose that's as close as I'll get!' he said, disgruntled, as the Beale College lot sped in the opposite direction. I'm not used to seeing Jonty like this – he's usually so even-tempered. 'They've only got two more whole days,' he said.

'Well we've only got *three*,' said Linden.

'Three? Is that all?' I couldn't believe it. Only three more days with Red. We were all cast into deepest gloom. Red held my hand very tightly.

The boat pulled up by the submarine and we were handed down the steps. It was like getting on a plane except that you went down instead of up. It was very narrow down there. I tried not to think about claustrophobia. All I wanted to do was cuddle up to Red and watch those fish go by, but he was entranced – glued to the porthole. 'Wow! This is excellent, man! I've never seen so many of those rainbow fish before. Look at that, would you!'

There were a couple of wrecks down there – great playgrounds for the fish – but they made me feel sad. I couldn't help thinking of *Titanic*. Dad and Fay were still tense – they obviously hadn't resolved their shopping squabble. My headache was getting worse and I tried not to think about being claustrophobic. Red was going on and on about blasted fish. I put my head in my hands and shut my eyes. Is this how a baby feels in the womb?

'Maddy! Maddy! Just take a look at that, man! Jeez, do I wish I had the camcorder!' Red was getting hyper.

'What's that one called, Red?' Linden was crowding me out.

'Something wrong, Mads?' Jonty saw I wasn't enjoying myself.

'I'll be fine,' I said, without opening my eyes. 'I'll just be glad when we start going up again.'

'Bad luck!' said Jonty. 'You're missing a treat!' He pushed up against the porthole too. 'Wow! There's millions of them all around us! What are those ones, Red?'

I felt wretched. It seemed an age before the captain announced that we were going up again. Probably keeping my eyes shut made me more claustrophobic than if I'd had them open – at least I might have been distracted by the fish.

It was wonderful when we finally got out in the fresh air

again, though the bright light did nothing for my headache.

On the way home in the bus Red still couldn't stop talking about the reef. 'Please, Red,' I said. 'I've got a cracking headache and you're not making it any better.'

'Sorry,' he said shortly. 'I didn't know I was boring you.'

'That's not what I meant.'

'That's how it sounded.' He looked out of the window.

'Red – don't be like that.'

'Like what?'

'All grumpy.'

'Well, I feel like an idiot. I thought you were really interested too.'

'I am, Red. I just can't help thinking about my other problems and my head hurts.'

'For goodness' sake, Mads. Let's find you a headache pill!'

'If only it was that simple!' I knew I was being peevish.

Red sighed. 'I'm going to find you an aspirin.' He stood up and pushed past me to Fay, of all people. I saw her delve into her bag and hand him some tablets and a small bottle of mineral water. He sat down by me again. 'Here!' he said. 'I saw her popping a couple in that bar in the harbour. I just know that you're not a natural grouch.'

'I don't know which came first – the headache or the worrying.'

'Maddy – *please* quit worrying about your parents – just for three more days? Then you can worry all you want!' It was meant to be a joke.

'Huh! Thanks.' I knew I was spoiling for a fight. 'My whole world has been turned upside down, Red – twice – and you expect me to switch my feelings on and off for your convenience?'

Red didn't get a chance to defend himself because the bus pulled up outside the hotel and we got separated as we filed off. Fay's shopping bags were unwieldy and bashed up against people. It seemed as if none of us was speaking to the other. Actually, that's not true. Linden was bothering Red about something. My head was still bursting and I was full of pent-up fury.

Red finally caught up with me. 'Please, Maddy, I *so* do not want us to—'

'Red! Red! Maddy! Maddy! I'm back from seeing the doctor!' Bianca's little face was alight, but her mum and dad looked as tired and drained as I felt. 'Maddy, will you read to me? Please? I've got to go straight to bed and I want some stories? Please?'

'Of course, sweetheart.'

'You don't have to, Maddy,' said her mum.

'No, I'd love to. I'll come straight away.'

'Maddy, please!' Red had a hold of my arm. 'Can't we just talk a minute?'

'Let me go, Red. I said I'd read to Bianca. She needs me.' And I went.

'Bianca thinks she's getting better,' said her mum quietly to me. 'Of course, she's not – but we're going along with it, obviously. I'd love to believe that positive thinking worked miracles!' She gave a sad laugh.

'Right, young lady! What have you chosen for me to read today?' Bianca was in such a good mood it was impossible to believe that there was much wrong with her. Except that she was physically exhausted. By the time I'd read her three stories she was flat out.

I went back to our rooms. Dad and Fay were offering each other drinks and nuts and being polite to each other. Fay had a scowl on her face. 'Who is that child with the strange haircut who is always so over-excited? Her parents don't seem to know the meaning of calm restraint. She's certainly got *you* wrapped round her little finger, Madeleine!'

My jaw dropped. How *could* this woman be so horrible about Bianca? 'Tell her, Dad,' I said. There was no way Fay could redeem herself now. 'I'm going to lie down – my head's killing me.'

As soon as I drew the curtains and lay down, the phone rang. It was Red. 'Maddy! Good, you're back. *Please* can we go somewhere and talk? This is awful! I can't *believe* what's happening.'

'Red – seriously, I have a terrible headache.'

'Then how come you were able to read to Bianca?'

'Red! You're not jealous of *Bianca*, are you?'

'Only when she stops us making our peace with each other.'

'I can do without this, Red. I've got a headache now. Bianca needed me to read to her. Please.'

'And I *need* you to talk to me!'

I managed not to put the phone down but I was speechless.

'Maddy – I need to talk about this business of Dad's film, too.'

'You mean the message you didn't pass on. Well, you needn't worry, because Linden did. Red – I'll see you later. GOODBYE.' And I did put the phone down. First Dad. Then Mum. Fay, of course. And now Red. Everyone out to get me. I hate them all. And in that dire frame of mind, I fell asleep.

Late in the evening the phone rang again. I reached for it sleepily. 'Maddy, it's Linden. You've really upset Red, you know. You don't know what my brother gets like when he's really upset. He's gone off for a walk somewhere. I just hope he comes back, because if he doesn't, it'll be your fault.'

'Linden – I went to bed because I was feeling lousy. Red knows that. And I'm still feeling lousy, so get off the phone and let me get back to sleep.'

'He really doesn't want you to talk to Dad about a part in the film, either. I think he's worried you'll make a fool of yourself. He was really mad at me for telling you, anyway. OK. I'll let you get back to sleep. Bye now.'

Needless to say, after that little tirade it was some time before I got back to sleep. Oh yes, and I hate Linden too.

THIRTEEN

When I woke up in the morning I had my period. That explained a lot. It was late and Dad and Fay had left a note saying they were off playing golf for the morning. I had a lovely bath, found some magazines, made a hot drink, took some fruit and put myself back to bed. Sometimes a girl has to pamper herself.

But then everything started coming back to me. 1. I've had a row with Red! How did that happen? 2. Mum is going to have a baby with the awful man from down the road. It's gross. How can I go back home to that? 3. Dad is forcing me to share *my* holiday with hamster-woman. Let's hope she's a bit past it for having babies.

I want to go home – but what *to*? I'm not sure that I want to stay here with Fay. Why oh why do adults do this to us? Why are they so selfish? I feel as if there's nowhere to turn. My own life is giving me claustrophobia!

I sat up in bed and hugged my knees. I was frowning with concentration. At the end of all this, there was only *me*. Whatever my parents did, even if they died – especially if they died – I was on my own. *I* was all that really mattered to me. The older I got, the more I had to make my *own* life. These thoughts seemed very profound. I pondered them for a while. They were leading somewhere, and what they were leading to was Oliver O'Neill and a part in his film. Me! A film star! I could handle that! Hmmm.

Then I remembered Linden's bizarre phone call. Something about Red not telling me in case I made a fool of myself? How dare he! Why would Oliver have offered to see me if he didn't think I had something? I *would* give him a call, dammit.

The number was one digit different from Red's. I took a gamble on it being one higher.

'Hi, this is Madeleine Dumont—'

'Hello? *Maddy*?' Hell! It was Linden! I put the phone down and dialled the number lower than Red's straight away before I lost my nerve. I'm only calling the most famous film director in the world.

'Yes!' It was definitely Oliver O'Neill's voice barking in my ear.

'Er, hello. This is Madeleine Dumont. I had a message to call you.'

'Who?'

'Madeleine Dumont. Your son – your daughter told me you said I should phone you.'

'Yes?'

'About *West Side Story*. I'm a – a dancer.'

'And?'

Did he even know who I was? 'And you said you might see me about a part in your film. Your daughter said.'

'And you're a dancer, you say?'

'We have met,' I said cautiously. 'I'm staying at the hotel.'

'Uh-huh.' I got the impression he was doing something else as he spoke, making coffee or reading the paper.

'So when could we meet?' No point in being timid.

'Six o'clock. Reception.' He suddenly stopped being vague and went all businesslike. 'We'll pop out somewhere for a drink.'

I had a shower and dressed. I couldn't help feeling that I was doing something wrong. I wasn't convinced that Oliver O'Neill knew who I was over the phone. I'd said I was a dancer – but it didn't seem to ring any bells with him. Shouldn't he have said something like – 'Oh, Red's girlfriend!' or 'the sensational English girl' or something? And then I remembered Linden on the subject of her father and young women. But I didn't have to believe Linden, did I? Anyway. It was done now. Six o'clock.

It was nearly lunchtime and I wasn't quite sure what to do with myself. I'd somehow expected Red to ring me, but he hadn't. What was everyone up to? The cricketers and Holly? The Hayters? I felt isolated.

I forced myself to go out and down to the beach bar. I went via the restaurant, the pool and the beach. I saw no one I knew. Flavia was at the beach bar with her jockey. He still looked lugubrious but she was drinking a ridiculously huge pink drink and laughing her braying laugh. 'They're all off on the pirate ship!' she said. 'I always thought it was simply an excuse to get sloshed, but Ma and Pa insisted on taking everybody. Trying to cheer up my little sister and brother, I think. Honestly, anyone would think they were in *mourning*, and their friends on the school trip haven't even gone yet!'

'Did the O'Neills go, too?'

'Yah. I think the O'Neill *kids* went.' (How long ago was it that she had been madly in love with Red?)

'Well, that's great. Obviously no one thought to tell me.'

'Someone said you weren't well. Your mother, was it?'

Flavia really was the pits. 'Do you mean my father's girlfriend, Fay?'

'Yah.'

Honestly. That girl is so thick-skinned. I didn't know what to do next. I could see the pirate ship with its big cross on the sails moored out in the bay. People go out there for a sort of big party – drink a lot of rum and do silly things. It would have been fun with Red.

I set off back to our rooms to get a towel and my script. I'd spend the afternoon learning it by the pool. And then it hit me like a sledgehammer. RED! Oh Red, what had I done? We only have two whole days left after today. Is he really angry? I couldn't even quite remember what we'd quarrelled over. Wasn't it all to do with him wanting me to forget about my parents for a while and concentrate on him? Well, I couldn't forget about them to order, could I? I mean, it's not every week you discover that your father has an appalling girlfriend and that your mother is going to have a baby, is it?

I let myself into our rooms and changed into my swimming gear. I didn't feel too great actually. Perhaps a quiet day away from everyone was what the doctor ordered. My brain was still a jumble of confused thoughts. Mum. Dad. Red. I felt alternately calm and then seething with anger. How could they? How could Red expect me to put them on one side? Why hadn't he passed on Oliver's message? How dare he think I'd make a fool of myself? I'd show him! I'd show them all!

I gathered up my script and towel and sunlotion and went down to the pool. I stretched out on a sunlounger under a beach umbrella and soon Maria's anguish blotted out my own. All the lines in the songs seemed so horribly relevant – I could *be* Maria. I could get under her skin all right. I under*stood* about love and families. Once he'd heard me, Oliver O'Neill wouldn't want anyone else.

By five o'clock I felt calm and focused. I went back to my room. I showered and changed into my surfie dress. It's flattering, but not over the top. I kept wondering if Red would phone, but he didn't. Perhaps Linden wasn't exaggerating – perhaps he *was* really upset with me. Well, I was pretty upset with him. Then again, perhaps he just wasn't back from the pirate ship. By ten to six I kind of hoped Dad and Fay wouldn't come back before I went out. It would be far easier to leave them a note to explain. Fay would be bound to try and stop me. I spent five minutes working out what to put in the note and ended up writing:

GONE OUT TO BAR, BACK BY NINE, LATEST. I even figured it might be good if someone started worrying if Oliver kept me out more than three hours.

I felt rather self-conscious waiting in Reception. Everyone else was passing through and I kept thinking Dad and Fay, or the Hayters, or even Red and Linden might walk in and wonder what I was doing. Well, I'd tell them, wouldn't I? I was pretty flattered that Oliver O'Neill thought I might have what it takes, wasn't I? I wasn't ashamed about talking to him about a part in his film, over a quiet drink.

At last, about half an hour late, I saw him approaching up the main drive. He looked dead cool in a pale linen suit and a dark casual shirt with trendy shades. And he was coming to take *me* out! I stood up so that he should see me. I could see him looking out for someone. I waved my script, but as I did that an ambulance came haring up the drive behind him. He jumped out of the way. The ambulance screeched to a halt and two ambulance men ran into reception. 'Room eleven!' they said. 'Bailey. Bianca Bailey.' They shot off in the direction of Bianca's rooms. What had happened? And then this tiny figure was brought down on a stretcher, an oxygen mask over her face.

'Bianca! What's happening?' I asked her mum, but she was too distressed to listen to anyone other than Bianca and the ambulance men. I just had to stand back to let them through.

And then, from nowhere, Red appeared. 'Oh my God,' he said, watching what was going on. 'Is she all right?'

'I don't know, Red.'

And then Oliver came up to us both. He only addressed Red. 'I had myself a date with a hot little dancer called Dumont. Any idea which one she is?'

Red stood slightly in front of me. 'No, Dad,' he said, 'I haven't. I expect she thought better of it.' He looked back at me with a strange, cool expression, took his father's elbow and walked him towards the bar.

My legs felt weak. I crumpled on to one of the fancy sofas in the foyer. What had I done? What was Red thinking? And Bianca? What were they doing to her? Would they tell me? I couldn't bear it if she died. My headache was coming back. I felt claustrophobic – here, in the hotel!

I got to my feet and went out to the front of the hotel – I sat down on a wall in the shade of a sweetly smelling forangur tree. I tried to marshall my thoughts. Dad's girl-friend, Mum's baby – right now they were nothing to how I felt about Red and Bianca. I desperately wanted to talk to someone who would understand. Someone like Holly.

Without really thinking, I set off in the direction of the chalets Jonty had pointed out that first morning. Someone there would know where Holly was.

All I wanted was Holly. I forgot everything else. I walked on and on. After about ten minutes rainclouds gathered, and by the time I reached the place I was completely drenched. Like a mad old crone I went round the buildings peering in the windows. The boys slept four to a room, but all the rooms were empty. Finally I stood outside a room that was lit up against the wet evening. I pressed my face against the steamy window. They were in there, eating. All I had to do was get in.

I staggered round the outside of the building, looking for an entrance. I found one, went in and followed the sound of voices down a corridor until I came to their dining room. The door was open. I stood in the doorway, dripping. Suddenly the room went silent. 'Maddy!' Holly had seen me. 'Whatever's the matter?' She came over to where I was standing – and I knew no more.

When I came to, I was lying on her bed in the little room that she shared with Abby. Holly sat on Abby's bed. Some-one had wrapped me in a blanket and made a sort of turban from a towel round my wet hair.

'Blimey, Maddy! You frightened the life out of me! You passed right out! What's going on? Mum's ringing your hotel, trying to get hold of your dad, but they can't find him.'

I sat up. I was warm and wet under the blanket. 'Could I borrow some dry clothes, Holly?' It was all I could think of. 'And I've got the curse – have you got any stuff?'

'Yes to both questions.' Holly was very practical. She found me a complete set of dry clothes – underwear, top, trousers, flip-flops, disappeared to the loo and came back telling me that I'd find everything I needed there. 'Sort yourself out and then come and talk to me. I'll get us a drink and something to eat.'

Food. When had I last eaten? Breakfast? Holly had made Marmite sandwiches. *Marmite sandwiches!* Bliss! And there was a weak orange squash! It was horrible and comforting and thirst-quenching all at the same time. One of the best meals of the whole holiday.

'Well, go on,' said Holly.

'I don't know where to begin,' I said.

'Anywhere,' said Holly. 'Work backwards.'

'I know that I really wanted to talk to you.'

'Why, especially?'

'Because Red gave me a look that shot icicles into my brain.'

'Why?'

'We had a row yesterday.'

'You and Red? I don't believe it!'

'He wanted me to be all cheerful and stop worrying about my parents.'

'What – your dad and Monstrous-Woman?'

'Them and – oh Holly, I've got so much to tell you!'

Holly's mum knocked on the door and came in. 'Hello, Madeleine.' She had a lovely soothing Scottish accent. 'I've left a message with the hotel for your father to ring us as soon as he gets in. But I'll be keeping you here until he comes in person to fetch you. I think you need a bit of looking after, dear.' She clucked sympathetically and backed out of the room.

'You were saying?' said Holly. 'Your dad and Monstrous-Woman—'

'Not just my dad. My mum as well. You see, *she* rang because she had some news for me, but we kept missing each other, and then I rang her and – and – her *news* was that she's pregnant again.'

'So irresponsible, these adults, aren't they?' said Holly, frowning but almost laughing. 'Is that such bad news? I thought you really adored your little sister. Babies are cute. I'd *love* to have a baby to play with!'

'I hadn't thought about the baby so much as its father. Roddy. He's a pain.'

'I thought he didn't live with you?'

'He doesn't. But I'm sure he will if there's a baby involved.'

'Face that one when you come to it. You've got a few months to blackmail everyone into making your room the perfect bedsit – you know, TV, kettle, futon, your own phone. Could be good.'

'Maybe. Holly, you're amazing. I *knew* you'd be able to help.'

'OK. So what else? As if that wasn't enough!'

'Well. I had the row with Red – yesterday, after we came off the submarine. Everyone was in a filthy mood. Then Linden cheesed me off by ringing up and saying that I'd really upset Red.'

'She's a liability, that girl.'

'Then, this morning I woke up with the curse and by the time I got up no one was around.'

'Our lot have been here all day, sorting ourselves out so that we can have a civilised last day tomorrow. I didn't even get to see Jonty. We're leaving early on Friday morning. Mum and Dad have said Charles and I can spend tomorrow evening with you and the Hayters, if we want, which is pretty cool of them. They know they'll get no peace if they don't let us!'

'Jonty and Dilly and the O'Neills all went on the pirate ship.'

'Lucky things! That's considered far too boozy for us "youngsters"!'

'*Anyway . . .*'

'You mean there's more?'

'Much more. I did this really stupid thing, you see. Linden's been winding me up about auditioning for Oliver O'Neill's *West Side Story*.'

'Wow! Do you think he'd give you a part?'

'That's the thing – no. Not really. But Linden's been saying things. Actually, Red said that his dad thought I might have "something" – after he'd seen the video of us dancing. But that was only because we'd had this misunderstanding when he saw me with the script. Oh, it's all so confusing, Holly. Red tells the truth, I know, but no one else does.'

'So what's the really stupid thing? I bet it wasn't that stupid!'

'I rang Oliver O'Neill on his mobile, told him I was a dancer, and arranged to meet him for a drink.'

'Ah. So it *was* that stupid.'

'In every possible way. But, Holly – you know, I just wanted to do something for *me*. Everyone around me is so blooming selfish. I really believed he did want me to call him, though if I hadn't been so mixed up in the first place I'd never have done it. Anyway, needless to say, he thought I was some little bimbo groupie. He hadn't a clue who I was on the phone. Do you know what he said to Red? He said – "I had myself a date with a hot little dancer called Dumont"!'

'It was a close thing then.'

'Yup.'

'So do I gather Red was none too pleased at you arranging a cosy little rendezvous with his father?'

'He just looked daggers at me. But do you know what actually got in the way of me meeting up with Oliver O'Neill? I mean, thank goodness it did, I was way out of my depth, but it was awful – an ambulance coming for Bianca. They brought her down all wired up, and I don't know if I can see her at the hospital, or what.'

'Tell you what,' said Holly. 'Let's get my mum. You know she's a nurse – she might know the score on Bianca. In fact, let's get phoning. I'm going to phone Red.'

'You what?'

'I'm going to tell him you're here and you're in a state and you're not coming back till tomorrow and that you're upset and that there have been all sorts of misunderstandings but that you're still completely potty about him. How's that?'

'Potty?'

'Uhuh.'

'Oh. OK. Thank you, Holly.'

'Good. That's that settled then. Here, write down his mobile number for me. I'm sure you know it off by heart. Mu-um?'

Holly's mum bustled in. 'What is it, dear?'

'Tell Mum about Bianca, Mads.'

'Is this the little leukaemia girl?'

Holly went off to phone Red, and her Mum told me all about leukaemia patients and how they sometimes got infections, and that it sounded as if that had happened to Bianca, but that it didn't necessarily mean she was about to die. She was so kind – I couldn't imagine her moaning about all the rich people or suggesting that Jonty wasn't right for Holly. But that's other people's mothers for you, isn't it? With people like Holly and her mum around, the world isn't such a bad place. I realised how at home I felt – it was quite a relief to be with *normal* people for a change!

What's more, the rain had stopped raining and the evening sky was clear and full of stars.

I heard the phone ringing and Holly answering. She passed the call on to her mum and came back in. 'Right. Well, that was your dad. You'd left them a note apparently, saying you'd be back by nine. He'd just started to worry when he picked up the message at reception. I've put him on to Mum. She's determined that you're going to stay here tonight.'

'What about Abby?'

'Oh, Mum's already moved her in with the other little girl.'

'So I just stay here?'

'That's right. Shame we couldn't do it for longer!'

'Holly, we really will meet up at home won't we?'

'I hope so. By the way, do you know someone called Hannah Gross?' Holly asked.

How funny. A picture of Hannah and her anxious face floated into my mind. She and Sophie and Charlotte seemed to belong in another life. 'Hannah Gross! Of course I do, she's one of my best friends. Why?'

'Oh, some of my friends go to her school and they're all going on a music course together. I thought she lived over your way.'

'Wow, what a coincidence!'

'That's London schools for you. Someone always knows someone. Anyway, Maddy – we're forgetting the *important* phone conversation.'

I knew I was putting it off. 'OK. What did he say?'

Holly held the thumb and little finger of her right hand to her ear. ' *"Red? Hi. It's Holly."*

"Holly. Hi! What's up? Is Maddy with you?" (See – he cares!)

"She's staying over, Red, with us. She's OK now, but she passed out earlier."

"She WHAT? Is she OK? I mean, can I come over and see her?"

'I thought I'd lay it on a bit. *"Well, I don't think she ought to see anyone just now, Red. She's been through emotional hell."* '

'You said *that*, Holly?'

'Yup. Well, you have been through emotional hell. I know you have. Anyway, it had the desired effect.'

She held the imaginary phone to her ear again. 'This is Red. *"I know she's pretty upset about her parents. But hey, we've all been through it—"*

"Maybe, Red, but she's upset about you, too, and all this business with your dad. She'd no idea Linden had set her up. She feels terrible."

"I feel awful bad about that. I should have told her straight out – Dad only deals with agents. I guess it's a world I understand, but how could she? Holly, are you sure I can't come over?"

"No, Red. Certainly not now my mum's on the case."

"Which reminds me. Bianca. I suppose Maddy's scared about her, too?"

"As if she wasn't feeling bad enough already." I wasn't going to let him off, Maddy.'

I was beginning to feel sorry for Red at Holly's hands. 'Couldn't he come over, Holly?'

'Absolutely not. I'm not joking, Maddy. You've been through enough today. Let him sweat a bit. Anyway, my mum couldn't possibly say No to your dad but Yes to Red, now could she?'

'So what did he say then?'

'He said, *"Tell her I'm real sorry, Holly. Tell her I can't wait to see her. Tell her – no, don't, I'll tell her that myself when I see her. She will be back in the morning, won't she?"*

"She will, Red."

"Tell her to call me if she feels up to it. I so want to talk to her."

"OK, Red, I'll tell her. Bye!" ' And she put her imaginary phone down. 'So, I'd say you have nothing to worry about. And don't you *dare* call him. You want the upper hand,

remember?' She stood up and readjusted the hairband round her ponytail. 'The boys have a snack before bedtime – d'you want to come and join us?'

I could get used to this well organised institutional life. How am I ever going to get used to slumming it with Mum – *pregnant* Mum – again?

FOURTEEN

In the morning Holly's mum woke us with a cup of tea. It was wonderful. She sat on Holly's bed while we drank it. 'Right, girls,' she said, 'I've been on the phone to Maddy's father and he'll be over in about an hour – so you can have breakfast with us, Maddy. And I've also rung the hospital to see if there's any news on wee Bianca. I had a word with her mother, and she says the child's stable for the present. You can visit this afternoon if you want, but sadly she'll have to stay put until she's strong enough to fly home to a hospital in England. Poor wee mite.'

My clothes had dried in the early morning sun. They were lovely and warm and slightly crisp when I put them on. I even enjoyed having cereals for breakfast. I was dying to phone Red, but since there was only one payphone in the place I didn't get the chance. Before I knew it, Dad had come for me in a taxi. On his own. Holly's mum brought him to our room. She'd obviously had a word or two with him (it's clear she thinks he's hopelessly irresponsible) – his expression was one of concern. I was so pleased to see him. 'Daddy!' I gave him a huge hug. He clung on to me.

'Sweetheart,' he said in the taxi, 'whatever's been going on? You must tell me!'

So I decided to tell it how it was. I told him all about being upset by him and Fay, by Mum being pregnant, my row with Red and the decision to call Oliver O'Neill, and being saved, as it were, by the ambulance coming for Bianca.

'And I just wasn't there for you, was I? I do sometimes think I wasn't cut out for fatherhood. Has it all gone *horribly* wrong?'

'I think Red understands now. Holly told him everything.'

'I'm pretty disgusted by Oliver's behaviour.'

'Always someone worse than yourself, eh, Dad?'

'Well, he told me himself that he was impressed by your dancing.'

'Which of course is quite a different thing from working with professional casting agents. I should have known myself, Dad – even at my Saturday morning place we're dead professional when it comes to auditions and casting. I don't know what came over me.'

'Well don't punish yourself too hard. I'd say it was an understandable mistake. I blame him. Hot little date, eh? I'd like to give him a piece of my mind!'

'Well don't, Dad. That will only make matters a million times worse, and he *is* Red's father.'

'So how are the young lovers? I'd say you were faring marginally better than the old ones on current showing.'

We were pulling up outside the hotel. I saw it with fresh eyes – like a palace for the incredibly privileged. Dad *had* brought me here as his little princess. He hadn't wanted to spoil that first week by talking about Fay. Maybe he'd known in his heart of hearts it wouldn't work out with her. I gave him a quick kiss before we got out. 'Love you, Dad. I'm fine now. It's all been brilliant, really.'

'Go and sort it out with Romeo. Look, he's over there, waiting for you.' Do you know, I hadn't noticed Red standing outside the entrance? And when I looked at him, before he saw me, he seemed smaller somehow, diminished.

'Maddy!' He rushed over and caught me up in his arms. I

recoiled slightly. He stood back. 'Maddy – we are OK, aren't we?'

'Sure,' I said lightly. I *wasn't* a hundred per cent sure, though. 'Red, let me just go up to my room, have a shower and stuff. I'm feeling kind of icky.'

He looked wary. 'OK. Sure,' he said, nodding. 'See you down by the pool?'

'Somewhere cool and shady.'

'I'll find a spot by the fountains.'

'Give me an hour.'

I had to get my head straight. It wasn't so simple to forget that I *had* been angry with Red. But then, he'd only been wanting us to enjoy our time together, hadn't he? Bit like Dad, really, not wanting to mention Fay. Both of them just wanting to live for the present.

If Red wasn't to blame, why did I suddenly not feel so enthusiastic about being with him? My hormones might have had something to do with it. But it wasn't just that . . . Of course! That was it! We'd had our first row! We'd become human and the magic had worn off a little. Red has an ego and pride, weaknesses, confusions. I hadn't noticed them before. Our romance so far had just been a series of sunsets and kissing. A real holiday romance – the genuine article. But was that *all* it had been?

I put a sarong over my bikini and sat at the dressing table to dry my hair. I'd been totally *in love* with Red, blindly in love. And now that bubble had burst and I wasn't sure whether I *loved* him or not. There is a distinction, isn't there?

I packed my beach bag. There was a small paper bag at the bottom. It was the ring I'd bought Red in the market – I'd never had the chance to give it to him! Maybe I never would. I was completely, utterly confused. I set off for the fountains.

*

Red had bagged us a couple of sunbeds. He looked as hunky as ever in his swimming shorts – I wasn't going to have to *pretend* to find him attractive! Though I did notice, as I hadn't before, that his blond eyebrows nearly met in the middle and that his hands were smaller and neater than I remembered.

He had a cold drink all lined up for me, too – still thoughtful. 'They've got it all mapped out for us – can you believe it?'

'Who? What?'

'The Hayters. For Dilly's and Jonty's last day with Charles and Holly. Afternoon out on a boat – you know, the sort you can swim from – and dinner this evening at that place where the turtles come up the beach. Steel band. The Hayters want to pay for you and me too. And Linden.'

'Where is Linden?'

'Keeping her distance from me, I expect.'

'Why?'

'*Why?*'

'Should I know?'

'Maddy, she only did her best to upset us both – all that about messages from my dad. She played one game too many and I told her just to keep out of my way for a while!' Was Red putting too much of the blame on Linden? I didn't know. All I knew was that I couldn't take anything at face value any more.

'Won't that be a bit awkward this evening then?'

'We'll make sure it's not!' Red put his arm round me and tried to kiss me, but somehow we couldn't get comfortable.

'I can't go on a boat this afternoon, Red. I want to visit Bianca.'

'So would I, if I'd known it was on the cards,' he said. He sat up. 'Maddy. I want you to look me in the eye.' I tried. It wasn't easy. Red's face was troubled. 'Something's changed, hasn't it, Maddy? I recognise the signs. I'm not stupid, you know.'

Tears came into my eyes. 'Red, I'm sorry. Believe me – I don't know what's changed. I only know it has. We were on such a high. Now – just knowing it's got to end . . .'

Red looked away. I knew I had hurt him by not responding like I used to. 'I thought . . . that maybe . . . somehow . . .' he trailed off. I had to hug him, make things better between us. 'Don't do that unless you mean it,' he said, trying to shake me off.

'Red?' It was my turn. 'Now I want you to look me in the eye.' He tried, but he blinked a lot. 'Listen. Perhaps it's better this way. We were going to be separated in a couple of days, whatever happened. Can we just spend the rest of our time together kind of – starting again? As if we'd been parted and then met up again as holiday romance couples do? Only for them, seeing each other in some dreary old town in the rain, it's almost always a disappointment. For us, it's just that we know we're both human, warts and all – and we can be just a bit more realistic? Please, Red?'

He wasn't going to make this easy. 'But, Maddy – I'm still crazy about you. Nothing's changed for me. Nothing apart from your feelings.'

'Red – I know you don't think all this stuff about my parents is important—'

'I do now – honestly. I feel real bad about how I trivialised it. I just felt *we* were so much more important, and our time together was so short—' I caught his eye, and before I knew it, we were kissing, desperately, and both our faces were wet with tears. Good job the fountains were so close by. 'OK,' he said after a while. 'Let's start again. Maybe I like this idea.'

'I'm more confused than ever now, but maybe I do too. Let's see Bianca, go to dinner with the Hayters, have a fabulous day tomorrow and—' I looked at him. I liked his funny eyebrows. I liked his sensitive hands. 'I think I'm crazy about you all over again.' We kind of stopped talking for a while after that.

*

Bianca lay in a large cot in a bright ward where the walls were covered in children's paintings. A breeze blew the muslin curtains at the window and nurses and children clattered about, almost drowning out the large TV that blared away in the corner. Bianca was asleep, breathing lightly. Her parents looked exhausted.

'I'm afraid you won't be able to see her tomorrow,' said her mother. 'They've got to do a biopsy under anaesthetic, so you'll have to say your goodbyes today.'

What a shock. I had no idea how I was going to get through the next few minutes. I sat down by the oversized cot. One side had been let down. 'Bianca, sweetheart?' I whispered, stroking her downy head. She shifted and half opened her eyes.

'Maddthy!' she slurred. 'Have you come to read to me?'

'Yes, angel,' I lied. And then, so it wasn't a lie – 'I've come to tell you the story of Bianca and the Banana Boat.'

'Goodth,' she said, closing her eyes again and smiling. 'I like that one.'

Fighting against the sadness that was choking me, I began. 'Once upon a time there was a beautiful little girl called Bianca who loved bananas.' (Was that the best I could do?) 'She ate bananas for breakfast, bananas for lunch and bananas for tea. That was because she loved everything to be bright yellow like the sun. Bright yellow made her feel happy. But best of all, she liked to cool down by going out on the Banana Boat. Out there in the sun and the wind she felt free as a bird, racing, flying through the rainbow spray . . .' And then I found myself softly singing, 'Hold my hand, I'll take you there . . .' instead of finishing the story. Bianca's hand lay limply in mine. She was asleep again, her little face delicate and peaceful. I couldn't have gone on anyway – I was crying too hard and my voice just wouldn't come out. I released my hand, kissed my finger-tips and planted them on her forehead. 'Bye, Bianca,' I said, and rushed out of the ward before she woke up and saw my tears.

Red came out a few minutes later and joined me on the bench in the hospital corridor. We held each other and cried and cried and cried.

'Let's go outside,' Red managed to say. 'We're upsetting people.'

The hospital was in town, but it had a small garden where we could sit together in the shade. There was nothing much we could say. The cruelty of knowing that we would never see that smashing little girl again, ever, was more than either of us could bear.

But there did come a time, after an hour or so, when we both felt all cried out. Red looked at his watch. 'We've got a couple of hours until this dinner. What's the best thing for us to do?'

'I keep telling myself that she's still alive. It's not fair on her for us to behave as if she's just died, is it?'

Red looked at me, as if to say, but that's how it is.

'I have to believe that maybe I'll be able to write to her or talk on the phone or something once she comes back to England.'

Red carried on looking at me. We both knew that Bianca had very little time to live. And then I had a thought. 'Red – let's go back to our rooms. I'm going to do just that – write to Bianca. I want to. I'll tell her all about what we're going to do tonight and about what we're going to wear and everything – just as if she was Lo-lo. That's what she'd want to know. And I'll tell her about the new baby and how Dad and Fay probably won't stay together. And I'll tell her about Holly and Jonty—'

Red pulled my head on to his chest. 'Do it,' he said, and then, quietly into my hair, he whispered, 'I love you, Maddy.'

We walked to the cab rank. 'Will you write me letters like that? E-mails?'

'You won't be as far away as she is,' I said.

Dinner was a laugh. Looking back, I wouldn't have thought it possible to go from one such extreme to another, but, thank goodness, it was. I was living for the present. Sometimes you have to. How else do people cope with grief lurking around the corner? I was with Red all the way for simply enjoying the time we had together, though our relationship had definitely entered a different and deeper phase. But dealing with saying goodbye to Bianca had somehow prepared me for saying goodbye to Red. Holly, Jonty, Dilly and Charles all knew they would be able to see each other again, though there was plenty of kissing and crying at the end.

Red and I spent Friday on the beach. Linden hung around with Dilly and Jonty and didn't bother us. It was as if we were survivors and she knew she couldn't touch us. We bumped into Red's father in the bar before dinner. I was terrified he'd make the connection, but Red reassured me that 'his son's girlfriend Maddy' and a 'hot little dancer called Dumont' wouldn't come under the same category in his father's highly compartmentalised brain. 'Do you two want to have a drink with me?'

'Come on, Mads,' said Red. 'Take your mind off things.' So we had a very civilised drink with Oliver O'Neill, and he asked all sorts of fatherly questions about school and home and my family. He even looked at the two of us and said – 'And how are you two lovebirds going to cope when cruel fate tears you apart?'

'Dad!' said Red, embarrassed.

'No, I mean it,' said Oliver. 'I'm not scared to mention it. It's obvious that you two are crazy about each other. I was wondering if we should invite the young lady over the US of A some time?'

Red was still embarrassed. 'We'll just have to see, won't we, Dad.'

'Well, you're such great kids. I'd hate to see either of you pining away. I'm just saying it could be arranged. Don't be afraid to ask, son.'

'OK, Dad. Thanks.'

'Thanks, Mr O'Neill,' I said.

'Call me Oliver, please.'

Red and I sat out in our favourite place under the stars. Dad said I had to be in by eleven because of our early start and in a funny sort of way I was glad to know the limits on our time. 'I wonder where Bianca is now,' I said.

Red knows my lines better than I do. 'About halfway there, I should say. And where are we?'

'I've done so much thinking, Red. I'm getting quite philosophical in my old age. Bianca's parents will have to think of her whole life as a sort of bright capsule of time. And that's how I think of this holiday with you. For a while nothing touched us, did it? And then my stupid parents got in the way. But then, when Bianca did too, she kind of made it richer, more intense. I can't quite describe what I mean.'

'You're doing good,' said Red. 'Go on.'

'Well, our time together is like this bright little light. It won't go away. I can't even think of saying goodbye to you, but I know that little light will always be there, bobbing along with Bianca's. And we'll write. And then one day we'll see each other again, and – and—'

'I don't want to talk any more, Maddy. I can't hold you in a letter. We've got just half an hour to make more memories.'

Red and I said goodbye that night. It was a bit like with Bianca. It was good to know that we were still in the same building for a while longer. In the morning Dad and Fay and I went to the airport together, though Fay was on a different flight from us, thank goodness. They said all the right things to each other when they parted, but it seemed pretty unemotional to me. All these goodbyes – I hadn't forgotten that soon *I'd* be saying goodbye to Dad again too. I remembered how upset I'd been when he said Red was just a holiday romance, but he was my father. Dad goes away, but he always comes back, some time.

I thought about my 'holiday romance' and how I'd process it for the others when we got together at the end of the holidays. The romance with Red had been so perfect, but it had been balanced in a subtle and complex way between a 'romance' with Dad, and another with Bianca. And I was forgetting. There was someone else. More constant than all the others. Holly. I'd made a terrific new girl friend, who would still be around when I got home. Because, when it comes down to it, aren't your female friends more important than anyone?

That's a difficult one. Because with Red I touched on *love* in a way that I never have before. Already I reach out and find that he is missing. Nothing's quite as bright as it was when he was around. And however much I hold on to that little bubble of light, right now it's not enough. I twist a funny little necklace round my finger. It is a present from Red – three beads on a thread: a gold one for me, a red one for him – and a white one for Bianca. He bought it for me outside the hospital that afternoon. And of course I gave him the ring. At first I worried that I'd bought it on that awful day of the submarine, but then I thought it was good, because it was a reminder of the time we discovered we were human after all.

EPILOGUE

The sleepover was at Hannah's house. First I had to read to Lo-lo and play Barbados with her Barbies. I talked to her a lot about a little girl called Bianca. Bianca died two weeks ago, after making it home. Her parents wrote to me. I keep their letter with some photos of her and the video that Red sent. The video is completely brilliant, especially the underwater stuff! Red is a genius as well as everything else. I miss him like anything, but somehow he's already part of the past. Then I made Mum a cup of tea and left her sitting in front of the TV. Roddy hasn't moved in yet, and his technical support job means that he often works in the evenings, all of which is fine by me. I'm working subtly on the bedsit scheme. Mum is really pleased about the baby and Lo-lo seems quite intrigued by the whole thing. I have this sentimental desire for it to be called Bianca if it's a girl.

I finally got my make-up on and loaded on the Hugo Boss. My tan seems to be fading fast. I've already made contact with Hannah and Charlotte, though I haven't said much about Barbados, I was too gutted about Bianca. Sophie's the one I'm most interested in, anyway.

'Maddeeeee!' There was a squeal as I crossed the road and Sophie was on the other side, waving frantically. I threw my arms round her.

We quickly compared forearms. 'Your tan is fresher, that's not fair!' I said.

'But yours is pretty incredible, Maddy,' said Sophie. 'So go on, then! Spill the beans!'

'Well, Hannah met a guy called Jonny, I think, and Charlotte hasn't said much – not that I think there'll be much to say!'

'No, idiot! *You!* What happened to you? Was he gorgeous?'

'What makes you think I met anyone?'

'Stop teasing! You always meet someone. You only have to go on the bus to meet someone!'

'Yes, he was gorgeous. So what about yours?'

'Well, he was gorgeous too, but – it was complicated.'

'So was mine. Though really it was everything else that was complicated. And something really really sad happened too.'

'Oh, Maddy!'

We'd reached Hannah's mansion (it is, compared to our place). 'Yeah, well. I haven't got over it yet. But I'll tell you more some other time, on your own, OK?'

'OK.' We rang on the doorbell and waited for Hannah to come and let us in. 'I'm dying to know what happened to the others. I bet it was more than you give them credit for, especially Hannah with her Jonny. She's a sneaky one!'

'Well, I'm going to quiz Charlotte about that Josh. It seems he might be coming to London next term.'

'So what about your gorgeous guy in Barbados?'

'He lives in America, doesn't he? And he's the one that taught me to live for the present – because, well, you never know what's going to happen to people, do you?'